DISPOSABLE SOULS

PHONSE JESSOME

D1057178

Vagrant
PRESS

ADVANCE PRAISE FOR DISPOSABLE SOULS

"Move over, Harry Bosch. Like Michael Connelly's hero, Jessome's detective and patch-wearing biker Cam Neville views the world like a guy who's been to hell and back, and still carries the scorch marks. Written in a drop-dead style, *Disposable Souls* is hardboiled crime writing at its best and grittiest. Welcome to Halifax Noir."

–ANNE EMERY, author of *Children in the Morning*, winner of the 2011 Dartmouth Book Award for Fiction

"A compulsively engaging tale featuring a bruised and brooding Halifax—a place, not unlike Detective Constable Cam Neville, with a mysterious and murderous past forever shaping its tortured and troubled present. Certainly, I like my hard-boiled mysteries with kinetic energy, colourful characters, and compelling atmosphere. In *Disposable Souls*, I have it all and more."

–STEVEN LAFFOLEY, author of *The Blue Tattoo* and *Hunting Halifax*

"A riveting tale, skillfully told. Phonse Jessome has crafted true-to-life characters evocative of Elmore Leonard as they rise and fall from the mean streets of Halifax."

–RICK MOFINA, international bestselling author of *Free Fall*

"Only a writer who has been inside the yellow tape knows the scene well enough to tell a story like this. Gritty and authentic writing."

–MATT JOHNSON, Detective Inspector (rtd.), Scotland Yard Murder Squad, and author of *Wicked Game*

"For most crime writers, the scene of the crime is that awful spot where he spilled bloody red wine on a spotless white carpet. Phonse Jessome is not one of those writers. In his long career as a journalist and author, Jessome has been at the scene of many real and horrible events…. His long history covering crime resonates on every page of *Disposable Souls*."

–DON CONNOLLY, co-host, CBC *Information Morning*

PRAISE FOR PHONSE JESSOME

"Phonse is known to be a fair and accurate journalist who researches his Outlaw Motorcycle Gang [OMG] stories for the interesting details that catch the reader's attention…. Understanding the biker subculture is a lot of work for an outsider. Developing valuable sources in these gangs is even harder. Phonse did both."

–BRUCE MACDONALD, Sgt. (rtd) OMG investigator, Nova Scotia

"As a homicide investigator within Halifax Regional Municipality for fifteen years, when I arrived on a scene I knew I was going to deal with two certainties: at least one deceased and Phonse Jessome. He was at so many murder scenes before me that, over the years, he became one of my main resources for factual information."

–TOM MARTIN former Halifax Regional Police homicide investigator, now private investigator at Martin Investigations

"When the cops called the Darksiders a criminal gang, they were wrong. We're a club, nothing more. Phonse Jessome came to our house and asked for our side of the story. He stayed until he understood it. If anyone is going to write fiction about outlaw clubs, it shouldn't be the cops writing phoney releases, it should be Phonse writing an entertaining story like this one."

–LESTER JOHNSTON, president, Darksiders MC, Dartmouth

"Police tape divided our work space as both Phonse Jessome and I attended a variety of calls over the years. From motor vehicle accidents to homicides, day or night and in all kinds of weather, I have seen Phonse doing his job while he watched me do mine. I look forward to reading his new novel."

–SERGEANT SANDY JOHNSTON, Halifax Regional Police, former forensic identification officer

Nimbus Publishing Limited
3731 Mackintosh St, Halifax, NS B3K 5A5
(902) 455-4286 nimbus.ca

Printed and bound in Canada

NB1255

Cover: image copyright © Allen Crooks
Cover and interior design: Jenn Embree

This is a work of fiction. Names, characters, incidents, and places, including organizations and institutions, are either the product of the author's imagination or are used fictitiously.

Library and Archives Canada Cataloguing in Publication

Jessome, Phonse, author
Disposable souls / Phonse Jessome.
Issued in print and electronic formats.
ISBN 978-1-77108-417-8 (paperback).—ISBN 978-1-77108-418-5 (html)
    I. Title.

PS8619.E794D58 2016   C813'.6   C2016-903734-7
                                          C2016-903735-5

Nimbus Publishing acknowledges the financial support for its publishing activities from the Government of Canada through the Canada Book Fund (CBF) and the Canada Council for the Arts, and from the Province of Nova Scotia. We are pleased to work in partnership with the Province of Nova Scotia to develop and promote our creative industries for the benefit of all Nova Scotians.

FOR BARB
THEN. NOW. ALWAYS.

━━━

PROLOGUE

THE FRONT DOOR WAS OPEN ABOUT AN INCH. I MOVED UP THE STEPS and pushed it in with the barrel of the shotgun. I should be waiting. I should have MacLean and Dill stacked up behind me. There is a right way to do it, a safe way. First officer in breaks right, second breaks left. You chase your gun along the wall looking for targets, knowing the middle of the room is covered by the third member of the team. I wasn't waiting for backup. I didn't want witnesses. I knew the house well enough to play the odds. If she was inside, the girl would likely be all the way in the kitchen or down the hall hiding, not lying in wait inside the small foyer. I rushed in and dashed across the floor, slamming my back against the knee wall that jutted into the kitchen entrance. Nothing. I dropped to my stomach and eased my face around the wall. She'd be looking higher if she was waiting. The kitchen was clear, boiling water spilling out of a pot popping and hissing on the stovetop. I saw the pot before I heard the hiss. That was a problem. My pulse pounding in my ears blocked everything else. I had to take a deep breath and gather my senses. Not hearing is as bad as not seeing; it could be fatal.

The sound of the gunshot was unmistakable, and I probably would have heard it even with my pulse pounding in my eardrums. I rolled back behind the knee wall and pulled my legs under me. The shot came from the hallway beyond the kitchen. I was calm. Being under fire is easier than thinking you might come under fire. When it's real, you can fight back. I dumped a round high into the open doorway to keep the shooter down as I ran past to take a position in the kitchen. I leaned out and took a quick glimpse into the hallway.

The girl was sitting on the floor, staring at the gun in her lap. She was small, looked to be maybe thirteen. The front of her dress was covered in blood. I thought maybe I'd hit her, but she raised her head and looked at me. She lifted the gun, and I dove to the right. I slid into the patio door in a shower of broken glass as I heard her second shot.

"Get out. Get out," she yelled. "I won't go back. No more. You don't own me. You bastards can't make me. Fuck the Stallion."

I could hear the sobbing from the hallway, a tiny, broken girl with a gun in her lap. I couldn't kill her. I had to disarm her before she shot anyone else. I moved to the wall and inched my way past the kitchen table to crouch next to the opening to the hallway.

"Hey, are you still there?"

She answered with another shot. The pot jumped from the top of the stove, spraying water over the floor. She wasn't aiming, just shooting. I wanted to rush her, but it would be suicide.

"Hey, let's talk. Just you and me. Okay?"

"Fuck you. Fuck every Stallion. I know why you're here. You wanna kill me."

"Hey, come on now. Why would I want to do that? Just calm down, okay?"

"I didn't do anything. Just leave me alone. Fuck that midget. He shouldn'a told me he killed that cop. You can't blame me. I won't tell anyone."

I waited, didn't know what to say as her sobs grew louder. I looked around the kitchen for a way to distract her so I could disarm her.

"You don't want to do this. Please, there has been enough killing."

"Just leave me alone." She punctuated it with another blind shot into the kitchen. The sobs stopped; she was angry again. Good, angry is easier to deal with.

"Look, I am not going to hurt you. No one is. We can sort this out."

"No, you're going to kill me because of that dead cop. I know it."

She wasn't making sense, but she wasn't in shock. She knew I was wearing the colours. She did not see my back. She had to know the club well to call it from the few badges on the front of my cut. She had to be the dancer Blair had gone to see. He said she looked like a kid.

"Hey, come on, kid. You work with us, right? I just want to get you out of here. The cops are coming. You hear that?" The sirens outside seemed constant as more and more officers arrived.

"I'll kill them all. I'll kill you."

Her voice sounded different, calmer. Not a good sign. I heard movement. She was standing. I pressed my back into the wall and pulled the shotgun tight to my chest, tilting it slightly toward the doorway. She walked out and swung the gun my way. She wanted out, and I was her ticket. I hesitated and felt the burn as she took a shot.

The kick of the shotgun hurt more as the butt punched the inside of my left thigh. She fell back into the hallway; her gun dropped beside me. I kicked it away and rolled into the doorway.

She looked like a broken doll on the floor in front of me. Blood poured from a hole just below her throat. She looked so young. I'd seen dead kids who were a lot younger. You could never unsee them. This one was mine, and there was nothing I could do to change it. Her head was tilted to the side, facing the open door to Sandy Gardner's bedroom. I wanted to turn it away from that place. I picked up her left wrist to check, but I knew I'd find nothing.

CHAPTER 1

Thursday morning, near dawn

I JAMMED THE SHIFTER INTO PARK AND KNEW IT WAS MURDER before I killed the engine. One glance told me that. Every cop had the vibe, the extra energy that only comes with the big show. No one takes the oath to hand out parking tickets or lock up drunks. Catching killers, that's what the badge is really about. I grabbed my questionable cop credentials and stepped out to the rhythmic snap of yellow crime-scene tape fighting an ocean breeze. Home.

I stood beside the car, tasting the salt brine in the pre-dawn air, pulling it into my lungs, savouring it. It tasted good. I felt good. Don't get me wrong. Death isn't my feel-good thing, but murder, well, I wanted a good murder. My badge felt heavy and dull when I clipped it to my belt. It needed something to give it back that sheen. People die every day, every second. We all come with an expiry date. Why shouldn't one man's death be another man's break?

Two cruisers sat nose-deep in the ditches at either side of a gravel road. Gatekeepers protecting the dead. Red-and-blue lights cut into a heavy fog. The tape making the racket strained away in a wide arc, anchored to the roof racks beneath the spinning lights. More tape stretched from the cars to nearby telephone poles. Beyond the thin plastic barricade, the road twisted its way up the blackened hills of the old city dump. The sky beyond was shedding the deep dark of night. Sunrise was still twenty minutes away, but a soft blue was already bleeding into the dark. I couldn't see the water beyond, but I could feel its chill, hear the waves slamming the rocks along the shoreline. I glanced left into purgatory.

The cranes in the Fairview Cove Container Terminal rose into the fog. Beneath them was the construction-trailer-turned-cop-shop where I'd shuffled paper for the past two years, waiting for something, anything, to happen. This felt like something. When he stuck me behind that desk, the chief told me the waterfront anti-terror squad was a glamour gig. He lied.

Halifax is the off-load port for millions of tonnes of cargo piled onto container ships too big to fit into New York's piers fully loaded. Crews here peel the top few rows of containers off the ships. Those boxes hit the rails while the ships, sitting higher in the water, head to the Big Apple. That means nasty guys with bad intentions might just try to slip a surprise through the container terminal. Thus, the anti-terror squad. Two years, no dirty bombs, no terror plots, and, until today, no yellow tape snapping in the breeze. I knew the chief stuck me on the squad because he was tired of getting complaints about the biker with the badge. Well, he was the one who pinned it on my chest.

I pulled the badge and handed it to a rookie standing between the cruisers. He slid into one of the cars and punched the number into the remote terminal. Everyone entering or exiting an active crime scene is logged.

"Here you are, Detective Constable Neville," he said.

We didn't know each other, so I figured the terminal gave him my name when he entered the badge number. Guess it hadn't expired. I ducked under the yellow line and back in time. Couldn't help smiling. Walking into a real crime scene again, owning it.

Halfway up the hill there was a dead guy face down in the dirt. He was naked; plasti-cuffs locked his hands behind his back. Like I said, murder. My detecting skills were still sound. I grabbed my left wrist as I looked at the tight cuffs holding his hands together. I massaged the scars, felt a distant pain. I released my grip, massaged the scars on my right. Permanent reminders of rusty shackles, thick chain, and no hope. Both wrists ache when it's damp; so do my ankles. In Halifax, it's always damp.

Sergeant Carla Cage was crouched beside the body. She was the best in the forensics game. A third-generation cop. Her grandfather was chief of the old Dartmouth police force, and her father still ran our patrol division. She was raised to be a cop. Having her here was a break.

"Hey, Sergeant."

"Cam Neville, in the flesh. Are you lost, Detective?" She glanced my way and then turned back to the vic.

"Took the call, just like you." I pulled out a notebook and jotted down a few first impressions. Show the good sergeant I was in the game. She looked over again.

"Really? Guess the horseshoe finally fell. Give me a minute, and this one is all yours." She lingered on the "all." I didn't like that. Didn't much like the horseshoe shot either. Cops call the anti-terror task force the golden horseshoe squad. They also claim our horseshoes are lodged in a very uncomfortable place. Lucky us.

"Sure, Sarge, take what you need. I'll look for that horseshoe." I knew Cage was a good cop, and she didn't carry any of that holier-than-the-biker bullshit, so I didn't mind the remark coming from her as much as I did some of the assholes in uniform who think the chief gave me an easy ride.

I pushed two tiny plastic buds into my ears and ran my finger over the menu on my iPhone. Lynyrd Skynyrd's "Vicious Cycle" seemed appropriate. The music started as I walked up a steep mound of hard-packed clay. Murder investigations are about the kind of truth that changes you. You can't avoid it. There is a purity of purpose that can make you stronger, but there is also a darkness that can eat you whole. Music grounds me. It can get me to that purity and help me fight the darkness. Skynyrd is as good a shield as I've found. I turned when I reached the top of the hill and looked around.

The body sat at the end of a perfectly maintained access road that led to a place no one needed access to. Government property. Thirty years ago, the city closed the dump. Somebody realized the harbourfront probably wasn't the place to bury garbage. They covered everything in clay and hoped for the best.

From the top of the hill, I watched Sergeant Cage work the body for a few seconds before turning away. I'd carry the dead guy with me for the rest of my life and wasn't ready to pick him up just yet.

I've killed people and I've solved a few murders. The people I kill and the people I set out to avenge belong to the same club. Their dead eyes are as much a part of me as my scars.

Flashbacks are nothing like you see in the movies. Sometimes they are about a smell, taste, or sound. Sometimes it's a visual image but nothing really clear. It's not what you see, hear, taste, or smell, though. It's where those things take you. It's a full-on fight-or-flight feeling, with no one to fight and nowhere to run. They set off the adrenaline, the panic, and pin the anxiety meter in the red. You can drink or drug them away for a while, but they come back. PTSD is a motherfucker, plain and simple. A cold-hearted bitch. No cure and no point dwelling on it. After all, I'm still alive; the guy face down on the hill is not.

To the left I could see a dark shadow in the fog. The spire of a small wooden church, a testament to the racism most people in Halifax will tell you never existed here. For 125 years, the descendants of African slaves lived along the shoreline here. They built a tight-knit and proud community in isolation and poverty. Africville was part of Halifax, but the city didn't want it, wouldn't provide sewer, water, or even police protection. As far as the good people of Halifax were concerned, Africville was a shantytown to be ignored. The city put the open-pit dump beside it and set up sewage lagoons nearby to drive home the point.

Then, one day, Africville mattered more than it wanted to. The people were evicted, and late one cold night in 1969 heavy equipment swept in and demolished the church. The last house was flattened within a month. The city called it urban renewal. Halifax needed a new bridge, and Africville was in the way. The suddenly homeless people were jammed into inner-city slums and ignored for decades. Some of the toughest gangs in the city came out of those inner-city kitchens where bitterness and frustration still simmer.

The spire in the fog was what passed for an official apology. The replica of the Seaview African United Baptist Church was built a few years ago after the mayor told a room jammed with TV cameras the city was sorry. Halifax is still a racist city; it just hides it better now.

I turned to look at the container terminal on the opposite side of the dump. I figured the victim had nothing to do with our ugly history. I hoped he wasn't connected to the billion-dollar flood of goods that rides the tides into the city every year. A murder outside the port is just a murder. If it's linked to what happens inside, it's an international incident. I wanted a case to work, but not that case.

The scream of steel on steel cut through the fog. Intermodal containers dotted seventy acres of concrete and asphalt below. All of them, it seemed, in motion. Ship-to-shore cranes lifted boxes from the decks of two ships. Forklifts hauled them away as soon as they hit the dock. Each one rushing to the trains and trucks that would feed them to the waiting Walmarts of North America.

I looked at the fence wrapped around the terminal. The towers standing sentry above it held cameras, lights, motion detectors, even heat sensors. All the gadgets a paranoid society needs to sleep at night. How did a dead guy land beside such a secure bit of real estate? There'd be hell to pay for that. Might be mine to pay. On the upside, that dead guy had me back in the real world.

I turned back to the vic and saw my partner, Blair Christmas, heading my way. I pulled the buds from my ears and stuffed them in my pocket. At six four, Blair pushed the scales to 260. None of it jiggled. I fought as a middleweight, but I walk around in light-heavyweight shape. Still, my partner has me by 50 pounds. When we spar, I feel it. Blair moved with long strides, his black shoulder-length hair swinging with each step, a middle finger raised to the lazy cops who blame him for their stalled careers. They call him a quota cop. His badge just a check in a box on some affirmative-action spreadsheet. They ignore the spreadsheet showing the cases he's cleared. Blair claimed his Mi'kmaw heritage gave him the right to wear the traditional hairstyle. The white shirts didn't argue the point. We both knew he didn't care much about heritage. He just liked long hair. I ran a hand through the curls on the back of my head, felt them brush my collar. I also felt the scar back there and wondered when some asshole with rank would order me to chop off the curls and sport a regulation cut. I don't care about long hair, just don't like answering questions about the scar.

Blair's deep-set eyes scanned left and right as he walked. Brilliant white teeth blinked through a broad smile. I'd seen men mistake that smile for softness. They were left picking up their own teeth. My partner was not subtle.

He looked down at the port. "Never seen it from up here," he said.

"Me either. Someone might make an issue of that now," I said.

"Can't see it. We keep the guns and bombs out of the containers. What happens out here, not our problem." He shoved his hands into the back pockets of his jeans and turned his gaze to the body below.

He was probably right. Unless the dead guy was sprinkled with anthrax or sporting an *Al Qaeda Rocks* tattoo, he probably wasn't going to be our problem. I didn't want him to be a terrorist, but I did want him to be our problem.

"Let's just play cop a bit. Find any clues?" I asked.

"The dockworker who found the body is in the clear, and I got us a timeline. That help?" The smile again.

"Let's have it." My kind of quota cop.

"Okay. I talked to Billy Oikle; you remember him. He found our recently departed." He nodded toward the body. "Billy's a head case. Worked thirty-five years down there before retiring last month. Now, he spends his time prowling the fenceline keeping an eye on what he calls the slackers inside. You believe that? Guy needs a hobby," Blair said.

"He mean us?"

"Nope. The guys on the cranes. He says we'd have to do some work before he'd call us slackers. Means it, too."

"Bull work or no work." We'd heard it from the longshoremen for two years.

"Yep. Anyway, he says he left at sunset last night. Came back at four-thirty this morning to watch one of those fat-ass post-Panamax boats. Security guys at the gate say that fits his pattern," Blair explained.

"They see him leave last night? They see anything?"

"Patience, partner, they weren't here last night. The night-shift guys are on the way back in to talk to us. Anyway, I called Billy's wife, and she says he came home about nine o'clock and didn't leave again until this morning. He tells me there was no dead guy when he left last night, so there's our timeline."

Carla Cage walked up the hill toward us. A beauty in a baggy blue bodysuit and booties. A matching hood covered her hair and most of her face. Crime-scene couture. Ravishing. We almost had a thing once. She let me know she was interested. I walked away. Sometimes I regret that.

"Hi, Blair. Nice to see you. Cam, the body's free now. Medical examiner will give you an exact cause, but I can tell you he was strangled and stabbed. No sign of either weapon. If they're here, we'll find them." She nodded toward two police dogs leading officers around the dump.

"Hey, Sarge. Great to see you." Blair's smile broadened. He's like that.

"Thanks, Sergeant," I said.

"Good luck, gents, you'll need it on this one." She touched my arm, her smile broader than Blair's. She turned and walked away. Go figure.

The first rays of sunlight cut over the city, chasing the fog from the dump. Time to visit the star of the show. The dead guy looked to be in his late fifties. Hard to tell for sure, but even with the rigor his skin sagged, and he wasn't fat. I squatted low beside the body as Blair moved around to the other side. I needed time with the victim; so did he. We fell into the old pattern easily. Tomorrow we would have crime-scene pictures and notes, but nothing beat a fresh corpse. This guy had a story to tell. We were here to listen.

Opaque plastic flex-cuffs locked his wrists together. The kind the cowboy cops in the public-protection unit use. We used to call it the riot squad, but that's frowned on now that PR suits dictate police policy. The cowboys resent the name change, but they still get to carry batons and bust heads, so they stay quiet about it. Electricians carry similar ties for bundling cables, so I wasn't going to haul in the protection squad. They were probably good for a few crimes, but maybe not this one.

I pulled a pen from my pocket and tapped it on the plastic. Tight, no wiggle room. The victim's right hand was above his left, both palms up. His arms were locked straight back, hands at the base of his spine. The sun glinted off a gold band. A newly minted widow would get the next-of-kin notification. Bruises filled his upper back and shoulders. Lividity. More bruises and scrapes covered his elbows. I pulled out my notebook and jotted a line. He'd been on his back with his arms pinned beneath him at or near the time of death. The scrapes told me someone dragged his body. The ME would have the final word on that, but I like to note my first impressions. Darker marks ran across the back of his neck. I could feel my shoes sink into the mud as I leaned forward to check them out. His head was turned to the right, toward Blair. I could see the marks on the back of the neck changed from bruising to cuts as they moved to his throat.

"Well, shit." Blair stepped away from the body.

"What's up?"

"I think we should go chase terrorists. Now."

If I didn't know him better, I'd say the big guy was afraid of something. I moved around the body.

"Blair, that's not—" I swallowed back the name.

"Like to say it's not, but I do believe we're looking at Pastor Sandy Gardner. The great man himself. The saviour of the lost children and all that crowd-pleasing shit," Blair said.

"Fuck." I moved away and joined Blair.

"Well said."

I recognized Gardner's face, even dead and coated in dried mud. The bushy brown moustache, matching eyebrows, that famous dimpled chin. The small L-shaped scar on the right cheek sealed it. I turned toward the squad cars at the bottom of the hill. Gardner's face smiled back from a billboard across the street. Nice tan, no mud. The bigger-than-life Sandy Gardner was surveying his domain from above. The billboard text invited wayward souls to come home to his Church of Salvation.

Gardner worked the Bible-thumping big leagues. He ran his Halifax based adoption agency with an evangelical zeal. He sliced red tape with a Jesus-powered lightsaber. Bringing Third World orphans to new homes in North America with little or no delay through his Little Maria Foundation, named for the first orphan he rescued. Pastor Gardner's televised services drew a global audience. Donations poured in, and the orphans kept coming. The healing power of TV. I caught Carla's eye. She smiled. Cute.

"Relax, Blair, this one is too hot. The major-crime guys won't let us near it." Maybe I didn't want this vic after all. Hell of a case if we could crack it. Permanent proof for the assholes who say we are sub-par cops, if we couldn't.

"Sure, partner. I can see the line forming now. This town's gotta be lousy with cops wanting this one." He gestured at the late pastor.

"Hmm," was all I had for him.

I walked over to Carla, hoping I didn't look as sick as I felt. No point in ruining my frosty rep.

"You better break out the tent poles and canvas, Sergeant. Cover him up; we won't be moving him any time soon."

"Expecting rain, Cam?"

"Some kind of storm, yeah." I swallowed.

"Locusts would be biblically appropriate, I guess. Probably with long lenses, too," she said.

The smile again. I thought punching her in the nose would be a little too much, so I headed back to join Blair and Sandy Gardner.

I looked down at the body. Blair stood beside me. We both pulled on purple latex gloves.

"Let's see what he says."

"Sure. But let's be clear. We want to shake this case," Blair said.

We circled, looking down.

"Oh, sure. Just curious," I said. "We go back to the task force when reinforcements arrive."

"Exactly." Blair moved to Gardner's head. I knelt on a dry rock near the dead man's feet. "Take a look at this: bruising around his ankles."

Blair crouched beside me.

"Looks like cuff marks."

"Yep."

"So, why remove them and leave his wrists bound?" Blair took a closer look at the plastic ties holding Gardner's hands behind his back.

"Not sure. Marks look fresh. Maybe the cuffs are still with the killer or where he was killed."

I didn't think he was murdered in the dump. Not enough evidence. Naked guy in the mud, that's it. No blood, no clothes, not much of anything turned up by the crime-scene team. This was looking like a real whodunit.

"You figure a body drop?" Blair moved back to the cuff marks on the ankles. He took a pen from his pocket and held it lengthwise along one of the bruises.

"Yep." I watched as Blair took the pen and held it to the plastic cuffs on the victim's wrists.

"Ankle bruises don't match. Too wide. Real cuffs maybe," Blair said. "The poor slobs who catch this file can sort it out. You have any idea why they called us out?"

I lowered my right cheek and tried to see where the ankle bruising moved to the front of the legs. A sour smell rose from the mud.

"I figure they want us to have a look because he was found beside the terminal. See if it's connected." I raised my head. "Fun playing cop, though. I kind of miss the real thing. You?"

"Sure, fun for a minute or two. Sandy Gardner is not in the shipping business, though. This should be a fast toss back to the rock stars in major crime," he said. "We both know a famous vic is poison, right? Too many people watching, second-guessing, and micromanaging. We don't want that, even if we do miss the real thing."

"Absolutely." I moved back on my haunches and looked toward the main road and the entrance to the Fairview Cove Container Terminal. Why here? I looked across the street.

Just beneath Gardner's smiling billboard was the Satan's Stallion compound. The Stallion is Halifax's toughest motorcycle club. My father founded it, and in another life I rode under the Stallion colours. A body this close to an outlaw clubhouse would bring the Outlaw Motorcycle Gang unit out. Perfect. The club wouldn't dump a body so close to home, but the OMG team would link it to the Stallion if only to justify the fat budget that comes with fighting the big bad bikers.

I figure the OMG guys were behind the chief's decision to side-line me in the anti-terror unit. Well, that and the three men I beat into the ER from the courthouse steps. They started it. I ended it. Trouble is, nothing ends that easy in this town. Halifax is a city of world-class whiners, and Twitter is their town square. We are a provincial capital filled with government workers. We have a fast-growing international finance sector and five universities. A whole city full of big brains who know everything about everything. Even if they haven't actually done anything.

The Twitterverse exploded with opinions about the outlaw biker and cage fighter who carried a badge and beat people bloody in their pretty city by the sea. Every twit had an opinion. Online petitions calling for my badge flew across the web. Facebook echoed the cry for my blood. Never mind that the three guys were hard-core dealers flooding the streets with crack. Never mind that I stepped in when they were threatening a witness outside a courtroom. I was an asshole, and they were victims, no room for debate.

The fight did get me some credibility on the force for a while. Other cops pushed their chests out; suddenly I was one of them. I was proof the uniform must be feared and obeyed. Of course, my uniform got pulled. I was stashed out of sight. First, the chief stuck me with Blair in major crime. Hands down my best three years as a cop. I felt like a real investigator, not some reformed thug-turned-military-hero. A trophy badge the chief kept in his collection. I'm no hero, but I did give up the thug life. The OMG guys didn't like my new assignment. They work under the major-crime flag, and no way would they share that with a former Stallion. They kept hammering at the chief. Blair heard they built a file with informant statements saying I'd beaten the crack dealers to protect Stallion turf. Like the club needed me to do that. Finally, the chief folded, and I was off to the port. Blair raised a little hell, and they tossed him in with me.

This case could be our ticket back. It had leprosy, though. Best-case scenario: a sex crime involving a prominent preacher. That's a bad best case. A Stallion link would take it to a whole new place. No sane cop would want this mess. I wondered how sane I was. Languishing in an anti-terror squad on the waterfront wasn't working for me.

"Hey, take a look at this." Blair moved crab-like from Gardner's feet to his torso.

"What have you got?"

"Tattoo. Here at the hip. Let's roll him over," he said.

"Better wait for the ME. He should be here by now, anyway." I looked toward the parking lot. "Like you said, the second-guessing desk jockeys will be all over this, so let's keep it by the book."

Blair dropped into a push-up stance next to the dead hip, keeping his clothes out of the mud as he tried for a better angle.

"Anything?"

"Well, I can't be sure, but it looks like a horse," Blair said.

"Let me have a look." I crouched low as Blair moved aside. "Could be. Can't be sure, with that mud smeared around it."

"Hope the ME gets here soon. I'd like to have a look before we hand this thing off," Blair said.

"Yep, me too. Just to see what it is. Tattoo on a preacher. I could see a cross maybe, but a horse? Might mean something."

"Yeah, maybe," Blair said.

The A. Murray MacKay Bridge climbs skyward from Africville. It arches across the narrows to the Dartmouth side of Halifax Harbour. The four-lane span dumps an endless flow of commuters into the North End of the Halifax peninsula. The steady whine of rubber marked the start of the morning rush. The hacking and spitting of Jake Brakes mixed in as truckers slowed big rigs bound for the container terminal.

Engine popping and banging of another kind pulled my attention from the late Sandy Gardner. The familiar symphony stirred something deep inside. I turned to see Snake Howard lead a Satan's Stallion formation toward the club compound. I was ten the first time I saw and heard an outlaw formation, seventeen the first time I rode in one. Something about it still pulled hard. I knew better now, but it still made me twitch.

For me the outlaw life wasn't so much an anti-social statement. It was the only option I had, at least I thought so then. My old man was the original Stallion, and the only role models I had were his bros. My father didn't give a shit about me or anyone else, but the club's co-founder, Grease, took me in. I spent more time in the shop with him than I did in school. Just as well. In school, there were two kinds of kids: those who avoided me because their parents said I was trash and those who wanted to fight me to prove something. I preferred the fights. The teachers weren't any better, either afraid or disgusted by the outlaw's kid. My older brother, Gunner, had it just as bad, so he dropped out in Grade 10. I never would have made it through high school if I hadn't met Glenda. I just followed her to school, and by the time we were eighteen we were married. Thinking about her still hurt. She believed in me the way no one else did, not even me. I was bigger, better with her, and I let her down. I went off to war to play hero, and the wrong one of us ended up under a headstone. Glenda was born with a bad heart; I knew it, she knew it. We ignored it, and it killed her. I headed to Afghanistan and left a beautiful wife behind. I got my dumb ass captured and never saw her again.

If I wasn't chasing Glenda or fighting behind the school, I was in that shop with Skynyrd blaring and wrenches flying. Grease taught me to strip a Harley and build it back up faster and louder. I still do all the work on my own ride. He put me up as a prospect when I was seventeen and patched me into the club as a wedding present. I still miss working with Grease, but he took it pretty hard when I walked . away from the club after the war.

I watched my former brothers roll. Snake's blonde hair twisted in his wake. It slapped his denim-covered shoulders just above his club patch. I smiled. Snake, the only Stallion still wearing an original cut. No leather for the pres. When the club formed, members cut the sleeves off their denim jackets and sewed crude patches on their backs and called the creation a cut. Leather vests long ago replaced the faded old denim, but every outlaw still called his vest a cut. Traditions don't die hard in outlaw culture. They don't die at all.

Snake's hair danced around blue flames rising from the horns of a Gothic demon. The split tongue reaching beneath the demon's chin was an identical blue. Even from this distance I could see Snake's left hand pull the clutch lever into the handlebar as he stomped a heavy leather boot on the shifter. The twelve Satan's Stallions following their club president downshifted as one. The parade of big bikes slowed, their engines backfiring and coughing again. A parked car's alarm squealed against the rumble as the bikes passed.

As vice-president and sergeant-at-arms, Gunner rode to the right, slightly behind Snake. He grabbed the pearl-handled pistol grip that topped the suicide-shifter beside his gas tank. His left boot pushed and released the foot clutch as he shoved the pistol forward. I knew his bike was a bitch to ride and marvelled at the ease of his movements as the group rounded the sharp corner near the terminal entrance and headed toward the clubhouse. Gunner gave the throttle a twist, and his bike rolled up wheel to wheel with Snake. He pointed to the police cars and yellow tape below me. Snake held up two fingers, gestured forward, and kicked his bike down another gear, setting off the backfiring and popping again as the procession slowed with him. Gunner grabbed a handful of brake and forced his bike to a stop at the shoulder of the road.

He planted his boots on the pavement and turned to watch his brothers. I smiled. The Satan's Stallion Motorcycle Club was an ominous spectacle, even to a born-to-it Stallion like Gunner. The club name arched shoulder to shoulder at the top of his back. Letters in blue edged in an icy silver. Beneath it, Satan grimaced at the world. At the bottom, curved upward, the rocker that named the territory: *Halifax*. Air-brushed blue skulls bathed in flames burned across most gas tanks. Barbed wire lined a few others. *SFFS* stamped on every bike. *Stallion Forever Forever Stallion*, brother.

Jimmy Williams, his greasy locks trailing back in the wind, rode the final bike in the group. A radically raked trike with two wide skins in back and one skinny-ass tire stretched way out front.

Williams wore a prospect's patch, the mark of a rider still trying to earn full club membership. He had a blue-and-silver *Halifax* curved along the bottom of his back, but no Satan's head or club name above it. Gunner signalled for Williams to join him. The trike pulled in behind Gunner's bike and stopped. Neither man spoke.

The Stallion train rolled on, making a hard right turn beneath the smiling face of Sandy Gardner. The bikers rode between the posts supporting the billboard and past a slowly opening steel gate into the club compound. His club safe at home, Gunner jammed his left foot into the clutch again and shoved the shifter lever without saying a word to Williams. He didn't have to; the prospect would follow. He turned his bike away from the clubhouse and into the parking lot below. That was going to be a problem. I watched as he twisted his right hand hard on the throttle. The big bike howled and slewed violently and then straightened as he raced across the lot, stopping just short of the yellow police tape. The trike carrying Williams screeched to a halt beside him. The two let their bikes idle at a deep rumble as the cop I had badged earlier walked over.

I didn't know what the cop was saying but watched as Gunner raised his hands and placed them on the handlebars in front of him, making sure the young cop could see them. Williams did the same. Not exactly surrender, just relaxing.

I saw the rookie make a move with his right hand. Looking for comfort from the gun. Never say things can't get worse. I looked down at Gardner's lifeless form. He'd wait. I headed to the parking lot to try to keep the body count at one.

I placed a hand on the rookie's shoulder as I moved past him. Felt him relax. Gunner smiled, all innocence. His ink spoke for him. A blood-red *FTW* rose from his left shoulder to his ear; *FTP* matched it on the right side. *Fuck the world. Fuck the police.* Jimmy Williams's bare arms showed more ink than a daily newspaper. Gunner stood just over six feet tall and had that prison-yard build that came from too much time behind iron bars. It had been years since he did any serious time, but he still had the hard body. It was Williams at only four foot three I worried about. The fat little man was unpredictable. Gunner had nothing to prove; Williams did.

I reached over the elevated handlebars on Gunner's ride and pushed the kill switch beside the throttle. The engine died. I glanced at Williams; the little man on the trike looked down and killed his engine. I grabbed Gunner's extended right hand, pulled him forward on the bike and embraced him, slapping his patch with my left hand as we hugged.

"You harassing the troops?" I asked.

"Other way around." He spoke to me but gave the young patrol-man a hard stare. "Why you bringing your gang into our territory?"

"Gunner, this whole city is my territory. I just let you ride in it. Now what drags you out of bed at this hour?" I asked, moving to stand between him and the uniformed officer.

"Haven't been to bed yet."

I looked over toward Williams.

"Officer, do you have a Breathalyser unit in your car? I think I smell alcohol off this one," I said.

"Fuckin' cops," Williams muttered.

"Don't say another word, prospect," Gunner ordered.

"What? I'm not your hero anymore, Jimmy?" I asked

"Fuck you," he answered.

"Your hero days ended when you crawled in with that crowd." Gunner nodded toward the officers beyond the yellow tape.

I didn't have to turn. I knew all work on the crime scene had stopped. Every eye on the parking lot. I'd bet another hand or two made the move to rest on a gun butt. I could feel the hate flow through me in both directions. Once again, I stood between the bikers and the badge. That movie was getting old.

"Unless you have something to share about the dead man over there, you should head to the clubhouse, big brother. Tell Snake I'll be over to speak with all of you shortly."

"Not coming in behind a badge, bro. Who's the stiff?" Gunner asked.

"Go away, Gunner. Tell your fearless leader I want to take a look at the club surveillance tapes from last night."

I locked eyes with him.

"Well, look what we have here." Blair arrived, looking to toss some fuel on a fire I had under control. Always perfect timing, my partner.

"We rarely get to see actual criminals at a crime scene. Care to confess, lowlife?" he said to Williams.

"Fuckin' cops." Williams turned away from Gunner as he said it.

"Brilliant retort there, Tiny. Show me the papers on that tricycle," Blair said.

"Not now, partner," I said. "They're leaving. Like I said, take off Gunner. Now."

Gunner's eyes stayed on me as he reached down to the kick-start pedal; he eased it down once with his foot to prepare the engine and then released it. He moved his eyes to the young patrolman as he jumped into the air and came down on it hard. The engine exploded back to life. He rolled off to the left in a tight turn. The bike leaned as though it would drop to the pavement before he twisted the throttle, and the engine's torque pulled it upright and away. Williams followed close behind. The horned demon's head stared back from Gunner's patch. Williams seemed to have horns of his own.

I turned to the patrolman and looked at the name on his Kevlar vest. Kid was maybe twenty-three.

"Constable Barber, you reach for that gun, you better plan to pull it, and if you pull it, you better be ready to use it. That *High Noon* shit will get you or someone else killed. Clear?"

"Yes, sir." He looked at the ground.

"You know, Cam, just because he's your brother doesn't mean you have to be nice to his friends," Blair said as we moved away.

"I know. But if this was Stallion business, the body wouldn't be so easy to find. Besides, if the clubhouse wasn't underneath his billboard, they wouldn't know who Sandy Gardner was. Probably still don't."

I looked up. The paper pastor beamed agreement as the two bikes rolled beneath him through the clubhouse gate. I headed back to the real thing. No beaming going on there.

"Let's go grab this career-ender and see what kind of shit we can shake out of it." The fog was gone, and the fresh morning air was rich with possibility.

"Great idea," Blair muttered. "Can't imagine a better plan."

The medical examiner worked the body. Blair and I waited. Our vic rated the top doc. Dr. Henry Ian was chief medical examiner for the province of Nova Scotia—the first Canadian province to have an ME, he'd tell you if you gave him half a chance. The heavy-set balding man had stubby fingers that worked magic with a scalpel. Of course, his patients were dead. He rarely left the office, but a famous vic brings out the big players. The ME wore a set of crime-scene coveralls but no hood or mask. He wasn't trying to keep trace evidence off the body; he was trying to keep the body off his suit. He was taking his time examining Sandy Gardner's neck.

The sun felt hot on my face, the fog already forgotten. I looked down the hill. A TV cameraman was pulling gear from the back of his truck. Two others were shooting from behind the yellow tape. Murder moved our evangelical preacher to a new place in TV land. No more preaching the good word for Sandy Gardner; now he was in the breaking news cycle. Crime scenes, burned buildings, and car wrecks fight to fill the space between the commercials on the early newscasts. People like to start the day reassuring themselves that bad things still only happen to other people.

Two still photographers from the daily papers patrolled the outer edge of the tape, pausing for a shot and then moving on, looking for another. Their long lenses ready to freeze a moment in time, their pictures emailed back to newsrooms for the web.

A cluster of reporters gathered near the police cruisers. They typed away on smart phones. Tweeting the breaking news to the nation.

None of the photographers was pointing a lens at the billboard across the street. So far, the identity of the victim was a secret. I hoped it would stay that way. One of our computer techs would search the web for anything linking the victim's name to the crime. Killers were usually stupid people who tried too hard to distance themselves from a crime. Social media gave them all kinds of room to screw up. The Gardner name would surface on the internet pretty fast, and we'd want to find out who knew it first.

"And so the fun ends, my partner," Blair said looking at the parking lot. "Time for the hand-off."

I followed his gaze and watched Inspector Carl MacIntosh strain to duck beneath the yellow tape as Constable Barber pushed the line higher. The inspector walked to the body. The cameras all moved to him. The white shirt and gold insignia of a ranking officer: a stand-out shot at a murder scene. Any crime reporter with three bodies under his belt knows inspectors rarely step past the yellow tape. Now, they knew the victim was somebody important. They'd dig deeper, start calling sources. MacIntosh was a big man, an old-school Mountie who entered the force when size mattered more than anything. His close-cropped grey hair sat on a squared head that rose neckless above his shoulders. He looked like a goon, but the white shirt was proof he had political savvy. A survivor of the boardroom battles.

MacIntosh walked past the ME and stood in front of us. He folded his arms; the white sleeves of his uniform shirt were rolled up to the elbows. A horse silhouette reared from his wrist, covering a bulging left forearm. The inspector rode for two years with the famed Musical Ride of the Royal Canadian Mounted Police, and he made sure everyone knew it. The vic, Gunner, and now him; it seemed everybody was flashing ink today. I kept mine covered.

"Okay, gents, first things first," he said. "I will not listen to any bullshit about task-force duties or terror threats. You are seconded from that detail as of now. You are on this case. Conversation over." He turned and moved over for a look at Sandy Gardner. Giving us street tough and boardroom savvy all at once.

I was used to taking orders from Mounties, but some of the older members of the Halifax regional force still hate it. Halifax is an old city with new boundaries. It grew in one big spurt when politicians pushed the city limits out to cut service costs. Halifax swallowed its smaller neighbours, and those service costs grew.

The move forced the new city into a policing turf war. Before the shotgun amalgamation, the Mounties patrolled the rural communities while three municipal forces policed the old city and its two biggest neighbours, Dartmouth and Bedford. The municipal forces melted easily into one regional force, but Canada's national police agency kept its distance. The Royal Canadian Mounted Police force is big on tradition and not given to sharing it. As a national force, it works regularly with the FBI and Interpol on big cases. The idea of merging with a couple of small-time municipal forces on the East Coast did not sit well with the Mountie masters in their Ottawa ivory towers.

Practicality won out when the bigger force realized the new municipality in Halifax was planning to cancel its RCMP contract and expand its own new regional force through the entire city. The Mounties play nice now. They've added their considerable resources to the mix, making Halifax Canada's only city with a fully integrated municipal and RCMP service.

The ink wasn't dry on the deal when a couple of second-generation drug lords barely out of their teens decided to play king of the hill in the Spryfield area of the city. The drive-bys and body count pushed Halifax to second place on Canada's deadliest cities list at the time. Hard to call the police merger a success. I'm a Halifax city cop; Blair is a Mountie. At our level, the job is the same, no matter the shape of the badge. It works fine for us. It's the Royal Canadian Mounted high priests like MacIntosh who still struggle with it.

Blair leaned in. "Guess we'll get to see what that horse tattoo is all about."

"There's that."

It was shit for a case, but I could still feel the rush. I pulled my notebook out, logged the time and orders from the inspector. I drew a line under it and began to jot questions. What did that tattoo mean? Probably a minor thing, but until you know otherwise, nothing is minor. Where were the cuffs that left those marks on Gardner's ankles? Where did he die? Tracking Sandy Gardner's moves last night was critical. A visit to his home would be our number-one priority. Viewing surveillance footage from the container terminal and, with luck, the Stallion clubhouse made the to-do list next. We'd need a warrant to get near the Stallion video. I drew a heavy line under three questions: Who was Sandy Gardner with before he got himself killed last night? Where and when did he die? How did he end up outside the container terminal? Writing it down felt good. It's how I started every major case.

"Got a time of death, doc?" I asked, hoping to put something in the answer column.

"Hard to say for sure, Detective." Dr. Ian looked up as he pulled a thin rod from the body. "Liver temp may not be reliable. He is naked, and it was cold last night. It's safe to say he was moved after death, and that complicates it further. No way to know how long he was in the first location or what the ambient temperature there might have been. A little lab work will help narrow it, but I would guess some time around midnight. Just a guess, don't hold me to it."

"It's a start, doc. Thanks." I jotted that time next to the note on the surveillance tapes.

"Preliminary cause would be ligature strangulation. There is a stab wound, but it looks post-mortem. Again, hold me to nothing said here in the field." He went back to the corpse.

+-+-+

Inspector MacIntosh lectured Carla Cage and her crime-scene techs at the bottom of the hill. Blair and I went down to join the fun. The inspector explained his theory to Cage. He already had the whole case figured out. Drive-thru detecting at its best. Carla held her own, dismissing his musings with facts. Like me, she's a Halifax regional cop. The ranking Mountie didn't seem to intimidate her.

I glanced past them to the clubhouse across the street. I saw two security cameras pointed this way. There were probably more. I hoped my five years riding as a Stallion brother would buy me enough goodwill to see the tapes. I left the club in good standing, if not in good favour, when I got back from the war. They say war is hell, but anyone who's been there will tell you war is mostly days of boring routine. Now, combat, there's a head fuck that makes hell seem appealing. I came back more fucked than most. I blamed myself for the death of my spotter, the only real friend I ever had. I knew Ronald wouldn't blame me, but I did.

The six months I spent in chains in a Pakistani village shifted my priorities. It wasn't the daily whippings with the knotted ropes that did it. I watched from beside my rock as my Taliban captors traded poppies for bullets. I knew where those poppies were headed and didn't want to work the other end of the pipeline when I got back home. I didn't deal heroin as a Stallion, but I enjoyed some of the profits sent the club's way. I knew I could never party with that cash again. That doesn't mean I believe in drug laws. I just couldn't send money back to that place. I believed then, as I do now, the drug war is an unwinnable waste of time and money. Outlaw clubs are about freedom, and every member will tell you legislated morality is an attack on freedom of choice. It's an easy stance to take when you are raking in the cash selling sex and drugs.

I left the outlaw life, but I'm still tied to the club. My father founded the Satan's Stallion, so it's always going to be part of me. I have the lifer tattoo on my chest, my ticket to Stallion rides and parties. The only time I go to a club ride is when Gunner drags me along. My brother followed me to Afghanistan. When I got captured, he signed up for a second tour and went to Iraq to punish everyone he could find. He saw more combat than I did. He also saw things differently when he got home. To him, the drug trade here helps the rebuilding efforts there. He doesn't give a shit about rebuilding anything; he just plays it that way.

I drifted after I left the Stallion. For a while, I missed it, but mostly I drank too much and tried to hide from memories of Ronald, exploding bodies, and knotted ropes. I think Glenda got me through it, but I'm not clear on that. I have these images of her sitting beside me while my body revolted from the latest binge. I call them my good flashbacks. She'd stroke my hair and smile, and I'd feel safe. I'd sleep after that but when I woke she'd still be dead and I'd still be a drunk.

I know now it was probably Greg sitting at my side, the black sheep of the Neville family. Or the white collar. My baby brother, the priest. He pulled me out of the self-pity cycle in the end. Funny, I know I wouldn't be standing here without Greg, but I still don't think about him much. He just hadn't been a part of my life until those dark days. Gunner and I were raised in one world, Greg in another. He turned out fine, we didn't. Fractured families are like that.

Truth is, my drinking got so bad the club would have tossed me anyway. Getting loaded is expected; being a falling-down drunk is not tolerated. A real drunk might mumble secrets in the wrong ears, not a risk the Stallion would take. If they knew how bad I got, they would have killed me to be safe. Now I'm sober and what the club calls "out in good." It means I am in good standing and not a liability. It also means I must respect all Stallion secrets. That does not keep me in good standing with those OMG cops who want my badge so bad. Fuck them.

Blair is the only cop who really accepts my Stallion ties. I hoped they weren't going to hurt him now. I didn't like the idea of a case that would force me to put the club under the microscope. I knew I'd see things a cop isn't supposed to look away from, out in good or not. I turned back to the group in front of me.

"Goddammit, Detective Constable Neville, I'm talking to you." The inspector had turned his attention my way. "Give me something here. I'm going to be briefing the media in just a few minutes."

"Well, sir, we don't have anything Sergeant Cage didn't cover. We believe Gardner was dumped here, and strangulation is the likely cause of death. Both facts have to be hold-back."

Hold-back evidence can slam a cell door faster than a guilty plea. We always keep evidence away from the media and even the victim's family. A confession containing hold-back facts is a big club for a prosecutor to wield in court. It wasn't what he wanted to hear.

"So, what? You want me to waltz over to the cameras and say, 'Sorry, folks nothing to see here. Move along now.' They'll love that. Hell, why don't *you* try to sell it?"

"Sir, I don't care what they love. I only care about the case, and I'd like to get back to it. Blair and I need to get to Pastor Gardner's home and get the notification done before some reporter knocks on the door."

"What about your friends over there? I hear they came to see you." MacIntosh nodded toward the Stallion compound. "Why don't you go over for old times' sake? Have a cup of coffee and take a peek at their video. Let the media speculate on a biker angle. That should keep them spinning. Just don't get too comfortable in there."

"Going to be tough to get them off the club once they head down that road, no matter who the vic is," I said.

"A problem why?"

I locked eyes with the bigger, older cop, then looked at Carla. She avoided my gaze. I felt a hand on my left arm. "Let's go, partner." Blair pulled me toward the compound across the street. I stopped him mid-stride, shook my head.

"Stay with the body. Dr. Ian should be ready to flip him over, and you can get a better look at that tattoo. Get Sergeant Cage to get us a good picture of it."

"Ah, come on. I don't get to see the inner sanctum?" Blair flashed that smile.

"It's bad enough I'm going to piss in Snake's cornflakes. He'll go into full asshole mode if I try to take you in. We don't want him erasing any video."

Blair moved off. I watched as MacIntosh straightened his uniform and placed his hat carefully on his oversized head. Carla Cage began to peel off her bodysuit, but the inspector reached over to stop her. A real forensic cop in real forensic coveralls: good TV. The two moved to the cameras. I thought I was stepping back in time when I first ducked under the yellow tape just before sunrise. When I walked through the door on the other side of the street I'd be taking a bigger step. I was walking back into Gunner's world.

CHAPTER 2

Gunner moved down the short hallway into the warehouse the Stallion called home. The smell of stale beer, cigarettes, and gun oil filled the air. He listened to the three deadbolts slide into place as the door closed behind him. He stood where the hallway opened into the main room. A Skynyrd tune blared from the overhead speakers, a swampy groove. He smiled. Grease had finally figured out the sound system.

Gunner looked at his club president. Snake was in his leather recliner in the centre of the room, a big remote pointed at the theatre-sized screen on the wall. Two fighters were kicking and punching each other inside a caged octagon. The fight stopped as Snake stabbed the remote with a jewelled finger and reached for a beer. He flicked his long blonde hair as he settled back into the chair and opened the can. He punched the remote again; the fight resumed.

Further into the room, Grease sat on the floor, pulling a wire brush through the barrel of a MAC-10 machine pistol. Gunner nodded as Grease looked up and pointed the empty weapon with a grin. At sixty-two, Grease was the oldest member of the Satan's Stallion. He and Snake were the only original members left and among the few still in the game who had ridden with Gunner's old man. Grease had never spent a night behind bars and was a legend among all the outlaw clubs. His white hair and goatee were spotless. His clothes were not. The boxy jeans and long-sleeved T were tattered and frayed, and both were almost hard with the green-black stain of oil, tranny fluid, and thousands of hours of sweat. He could squeeze power out of a bike Harley's own techs never would. He was a magician with firearms, too. A good guy to have in any outlaw club. He pushed a set of small spectacles up the bridge of his nose and returned to the gun work.

A stage, stuffed with drums and amplifiers, sat at the end of the room. A chrome pole rose from the centre and got lost in the darkness overhead. The room was mostly black, the deep blue and silver club colours offering the only contrast. Every piece of furniture had a touch. Even the felt on the three pool tables was Stallion blue.

Gunner turned as he heard Jimmy Williams approach from behind. He grabbed a fistful of leather and slammed the prospect into the wall, pushing his chest into the small man's face. Williams stared into Gunner's chest and said nothing.

"Read that patch, prospect," he said.

There was no menace in his voice, a world of it in his clenched fist.

"*Gunner*," Williams said.

"I know my fucking name, prospect. Below that."

"*Vice-president*."

"And what does it say on the front of your cut? No, wait." Gunner spun Williams and pushed his face into a steel beam sticking out from the wall. Blood trickled from above his left eye. "Let me see what it says on your back. Not very fucking much." He released his grip and began to walk to the centre of the cavernous room. "You ever want to fill that back with a patch you better learn to shut up when I tell you, prospect." Gunner could feel the rage build.

He knew it wasn't the prospect. Seeing Cam behind that badge, hearing him give orders like every asshole cop Gunner had ever met. Maybe his brother was just another fucking prick.

Grease was still fidgeting with the MAC-10. On the floor beside him a partially assembled Harley engine sat bolted to a steel cradle. A few parts covered dirty rags beside it, tools filling the top tray of a red trolley nearby. The bottom tray held solvents, lubricants, and an assortment of tubes and bottles. Some for the engine, others for the gun.

"What's the prognosis?" Gunner asked as he knelt next to the engine.

"Circlip snapped off. Just like I said." Grease put down the MAC-10 and crouched beside Gunner. "Look here, see the scoring." He pushed the rod he was using to clean the machine pistol inside the exposed cylinder. Gunner nodded although he didn't know what to look for.

"Can you work on it now and lose the 10? We may have company."

"Who?" Grease moved around behind the bar, and snapped the components of the MAC-10 together.

"Cops. Cam maybe," Gunner said.

Grease dead eyed him and moved away with the gun. The old biker hated Cam's badge more than any other Stallion, maybe even more than Gunner. He let the hard stare go and looked at the stage where his guitar leaned against an old Fender amplifier. Gunner could squeeze the blues out of that guitar better than some of the pros. He looked at it now and thought maybe he should crank it up. A little Slash might help him take the edge off. Fuck it, Grease was in a dark place already. He might just put a bullet through the amp. Gunner dropped into the chair beside Snake.

"Problem with the prospect?" Snake asked.

Gunner reached between the chairs and pulled a can of beer out of a blue-and-silver cooler. Snapped the top open and took three long swallows before answering.

"Talks too much." He wiped the back of his hand across his mouth. "The real problem may be little brother."

He and Snake looked at a framed picture above the bar. Cam in blue-and-silver trunks standing in the middle of the octagon. The Stallion tattoo prominent on a cut left pec. Every muscle in his six-foot frame popping in the ring lights. That mop of black curls matted to his sweat-soaked head, his smile defiant. A ref holding his hand high while doctors worked on an opponent on the canvas behind him. Hell of a shot. Made the cover of a big mixed martial arts magazine. Made Cam a legend in the Stallion world.

"Guy had such promise," Snake said as he pulled on his own beer.

"War fucked him up." Gunner raised his beer to the picture.

"You came back okay."

"My ol' lady didn't die while I was chained to a rock in East butt-fuck Pakistan," Gunner said before taking another drink.

"True enough. So what's he want?"

"Somebody got killed over there, and he wants to come see if our cameras caught anything."

"Like fuck."

"What I told him," Gunner said, returning to his beer.

He watched Jimmy Williams hover near the pool tables, waiting for permission to go to bed. Not likely.

"Prospect," Snake said.

Williams moved quickly. His exaggerated swagger rocked his shoulders from side to side. Tiny little prospect showing big-time biker attitude. How the hell could Snake want to pin colours on that? Gunner wondered, not for the first time.

"Go to the office and check last night's tapes. Watch the dump. I need to know if there's anything more interesting than gulls fucking over there. Do it fast but don't miss anything. Go," Snake said.

Williams hustled across the room and disappeared behind a sliding door.

Gunner pulled the tab from his third beer as he stood behind the bar. This one held the cure. He emptied it in one long drink. He crushed the can in his fist, the inked silhouette of a naked woman dancing on his forearm as the muscles flexed. He looked at the fight playing out silently on the big screen.

Gunner had been nursing the same buzz for eight months. A fast beer before bed with one on the floor for the wake-up. Beer was the only sensible way to smooth the edges between the days. He'd seen the hard stuff suck the life out of too many bros. Gunner had drinking rules and he rarely broke them. He waited until he was up five hours before letting Jack lift him higher. Tough rule to follow today; he could hear Jack calling from behind the bar. He hadn't been to bed yet, so maybe the beer rule didn't apply. Problem was his second rule did. The buzz was turning dark. Adding Jack to a bad buzz could stoke the hate. That never ended well. Seeing Cam with all those fucking cops shoved his head into an ugly place. How could the brother he raised turn on him, on the club? He needed to hurt someone. Maybe go back into the office and kick the prospect around.

He shook off the idea and pulled an orange-and-black oil can from under the bar. It was a decorative piece of Harley junk someone had left in the clubhouse. He pulled off the lid and savoured the sour smell. He grabbed the small blue-and-silver pipe and pinched off a bit of the pot that filled the can. Just enough to chase the darkness away. It was prime pot from Bear River in the Annapolis Valley. It blew the leaves off the famous BC bud.

Gunner decided he'd take the two-and-a-half-hour ride to Bear River in a day or so, keep his growers honest with an unexpected visit. The long solo run would do him good. His grow-ops there were his biggest earners. He had a sweet deal with a Mi'kmaw lobster crew fishing out of St. Mary's Bay. They took the crop out to the Canada-US line and handed it over to a crew from the Aroostook, Maine, reserve. The fisheries patrols stayed away from First Nations boats. Their last attempt to interfere with the traditional native fishery left wharves and boats burning along the coast. There was peace on the water now, and the government didn't want to do anything to change that. Gunner's crop quietly made its way to Boston, and the cash flowed back.

He pushed the tiny bits of grass into the pipe and held a lighter to it. There was an air hole on the smooth front edge, and Gunner placed a finger over it as he drew on the pipe. As the grass glowed red, he removed his finger and inhaled quickly, taking the smoke deep into his lungs, chasing a hard hit. He coughed it out and put his stash back under the counter. An intense body-numbing rush spread to his limbs, smoothing out the alcohol buzz. He smiled. Perfect.

He dropped back in the chair next to his now sleeping club president and let his mind float. He remembered smoking pot with Cam in the shed outside their mobile home. It was Cam's first time, and Gunner was his guide. Always the guide for little brother. At least, until Greg stepped in and pulled him away from the club. Greg, the brother Gunner really didn't know, didn't understand, didn't want to. Guy was a priest for fuck's sake. Off on some pilgrimage in Spain now, total head case. The old lady blew her brains out on a bad meth trip a month after he was born. At the time, Greg was in the hospital coming down off his own addiction, a birthright. Their grandparents took Greg from the hospital and turned him into a Jesus freak. They left Gunner and Cam to fend for themselves with the old man. That went well. Shit, his mind was floating back to the darkness. He tried to shake off the ghosts. He thought maybe another small hit would do it. He sat stuck to the chair pondering that.

Gunner turned at the squeal of the big steel office door. Williams was back already, waddling across the room with a stupid grin on his heavily pocked face.

"You smoking my pot back there, prospect?" Gunner reached down and pulled another beer from the cooler.

"You can't possibly be finished looking at all that video." Snake was in the conversation, like he'd never been asleep.

"Don't have to," Williams said, still grinning.

"The fuck you saying? I gave you a clear fucking order." Snake slapped Williams on the side of the face with the remote. The grin stayed. It was a glancing blow.

"You said you need to know. Anything interesting, and you need to know. I saw something." Full-on, shit-eating grin now.

"What did you see?" Gunner stood. "Show me."

"Let's go," Snake said as he stood.

The grinning prospect led the way. The Satan's Stallion office sat at the end of a storage room that ran the length of the warehouse. The door opened in the middle of the run. To the right, floor-to-ceiling shelves lined the walls. Harley parts filled every shelf, most hot, Grease's stash. To the left, a row of dented metal lockers covered the outer wall. They held leather vests with Stallion colours. The Stallion patch belongs to the club, not the brother wearing it, and most members leave them locked here in the house when not on club business. The habit became popular when the cops seized a full patch during a drug raid on a brother's home. Seeing the cops show it off on TV was more than Snake could handle.

The lockers were plastered with decals featuring quotes from the biker bible: *Helmet laws suck; Loud pipes save lives; FTW; FTP; Doesn't play well with others;* and of course, *We don't dial 911*. The silver-and-blue *SFFS* and *SSMC* badges topped every locker. The *Stallion Forever Forever Stallion* and *Satan's Stallion Motorcycle Club* stickers also marked the club bikes. Better protection against theft than any insurance policy. Pin-ups of naked women posed on member's bikes drew the eye away from the decals. Each autographed with a pledge of devotion to the locker's owner. Gunner touched the pin-up on his locker as he walked past it; Snake did the same to his. Jimmy Williams had no locker and kept his hands to himself.

Phil Murphy sat beneath a bank of monitors at the end of the room, the back of the chair a small slab of leather between his shoulders. He stood as Gunner approached. Murphy was the top enforcer with the Litter Box Boys, the street gang handling Stallion drug business in the profitable Spryfield area of the city. Jimmy Williams ran the gang. He was a fuck-up as a prospect, but he kept the Litter Box clean. Had to give him that. Gunner remembered his days in the Box when murder was just a part of the game. Under Williams, the body count had dropped and the police attention faded. Always good for business.

Murphy shoved his hands in his pockets and backed up against the wall, afraid of the little prospect. Gunner shook his head. Williams took the chair and began to work the computer controls. The monitors showed every angle of the property through the security cameras outside. The monitors went black, and then they all showed the same image as Williams pounded the keyboard.

"Here it comes." The screens showed the glow from the Fairview Cove Container Terminal. "Watch to the right." Williams pointed to the monitor nearest him. A blur emerged where the road passed in front of the clubhouse. It was silhouetted by the lights from the cranes. A dark vehicle: small, high, an SUV, for sure. It stopped in front, hidden by the gates.

"Is that it? Can you make it clearer?" Snake leaned forward, putting his hands on the desk beside Williams.

"Hang on," Williams said. "Just wait." Giving orders now.

The front gates opened, and a small shadow raced inside the compound. The gates closed before there was a clear view of the SUV. The cameras were useless; you could see the person, but it was so grainy you couldn't make out any detail.

"Now what?" Gunner asked.

"Nothing for five minutes." Williams punched the keyboard, and the numbers in the top left corner of each screen skipped ahead.

The shadowy figure walked out through the compound and slipped between the gates. The vehicle emerged from behind the wall and drove up into the dump. Williams punched the keys, and the time code began to race again. He slowed it just as a set of headlights came down the hill and blinded the cameras. A second later, the SUV was gone.

"Fuck," Snake said. "Who the hell was that? What time did that happen?"

"Three-thirty this morning." Williams pointed to the time log on the monitors.

"Who the fuck would come here and dump a fucking body? Fix the image." Gunner slapped Williams in the back of the head.

"It's the light. The light from the terminal is blinding our cameras. It won't get any clearer." He tapped on the computer keyboard. The image on the screens got worse. "See?"

"What about the side door? Did he get inside? Search that tape again. And put the live feed back on the top row. I want to see what the fucking cops are doing," Snake said.

Gunner turned and headed back past the lockers. Grease was the only one who hadn't gone on the run last night. If someone knocked on the clubhouse door at 3:30, Grease was the brother who opened it.

+—+—+

Gunner found Grease back at work. The old man knelt on the floor beside the cradled motor. Black-rimmed glasses and a visor with an LED light helped him see the work. He held a dome-topped piston in his right hand; with his left, he steadied a connecting rod that stuck out above the open engine cases. The cylinders were gone now. Gunner knelt on the opposite side of the cradle. He knew when not to interrupt Grease.

"Hold the rod," Grease said without looking up.

Gunner wrapped his fist around the thin steel connecting rod. It was about an inch wide where he held it and widened around a circular opening just above his fist. He'd never helped Grease before and didn't understand how the engine worked. Holding the rod gave him a connection to his own ride he'd never felt before. He realized it was also a connection to Cam. From the time he was old enough to hold a wrench, you couldn't pull Cam away from Grease.

There was a channel at the base of the piston, and Grease lowered it in place. The opening in the top of the rod lined up with two matching holes, one in each side of the piston skirt. Grease reached for a stainless steel tube not much bigger than his thumb. He slid it through the smooth tunnel, marrying the piston to the rod.

Gunner released the rod as he watched the white-haired biker grab what looked like a pair of pliers with a rounded blunt end. He eased a small metal ring onto the nose of the tool and pushed it into the opening in the hollow stainless steel tube. There was a groove cut into the outer edge of the piston to hold the ring. There was a small snapping sound, and Grease removed the tool. He repeated the move on the opposite side. The tube could no longer slide out of the piston and connecting rod. He looked up.

"Locked and loaded. That was the bastard. Tiny little clip. Fucking motor company buying Chink garbage now. Two-cent clip wrecks a five-thousand-dollar power plant. Fuck." He wiped sweat from his forehead with his sleeve and picked up the second piston.

"Hey, Grease, hang on a minute."

Grease held the piston in his hand.

"Who was here last night, bro?"

"Couple of the boys from the Box stopped in for a beer, imported some real fucking music and showed me how to use your stereo, too. All Skynyrd, all the time now, bro." He smiled as he moved to position the second piston.

Gunner could almost see the oily fingerprints on his touch screen.

"Anyone else? Tape shows someone at 3:30 this morning."

"What?" Grease leaned in over the engine, adjusting the black glasses. "Oh, yeah. The dancer. I didn't let her in."

"Dancer, what dancer?"

"That little bitch with the schoolgirl gig. Don't know her name."

Gunner knew it.

"What did she want, Grease? It's important, bro."

Grease lowered the piston to the floor again and wiped his hand in a rag.

"She was bitching about some trick gone bad. Said she needed the club to fix her shit."

Gunner ran his hand through his close-cropped brown hair. The dead body was a Stallion problem after all.

"What did you tell her?"

"Told her to fuck off outta here. I'm not into helping strippers. Those bitches always have some drama going on, man. You know that."

"Shit."

"What?"

"Nothing, man," said Gunner. "Nothing. Dumb bitch dumped that body across the street, and now we've got cop trouble."

"Body? She didn't say shit about a body, bro. I woulda made sure she got it the hell out of here if she said she had a body."

"No worries, bro. We'll deal with it."

Gunner stood, and Grease returned to his work. There was no way to undo the damage. Distancing the club was the only option now. He wanted to go question the dancer, maybe kill her, but the cops might be on to her by now. There was no way he could get close. Williams would have to handle it. The dancers were his problem anyway, and if he got busted, well, fuck him and the Harley he rode in on. Wasn't much of a prospect, anyway.

CHAPTER 3

I BANGED ON THE DOOR WITH THE SIDE OF MY FIST, HEARD A MUFFLED voice from inside.

"Sorry. Everyone went to bed. You'll have to come back." Jimmy Williams, I was sure of it. Mostly because the cover on the peephole didn't move. He was too short to use it.

"Fuck off, prospect, and open the door."

The deadbolts began to slide open. Good to see the club tattoo still carried clout with the prospects.

I pushed past Williams and headed down the hallway. Snake and Gunner were standing near the bar. I saw Grease huddled over a stripped-down twin cam. He had two pistons sitting on top of the connecting rods and was ready to lower the cylinders over them. He'd need help with the rings. I fought the urge to go help him. Figured he had a gun nearby and might use it. Losing that old man's respect is the biggest price I paid for my decision to walk away. I shook off the regret.

"Offer a brother a coffee?" I said to Gunner.

"Something better in the cooler." Gunner nodded toward the centre of the room.

"No, Gunner, he's on duty," Snake said as he moved toward me. "Oh wait, he can't be on duty or he wouldn't be in the middle of my fucking clubhouse." He eyed Williams as he spoke.

"Now, Snake, don't shoot the prospect. At least not on my account. I checked my badge at the door." I reached into the cooler and pulled out a can of beer. I'd regret it, but I needed to put Snake at ease.

Snake and Gunner walked over and did the same. Three brothers-of-the-road drinking in silence; what better way to greet the day? Long time since I'd felt the cold bite of a morning brew. Williams stood nearby without a beer. I think he was pouting. What was the club coming to? I glanced back and forth between my brother and the president of the Halifax Charter of the Satan's Stallion Motorcycle Club. Gunner was wearing an Under Armour workout shirt. His muscles rippled through the black fabric with every move, his biceps popping below the sleeves. Big brother was getting bigger. Snake was, too. He was showing the strain of too many years and too many beers. His paunch fell over a chrome pistol belt buckle that fought to stem the tide. His long blonde hair looked bleached, grey stubble on his face telling the tale. I tipped my beer to the framed picture of my proudest moment as a mixed martial artist. As long as it hung in the house, I knew I still had some status.

There are no gold watches for retired outlaws, a body bag sometimes, but no watch. Those of us who get out alive are attached to the club for life. As the tattoo says, *Stallion Forever Forever Stallion*. I was the only man to ever wear the Stallion patch and a badge. Most bikers and more than a few cops will tell you the body bag was the better option. It's good they agree on something. Members out in good standing are welcome in any clubhouse for a beer, a game of pool, or to work on their ride, as long as it is still a Harley. Snake didn't want me standing there, but he would never violate the Stallion code. That's the one-percenter's way. Guys drop out, condemn society's rules, and choose to live under an even bigger thumb. I was out from under it, but the Stallion tattoo will always remain over my heart. It was my father's baby, love the prick or hate him.

Even a founder's son out in good standing is banned from church, the weekly meetings where club business gets hammered out. I figured drug deals, prostitution, and extortion were still the big-three money-makers. Not every Stallion is a criminal, but every patch knows the score. The guys in the OMG unit say just being a Stallion makes a man a criminal, that wearing the patch is a form of extortion. I can't argue it. A Stallion rolling is a message to anyone dealing in drugs or sex. The streets belong to the club, and it better be getting its share. The rumble of a Harley can be the most terrifying sound in the world. To some, it speaks of violence and death. I knew it when I rode under the patch, and I know it now.

"So, bro, what's with the clowns outside?" Snake broke the silence.

"If I could pick up my badge for a minute." I put the half-finished beer on a table. "We have a dead body over there, Snake. Famous one, at that. It's that guy on the billboard out front. Appreciate it if you could keep that secret for a while." No point in hiding it. The news guys would have it soon, and offering Snake some inside information, even short-lived, might pay off.

"The preacher? No shit."

"The one and only. I need to take a look at your tape from last night. You have a pretty good angle on the street."

Snake ran his hand through his blonde hair and looked at Gunner.

"You're asking from behind the badge, not as a bro. So the answer is 'fuck off.' Pick up that beer or hit the road. Your call, pig."

I stepped in closer, my fists tight at my side. Snake held his ground. We eye-fucked each other. You can't give quarter in a clubhouse, not even with the president.

"I'll ignore that this time. You're tired. But remember, I am still that guy, bro. Always will be." I stood a second longer and then eased back, took another drink, and nodded to Gunner as I headed out. As the door slammed behind me, I heard the crash of a beer can. The prospect got a taste, after all.

My adrenaline spiked, keeping me jacked and on edge on the way to Sandy Gardner's home. Blair can read me better than most; he stayed quiet during the drive. Being called a pig didn't mean anything, but having it come from Snake inside the house was a problem. It was an insult to Gunner I couldn't let pass. Still, I regretted threatening Snake. We needed that video.

We drove silently through Waverley on a highway that hugged Lake William and offered a great view of its small tree-covered islands.

Realtors call the highway "an idyllic meandering road." They also advertise private lakefrontage with the top-dollar properties. They don't mention the highway that slices between the front door and water beneath the overbuilt hilltop homes. The private docks and power boats dotting the lakeshore are proof there is no shortage of people willing to dodge a little traffic to get to their private paradise.

Gardner's estate was an exception. His seven-acre peninsula jutted into the lake on the side of the highway. There is serious money in the God game. Those same realtors would call his house "a classic rancher." I thought "strip mall" worked, too. The V-shaped single-storey home sat at the end of a long driveway of multicoloured brick pavers. The inner drive opened to a circular plaza big enough to be called a concourse. A sculpted cherub, surrounded by flowers, was pouring water from a vase into a pond in the middle of the space. I knew a coke dealer who had a spread like this before downsizing to a small cell. A large copper-and-brass dollar sign sprayed water into his pond. Salvation was a different kind of drug, but the profit margin seemed to be the same.

The opposing wings of the house reached out from double doors to shelter the cherub and the parking concourse. A three-bay, two-storey garage sat tucked into the treeline on the left side of the driveway. A smooth slab on the opposite side was cut into three tennis courts. Beyond the courts, the lake wrapped around the side and back of the property.

I'd been here a couple of times. It always impressed. Little brother Greg convinced me to do a security audit for Gardner. Hard to say no to a brother who helped sober you up, harder still when he wears the white collar. Blair tucked the car in front of the garage. I made a mental note to call Greg. Pastor Gardner was a friend of his, and I wanted to fill him in before he heard about the murder on the radio. First, I'd have to deal with the more difficult notification inside.

We parked beside a white Ford Escape. A tan Mercedes sedan was parked on the other side of the small SUV.

"Hope the car doesn't leak anything on the driveway," Blair said, looking out over the sparkling silver surface of the lake. "Don't think the city could afford to fix it."

He tossed me a pack of gum. "I'm not asking," he said.

"It was work-related." I could taste the stale beer.

"Did I ask?"

"Thanks." I popped a piece of gum and stuck the wrapper in my pocket. "I'll lead; you read."

"Always."

It was the routine we developed when we worked major crime the first time. Blair would read body language and take notes. I'd lead the questioning. Death notifications suck; you can't let empathy get in the way. Next of kin are suspects first and bereaved second. Cold, but then police work is never warm and fuzzy. People tend to get killed by those who love them most.

An oversized oak door opened before we had a chance to ring the bell. Bobby Simms stepped out. His bald head shone above a tight silver dress shirt that fought to contain his muscles. A black tattoo peered above the neckline. A gold cross reflected sunlight from his left earlobe. He looked like a bouncer in a high-end strip joint. His crooked smile did little to soften the look. I picked Bobby for suspect number two on my list. The vic's husband or wife is always the front runner, so Mrs. Gardner was ahead of him.

"Cam Neville. Well, we don't often get to see the brother with the badge. Father Greg is a regular, of course. I guess his collar is a kind of badge though, isn't it?" The tone was welcoming, loose.

"Hey, Bobby." We moved up the two steps leading to the door. "We need to come in for a minute."

"Sure, sure. Come on in. My name is Bobby Simms." He reached past me to Blair. It was getting crowded on the stoop. He grabbed my partner's hand. "You are?"

"Constable Blair Christmas."

"Aren't you blessed to have our Saviour's name in yours? Come on in. What brings you here today, Cam?"

"It's business, Bobby. We need to talk with Mrs. Gardner. Is she around?" Simms closed the door.

"No. I'm afraid she isn't even in the country. She is in Africa on church business. Pastor Sandy is not here at the moment either. Can I help?"

Widow gets an alibi pass. Time to move Bobby up the list.

The foyer was isolated from the rest of the house by a knee wall. Beyond it, we could see the kitchen. An oak mantle capping the wall was filled with plants and framed pictures of Sandy Gardner, his wife, and their adopted son, Samuel. A white pillar stopped the wall at the entrance to the kitchen. Every surface gleamed. Floor-to-ceiling windows surrounding glass patio doors backlit the kitchen. They offered a clear view of the lake. The sun sparkled on the silver and blue waves. Fat white clouds slipped past the trees on the far shore. The view was proof that the best things in life are free. The pastor's kitchen was proof money still buys you the best seats.

The air was thick with the smell of baking bread and fresh coffee, a hint of some kind of cleaning agent just beneath it. I glanced around for signs of someone trying to clean up a crime scene. Nothing but sun sparkling in a gleaming kitchen.

I remembered an old Formica table covered in dirty dishes, cigarette butts, and empty bottles. A *Playboy* calendar pinned to the wall above it. I wondered where I'd be if I'd grown up in a clean, normal house like this. Of course, I've seen good kids come out of crack kitchens and evil pricks come from mansions. Still, a little more baked bread and a little less bourbon in our kitchen might have made a difference for Gunner and me. Well, maybe not Gunner. I've never been inside my grandparents' house, so I don't know what kind of kitchen Greg grew up in. More like this than ours, I figure.

"Did you see Pastor Gardner leave?" I asked Bobby.

"No. I drove up from the church like I do every morning. He was gone when I got here. Thelma is here. She'll know where he is. What is this about?"

Thelma Waters walked through the patio doors before I could answer. She was carrying fresh-cut flowers. The reds, yellows, and oranges of the blossoms gave a warm glow to her pale skin and white hair. The sixty-three-year-old retired teacher spent her days looking after the Gardner family. She was a founding member of their church and perhaps its most devout lay minister.

"Hi, Thelma, this is Constable Christmas."

"Good morning. Good to see you both. We are expecting Father Greg. He didn't say you were coming, Cam. We can't wait to hear about his Camino pilgrimage. Have you seen him since he returned?" she asked.

"Yes, he's thinner. Is Samuel around?"

"He's here somewhere." She smiled and moved toward the kitchen counter with the flowers. "Coffee is fresh."

A door on the left side of the kitchen swung open. Samuel Gardner walked in. Sam was small for a seventeen-year-old, bordering on frail. His eyelids dipped low into brown eyes, giving him a permanent sleepy look. Not that you'd ever get a good look at them. Sam's gaze was always on the floor. His deep tan and rich black hair hinted at his Honduran roots. Sam was among the first orphans brought to Canada by the Little Maria Foundation and the only one adopted by Pastor Gardner himself. He'd spent two years in a refugee camp after a hurricane-soaked mudslide erased his world. His family, every person he knew, his entire village and world gone in seconds.

Sam had become a featured attraction on Pastor Gardner's broadcasts. He'd get so caught up in Gardner's revival-style evangelical preaching that he'd walk slowly to the podium and begin to speak in tongues, his eyes shut, his hands raised. Others in the congregation would fall to the floor. I had no idea if it was real or staged. I figured he was so damaged by the early childhood trauma that his ranting could have been his way of coping with the pain. I hoped his faith was really that strong; he'd need a higher power to lean on right now.

Sam stopped as he entered the kitchen and looked quickly toward Thelma and then back to the floor. The kid screamed *damaged*, even after all these years in a good home. Some hurt can't be undone by a clean kitchen. I didn't want to drop more pain on his world.

"Constable Neville, it's been more than a year. I was convinced I'd never see you again. The Lord reminds me of the virtue of patience," Sam said. At least he remembered me.

"Be still in the presence of the Lord and wait patiently for Him to act, my dear." Thelma smiled.

"Those who wait on the Lord shall renew their strength," Bobby added with a smile of his own.

I wondered what the Bible verse might be for "Wake up and smell the badges." So far, no one seemed concerned about two police officers arriving unannounced. That's not healthy, if you ask me.

"Thelma, Samuel, can you both sit for a moment? I have some bad news." Blair did that disappearing thing, fading to a neutral corner to watch. There is no easy way to tell people. Your adrenaline spikes, your stomach falls. You need to be on top of your game, but you can't be. Not if you have any humanity left.

"Samuel, I'm sorry." I reached out and put my hand on the kid's arm. "Your father was found in the city this morning. I'm afraid he's been a victim of foul play. I am so sorry, Sam."

I watched as this frail boy absorbed the news. His shoulders hunched forward. He seemed to sink inside himself, his eyes looking quickly at me, then to Thelma, and back to the floor. Bobby Simms covered his mouth as a schoolgirl squeal slipped past his lips. Thelma reached for Sam as she took two steps in our direction before she fainted. I scratched her off the suspect list as Blair picked her up.

We were in tricky territory. The eight ball was rolling around on the table now, ready to drop. Section Eight of the Charter of Rights protects every Canadian's privacy. It also handcuffs every cop trying to keep them safe. Section Eight says we can't violate a person's reasonable expectation of privacy. That's where the judges went crazy. The courts have stretched the concept so far, we damn near need a warrant to step out of a squad car. The slightest suspicion that there could be evidence of a crime on private property makes it warrant territory. With the notification finished, we couldn't search the house. Just being inside risked scratching the eight ball. The smart move was to order everyone out, wrap the property in yellow tape, and sit on our hands for five or six hours waiting for a search warrant. I wasn't feeling smart. I needed to know where Sandy Gardner was killed. I couldn't burn six hours only to find out this wasn't our crime scene.

Besides, technically, we had no reason to suspect anyone, and that was wiggle room. I didn't think Gardner was killed in the house. Thelma Waters was part church secretary, part housekeeper and would have been through the house already, but Gardner's office was above · the garage and probably not part of her morning routine. A peek there could rule out the need for a warrant and let us move on. I knew there'd be some uncomfortable time in the witness box explaining my decision, but I'd swallow that medicine when the time came.

Thelma was sipping a glass of water and sitting beside Samuel. He was lost in a staring contest with the gleaming kitchen floor.

"Thelma, you do the cleaning here, is that right?" I asked.

"Yes, why?"

"Just wondering if you've been through the house today, if you noticed anything out of place."

"You mean like a robbery? You think someone killed Pastor Gardner and robbed him?"

"It's too early to tell. We may need to get a team here to search the house, and it will help them a lot if you noticed anything they should check first."

"No. Nothing. Do you want to go look now?" she asked.

"I would, but that's not how it works. We have experts to do that sort of thing. What I would like, if you don't mind, is to use the phone up in the office. I have to call and tell Father Greg what's happened, and I'd like to speak with him in private. I don't want to make a call like that on a cell." Blair shot me a look that I ignored.

"Oh, of course. Yes, Father will need to know. Please tell him we'd still like him to stop by if he could."

"I will. Now, I need all three of you to stay right here in the kitchen. Constable Christmas will stay with you." I looked at Blair. He nodded. The eight ball scratch was mine, not his.

Thelma gave me a key to the side door of the garage, but I didn't need it. It wasn't locked. It was going to be tough to convince a judge why that didn't make me suspicious enough to wait for a warrant. Oak handrails topped carved balusters on both sides of the stairway; plush red carpeting covered each step. Sunlight streaming in through skylights splashed back from gold-plated doves inlaid on each riser. A lot of money for a stairway. I thought of the coke dealer again. Maybe God was a better seller.

The door at the top of the staircase opened inward to reveal a long, spacious room running the length of the garage. The centre of the back wall, like the one in the kitchen, was all glass. It rose to meet the roofline at the peak and showed an even more impressive view. You could see the full length of the lake and the green-on-green patchwork of maple, birch, pine, and spruce trees covering the hillside across from the Gardner estate.

A glass-top desk sat beneath the glass wall, its high-backed leather chair turned away from the windows offering instead a view of a vanity wall. Pictures of Pastor Gardner with prime ministers and princes, presidents and paupers. At least a dozen showing him holding young children in Third World slums. I wondered if any were taken in Pakistan; some of the scenes looked like my village in the hills. At least the chosen ones saved by his adoption agency wouldn't be swinging knotted ropes at anyone.

Above the pictures, a shelf held an assortment of art objects collected from those same countries. Everything seemed to be in order. My concern about Section Eight eased, but the clean room did little to relieve the anxiety over not knowing where the murder happened. I still didn't think Gardner was killed at the dump.

There was a telephone on the desk. I walked over to make my call. I paused a moment when I saw a day planner, the old-fashioned paper kind. Old-school preacher, nice. I took a pen from my pocket and flipped it open to yesterday's date. A few meetings filled his final day along with a note to call Father Neville. A youth group meeting at the church was the last appointment in the book. Everything was in perfect cursive script. More likely it was old-school Thelma at work here. Yep, a note in a different hand ran down the left edge of one page. That would be Sandy Gardner, doodling maybe, while on the phone. *My Sweet Lo*, it said. Guess he hung up before he finished the lyric. Thinking of him hanging up a call reminded me to make one. I still wanted to give Greg a heads up, but seeing his name in the day planner meant I also needed to know if my brother had heard from Gardner yesterday.

I was dialling Greg's number when I noticed a flickering light at the far end of the room. I put the handset back in the cradle. I figured the office was at least fifteen, maybe twenty metres long. A cluster of chairs surrounded a coffee table in the space furthest from the door. An open laptop sat on the table. A leather wingback chair was overturned in front of it.

As I got closer, I could see handcuffs hanging from its curved front legs. A dark nylon cord hung from an open rafter on the ceiling. It stopped just short of the overturned chair. A looped slide show was causing the flicker on the laptop screen. I watched as one picture melted into another. The blue light just below the screen told me it was coming from a disc inserted into the computer.

Was I standing in the crime scene? If I was, the suspect pool was going to be a deep one. Gardner's office was the hub of his Church of Salvation and The Little Maria adoption agency. Hundreds of people came through this place in the run of a year. When I did the security audit, I found out Gardner had given keys to at least a dozen members of his congregation. I'd advised him to change the lock and that policy. I hoped he'd followed that advice.

The images on the computer screen punched a hole in my chest. Children, twisted and contorted into someone's idea of sex toys. Posed for a camera in graphic sexual positions. Some with adults whose faces were digitally blurred, most with other children whose faces were left clear. The screen filled with a young girl, six maybe seven, her blonde curls spread across a satin pillow. The hairy gut of an overweight man hung over her. The picture didn't show the man's head. I looked for tattoos or scars on his body, anything that would help the ICE team identify the bastard. The Internet Child Exploitation squad would have to scour every image on the disc. They could have that gig. I looked into the little girl's eyes as she faded from the screen, replaced by another child. I'd seen the look in bombed-out villages in Afghanistan. The kids there had lost limbs. The little girl on the computer had lost everything.

Two glasses of amber liquid, a candy dish, and a pill bottle sat beside the laptop. I made the liquid for Scotch; the multicoloured tablets in the dish had to be ecstasy. I didn't need a closer look to know there'd be a Satan's head stamped on every pill. Stallion approved. Blue football-shaped pills filled the bottle. I saw a small blood stain on the overturned back of the chair. A set of men's clothing sat on a chair behind the laptop. The way they were neatly folded told me Gardner had taken his clothes off voluntarily.

I stood there for five minutes. It felt like five hours. I needed every detail while it was fresh. I didn't want to look at the computer, but I knew those kids would be the fuel that would drive me now. Pastor Gardner didn't feel worth avenging anymore.

The scene didn't add up. If Gardner was killed here—and the cuffs, the clothes, and blood stain sure made it look that way—why move him? Moving a body is about hiding it. Usually, the body drop is off the side of a boat or in deep woods, not an open area beside a busy terminal. If it was just to lead us away from here, then why leave this scene intact? The obvious answer was post-kill panic. Even people who carefully plan a murder will often panic and make stupid decisions after the body falls. I'd seen people go to great lengths to cover up a crime and forget to get rid of a gun. Every cop loves post-kill panic. It solves a lot of cases. This scene looked like it could have been abandoned when the killer freaked. But, why drive past count-less small docks beside a nice deep lake and take a body to the old dump? There was another possibility I didn't like. The scene I was looking at was a fake.

It didn't look staged, but that was something I had to consider. The kiddy-porn crowd tends to dig up its garbage online. The ICE team finds it hidden in hard drives behind firewalls and false files. The computer disc was portable; anyone could have inserted it into the pastor's laptop and hit play. My instincts told me this was real, and the pastor had a serious problem. But was I being played?

Being a murder cop is a complicated gig. I made a few notes about my initial thoughts, and the doubts. Even if it was the real scene, finding it was adding to the mystery, not helping to solve it. It would be up to Carla Cage and the forensic team to tell me whether it was real and what it said.

I retraced my steps and headed for the stairway. I looked at the telephone on the desk and regretted touching it. As I walked down the stairs I realized that little mistake might just keep the eight ball in play. No judge would think I went up there believing it was a crime scene, and then touched the phone. Instead, I'd look like an idiot who stumbled into the crime scene blind. I could live with that.

I called dispatch and ordered up a crime-scene team. I didn't know if Sandy Gardner was killed in the garage, but I was damn sure what happened there was criminal. I decided our best bet was to accept that Gardner was a pedophile unless the crime-scene techs found something suggesting a staged scene. If he was a sick bastard, that offered motive, something we were lacking so far. An angry kill, and then a panicked killer, made sense. I'd share my initial doubts with Blair so we didn't get tunnel vision, but working the kiddy-porn angle felt right to me. Sometimes that matters more than anything.

+++

The kitchen looked shabbier. Same place, sunshine still sparkling from gleaming surfaces. It just didn't feel any cleaner than my old man's dump now that I believed a pedophile liked to chow down at the table. Kiddy porn leaves a big stain.

Blair was outside waiting for the cruisers to bring enough yellow tape and uniforms to lock the property down. By declaring this our primary crime scene I pulled most of the resources from the dump. I told Blair what I'd found in the office. It put him in a dark place, and he wanted to stay out of the house.

The images from the laptop played non-stop in my mind. I craved action, but I was stuck. I looked at the old-fashioned clock on the wall. I could feel the second hand pounding like a sledgehammer. We were racing toward that moment when red tape replaced yellow tape. Cops work murder for victims. Unfortunately, we do it in a system built for defence lawyers and their clients. Crown attorneys in Nova Scotia have been wimps since a judge bitch-slapped them for playing cute one of Canada's biggest ever wrongful death cases.

A couple of cigar-chewing mine managers walked away from twenty-six bodies in an underground sweatshop called the Westray Mine, because the prosecutors didn't play fair.

Now, they build a disclosure file that would fill a coal mine. They demand a log of every step taken by every cop. That means a file manager, usually a sergeant, must approve and record every move we make in the field. Before we make it. Tends to slow things down for the cops. Works for the prosecutors, though. They overwhelm defence lawyers with a kind of over disclosure that can hide evidence in plain sight.

Thelma was comforting Samuel at the table. Bobby Simms leaned against the kitchen counter, the smile gone. There was anger in his posture, defiance in his folded arms. Bobby used to be a dangerous guy until he ran into Jesus in the prison yard. Looked to me like there was still some hard guy in there. He'd have to come to the office for the long chat later, but I figured I'd keep it civil for now, just take him outside to ask a few questions. My phone beeped before I could ask him to follow me out. A text from Blair. I wasn't happy with what it said.

"Thelma, Father Greg is out front. Do you still want him to come in?" I asked.

"Please, yes, we do." She put a hand on Sam's arm.

"Okay, I'll send him in. Hey, Bobby, come on along. I want to chat with you outside for a minute."

A priest was a good idea for Sam and Thelma. I just wished it was a different priest; one brother a day is my limit. My relationship with my little brother is complicated. Greg pulled me out of that alcohol-fuelled tailspin when I left the club, and I am grateful. Unfortunately, he still thinks he's saving me and offers priestly advice when I don't want or need it. He forgets he's my brother, not my father. He didn't grow up with Gunner and me. We share parents and not much else. The old man was a full-on junkie by the time Greg came along. He didn't put up a fight when our mother's parents took him in. Living with the old man was a bitch, and we resented Greg for getting a free ride. He probably didn't have it much better, but we just couldn't see it that way. Our crazy grandparents believed he was born to atone for the sins of our meth-head mother. A gift from God they called him, and they promised to give him back. They pushed him from the cradle to the collar.

When Greg joined the priesthood, we resented him for that, too. We figured he was trying to prove he wasn't one of the white-trash Neville brothers. I feel differently now, but the old resentments can still pop up. Call it sibling rivalry, call it jealousy. Whatever it is, I didn't have the time or energy for it. I needed ice in my veins if I was going to get past the slide show still playing above the garage.

Greg was standing outside the front door. A young Mountie was with him. Guess the cruisers had arrived. She looked from Greg to me, smiling at the resemblance. We weren't exactly twins, but there was no mistaking the connection. Gunner and I have more in common, but Greg and I look like brothers. I ran my hand through my own hair as I looked at his unruly mop, the dark curls falling over his forehead into his eyes. Beneath all that hair, Greg's face was a golden brown, much darker than mine. His gunmetal blue eyes looked black behind the tan. The month spent walking through France and Spain had darkened his skin and melted away what little body fat he had. His face seemed harder. I wondered if I ever looked that tough. The tiny white collar looked more out of place now than ever. I asked the constable to take Bobby over to my car and wait with him.

"Pray for us, Father," Bobby said.

"I will, Bobby, I will." Greg touched Simms on the arm.

Greg watched them walk away, reached out, and embraced me. I returned the hug. It felt uncomfortable. I hug Gunner every time I see him and don't even realize I do it. With Greg, it always feels awkward. I slapped him on the back as he released me. No patch there, maybe that was it.

"You're going to have to get some meat back on those bones," I said.

"The Camino changes you, body and soul. You should consider taking the walk yourself."

"I think a ride out to Sturgis would be enough of a pilgrimage for me."

"I suppose you do." His eyes locked on mine. "Tell me about Sandy."

"Not much I can tell you, Greg. He was found dead at the old city dump this morning. He was murdered, but everything else is evidence I can't share."

He looked back across the driveway. "You don't think Bobby had anything to do with it, do you? He's a good man despite his past. He loved Sandy. I know that."

"Thanks. I'll keep it in mind. We don't have any reason to suspect Bobby or anyone else yet. I just want to talk to him. Sam and Thelma are in the kitchen waiting for you." I started to move toward Simms. Greg grabbed my arm.

"Cam, Pastor Gardner was a good man. His church has saved the souls of thousands. Bobby is just one example. But, he was also a man, and men have weaknesses. Try to protect his work; let us remember him as a beacon of Christ."

I pulled my arm free. Did Greg know? Could he be asking me to cover it up? I felt the knuckles in my right hand pop as my fist tightened at my side. Greg's dark eyes stayed with mine.

"What exactly do you mean by weakness?" I tried to keep my tone neutral.

"I don't know for sure; he confided in me. Well, he tried to. He told me he battled demons and wondered if his good works were enough to erase his sins." He pushed the dark curls away from his eyes. I caught myself reaching for my own and stopped.

"Did he tell you what those sins were?"

"No. I was giving him time. I was sure he'd tell me when he was ready. I couldn't offer him the reconciliation of the confessional and struggled with how I could help."

He placed the edge of his thumb against his breastbone. I knew he was feeling the crucifix beneath his shirt. My spotter Ronald's crucifix. It was a tell. Lies are tricks one mind tries to play on another. The body can't lie. It reacts no matter what the mind tells it to do. I didn't want to believe Greg knew about the kids on that computer. I touched his hand. The crucifix was my badge of guilt. If I had left our hide after three kills like Ronald had asked, he'd be alive. I was happy to let Greg have it. I wondered if he was touching it now to ease his guilt.

"Why don't you tell me about the prayer you are saying right now?"

Greg pulled his hand down.

"I am praying for the Church of Salvation. I should go see Samuel."

I nodded. There wasn't any point in pushing him. We had too much baggage. It's easy to unravel lies in a controlled interview when you are detached and professional. Any cop can do it. If you bring your emotions to the game, forget it. The ringing in my ears told me my emotions were pinning the meter. Blair arrived at my side.

"Father." He nodded at Greg and turned to me. "You want me to have a word with Bobby?"

"No, let me do that," I said. "Can you take Greg inside to see Sam and Thelma?"

"Sure." He looked at me, a question in his eyes.

"You and I can chat again later, Greg."

I took deliberate long breaths as I walked back to the car. I needed to shake the feeling that Greg might be worried about the legacy of a monster and not about the children he devoured. Bobby Simms would get the best of me. He was no virgin in this game. Still, I had to watch my own prejudices. I was in the dark, and it felt like I was jumping at the first shiny thing. He was the suspect from central casting, and, as appealing as an ex-con in the house seemed, he was probably too good to be true. Bobby looked glum and guilty sitting in the back of my car as I approached. Maybe he wasn't too good to be true.

Decorative stonework covered the ground around the fountain. The little cherub was still pouring water into the garden. I stretched my back, continuing with the deep breathing, thinking I should learn yoga. I took my time, wanted Bobby to be damn clear on who was in control. I let him stew in the backseat. The Gardner property no longer looked like an exclusive estate. One RCMP cruiser blocked the end of the driveway, and another was parked on the grass near the garage. Yellow tape ran from behind the garage to a large oak tree half the distance to the road; it looped around the tree and stretched to a stone pillar at the entrance to the drive. Another length of tape ran from the opposite side of the garage to a wooden newel post at the end of a small private dock behind the house. The inner-city charm of yellow tape. Nothing like it to send property values into the basement, even in a place like this.

The cruisers were here guarding the property, but I still didn't see the crime-scene trucks. I needed the techs to go through that scene to see if it was real or staged. I also needed them to clear it before Blair and I could have our time there. Waiting is torture; action helps. I headed for Bobby. I pulled open the door and asked him to jump into the front seat. Treating him like a guest now. He moved up front and stared through the windshield. We both watched as a German shepherd came from the side of the house. The officer at the end of its leash looked at me and shook his head. I felt bad for the dog. They live for that joyful scratch behind the ears when they find a piece of evidence. Not a lot of scratching going on with this case. Bobby smiled when the officer unhooked the leash and let the dog jump into the back of an unmarked police SUV.

"No dice today, pup," he said.

"Just one of the tools, Bobby. You know that," I said.

"Looks like it was a waste of time, like what you're doing here." He turned his gaze on me. A yard-hardened con stare.

"Relax, Bobby, you're no suspect, or I'd be reading you your rights. You know that. I just need some information. When did you last see Pastor Gardner?"

He looked at me and then toward the house. A smile formed and he leaned back into the passenger door, turning his body to me. An open posture, a sign of honesty. In most people.

"Last night. We had a short meeting after dinner," he said.

"Anyone else there?"

"Yes, Samuel and several members of the youth outreach team. We were discussing the summer retreat in Canso and looking for ways to draw more young people to Christ. Always a challenge." He smiled.

"Were you two alone after that meeting?"

"No. I was the first to leave."

He wouldn't be dumb enough to try a lie that easy to uncover. Still, I made a note to check it.

"Where did you go?"

"Home. And no, I can't prove that." His arms folded, and the smile was gone.

"Don't worry about that right now, Bobby. I can't prove I was home last night either, and, like I said, you're not a suspect." He relaxed his arms but didn't drop them, keeping his posture closed. "Let's talk about your relationship with the victim. How does a repeat offender like you end up working with a guy like Gardner? Hell of a life change."

"No. It's been more of a heavenly life change. As it says in Isaiah, 'To open the blind eyes, to bring out the prisoners from the prison, and them that sit in darkness out of the prison house.' Look at your life, Cam, and how Greg has changed it. You must believe God's hand reached out to save you," he said.

"Stop with the Bible quotes, Bobby. I'm seeking a different kind of truth. Just tell me how you met Pastor Gardner and what your relationship was." We both turned in the car as a large motorhome made its way in past the yellow tape and parked near the tennis courts. Our rolling command centre.

Bobby told me a story that sounded rehearsed. Like he'd told it from a pulpit too many times. I watched for tells, but his body was relaxed, his posture open again. His shaved head rolled back to rest on the side window, like he was watching the movie of his life. The move made it easier to see the neck tattoo above his collar. It was a lynx, its teeth bared. The tattoo worn by all the Litter Box Boys. A gang tat is a shield in prison, where Bobby's story of salvation started. On the East Coast, the lynx was second only to the Stallion tat in the prison yard. Everybody inside knew the Litter Box Boys were the dirty-deed disciples of the Stallion and had the club's protection.

Sandy Gardner ran a prison outreach program that Bobby claimed led him to his new path. Jesus got credit for doing the real heavy lifting and cleansing Bobby of the sins of his old ways. I knew the old Bobby, and wasn't sure I was ready to trust the new one.

I remembered him as the dumbest, most violent thug to fall short of the Stallion standard. When I still rode with the club, Bobby was a typical Stallion hang-around. Ready to prove himself at every opportunity. He thought he could beat his way into the club. No finesse. Bobby was a follower who thought he was a leader. Told the club he hacked up a girlfriend because she turned rat on him, thought he could make his bones that way. Claimed he gave her a Colombian necktie to silence her forever. When her body didn't turn up, we all figured he made it up. Besides, she wasn't ratting on the club. No one cared.

He did his first trip for aggravated assault. He tried to prove he was a man by putting a heavy beating into some guy in a bar. Did it because the guy looked at a full patch's ol' lady. The brother thanked him, slapped him on the back, and let him do his time. It was that beating that cost Bobby any chance of making it to prospect status. He lost control and made the patches look bad. Knocking a guy out for stepping out of line was okay, but Bobby kept pounding on the poor slob long after it was necessary. He got off on the violence a little too much.

The beating drew him a two-year sentence. Hefty for a bar fight. That dead girlfriend's body surfaced while he was doing that stint. She was a hooker, and the cops never linked it to him. Chances are she went down to a bad trick, and he used the whole thing as some bullshit attempt to impress the club. Didn't work. Murderer or not, he wasn't back on the street long when he took fall number two. This one for kidnapping and torture. The Stallion lawyer defending him was sure they could beat the charge until Bobby insisted on taking the stand. The final bust had him trying his bad luck in the pot-import market. All that, and yet here he sat, free and still a relatively young man. Have to love our revolving-door prisons.

"Without Pastor Gardner, I'd be at the clubhouse or back inside. You changed, you found a way out. Well, Christ led me away, same as you."

"It took a taste of hell before I walked away, Bobby. Different journey. What I need to know is do you still have a foot in it? I can find out," I said, reminding him.

"No, man, the Stallion world is empty. I know it now. Jesus is the only one I ride behind. He loves me, He makes me perfect. I don't need that false power. Matthew teaches us to beware of false prophets. The Church of Salvation is my club. Thank you, Jesus." He closed his eyes and touched his heart.

It could be that Bobby was a new man. It could also be that he was full of shit. I needed to know, and listening to him preach wasn't helping me decide. The garbage on the laptop should be hold-back evidence, but I knew it could shake Bobby up.

"What about the kiddy porn, Bobby? Matthew say anything about that? Is it the good pastor's private thing, or are you into it, too? You a couple of diddlers out here, or do you just get off on watching?"

He turned, leaning closer, moving his head into my space as he spoke through clenched teeth. "I had nothing to do with this. You know it. I can see it in your eyes, motherfucker." Old Bobby was still in there, one poke below the surface.

"Man, if I was a diddler, I'd be dead already. Shived in a shower long ago." His eyes were wide, his breath short as he looked through the windshield, checking for witnesses. He turned back to me. "So fuck you, Neville. And you better step carefully. If anything, I mean anything, comes out that hurts this church, the person who makes that happen will feel real pain. That means you too, asshole."

I put my hand on the steering wheel and pulled myself forward, forcing him back into his own space.

"You're a fucking parolee making threats to a cop, Bobby. Are you really that stupid? I could violate you right here. I don't want to toss you back inside, but I won't lose sleep over it either." Bobby leaned back. I tried to relax. "Whatever shit falls on the church is what it is. I won't start it or stop it. Now what was Sandy Gardner into?" He looked at me, silent. "Tell you what, you help me, and I'll see that we keep his bad habit away from the media."

Every piece of garbage we found up in the office would be public once the case hit the courtroom, but I hoped the lie would get him talking. If he was involved, he'd trip over his own lies; they always do. His reaction to being called a diddler felt like motive to me. If he was a full-on Jesus freak and found Gardner with kiddy porn, his prison instincts might have taken hold. Hard for a guy like Bobby to find out his hero in Christ is a toddler-stalker. Motive and opportunity looked good on Bobby.

"I don't know what his demons were. Like all of us, he had them. All men of God are tested, Cam. Do not throw stones at his memory, no matter his demons."

I didn't believe Bobby was in the dark when it came to demons. But I could see he was in control again. I had nowhere to go with him. He knew it.

┣━┿━┫

The yellow tape surrounding Sandy Gardner's property held back a fleet of cars, vans, trucks, and one very large motorhome now. They were white with the silhouetted Mountie on his rearing horse on the side, the red, yellow, and blue stripes of the national force prominent on each vehicle. No police merger when it came to branding. A lone Halifax Regional Police SUV huddled near the road, its blue on white looking faded. I recognized it as a watch commander's truck. At least we brought some rank to the party. As I turned toward the house, I realized just how much. Chief Simon Davis stood talking into a cellphone beside the motorhome we use as a mobile command centre. He wore a nylon windbreaker with *POLICE* in bold letters on the back. His navy blue ball cap was pulled down to meet a set of mirrored sunglasses, trying not to stand out. Tough when you're the top cop. Davis was the youngest chief in the history of the Vancouver city force more than a decade ago. He walked away from that job when we started chasing terrorists in Afghanistan. He commanded an armoured unit and picked up a chest full of ribbons. He walked away from that career after a couple of tours and found himself shortlisted for the chief's job here. Army's loss was Halifax's gain. We were over there at the same time, but I didn't meet him until I joined the force here. He waved me over, then opened the door to the motorhome and stepped inside.

The command bus was a couple of years old but never seemed to shed that smell of new carpet and leather. The fleet manager took extra care with it. There was no way to keep squad cars smelling anything even close to new, so the bus was probably a point of pride. We use it for whatever a crime scene calls for. It serves as a search headquarters, a coordination centre, or just a place to regroup and catch your breath. The chief sat in a small padded armchair set against the wall opposite the entrance. He took off the ball cap and glasses. The cap had left a mark along the sides of his close-cut hair. I didn't mention it.

"First of all, Detective, let me say I apologize for showing up at an active crime scene. I am not here to second-guess you, but this one is going to draw a crowd."

"Already starting to," I said as I took the seat beside him.

"Fair enough. I'll get right to the point. We are setting up a task force on this for obvious reasons, and, for now, Inspector MacIntosh will take the lead."

We both felt the same way about MacIntosh.

"Inspector MacIntosh?" I asked. "You sure he's the right guy?"

"Someone has to coordinate. You just worry about the investigating. I will elevate Sergeant Cage to the role of supervisor, so you'll be dealing with her on most things. She'll answer directly to MacIntosh and keep me in the loop."

Murders are solved in the field, but murder investigations are run from behind a desk, three desks actually. As team leader, MacIntosh would have ultimate authority. Most leaders don't interfere with the field work. Instead, the job is about keeping an eye on the paperwork, the budgets, and the flow of evidence. I wondered if MacIntosh would be willing to sit in the backroom on this. Probably not. Below the lead, two sergeants share duties. The file manager keeps the log, assigning task numbers for every step taken by the investigators and building the disclosure file for the crown. The supervising sergeant is where the desk meets the field. A good supervisor protects the team from the kind of insanity that an over-zealous file manager or team leader can impose on an investigation. Supervisors need to know the field and understand the dynamics of police management. Carla Cage was rock solid in the field, but was she up to keeping a bully like MacIntosh in the background in a high-profile media circus like this?

I tried a long shot. "The body was dumped downtown, Chief."

Team leaders usually get picked based on the old policing boundaries. If a body drops in old Halifax, it's an HRP lead, a rural murder gets a Mountie-run team. Like I said, the merged police thing works in the field, but at the highest levels there are still turf wars, and picking team leads is one way the white shirts on both forces piss on trees.

"I know, but you called this as the primary crime scene. Now the red, yellow, and blue circus is in town. They want it, and there is nothing I can do." He looked through the window at the house.

"Why'd they send him to the dump in the first place? Were they going to take lead even if Gardner was killed in our backyard?"

"I raised that. They say no. Say they didn't even know he was at the first scene. Seems he went on his own. Who knows what he was thinking. It really doesn't matter. It's his, theirs."

The politics of policing. The chief had to protect the shotgun marriage that kept that Mountie budget within reach. Handing a Mountie the lead in a high-profile case meant he was swallowing something he wouldn't like the taste of.

"One more thing you and I need to discuss." He turned back to me, a hard look on his face now. "I understand the inspector asked you to go to the clubhouse. I don't think that was a good idea."

"I don't think his reason for it was good, but we do need to work with the Stallion if we can."

"Like hell."

"They have security cameras pointing at that dump, Chief. We go for a warrant, Snake could erase anything they might have recorded. I think maybe I can convince him to give me a peek."

He looked back out at the house, and then returned his gaze to me, looked like maybe he was swallowing something else.

"Detective Constable Neville, you're a good cop. A good person, too. A hero, for Christ's sake."

"I'm no hero, Chief." I could feel a "but" coming.

"Look, I know how you feel about losing your spotter. I lost people over there, too, remember. No way to make that hurt go away. But, you fought your way out of a prison alone. That is heroic, no matter what you tell yourself."

"Killed a couple of kids and ran, Chief."

"Those kids had AKs and training. Never mind. What I'm saying is I don't regret fighting the fight with our Mountie partners to get you a badge. But, you've got to tread carefully around the gang. I don't think it's smart to remind people you have pull with a criminal organization."

I knew the chief had been forced to bend the rules to get me on the force. I wasn't the only Afghan vet with a checkered past he'd recruited, but I was the poster child for those who say his military loyalties ruined the HRP. I was never charged with anything when I rode under the patch, but my Stallion past makes me a guilty man to many cops.

"Might be that pull can pay off right now," I said.

"You really think he'll show you the tape?"

"Only if it's to the club's advantage. He doesn't want police attention, not even from me. If the tape shows something that leads us away from the club, he will want us to know."

"Then why not just get a warrant and give him the excuse he needs to turn it over?"

"He'll make a point of destroying it to show the club will never co-operate with the police. If he shows it to me, he can justify it internally."

He stood and walked over to the window overlooking the driveway.

"What if it shows something incriminating?"

"Then it's already been erased."

I stepped out into the sunshine, feeling its heat on my face, something hotter inside. Being told that my Stallion past is a problem still pisses me off. The chief gave me the badge, but sometimes he still acts as though it was a mistake. Makes me want to toss it back. Bobby Simms stood outside the car, leaning on the front fender, smoking. He smiled at me, like he could read me. I needed to get my head back in the case, so I headed inside to talk with Blair. I found him just outside the kitchen, thumbing his cellphone.

"What's up?"

"Just texting the boss. I expect I won't be home for dinner," he said.

Blair has a life away from the badge in the form of a beautiful wife, and he keeps her in the loop. The best I can hope for is the occasional smile from Sergeant Cage. I'd keep her in the loop if she didn't always seem to know more than I do. I told Blair about my meeting with the chief.

"Let's see if we can solve this thing before it attracts any more white shirts," I said.

"Too late." Blair nodded back toward the kitchen.

MacIntosh had managed to slip past while I was in the bus. Probably what the chief was looking at while he was giving me the outlaw lecture. It was MacIntosh's file now, like it or not. But what the hell was he doing here? The team leader's first job is to gather the resources needed to handle any big case. That usually means reassigning other detectives from colder files and sending them into the field to support the first responding officers. I knew we were going to need that help. Instead, here he was, sitting at the table talking into the cellphone that rarely left his ear. Thelma Waters was moving around the kitchen, coffee cup in hand. Looked like she was going to make him brunch. Greg was there too, sipping his own coffee and watching her. How much did he know about Sandy Gardner's habits? Could my brother hide something like that?

I gave the inspector a nod. He raised a finger to stop me as he kept talking into the little phone. I ignored him and walked over to Samuel, who was still sitting at the far end of the table. A gust of wind coming off the lake slapped the patio doors hard; the glass rattled in the frames, but he didn't flinch. Greg came over and rested a hand on Samuel's shoulder, a protective move maybe, a comforting move, for sure. I turned my attention to Samuel.

"Hey, Sam, you and I need to talk. Thelma or Father Greg can come along if you want. But I don't think that's going to be necessary. I just want to get some information about who attended last night's meeting."

I wanted him alone but had to be careful here. Like any seventeen-year old, Samuel had the protection of the YCJA. That little piece of legislation is a cop killer, let me tell you. It is supposed to protect kids who make minor mistakes: break a few windows, or get drunk at the high-school dance. Probably does that, but it also shields the hard-core little leaguers with the guns. YCJA stands for Youth Criminal Justice Act in a courtroom, but in the squad car it translates into "You Can't Jail Anyone." I couldn't talk to Sam without a guardian or a lawyer present. The only wiggle room a cop has is that, in theory, the YCJA only protects a suspect. I'm big on wiggle room. People are usually killed by loved ones, and technically that makes them all suspects. Sam was on the top end of the YCJA scale at seventeen, and that meant I didn't need a parent's permission to talk with him. As long as he wasn't a suspect. I told myself I didn't think Sam killed his father, so we could talk. He stood silently and glanced across the kitchen. He looked older now, something in his posture. Maybe losing his second father; maybe he knew what I found in the office.

"Do I have to go outside like Bobby?" he asked the floor.

"For a minute. Let's step out to the patio, if that's okay."

I could hear MacIntosh backpedalling on the phone, telling someone he had to make a statement. His voice quieted as he said he would be at headquarters right away. In trouble for talking to the media without getting his speaking points from the civilians on the PR team. Rank wouldn't protect him from them. I ignored his still-upraised finger and led Sam through the patio doors. I had police work to do and didn't want him interfering. He could deal with the bullshit downtown.

Sam walked to a large brick hearth built around a gas barbecue. He lifted the lid and looked at the grills absently. I wondered how often he'd seen his father tend to that grill. Well, it was his now. I remembered walking into the Stallion clubhouse the day after my father died, feeling a sense of power there I didn't have when he was alive. I sat on the arm of a cedar Adirondack chair; it was warm in the morning sun. I needed to go easy with him, let him open up on his own. I didn't want to drop into the chair and have him look down on me, but I needed him to see me relax. It's the kind of stuff we learn in cop school.

"So tell me about last night."

"Someone finally killed him, I guess," he said, closing the lid.

See, the relaxed posture worked. He was ready to talk. I moved into the chair as he dropped into one on the opposite side of the stone patio. It was the first time he had made eye contact. His eyes looked cold; I hoped mine didn't look too eager.

"What do you mean by 'finally'?" I asked.

"You don't care what I say. You didn't care last year. You don't care what happens to me, just him." The left corner of his mouth twitched. His eyes locked with mine. Showing me anger, and then just as quickly looking down into the patio stones. Where was this coming from?

Shit. I remembered it. He pestered me when I was doing the security check a year ago. Kept asking how the police protected the public. Wanted to know how much power I had. I wrote him off as another kid with badge worship. We see it a lot. Kids are never indifferent to the badge. There are two kinds: the ones who want to be us, and the ones who want to shoot us. His father was annoying the hell out of me that day, too, and all I wanted was out. I told Sam I'd be in touch, promised to chat with him another time. I blew him off. I'm no recruiter.

"Sam, if you're saying you wanted help a year ago, I am so sorry, believe that. No excuse. So please tell me now." He had me cold.

He stood and turned to the lake.

"To forgive is divine. It's a beautiful day the Lord has made, and I do forgive you." He turned back, looking down at me, in control of the conversation now.

I stood. This kid was mind-fucking me. A familiar pressure grew in my temples as my heart turned up the juice just a little. My left hand dropped to my hip. I felt the ridge of the badge clipped to my belt. Had to remember the colours I was flying and stay professional. Sam had every right to be angry, but I needed to take control.

"Let's have it, Sam." I kept my voice low, let a little ice in.

He dropped back into the seat. I sat down.

"I don't know what you want. Any of you. You want to punish someone for killing my father. What if my holy Father above did it? What if it was the right thing? You wouldn't help me; no one would. God did." The eyes came up again, accusation, maybe a little hate. "Luke said: 'There is nothing covered up that will not be revealed, and hidden that will not be known.' You refused to look last year; you can look now and see what was covered up." He was talking to the patio stones again. My heart valves struggled to slow the flow. Good cop and bad cop were at war, and I knew who I was rooting for. I knew who had to win.

"Sounds like a lot of people made mistakes, Sam. If you are telling me your father was abusing you, then we will get you help now. And believe me, I am sorry if I missed your plea for help. I said it twice. I mean it, but I'm not saying it again. Now let's get past this. He's dead."

I had questions but knew I couldn't ask them. Cheating Section Eight and finding the crime scene was one thing. The YCJA is a case buster. I had to walk away. If Sam was abused, he was a grade A suspect.

"Sam, I want you to go back inside with Thelma and Greg. I need to go ask Bobby a few more questions. I'll have to speak with you again a little later. When your mother is home."

He went inside without another word, the slouched shoulders barely moving. All the anger gone, all the energy with it. Maybe his trauma didn't end when he was rescued. He was the perfect target if Gardner was an abuser. Already shell-shocked and easily controlled by a powerful personality like the pastor's. The slide show upstairs was beginning to seem less like a plant.

I stayed outside, ducking Inspector MacIntosh. I walked in the deep shade of the hardwoods at the side of the house. The grass was soft, the air thick and cool. The police dog had been through, so I wasn't spoiling the scene. I stopped beside an old oak tree and pulled out my notebook. I jotted a few thoughts about Sam and what he'd said and logged the time. I leaned back against the tree and took a few deep, cleansing breaths.

There are times when I still miss club life. Not often, but it happens. I don't have the patience for by-the-book police work. I figure not many good cops do. Good cops weren't into sharing their feelings with an ex-biker, so I wasn't sure. The problem is simple. We fight above our weight class every day. Even when we land a good punch, it doesn't make a dent.

Figuring out the who of any crime is easy. Even a rookie can do that after a few weeks on the job. Want to know who is breaking into cars in the neighbourhood? Park on a side street and watch the fourteen-year-old sauntering home at 3:00 A.M. on a school night. Want to know who held up the young couple at the bank machine at ten in the morning? Drive to the nearest crack corner and watch the skinny junkie make a quick buy and then scurry out of the sunlight. Need to know who is keeping that crack corner stocked? Circle the block and watch the twelve-year-old run up to the passenger window of that Escalade and then dash away.

But figuring it out isn't worth shit unless you do everything by a set of impossible rules. Rules written by a crowd of second-guessing, liberal loons who've never seen a back alley or smelled fresh blood. Shake the shit out of the fourteen-year-old until the stereo components fall out. "Sorry, officer, that is not admissible. You had no right to touch that child." Shit, just try questioning him without whatever he calls a parent sitting in, and the judge will plug his ears to everything the kid had to say. The Escalade, have the traffic guys pull it over. But don't even look at that gym bag on the back seat. The rules that come with the badge are a bitch. The system is stacked against us. I wasn't sure if it was the boredom of the anti-terror task force, but I'd found myself second-guessing my choice to become a cop. This morning when I walked into the crime scene, it felt right, but that buzz was gone.

The outlaw life comes with its own rules. All the one-percent clubs have constitutions. The Satan's Stallion is no different. It's just that bending and breaking club rules is expected. Short of shooting a bro without consent, there isn't much you can't get away with in the name of profit. As for those who make a move against the club, violating their rights is mandatory. Don't get me wrong, I left the life for a reason. Not just the heroin. Too many assholes hiding behind the patch and doing nasty things to powerless people. Just like the badge, the patch can bring out the worst in some animals. At least with the badge, they usually can't hide forever.

This was no time to worry about career choices. I had to focus on the case. My nerves still jangled from the exchange with Sam, no matter how many cleansing breaths I took. It looked like I left him in the hands of an abuser for a year. I knew what that was like. You make judgment calls in this job. Sometimes they come back on you in the middle of the night, and then they own you. This was going to be one of those.

Sam made the jump from grieving kid to serious suspect, and that left me powerless. I could almost see the judge's robes fall from the clouds like a curtain for him to hide behind. It was by the book or bye-bye case time.

Inspector MacIntosh walked around from the front of the house. Shit just kept piling on.

"Detective Constable Neville, damn it, when I signal for you to wait, you need to wait."

"Just trying to get ahead of this one."

"Leaning on a tree helping?"

I raised the notebook.

"Logging my actions for the file manager." By the book.

"Well that's good, that's important, and it's why I wanted you in there. We need to be careful what we log here. Some details we need to be vague on."

"Not sure what you mean." I could see where he was going, but wanted to hear it.

"The things you say you saw on that computer. We have no idea how they got there. We can't ruin a man's reputation." The muscles along his jawline worked like he was chewing over what he had to say.

"Inspector, I don't think Pastor Gardner's reputation is our biggest concern right now."

"Grow up, Detective. It is until I say it isn't. Pastor Gardner was a close friend of the commissioner in Ottawa. That garbage could be a plant, left by a killer not satisfied with killing him. Someone who wants his reputation slaughtered as well. Until we know for sure, this all stays off the book. Clear?" He looked past me to the lake.

I didn't bother answering. I didn't care about the RCMP commissioner or his reputation. I couldn't argue his logic either. I had the same doubts upstairs, even if I no longer believed the scene was staged. Besides, he was dreaming if he thought he could keep this bottled up. A full ident team would comb the office. Too many cops would know, and cops can't keep secrets. The idea that the killer planted the porn on the laptop was a long shot. Still, the mess above the garage was puzzling. Did the killer want us to find the porn? Was leaving the body in the dump a statement? Was our killer saying Gardner was garbage? Good, my head was back in the case.

The inspector's cellphone chirped, and he slammed it against his thick ear. I headed back into the house. Blair was talking to Thelma Waters at the kitchen table. I took the spot against the counter beside the coffee pot. Thelma was telling him she had no idea who could have brought such evil filth into this holy home. Blair had gotten to the kiddy-porn question. No surprise in her denial. She was the church's most devout lemming, and the idea that Sandy Gardner shared his party favours with her was unlikely. Her devotion to him meant some serious soul-searching ahead. Guess I wouldn't be the only one.

Thelma was wringing all the air out of a napkin on the table in front of her. Her ankles kept shifting under her chair, crossing first with the left in front, then the right. Any cop could read the body language she was projecting. Left in front for lies, right for evasive answers. If Blair wanted any truth, he was going to have to find her a third leg. I caught his eye then looked toward the door. He nodded, and I headed out to wait for him.

━┼━

I walked into a day tilting to hot and humid. The rich sweet smell of cedar filled the air. I looked down at the flower beds along the front of the house. Small red chunks of bark topped the beds. A decorative way to keep the weeds down. Smelled good, too.

I glanced at my car and saw Bobby stewing in the front seat. Probably didn't smell so sweet in there. I wasn't sure why he'd gotten back into a hot car. Maybe one of the officers on the scene told him to. I stretched, pushing my hands into my lower back before moving over to let him out. He'd suffered enough. I looked at the command centre near the tennis courts. My brother Greg was standing beside it, talking with a couple of uniforms. I figured the chief was gone. I could take Bobby over there for another chat. I needed to know if he'd seen any signs of abuse between Gardner and Sam. Bobby was still a better bet as a suspect. I couldn't see Sam hurting anyone. What passed for his angry outburst at me seemed to deflate him. But if Sam was abused, Bobby might know.

I opened the door and he rose from the car in a fluid motion, staring at me as he rocked his head from side to side. I could hear his neck crack and pop as ropy muscles bulged and dropped with each shift. Sweat plastered his shirt to his chest where the pecs were dancing, too. Big boy, our Bobby. He eye-fucked me yard style, said nothing. Good that he still had the technique, might need it again.

"You know, Bobby, I'm disappointed. I thought we were coming to an agreement." I spread my legs a little. Tilting my own head to loosen things up.

"That so?" He kept his temper in check, but I could feel the heat coming from him, and it wasn't from the time spent in the car.

"Yeah. I mean you want me to tread lightly around the reputation of your church, and I want you to be upfront. Told you I'd do what I could to keep the kiddy-porn mess contained. So why the fuck didn't you tell me your beloved preacher was abusing his kid?"

"Cam, why do you treat me like something I am not? I have found my salvation. I've been praying for you here. Satan is at work. I can feel him, and you must try to fight him. He is real, Cam, not just something you slap on your back to ride a motorcycle. He is right there in your eyes." The change was a physical thing; the God-fearing Bible-thumper replaced the con in a heartbeat. He eased back and leaned against the car. His anger gone.

I could feel mine grow. My temples ached. I didn't want Bobby cool. I wanted him fiery. I wanted him to push. More than anything, I wanted to push back. It might have been the guilt over missing Sam's plea a year ago, maybe the bruised ego over letting the kid get the better of me today. Either way, a little dust-up might set me straight, and I knew Bobby was good to go. I felt it when he stepped out of the car. I moved in closer, and then spun as I felt a hand grab my shoulder. Greg stepped back quickly. The shift in Bobby's body language wasn't about the Bible. It was for my brother. He saw Greg coming. Man, I couldn't get ahead of the curve on this thing.

"Sorry, Cam. Did I startle you?" Greg looked at Bobby and back at me.

"Yeah, I guess so, Greg." I kneaded the arch of my back a little more. It didn't help. "Listen, I have a few questions for Bobby here. Can we chat in a minute?"

"Sure. I just wanted to tell you both about the TV cameras at the edge of the driveway. They seem to be shooting anything that moves here." He was saving me some grief.

"Thanks, Greg. Appreciate the heads-up." I hoped he could see the gratitude in my eyes. Popping Bobby would have felt great until it hit the TV news. I turned back to him.

"Let's take this inside the bus, Bobby."

I glanced toward the driveway and the Waverley Road. Those familiar circles of glass were tracking my every move. Guess the word was out. The dead guy in the dump was a solid-gold hit in the newsroom. Top of the clock, every hour.

We got about halfway to the bus before Inspector MacIntosh caught up with me again. He nodded at Bobby.

"Detective Constable, where are you going?"

"Into the bus, Inspector. We have cameras out here now, and I don't want them to see me questioning Bobby. Don't want them to start reporting that we have a suspect."

"Well, it's a little late for that. If you take him into the bus, they will. Let's do our questioning downtown, shall we? I'll take him with me. We've got other detectives assembling now, and I'll have a couple of them do the questioning."

"But won't that make him look more like a suspect?"

"No, I'll tell the reporters he's one of our witnesses." He started to lead Bobby away.

No cop in the world identifies a witness while a killer is still at large. He'd be putting a target on Bobby's head. I knew what was really at play. Bobby looked like a thug. The cameras were going to make love to him. The inspector wanted to get on TV leading a thug from the scene whether Bobby did anything or not. Fuck me. I should have stayed in bed.

+‑+‑+

The sun still shone, the birds sang, and the smell of early summer was still intoxicating. But there had to be at least one dark cloud up there, hanging over my head. I could not catch a break. Inspector MacIntosh slowed his car near the cameras as he headed out. Telling them about his witness, no doubt. Well, Bobby, if you're not guilty you'd better start sweating now. I had to stay away from Samuel until we heard from his mother in Africa and she lawyered him up. With those two off limits, I thought maybe I'd go get a haircut or mow my lawn.

"Hey," Greg said, as he walked over to me from the front of the house.

"Hey. Thanks for that heads-up with the media," I said, nodding to the end of the driveway. They were still there, leaning over the yellow tape, looking for an exclusive.

"Looked like maybe you were about to slip back into your old ways there, slugger. Didn't think you wanted to make a comeback on the evening news."

"No, my cage-fighting days are over, Greg. Just had to let Bobby know who was in charge."

"Oh, but Cam, you're not," he said as his right hand moved to the spot above the crucifix. I smiled and raised my hands in surrender.

"Can we keep God out of this for just a minute, Greg? Got beat up pretty bad by the Bible over there." I nodded back to the car.

"Yes. I suppose so. Bobby has an amazing recall for the Word, doesn't he? Certainly better than mine."

"He does at that, although I can't speak to his accuracy. Let's grab a seat away from the cameras."

We walked around the side of the house. A stone patio curved away from the foundation, filling the space between the tennis courts and the lake. I should have tried to duck Inspector MacIntosh on this side. It was nicer here. A wrought-iron railing surrounded a fire pit in the middle of the patio. A couple of tables, a grill, and a few Adirondack chairs circled the pit. How many barbecues did Gardner need? The God gig must be T-bones and beer every day, at least on the evangelical side. I knew Greg lived in a small room in the rectory beside the basilica downtown, and I wondered if he was second-guessing his choice of church. Maybe it was a family trait, although Gunner was sure where he wanted to be. We sat in the wooden chairs. We could second-guess together.

"Nice spot."

"Yes, I've been to a couple of church barbecues here. It's even nicer at night," he said, as we both looked past the fire pit to the lake beyond.

"That's what I want to talk to you about. I wanted to ask you this last year when you had me check on security here."

"What?" Greg leaned forward in his chair. His look was earnest, probably the kind he gave parishioners when he wanted them to know he cared. It was a good look. We looked a lot alike; maybe I could learn it.

"Well, Sandy Gardner was a Bible-thumping TV star who reached out into the purses and wallets of the world. Where do you fit in his evangelical collection scheme?"

"That's unfair, Cam." He leaned back, the pleasant look gone. "It's true he pushed hard for donations, but look at the work his church accomplished. Look at the orphans who now have homes."

"I've seen his work close up, and I'm looking at the home those donations built," I said. "Let's just agree to disagree on whether it was greed or God at work. I still can't figure you in the mix. How often did you come here and why?"

"Fairly often, I suppose. At least once a month. We both belong to the—belonged to, I guess it is now—the Halifax Ecumenical Council. He was busier than me, so I'd come here to meet with him." A sadness crept into his voice as he moved to the past tense. "I know I got to see a side of Sandy Gardner you may never grow to believe in. I know it was real." He ran a hand through that thick unruly mop, and before I realized it, I was stroking the curls on my head. I liked the look of Greg's hair and decided to let mine grow until I got busted by a white shirt. I gave Greg my best earnest look.

"Well, I'm sorry you lost a friend, Greg." Sandy Gardner may well have been an evil man who needed killing, but I could feel my brother's loss.

"Thanks, Cam. I guess that's why I spoke out of turn earlier. But I know you have to do what is right. I do worry about how this may change how people feel about him. He built his church into a world force for good from a Bible group that met in his basement fifteen years ago. Did you know that? Amazing, really."

"I know the legend of Sandy Gardner. What I need to know is the man. It's clear he was not what we all thought."

"How bad is it?"

"Kiddy porn for sure. Looks like he might have been abusing Samuel, as well."

He looked away. I hated to dump it on him, but I needed his help. Kicking the crap out of his image of Gardner would help. It's possible he'd seen signs and dismissed them.

"That is bad. Worse than I could have thought. Poor Samuel. I should go to him," he said.

"Sure, in a minute. First tell me about Sam. That whole speaking-in-tongues thing. Is that an act or is he crazy?" What I really wanted to ask was: Is he crazy enough to kill his father?

"That's not a fair question, Cam. It is not an act, and he is not crazy. Many people become so overwhelmed by the power of the Holy Spirit that they enter a trance-like state. Faith, real faith, is a life-changing thing."

"That ever happen during one of your Masses?" I asked.

"No, but the Catholic Mass is more structured, restrictive maybe, than an evangelical service. Pastor Gardner and many evangelicals encourage their followers to give in to the power they feel. It is quite common to hear entire congregations speak in tongues at a service like that."

Sounded more like mob mentality than miracle to me, but I wasn't looking for a theological lecture from my brother, so I kept that thought to myself.

"I really should go to him, Cam," he said.

"Thelma is with him. Just give me one more second. I need you to think, Greg, think hard. Is there anyone in his church who could have found out about these things and reacted this way?" I was thinking of Bobby, and he knew it.

"I will think, Cam, but I have to tell you, everyone I've met at the Church of Salvation is an inspiration. That includes Bobby. Their faith is strong, and their belief in the teachings of Jesus would rival the strongest Catholic."

"Fine, but think, and call me if the slightest inkling crosses your mind. It may be nothing, and that's fine, but feel free to waste my time with it." Time I had. There was no one left to interview except members of the youth group, and they were unlikely candidates. "Let's go in. You can sit with Samuel. I need to bring Blair up to speed."

"One thing first." He placed a hand on my arm. I relaxed back into the chair.

"I did a lot of thinking during my Camino."

"Hard not to, I imagine."

"Well, it's the point of the journey, so yes, it's hard not to."

"And."

"After the first week, all I thought about was you and Gunner. Well, the three of us, actually." I waited. I didn't know much about El Camino de Santiago. Greg walked eight hundred kilometres from France into Spain. If his exhaustion on the pilgrimage led him to believe he could convert us, I figured he must have suffered sunstroke. I definitely wanted to be there when he explained it to Gunner. I went to Greg's Masses occasionally, but that was just to support him.

"I thought you were supposed to think about Jesus, not the three of us."

"You can't force the Camino. If you let it guide you, though, release yourself to it, Saint James will step in and lead your thoughts."

"And this saint had you thinking about us?"

He reached to his chest and stroked the crucifix again.

"He did, yes. We don't see enough of each other. Not the way brothers should."

"Look, Greg, this sounds like it is going to be a longer conversation than I can afford right now. I'd love to hear more about it, but I'm on a pretty big case." It was a lie. I didn't want to hear more no matter how much time I had. He'd forgive me for the lie. It was his job.

"Of course you can hear more, Cam, that's all I'm asking." He smiled, a grin really. He had me with my own words. "I spoke with Gunner yesterday. I am doing the blessing in Peggys Cove this year, and he has agreed to ride out to our mother's grave for a visit afterward. We want you on the run and with us at the grave. We can talk and bond a little there." The grin again.

I couldn't believe it. He'd sandbagged me. Did I leave my street smarts home? Did I even have any? Everybody was kicking the shit out of me today. Even a priest.

"If I can, I will, but like I said, it's a big case."

"That's all I ask. I'm going back to be with Samuel now," he said.

I watched as he stood and wondered why he cared so much about me, and now Gunner, and what he had in mind for that ride. The annual blessing of fallen bikers is a Stallion-sponsored ride. Mostly a PR stunt. I couldn't believe Gunner had agreed to leave it and go to our mother's grave. Greg must have found him when he was heavy into the Jack. Sandbagged him, too. Well, no way I'd have time, and Gunner would forget he'd agreed to anything. Sorry, Greg.

He smiled down at me and rubbed his right thumb against his shirt, feeling the tiny crucifix below. The move took me back to another brother. One I'd lost in a shithole called the Place of the King. It was in the Paktia province in Afghanistan. Greg walked away. I felt a dryness in my throat. I began to think of Master Corporal Ronald—don't call me Ron—Gosse.

+-+-+

March 2006, mountain range, Paktia Province, Afghanistan

Every time I killed someone, Ronald said a prayer. It spooked me, but I didn't tell him that. When a brass shell popped from the side of my rifle, he pulled the gold crucifix from under his ghillie. He'd ask the Lord to let His perpetual light shine on my latest kill, as I pushed my eye to the scope and looked across the valley for the next guy.

"You ever think about trying a Muslim prayer?" I asked. "They might appreciate it more." I moved the scope slowly into the dust cloud kicked up by the 50's recoil. I could taste it on my lips, a dry, almost sweet taste. Afghan death.

"It's not a prayer if I don't believe in it. Just words, brother." Ronald's eyes were back on the spotting scope now. He'd find me someone else to kill.

Ronald was the brother I should have had. He was a perfect combination of Gunner and Greg, a fight-to-the-death soldier with a faith that was a physical thing. We chewed that dust together for six months. I'd die for him. He'd do the same for me.

"You think they pray for us when they get a kill?" I rubbed my sleeve across my lips and shifted the heavy TAC-50 slightly on its bipod, kept scanning.

"I asked the Imam. He says the Quran forbids it. We are not believers, so they can't pray for us."

Ronald: Christian, but not stupid about it. Spent his free time with the Imam back at the airfield where we bunked. He needed to understand Islam. I didn't. One reason none of the other snipers wanted to work with the Master Corporal: he liked preaching about Christ or explaining Islam. That can rattle guys who kill for a living.

Me they avoided because of Gunner and the outlaw club we belonged to back in the world. Gunner can be an asshole about the outlaw thing. He killed too fast, even for Trashcanistan. He pounded guys on our side senseless. Perfect war machine, Gunner. He was one of the door-kicking urban assaulters, of course. Guys in the sniper teams are quieter, more philosophical, about killing. They decided my past meant I wasn't sniper material. Fuck 'em.

"Got one." Ronald shifted his weight, pressed his hips into the ground, as he worked the dials on the scope. "Okay, let's do this guy and then find us a new house."

He fed me the wind and elevation adjustments. The guy was just over two thousand metres out. The TAC was good to 1,800, but at this altitude two clicks was more than doable. I filled the scope with him, saw the long barrel of his rifle. He was sprawled on his chest at the base of a jagged boulder on the opposite side of the Shahi-Kot. Couldn't see a spotter. Sometimes those Taliban shooters worked alone, seriously badass. He moved, got on his own scope, settling for a shot. Some poor Marine on the valley floor just walked into the space where life and death are measured in the speed of a trigger finger. Whose was quicker, the Taliban shooter's or mine?

I welded my body to the rifle stock, married it to the hard rock below me. I let the breath leave my lungs slow and easy. Waited, felt the trigger break on its own. My muzzle jumped as a .50-calibre armour-piercing shell started a supersonic race to save a Marine's life. At that altitude the Shahi-Kot was a four-second bullet ride, ridge to ridge. I settled my scope on him again before my shell finished the trip. There is nothing clean in a sniper kill. A 50 hits hard, fast, and ugly. I watched a tangled mess of detached arms, legs, and rifle parts spin in the air and fall out of sight. I re-racked. A brass shell popped, and Ronald was back on the cross.

"So now we repo. This spot is on fire," he said, as he fingered the crucifix.

"You saw him, Ronald. He was on the trigger. Guys down there are in it, bro. That's why we're here." I said. "Take us half a day to find another spot. How many of them you think will die in that time? How many did we just save?" I looked at him.

Ronald was sure three was the best-before number for a sniper hide. You kill the first one, the other side starts thinking about you. Number two, they start looking. By number three, they're looking hard. We'd taken out the tenth target at dusk the day before. The guy we'd just put down was number sixteen since we first set up. I figured this was the sniper hide that just kept giving. He figured it was scorched earth. I watched him squeeze the cross between his thumb and index finger. He kissed it and dropped it back inside the ghillie.

"You shoot better than anyone out here, but you're definitely an asshole, Cam. It's in your white-trash DNA, some hero flaw. Can't be helped I guess." He smiled and gave me the single-finger salute as he moved back to his scope.

I returned the gesture and settled back into prone, hunting for number seventeen. We stayed quiet, searched the ridge line for movement.

"Got one," Ronald said. Then, the world turned upside down.

The rock below slammed into my chest. I sucked down a mouthful of that sweet Afghan death, wondered if it was mine. Rock, dirt, and shrubs pounded me. Thick smoke stung my eyes. We were tucked beneath a brush-filled overhang. The dry wood cracked and popped as a fire spread through the bushes. I recovered just before the second mortar hit. A chunk of rock took the scope off the 50. My gun was dead. We were out of the war and into a fight for our lives. I crawled to Ronald, pulled his arm, and shouted, "We gotta get back, come on. Let's move."

My hand came away bloody. I rolled him over. Blood poured from a three-inch gash above his hairline. A wet stain grew across his chest from an ugly hole there. We didn't wear helmets or flak jackets. Recommended but not required for sniper teams. I always thought it made us hard.

"Hang in there, man. I'll get help." I crawled over him and grabbed the radio from his kit. It was in worse shape than my gun. An Apache helicopter rose into view a hundred metres away. Drawn by the smoke. I locked eyes with the pilot. He gave me a thumbs up, and spun the chopper around, hunting. A beautiful bird of prey.

"We're good, Ronald. See that, easy ride home, man. No humping out for us. Hang on." I pulled him further under the overhang to wait for the Apache crew to kill the motherfuckers lobbing shells at us.

Sparks flew from the helicopter gearbox. Oily black smoke trailed as it spun lazily and plunged below the ridge line. I could hear the quick rattle of machine guns getting close. I grabbed my C7, flicked off the safety, and set it for three round bursts. I leaned across Ronald for his. He grabbed the front of my ghillie. I dropped the rifles and held his shoulders. His eyes locked on mine. I didn't see fear. I did see death. Not a distant sniper death. This was up close and personal. His bloody right hand worked the tiny crucifix at his neck. I reached over and squeezed his hand and the crucifix. Felt the life leave his body.

"Grant him eternal rest, Jesus. Let your perpetual light shine on him. May he rest in peace." I knew it wasn't exactly right. Wished I'd listened more carefully when he said it. I reached behind his neck and unhooked the chain, put his crucifix in my pocket, grabbed the C7s and got ready to die.

CHAPTER 4

Thursday, noon

LOLITA SHINES RAISED A CIGARETTE TO HER LIPS WITH A SHAKING hand. She looked into the mirror and adjusted the white ribbon on one of her pigtails. She closed her hand around the cool hair and ran it to the end then reached across with her left hand, and repeated the move with the pigtail on the right. Both were smooth, black, and shiny. She pulled open the front of her white shirt, revealing more cleavage. She retied the shirttails, knotting them just above her plaid skirt, making sure to leave just a little skin showing. She looked down. Both white stockings stopped just below the skirt. Dressed to undress.

She turned from the mirror and dropped into a tattered couch in the corner. She looked down. Fuck, her stockings had slipped again. She ignored them and listened to the music coming from the front of the bar. The rolling bass line soothed her. Not because she liked the song, but because she knew it meant Sheilagh was dancing to the final tune in her set. She needed Sheilagh right now. A healthy distraction. There were dancers in the rotation between them, so they'd have time together. Lolita smiled for the first time today. She knew Sheilagh would fill that time with non-stop chatter, mostly about her daughter but also about the life. Sheilagh didn't have a clue about the life; she never left Halifax. That's what Lolita loved about her.

The Fog Bank was like every other strip bar in Canada. It kept a stable of local dancers who were more clock burners than cock teasers. Something to stretch out the space between the shows put on by the headliner of the day. The men bought more beer and spent more time at the poker machines when the local girls danced because most of the local girls weren't worth watching. Well, the pervs would stay in perv alley next to the stage. They never left their seats when there was pussy to stare at.

Lolita shuddered and took another pull from the cigarette before stuffing it out in an ashtray shaped like an oversized dick. Definitely designed by a man. She had seen enough to know it would take two and a half men to fill that ashtray. She'd also danced long enough to know the club owners didn't even like headliners. They needed them to fill the club but resented them because they had to pay them top dollar. Well, not Lolita, but the others, the porn stars especially. The stingy fucks didn't like to pay anyone. Most of the locals danced for tips. Lolita, at least, got a room, some food, and cigarette money on top of her tips.

She would headline here at The Bank for two more weeks, then it was back to Montreal for a short stint before heading to Vancouver and starting her cross-Canada tour all over. She wished she could leave today. She wished her mind would stop racing and her hands would stop shaking. She wished Sheilagh would get the fuck off the stage and come distract her. The bass line stopped, and she could hear the familiar vocal from "Sheets" fade out behind it. It was Sheilagh's final number. Imagine closing the set to a Carleton Stone tune. Only Sheilagh. Lolita smiled again; she wouldn't mind dancing for the shaggy-haired singer, but dance on stage to his music? Never. That was Sheilagh. She had a crush on a local singer she'd never met and thought she was doing him some solid by closing to his music. Lolita was the little schoolgirl who packed The Fog Bank, but Sheilagh was the one with the schoolgirl heart.

Lolita reached for another cigarette. She waited for Sheilagh to walk around the bar wrapped in a towel. She'd go from table to table, hoping one of the men would hire her for a private dance, the real money-maker. She'd be here soon. Just as the wavering flame reached the dancing tip of the cigarette, she heard a faint knock on the dressing-room door. Fuck, fuck, fuck. The only person who knocked that softly was the biggest man she'd ever seen. Phil Murphy. If the giant was at the door, the midget who pulled his strings wanted her. She glanced up to the ceiling where she knew the hidden camera was. Fuck, why wouldn't someone put a bullet in Jimmy Williams? She retched and coughed out smoke as she slammed the full cigarette into the dick on the table. She glanced at her locker. Her purse was inside and so was her switchblade. Maybe she should just stab the little fucker. She stabbed a man outside a Boston strip club once, and it was pretty cool. He'd tried to rape her, but she stuck hers in him first. The club freaked and had her in a van halfway through New Hampshire before the guy got out of surgery.

The dressing-room door opened and Sheilagh walked in, smiling and clutching a small bag full of tips. Not a single piece of paper showed. Lolita could see Murphy, his back to the open door.

"Hey, hon, Phil wants you," Sheilagh said, as she dropped her towel and walked naked to her locker. She dumped her tips into a pink plastic container and pulled out her robe. Lolita felt a pang as she stared at Sheilagh's simple beauty. Skin whiter than Lolita's and perfectly clear. Green eyes, waves of soft red hair on top, a perfectly groomed red landing strip below. She could be a money-maker if she didn't have that telltale sag below the navel. Mommy dearest was what men wanted to forget. Lolita walked over and reached up, pulled Sheilagh close, and kissed her long and hard. God, she wanted to stay here. She walked to her locker and slipped on a navy blazer: the finishing touch in her stage outfit. She grabbed Lucky; the ragged one-eyed teddy bear worked the stage with her. Best to take him in case Fuck Head kept her in the office too long and she had to go directly to the stage.

"I'll try to shake the midget and come back before my set, sweetheart. But don't count on it." She turned for the door.

"It's okay if you can't."

God, with Sheilagh everything was okay.

Lolita followed Murphy down a narrow hallway. The man filled it with his wide shoulders, and she wondered absently if maybe he could fill the ashtray. They walked to the back, away from the music out front. She knew there was an exit beyond Murphy and fantasized about walking past him out into the sunshine. The Fog Bank sits in the side of a hill above Halifax Harbour in the Burnside Industrial Park. It's a short hop over the MacKay Bridge from the Satan's Stallion clubhouse. That was enough to keep her from running. She'd danced here a thousand times and still didn't know the place well enough to hide if she tried. Burnside is an ugly cluster of warehouses and industrial shops shoved into the side of a hill. The Fog Bank sits halfway up, giving it a perfect view of the bridge and the city beyond. Not the view the customers come for. Dancers strutted and stripped from 11:00 in the morning until 2:30 the following morning. The lunch crowd was out front now. Truckers mostly. Big rigs run in and out of the industrial park all day and all night.

Murphy stopped and turned, sadness in his eyes as he opened the door to Jimmy Williams's smelly office. Lolita sighed and walked into the four-by-five metre room behind the club's kitchen. There was a riser built into the floor along the wall to her right. Williams sat behind a cheap metal desk on top of the riser. He was turned from the doorway with his cowboy boots perched precariously on the edge of the desktop. His greasy I-want-to-be-Snake hair draped over the back of the chair. A black leather couch sat beneath a bank of security monitors opposite the desk. Lolita glanced up to see the parking lot, the stage, the area behind the bar where the cash register sits, and the tables where customers watch the dancers. She knew if she wasn't in the room one of those screens would be showing Sheilagh walking around in the dressing room. What kind of sick prick runs a strip bar and needs to peep at his dancers? God, they were naked most of the time, anyway.

The solid bass thump of AC/DC shook the walls. Lolita dropped into the leather couch to wait for his fucking majesty to address her. She toyed with Lucky and tried to remember the name of the dancer whose set opened with that song. Williams continued to ignore her.

"What do you want?" She couldn't stand the wait any longer.

"What I want is some answers." Williams stood behind his desk, making sure to use the riser to full effect as he glared down at her. He still had to look up at Murphy, but so did everybody. "What the hell were you doing at the clubhouse last night and who were you with?"

Lolita picked at Lucky's remaining eye and said nothing.

Williams pulled a handgun from a drawer and tapped the barrel on the desktop.

"I asked you a question, bitch."

She kept her head down and picked at Lucky. Making the little man and his big gun wait on an answer.

"Wasn't near the clubhouse." She flipped Lucky over and adjusted the yellow ribbon around his neck.

"The fuck you say?" Williams moved around to the front of the desk still not leaving his riser, she noticed. The gun slapped the side of his leg as he stared down. Lost for words. "Wasn't there," he finally said, seemed to be trying to put menace in it. Even the gun didn't give him menace.

Shit, even that shiny new Stallion cut with the prospect patch didn't do it, Lolita decided. She thought about her switchblade and smiled.

"The fuck you grinning at?" Williams demanded. "You lie to me again, you little whore, I'll put a bullet in your head. You're on the fucking video, and Grease spoke to you at the door."

She turned her slate-grey eyes up. She knew there wasn't a prospect alive with the balls to shoot a Stallion money-maker.

"Grease is a meth head. He don't know me from any of the other girls. I wasn't there. Shoot me or let me get ready to work." She turned her attention back to the bear.

Williams jumped down from the riser, grabbed a pigtail, and yanked her head up. It hurt, but she'd felt worse. He shoved the gun against her forehead. It was warm. He must have been playing with it before she came. She cringed at the thought.

Murphy moved toward the sofa.

Williams glared up at the big man. "The fuck you think you're doing?"

Murphy backed away.

"I am not fucking with you here. This is Stallion business, bitch. We need to know who killed that preacher and why." He slid the gun barrel down over the bridge of her nose and rested it against her lips.

"I wasn't there." She reached up and caressed the barrel with her fingertips as she parted her lips and began to lick the underside of the gun. She hoped he hadn't really played with it, like ever. Slowly, she took it deep into her mouth, looking up at Williams with nothing in her eyes. Every stripper had that look.

The gun cut her upper lip as he pulled it from her mouth, jammed it into Lucky and pulled the trigger. The tiny bear did little to dampen the gun's heavy blast. "Get the fuck out."

Lolita stood and pulled the still-smoking Lucky from the couch. She smiled as she walked out. She'd get a little time with Sheilagh after all.

+++

Sheilagh smoked on the couch just inside the dressing room. She still wore the tattered robe. Lolita sat beside her, felt the familiar warmth as Sheilagh moved close and dropped her head onto her shoulder. It didn't stay long.

"Oh my God, what happened to Lucky?" She grabbed the bear from Lolita.

"Little asshole shot him. Trying to prove he's the big man," Lolita said, looking at the damage for the first time. Lucky's light-brown belly was scorched, stuffing leaking from a small hole in the middle. He could be fixed.

"Why'd he do that? My God, did he hurt you?"

Lolita grabbed a cigarette and lit it. Her hand was no steadier.

"No, just Lucky. Let's forget about him and enjoy a few minutes before I go on." She pulled Sheilagh's head back onto her shoulder and took a long pull on the cigarette. That soft knock on the door again.

"For fuck sakes. He can't be serious."

"You can't go." Sheilagh pouted. "Just tell him you have to go on."

"Don't worry, hon. I'll go. He's afraid to hurt me."

She opened the door, and stepped out to join Murphy again. He shook his head and looked in at Sheilagh.

"He wants to see her," he said.

"That little fucker. Why don't you do something for us, Phil?" Lolita touched his chest. He backed away. Sheilagh was standing beside them now. Her turn to say, "Don't worry." Lolita watched the two walk down the hall and disappear into the office. She looked back into the dressing room and then walked down the hall herself. As she passed the office the door opened, and a sad-eyed Murphy stepped out and closed the door behind him.

The sin was Lolita's, but she knew Sheilagh was about to pay the price. She glared at Murphy and walked to the exit. Outside, she leaned against a dumpster and let the sun warm her face as she finished her cigarette. She thought again about running and wondered if any of the squares in the real world would take in a nineteen-year-old dressed like a five-year-old. Fat fucking chance. She looked at the big rigs lining the parking lot. Spotless paint and shining chrome glistened in the sunshine. Could it be that easy? She could fuck a trucker all the way to freedom. She reached into the blazer pocket and pulled out her cigarettes, lighting a new one from the tip of the old. Her hands were steady. That was a sign. Her decision came in an instant. She'd do it.

Just as quickly, her hand shook harder. This time it was a sound, not a sign. Lolita sagged against the garbage bin as she watched the sun glint from a familiar coat of paint and even more chrome. She was no piece of patch pussy trained to recognize every Stallion ride. Still, even she knew the movements of this biker as he rolled into the lot shifting and making his bike bark and howl. Gunner.

CHAPTER 5

GUNNER STEPPED OFF HIS BIKE, PULLED THE SKID LID FROM HIS head, and dropped it over the mirror. He tossed his fingerless riding gloves into the helmet with one hand then reached into his pocket and pulled a crushed pack of cigarettes out with the other. His cellphone played a familiar Skynyrd riff. The fuck does he want? He tapped the green button on the small screen.

"Seen enough of you today, little bro." He then listened, trying to shoulder the tiny phone so he could light his fucking cigarette. Gave it up.

He spotted the dancer leaning against a dumpster and waved her over with his unlit cigarette. She gave him a light. He waved her back to the dumpster.

"Look, man, I got club business going here. I don't know shit about Mom's grave. All I remember is him saying he'd do the blessing." He sucked a satisfying drag from the unfiltered cigarette. "Seriously, bro, I got shit going on. You just get your ass to the run. Fuck Greg." He took another drag. "Don't give me that shit. This is one ride you don't miss. I'll scrape your fucking tat off myself. See you at the house Saturday."

He punched the red button, pocketed the phone, and walked to the dancer. As he got close to the rear door of the club, he could hear a solid guitar riff peeling the paint off the ceiling inside. GN'R. Fuck, a stripper with taste. He decided he'd take a piece of that. He looked down at the dancer in front of him.

"Follow me, bitch." There was no disdain in it; it was like another man saying, "Follow me, dear."

In the hallway ahead he saw Phil Murphy standing outside the main office like some hulking doorman. Gunner admired Murphy's loyalty, even if he couldn't stand the man giving Murphy his orders. The real reason the gunplay had stopped in the streets was that Murphy was a soulless killer who did exactly what Jimmy Williams told him to do. He'd once scooped another man's eye out with a spoon in front of a dozen witnesses. Williams hadn't even meant it when he told Murphy to do it; it was just to scare the bastard. The eye was gone before he could say "Wait a second" to his enforcer. Street lore had it the little freak pissed himself laughing. Gunner never asked Williams about it and never would.

He walked up and reached for the doorknob. Murphy moved to block him. Shit, he didn't need that. Gunner's play was forced. He moved away from the door and looked up at Murphy. Gunner was comfortable with his size; he was big, broad, and intimidating. He figured most men felt small when they squared off against him. He rarely got that feeling, but he had it now. He broadened his stance as he watched the struggle play out slowly in hollow eyes hidden beneath an overhanging forehead. Murphy was at least smart enough to know he couldn't stand in the way of a full patch. Also, smart enough to know what Williams would do to him if he let someone pass. Poor fuck.

"He tell you to keep everyone out?" Gunner asked.

"Yeah."

"You gonna try to keep me out?"

"No."

"You just did."

"Yeah."

The fucker's smarts ended somewhere short of lying. Hell, Gunner wanted to cut him loose. Wanted him to make up some bull-shit excuse for the move. Too fucking honest. Shit. The punch hit the cement jaw before the cigarette hit the floor. It was hard but not as hard as it should have been. Gunner didn't pull it. Didn't rotate his hips to follow through. Made it an arm shot. Still, it came from a powerful arm. Murphy's head rocked up and then dropped back into position. His hands didn't even close into fists. He ate the hit. Perfect fucking soldier. Too bad he was wasted on such an idiot.

"Go watch my bike," Gunner said as he turned to the office door. He opened his hand wide, spreading his fingers apart to try to get some feeling back before he grabbed the knob.

Inside, some redhead was kneeling with her back to the door. Her hair bouncing. Jimmy Williams stood in front of her, looking down, his hand on her bobbing head. The girl's ass was planted on her heels to get her head low enough.

"Get the fuck up," Gunner said, as he moved into the room. The girl jumped to her feet. Williams nearly fell to the floor as he struggled to get his dick back in his pants. Gunner took a step forward with his left leg, lowering his right hip as he rolled his elbow back, and brought one all the way through. It found a smaller, softer jaw, but damn, the hand still hurt like a motherfucker. Williams landed up against the wall in a heap. The girl was grabbing clothes from the sofa and keeping her eyes away from Gunner.

"Out," he said and then turned to the dancer in the hallway behind him. "You get in."

The redhead closed the door with a quiet click behind her as Gunner moved up onto the riser and sat on the edge of the desk to wait. It didn't take long. The little man could take a hit, too. He sat up with his back propped against the wall and moved his chin back and forth with his right hand. He looked at Gunner to see what was coming next.

"Here's the thing, prospect," Gunner said, as he stepped down from the riser to tower over Williams. "I sent you here to find out what one of your girls was doing at the clubhouse last night. You don't come back, so I gotta make the ride here. I find the girl I need standing outside while you fuck around with the wrong bitch in here. You really that stupid?"

Gunner wanted to build himself up to another shot at the fuck, but Williams looked too pathetic. He dropped into the sofa, throwing his legs out, the big boots clunking on the riser across from him. Williams stayed on the floor. Gunner caught him looking over his legs at the dancer by the door. Or maybe just hoping for Murphy. Gunner pulled a cigarette out to replace the one he'd dropped in the hallway. He tossed the pack into Williams's lap, letting him know the beating was over. Time for business.

"You talk to her?" He nodded at Lolita.

"Yeah, she says Grease was on meth, she wasn't there. The one you just kicked out is her lover. I was helping her shift loyalties." He popped a cigarette into his mouth, lit it, and then rubbed at his chin as he took a long pull.

Gunner looked down at the prospect on the floor, saw his eyes were starting to clear, could see defiance there. Good. If he wanted a full patch, he'd better show something after a sucker punch like that.

He thought about the stripper's story. Grease did like those little chunks of ice. He was no addict—he'd lose his patch over that kind of shit. Still, he'd stayed behind during last night's run, and he did like to indulge now and then. Gunner thought back to the conversation over the engine this morning, remembered the clarity in Grease's eyes as he worked.

"Naw, she's full of shit. Grease was clear as crystal today, not using it."

"That's what I figured. I know you don't want her marked, though, so I was working on the other one."

Gunner nodded. Neither man looked at Lolita.

Gunner slumped in the passenger seat. Murphy was behind the wheel, Williams somewhere in back where a prospect belonged. The van smelled like shit. Gunner powered down the window and lit a smoke to mask it. He pulled a pair of earbuds out of his pocket and stuck them into his phone. He rolled through the music for something to clear his head, stopped on "Sympathy for the Devil." The Motörhead cover. He let himself melt into Brian May's smooth licks as Lemmy's vocals growled over the top. Damn if it wasn't better than The Stones. He stayed with the music as he thought about the stripper. He wanted more time to push her on her bullshit story, but two things stood in the way. Both of them money. First, it was time for her headline act. The Fog Bank couldn't afford to sit down the headliner during the second busiest show. Lunchtime is money time.

The second reason was that prick Nicholas Mapp. Guy kept the cash flowing, but Gunner longed for the day he'd be stuffed into one of his own money bags and dumped offshore. Mapp had called, asking for a meet to discuss the preacher, like it had any fucking thing at all to do with him. Mapp was Snake's man, but he called Gunner. Fuck it, he pulled on the smoke and let the music drive his thoughts.

Gunner was in the middle of the fourth run through the tune, watching May's fingerings roll across the back of his closed eyelids. He knew every phrase and lick by heart. Williams interrupted.

"Hey, man, we're in Lower Sackville. Gonna be at Mapp's in a minute." He touched Gunner's shoulder to confirm he'd heard it.

"Then tell me when we're there. You think I want to watch the finer scenery of this shithole or something?" He closed his eyes again.

Lower Sackville is a twenty-minute drive from the clubhouse. Gunner hated the place. Mostly because he'd shacked up with a crazy bitch for a miserable winter there. Well, it wasn't all miserable, but the chick took a knife to him when she decided he needed to buy her a ring. Wanted it that night. In the middle of a fucking blizzard. He looked out the window at an endless string of used car dealerships as Murphy began to slow the van. Used cars and used-up chicks, welcome to Sack-fuckin-Vegas. The van turned into a roadway with checkered flag paint covering the pavement. It led to the biggest pile of used metal on the strip. Mapp Motors. You couldn't see it from the strip, and there was no big neon sign like those outside the other dealerships. Nicholas Mapp brought in his customers with an endless barrage of dumb-as-fuck TV commercials. *You don't need a map to get to Mapp Motors,* was the tag line on every one of them. Well, you fucking well do, shithead, Gunner thought as Murphy pulled to a stop. He parked near the service bays and washing stations, where lemons were polished into gems.

They were here to meet Mapp, the drug dealer, not the car dealer from the TV commercials. Gunner pulled his Stallion cut off and folded it carefully before placing it on the seat behind him as he stepped out into the steamy heat of the early afternoon. It wasn't because of the heat that he'd pulled his leather. Mapp insisted the club not fly colours where its interests meshed with his legitimate business. Fifteen years ago, Mapp couldn't get inside the Stallion clubhouse. Now, he was giving orders, and even Gunner, the fucking VP, had to follow them. Williams dropped out of the side door onto the lot and walked toward Gunner, still wearing his prospect colours. Gunner slapped him in the side of the head. Williams spun and waddled back to the van. Hitting a prospect always took the edge off.

Mapp had started hanging around the club when Gunner was a prospect. He thought he could buy a set of colours. He'd inherited millions when his parents died in a yacht explosion. All that money couldn't even get him hang-around status. He was a slimy loser with no spine. Not Stallion material. That cash bought him something the club did respect, though. Friends in Colombia. He controlled the flow of so much snow, the club couldn't afford to cross him. If he cut them off, they could kill him, but they'd still be scrambling for a new supply.

Mapp's money-laundering empire hides in plain sight in an ugly cluster of buildings decorated with uglier flags. They sprawl in a wide oval, a race track in the middle. Keep Sackville's NASCAR nutjobs happy. Rows of shining cars filled the space behind each small building. Chevies behind the nearest building, Fords the next, the Jeeps after that. Beyond that, it was mostly imports. One building near the far corner sat behind rows of restored classic cars. Gunner noticed an old Vette. Paint the sucker blue and silver and take it home. Like fuckin' Mapp would give him a deal. Rather pay full freight somewhere else.

Nicholas Mapp walked out of the sea of clear coat in a loose-fitting white blazer over a black T-shirt. He wore matching white pants. Reminded Gunner of a cop on a TV show he and Cam watched as kids. Hated the show; fucking cops always won. Mapp stopped in front of Gunner and shoved out his right hand under a smile as white as the blazer.

"Appearances, my man, appearances," he said when Gunner hesitated.

Gunner shook his hand. Williams stepped up and reached out. Mapp looked down.

"Appearances, man," he said as he turned away from Williams and put his hand on Gunner's shoulder. Gunner held back a laugh as they walked away from the prospect.

"So what do we have? How bad?" he asked.

"We've got it handled." Gunner wasn't going to talk club business even if the club needed Mapp.

"Look, Mr. Neville, this is our business. Not just club business, okay? If this insanity blows back on you, then I'll need another crew to move my blow." He flashed a ten-thousand watt, twenty-thousand-dollar smile. "Is the murder of the good preacher going to land inside the clubhouse?"

"No, we'll make sure that doesn't happen. But there might be a small connection. One of our dancers maybe knows something." Gunner felt like he was betraying his bros. He made a silent vow: if Mapp's day ever came, he'd do the wet work.

"What does she know?"

"She isn't saying yet; I was working her when you called. Grease says she wanted help getting rid of the body." Gunner reached for his smokes and swore as he realized they were in his cut. Mapp must have caught the move because Gunner was looking inside an open silver cigarette case before he raised his head. He pulled one out, tipped it to Mapp, who already had a silver lighter out.

"Do the police know about her?"

"No."

"Then perhaps she should simply cease to be." Mapp pulled out a cigarette of his own and lit it, turning his back to the dealership. Appearances. "You have to understand something here, Gunner There are things in play that are much bigger than you or Snake. This unfortunate mess has—how shall I put this?—implications beyond your local concerns. It is important that you clean it up quickly." Giving orders now.

"Fuck this shit," said Gunner. "You know who you're talking to, so back the fuck off before you cease to fucking exist. I said all I am going to say. We'll deal with it. I came here as a favour because you wanted to know. You know. We're done."

Gunner headed toward the van. He paused mid-step when he heard laughter behind him. He spun and took two quick steps back. He pushed Mapp hard once, and the laughter stopped. In an instant, the old spineless Nicholas Mapp was backing away.

Gunner grabbed a fistful of that expensive silk blazer with his left and slid his right all the way back to fully cocked, ready to do twenty-thousand in damage. The cocked fist stayed there. He turned to see Murphy's meaty hand wrapped around his wrist. The giant had a pained look in those hooded eyes. Williams peered out from behind his strong man.

"You wanna do him here, that's cool. Just thought you might want a moment to pause. That's all. Let go, Phil."

Gunner's fist almost flew into Mapp on its own, but he stopped it. He smoothed the blazer and looked Mapp in the eye. "I think you got the point, shithead." He spit at Mapp's feet to drive it home.

He walked back to the van. He pulled the door open and reached in. He threw the leather over his shoulders and stood there, putting his back to the customers wandering around the dealership before he got in.

━━━

The van rolled over Magazine Hill. They were almost back to Halifax before Gunner spoke. He started with Murphy.

"You get a pass this time. Not saying what you did was right, but it wasn't all wrong, either. Tell you what, though. Next time you want to stop my fist, step in front of it and take the hit."

"Okay."

Just one word. But from Murphy it carried the weight of a speech. Shit. Gunner looked at the big man. Knew he meant it. If it came to it, Murphy would step in front next time. Fuck, if the guy showed one ounce of intelligence, he'd put him up for prospect himself.

He turned to Snake's favourite prospect in the back. "You gutless cunt, hiding like a bitch." He blew smoke back in Williams's face. "You ever get it in that greasy fucking head you know better than a patch, you'd better step up. You put the club first back there. Woulda been a ballsy move, if you stepped up to me, showed it. Might have earned you my vote. Instead, you show me pussy."

Gunner turned back to the front. "Get me to my ride."

He slipped the earbuds back in place and scrolled through the music in his phone. Needed something edgier this time. Went for Slash. Just right. The grinding guitar was pulling him back into his place. He could hear Jack calling from the clubhouse. Slash was grooving while Ozzy was singing about "Crucifyin' the Dead" when Gunner's head drifted to his brothers. Cam was a problem. Saying he couldn't make the run Saturday.

Stallion members out in good standing must ride in one club run a year to protect that standing. That meant Cam, especially Cam. The blessing was the only run Cam ever made. No way Gunner would let him miss it this year. The blessing was an all-clubs run. The First to the Fight assholes made it a point to fly their colours there. They wore an outlaw-style, three-part patch, and Gunner was pissed because he couldn't pull it. The Stallion protected its territory and made sure no one flew outlaw-style colours. Trouble with the First to the Fight pricks was that they were cops, firefighters, and paramedics. The club wasn't going to go to war with them over patches. As long as those pricks rode on the blessing run, Cam could ride behind the club, and no other cops could say shit. Missing the ride meant Cam losing his standing. Gunner still believed his brother would walk away from the pigs and become a true bro again. But if he lost standing, well, fucked if Gunner would sit by and let that happen. Cam would ride.

As for baby brother Greg. What the fuck had Cam said? Some shit about the three of them riding to the bitch's grave after the blessing. Like fuck. Could priests even ride? He knew Greg rode the shit out of the dirt circuit as a kid, but could he ride now that the Jesus freaks owned him? He smiled at the thought of little Greg on that motocross track flying from hilltop to hilltop. Little fucker could fly. Man, had to give him that. He had no memories of Greg that weren't at a dirt track. Only place they were allowed to see him. Thanks, Grandma. Bitch.

Lemmy was screaming at his doctor while Slash pounded that Les Paul to shit in the earbuds. He smiled at the song and at the image now playing out in his mind: Greg jumping up and kicking Gunner's bike to life, running that suicide shift like a man, lighting up the ass end. Crowd of squares staring at the priest in the outlaw saddle. Shit, that would be worth the price of a ride to the old lady's hole in the ground.

He opened his eyes as the growling vocal and guitar faded. His bike slid into view as the van rounded the back of The Fog Bank. No Greg, no crowd, no burnout. He pulled the earbuds. The van stopped and he jumped out without a word. He looked at the bike, turned away, and headed to work.

┿┿┿

Gunner pushed open the door. His boots clunked on the old plank floor as he moved into the dressing room. Two naked girls and one who might as well have been, looked at him, but said nothing. He took a look. Nice, but nothing to distract him. Two of the girls went about their business, avoiding him. One made eye contact. He moved to her. Tits were a little small. No pigtails.

"Hey."

"Hey yourself, Gunner Neville." She showed him a little pout and folded her arms under the tits. Didn't help much. Didn't hurt. He got a warm feeling but damn if he knew her name.

"Sorry, honey, if we hooked up I can't recall." He folded his arms and looked down.

"Oh, hon, if we hooked up you'd never forget." She turned and walked to a locker, showing him a serious ass and tight dancer legs.

"Lovin' the view, darlin', but come back this way." He watched her swing around, dipping her head to the right, showing enough black hair to get lost in. It settled over her right shoulder and draped over her breast. The hair accented her rich tanned skin and showed off brown eyes. The tan was perfect. Gunner knew the dancers lived in tanning beds, but something said this was all natural, and he noticed it was all over.

"What do you need? Or, is it what you're looking at?" She smiled. Better than the pout.

"Lolita, you see her?"

"Really?" The pout was back.

"Business, darlin', sorry." What the fuck was he explaining himself to this chick for? Careful, man.

She cocked an ear to the back of the room. Gunner could hear a thick bass line. Didn't know the tune.

"That's her finishing up. Room's mostly empty, just perv alley, so she won't be getting any private dances this time. Man, she worked the room at noon, though. Made a tonne." Her pout went to a frown and then over to the smile. "She shouldn't have to dance except lunch and evening crowds, you know. When I headline, fuck the two o'clock losers."

Jesus. Was this girl from that stripper's union in Montreal? Gunner knew about it, and if Williams let one of them in The Bank he'd rip the prospect patch off him and toss him off the bridge. Her smile broadened.

"Don't let me bore you with girl talk. I gotta get ready. I'm next. She'll be right in. Come check out my act when you finish that business."

Maybe, he thought, maybe. He watched her walk to the locker. She slipped into a tight leather skirt and shredded leather bustier as if they were greased. A long chrome bike chain ran from shoulder to shoulder, dipping to her navel. It swung forward as she slid into a pair of thigh-high leather boots. She grabbed a black riding crop from the locker and headed to the door, giving him a spin as she passed. No way he'd ask her name.

"Hey, what tunes you use?"

"Well, let's see, Gunner. A little Guns to get me hot, some Slash to match these." She ran black nails over the cuts in the bustier. "Then, it gets hard." She glanced down, turned, and walked away. Her boots doing the clunking now. Gunner looked at the thick heels, not stilettos. Good boots for hooking onto a set of pegs. Fucking ass looked even better in leather.

Gunner leaned on the edge of the desk, his arms folded, boots crossed at the ankles. He watched the monitors. He'd rather sit behind the desk to talk to Lolita, but he couldn't fit back there with the desk on the riser. Fucking Williams. He'd told Lolita to hurry the hell up and change, but now Gunner was hoping she'd take her time. The dancer was working the stage nicely, slapping that riding crop on her ass to the beat of "Night Train." Fast tune, she worked it like it was written for her. She looked directly at the camera, and he felt that warmth again. He looked at the other monitors. The few men not in perv alley were over by the poker machines. He could see they were turning away from the idiot boxes and watching the stage. She was headline stuff. He turned back to the stage monitor waiting for her to shed that top, even though he knew she wouldn't. Nothing comes off in the first tune. Long first dance making them wait for it; she had style.

The knock on the door drew his eyes from the monitors.

"Open it."

Lolita walked in, wearing a pair of ripped jeans and a Stallion support hoodie. It was too big, ran to her knees. If she was dressed to impress, it wasn't working. He glanced back at the dancer on the monitor. Still dressed, still prancing, and getting a little raunchier. She was swinging the bike chain now. He wished he'd seen her remove it. Lolita stood at the open door. Jimmy Williams was behind her. This tiny stripper was taller than he was. Gunner swore he would talk Snake out of patching that guy.

"Close the door, prospect." He nodded to the sofa, and Lolita dropped into the leather. She hugged knees to her chest and began examining her fingernails.

"All right, girl, we've got a problem, and I need to know how bad it is. So why don't you tell me?"

She kept working the nail.

"Told Jimmy. I wasn't at the clubhouse. I was here and then went to Sheilagh's place. Ask her."

No gain there. The girls were lovers, if Williams wasn't making that shit up. Even if he was, they were dancers, and they all lied for each other. With the time they wasted going to see Mapp, every girl in the club probably signed off on the lie. Gunner leaned forward quickly and slapped her hand away from her face. She looked up. Showing fear. Good, she knew she wasn't dealing with Williams.

"Little girl, you calling my bro a liar? I spoke with Grease this morning, and he was clean and sober. Told me about your little visit. Let's hear it again." He placed a boot on the sofa between her feet.

"I didn't do anything. He was already dead."

Fuck.

"Tell it."

"I went to see him like I was supposed to. I got there, and my brother was freaking out. I was pissed at the old bastard and stabbed him. Just once, and he was already dead. I swear. We figured we should get rid of the body, so no one would know. Thought you guys would be good at that. Guess not." She went back at the nail. Gunner let it pass.

"What do you mean, you went like you were supposed to? Who sent you?"

"You did." She shifted to a new nail. The backhand got her full attention, but the fear was gone, defiance showing now. Gunner slapped her again.

"The fuck you trying to pull, bitch? You want to find out how good we are at that sort of thing, keep that shit up." He leaned back on the desk. He didn't want to mark her, had to stop hitting her near the face. Of course, the trouble with strippers is: where the fuck do you hit them?

She held a hand to the side of her face and looked at him.

"The club, I mean, the club sent me. Not you." She kept the hand there ready to fend off another blow.

"Fuck, girl, if the club sent you, would I be here asking you about it? Talk to me. I'm getting pissed."

"Got the call on my cell, same as always. Caller said it was the house calling, same as always. Sent me to see him, same as always. It was the club. We figured you'd want us to get rid of the body." She dropped her left knee and went back to the nails.

Gunner ran his hand through his hair and looked up at the stripper on the monitor. The top was gone now, so was the crop. She was having fun running the chain across those tiny breasts. He took a deep breath.

"Give me your phone."

She reached into the pocket in the front of the hoodie and handed him a pink-shelled iPhone.

"What time you get the call?" He was scrolling through her re- cent calls list. Most were from Montreal. Made sense. That was home base, and he knew she was headed back there in a week or so.

"Don't know. Before the midnight show. I did my ten and was back in the dressing room talking to Sheilagh."

It was easy enough to find; there was only one call between ten and twelve. A blocked call. The clubhouse would sure as hell come up blocked. No way to prove anything with the phone.

"You trying to tell me Grease sent you to that preacher and then ignored you when it went bad? He was the only one at the clubhouse, and he didn't say shit about that to me."

"Not your clubhouse, man. Mine. I mean Montreal." She looked up at him now.

Well, shit, Gunner thought, that lie would be a little harder to chase down. It might even be true. The Stallion Montreal charter owned Lolita. Halifax took most of the profits when she danced at The Bank, but a piece had to go back to Montreal. If the bigger char- ter had a side business going with her here, it should share that money with Halifax, too. Should. Montreal had a habit of playing outside the rule book. Hell, Gunner ran side gigs hidden from his own charter sometimes. Everybody did it. He tossed the phone at her.

"Go put some ice on your face."

She got up and headed for the door. He was watching the mon- itor again.

"Wait."

She turned back.

"Who is that on stage now?"

A smile from her now.

"Cheyenne. I'll tell her you asked."

"You'll tell her nothing."

He reached for a cigarette as he heard the door shut. He blew smoke out to the screen, as Cheyenne bent over and dangled her chain in front of a drooler in perv alley. Didn't let the guy touch it. She walked to the centre of the stage, wrapping it around the chrome pole and leaning back, her hair trailing down to the stage. The music faded, and Gunner instantly recognized the opening notes of her finale. He was fingering the chords on his air guitar before Slash hit the third chord. Myles Kennedy was wailing about getting "Back From Cali" before Gunner realized what he was doing. He folded his arms again and looked at the screen as Cheyenne dropped the skirt and strutted the stage in her boots, swinging that chain. Cheyenne.

┼┼┼

Thursday, dusk

A bright yellow moon floated above the trees of Point Pleasant Park, the colour of the setting sun shading its surface. The sky ran from a brilliant orange in the west, to a deep blue where it met the waves in the outer harbour. The sky and water would be the same ink black when Thelma Waters returned at the end of her prayer walk. The moon and the tiny flashlight she carried in her pocket would be enough light to get her home. The park would be closed by then, but it was okay. She'd left her car outside the gate as she always did.

God put that moon there for her. Just as he shaded the eastern sky in the blues identical to the binding on the tiny leather prayer book she clutched to her breast. The soft, fine leather felt warm in her hand. Her thumb rubbed the embossed gold cross on the front cover. Her other hand held the balled-up tissue she couldn't seem to keep from her eyes. How could these eyes still produce tears after so many hours of crying? She fought to focus on prayer, but instead of

His glorious peace, dread pressed into her chest beneath the prayer book. This path was her personal connection with God. There was always the joyful meditation of repeated prayer here. Not tonight.

She was being weak. God was doing what only He understood, and she must accept it. This was a test, nothing more. Trust in the Lord with all your heart and lean not on your own understanding. Proverbs taught her that. Her faith would be purified in this horrible crucible. It would be stronger in the end. She knew that. Did not doubt it for a moment. But the pain and the panic were more than she could handle.

Again tears burst forth, tears of shame. How could she be worrying about her pain, about her state? Poor Pastor Brenda. Alone in Africa dealing with the loss of her husband, her partner, her pillar. The call to Brenda was the most difficult thing Thelma had ever done. When the police finished with their questions, she insisted on making the call herself. It took three hours for the Christian Service League to get a satellite phone to Brenda in the remote village where she was ministering. Now, it would take four or maybe even five days for Brenda to get out of that place and back here. Thelma couldn't believe she had to fight with the League volunteers to arrange transportation. In the end, it was another African aid organization that took control. She owed it to Brenda, her sister in prayer, to fight to get her home now. They shared a burden that no one could understand. Just as no one could truly understand Pastor Sandy, not the way they did. He was a man of God, a beacon of faith that shone across the globe, but still just a man. All men are born weak. Job tells us that. She clutched the tiny book tighter. It tied her to God, and to Pastor Brenda. They had identical copies, gifts from Pastor Sandy.

Thelma saw so clearly now what she could not see before. Pastor Sandy's death was a message from God, as are all difficult things. The symbolism is so obvious once you know where to look. She rubbed the edges of the prayer book and smiled a small smile. The first since she'd heard the news. The pain was real; it would not leave soon. She knew that. But in God's message to her, she saw the need for this pain. For as long as Pastor Sandy was alive she could not, would not, betray him. She ignored his weakness. No—more than that—she helped him feed the hunger he could not control. She looked away from her heart, from God, and served Pastor Sandy instead. It was wrong. Her smile broadened as she thought of the two police officers who brought her the terrible news. Messengers from God, who were not even aware of their role in the greater plan. One named for Christ, the other the brother of a priest. How could God be more clear? It was time for Thelma to stop the horrors, to tell all there was to tell. It would hurt the church, but the church would survive. She had told the others of her plan after the prayer service tonight. Now she was certain it was right. She would wait for Pastor Brenda, of course, but together they would follow God's command.

The moon brightened now. The yellow shade gone. The cool air filled with the salty brine of the ocean as the waves crashed in perfect rhythm. The tree frogs began their nightly serenade. Crickets joined. All of it for Thelma. God is everywhere if you open your heart. The path ahead began to narrow as she passed the rocks of the beach. She found the small opening in the treeline beside the main path used by the joggers and dog walkers. She entered and headed for her bridge. Not really a bridge—two wide planks some men from the church had placed across a stream that cut through the path. The city arborists left it there, used it in their running battle with some bug Thelma knew was invading the park. Waist-high railings of two-by-four lumber ran across each side. This prayer path was a Church of Salvation initiative, occasionally used by the joggers who discovered it. The godless fools at city hall would destroy it if they knew. Thelma knew even those who ran through here found a path to God. They, too, would be led to Him. All in His time. His plan.

She stopped partway across the bridge. She could no longer hear the waves crashing, but the gentle trickle of the stream was just as beautiful. She placed the tissue in her pocket and held the rail. The day's warmth still being released by the wood felt pleasant on her skin. Her heart calmed as she looked up through the canopy overhead to the moon and back down to the slivers of light dancing on the surface of the fast-moving stream. "Thank you, God. I feel you here."

Another brilliant reflection sparkled like a jewel beside her. It barely registered before the pain. Her sweet joy now a searing agony, heat now cold, light and dark as one. The moon jumped from its ancient orbit and rose above her quickly, directly above her now. How did that happen? The deep darkness of the pine trees on each side of the path framed it perfectly. A shadow moved across it, an eclipse, and then that glint once more. More pain, and a sound, a howling, an animal maybe. They said there were coyotes here in the park. No. Was it? Could that be her voice? She turned away from the sound, from that sliver of light that drove pain deeper. She could see her right hand beyond the planks. She watched as her fingers opened, and the tiny book slipped free. The reflection of light from the gold cross, and then darkness.

CHAPTER 6

Friday morning

THE TIRES MOANED AGAINST THE WEIGHT OF THE CAR. I FOUGHT THE
pull of the seat belt, stiff-arming the dash. The oil pan or something
else under the front end banged into cement. I said nothing but shot
Blair my best hard-guy stare. The toothpick in his mouth rocked up
and down. Better hard-guy look. He was driving, a clear advantage.
He manhandled the wheel and willed the car to stay in the hard right
turn. It did. We shot out of the dark tunnel and leapt from the parking garage beneath the temporary major-crime office in Bedford.
The ramp pointed us into a sun-filled morning sky. Did nothing to
improve my mood. Never think for a moment things can't get worse.

We arrived early and were waiting for the morning briefing to
start when the call came in. Blair and I kicked around his thoughts
based on the interviews at the house. Sam and Bobby remained a
double bill on the suspect list, but still untouchable, according to
the inspector. Neither one of us could get behind that, and we both
hoped it would change with the briefing. Sam, we agreed, remained
off limits. His mother was on the way, and he was blanketed by the
YCJA. But Bobby, man, that guy needed a round in the box. The
inspector was holding back, waiting until everything was in place, he
said. Like what, a defence lawyer?

We were set to raise our concerns with the inspector when the
new body fell into the mix. The inspector handed it to us. Teach us to
arrive early. I remembered the good feeling twenty-four hours earlier
when I ducked under that crime-scene tape and into the first real case

we'd had in two years. Somehow, I didn't expect this morning's scene to feel quite so good.

The car bottomed again as we left the mall parking lot and drove out the Dartmouth Road. The Halifax metro integrated major-crime team works out of a small office tower on Brunswick Street on the edge of downtown. We weren't there. Inspector MacIntosh decided his team needed separation to focus on the Gardner case. The new Mountie provincial HQ is in Burnside, and all the specialized units that investigate crime outside Halifax sit there now. The federal synthetic-drug section made the move, leaving behind a lease on some high-end digs in a glass tower sitting above a trendy shopping mall in Bedford. He placed us there. Gotta love that Mountie money. I figured MacIntosh was using this case to do a bit of empire building. Coffee there was good, so I was okay with his agenda.

"We've got maybe twenty minutes before Thelma Waters becomes priority one. Let's work Gardner through once more." I released my grip on the dash and eased back into the seat.

"You first," Blair said as he flicked the switch for the siren. Our car was unmarked, but it had all the toys.

"I'm liking Bobby. He has the violent history. I can see him falling back into the law of the jungle if he found out his pastor was a diddler."

"Big difference between the Church of Salvation and the prison yard though," he said.

"I know, I know. And I'm not the one to say a con can't change his ways. It's just a vibe I was getting off him."

Blair guided the car past slower traffic and began the downward trek toward the Dartmouth waterfront. I knew he would take the MacKay Bridge. The Macdonald was a shorter run, but even with the siren, the streets in that end of the city were too narrow, and at this hour, clogged. I watched Blair push the pedal down as the big police engine growled in delight. I still get a rush from a finely tuned engine doing its thing. I just prefer it between my legs, not under a hood. His knuckles whitened above the wheel. The toothpick flipped from the right side of his mouth to the left and pointed out the driver-side window. He was chewing over the options.

"What about Sam? There's motive we need to get at," he said.

"Yep, for sure. We need to bring him in. Both of them. Easier to work Bobby, no messy young offender shit to deal with."

"One good thing," he said as he began pumping the brake to bring us in for a landing at the bottom of the hill.

"What's that?"

"We can scratch Thelma Waters from the list."

Halifax is a Navy town. A military moron named Cornwallis was the first to claim it. He started his career as a bedchamber servant for King Edward over in England. He managed to sneak out of the royal bedroom long enough to slaughter hordes of unarmed Scots. The blood lust impressed the King who, although reluctant to lose a man good with a bedpan, realized he had a new bully ready for battle. With no one left to kill in Scotland, the good King sent him off to clean up the royal mess here. Cornwallis built a fort on the hill overlooking Halifax Harbour and headed off into the woods to make war. He couldn't find the French, so he drew Blair's ancestors into a little game called genocide. The British say he won. Cornwallis didn't procreate; Blair is here. I call that victory.

While the King's men and the Mi'kmaq took turns scalping corpses, the first Haligonians cracked open the rum kegs and got to work. That was the bloody summer of 1749. Couple of centuries later, city planners still fight a losing battle against their drunken design. A fort on a hill in the middle of a foot-shaped peninsula makes perfect sense in a world dominated by slow-moving warships. Throw in some narrow streets and fast-moving cars, and you have the little city we love to hate. A siren is only good if the people in front of you have enough road to get out of your way.

The bridge dumped us onto the peninsula at the foot's heel. We were fighting our way through the stop and slow morning ritual, trying to get to Point Pleasant Park at the big-toe end. The morning commuters didn't seem to care that we had a date with a dead woman.

We arrived at Point Pleasant Park without killing anyone, so I figured things were looking up. Then, I saw Greg just outside the yellow tape. Now my brothers were beating me to crime scenes. Halifax is a small city, but I knew for a fact there was more than one Catholic priest in it. I don't like coincidence, especially when it involves family.

Blair nodded toward him, as he shut off the engine.

"I know he's the chaplain. Didn't know he was getting called out now, too."

"Maybe he keeps a scanner in the rectory," I said as I opened my door and drank in the cool ocean air. Greg wasn't our biggest problem, and he wasn't the only one with a police scanner. The parking lot was littered with TV trucks and the point-and-click crowd. The lenses on the TV cameras swung our way as we headed to the scene. Nothing else for them to shoot.

Today's roll of yellow tape cut a diagonal across the huge parking lot. It blocked access to the walking-and-running trails that circle the park. A deep green urban forest bordered the right side of the lot and spread out to the tip of the peninsula. It was once flattened by a hurricane, but it was making a strong comeback.

Just beyond the paved lot, the swells of Halifax Harbour crashed on a small sandy beach. For decades raw sewage poured down the harbour's throat. The switch on the sewage-treatment plant had barely been thrown when the mayor of the day took a dip right here. Didn't get him re-elected, probably got him a shortened life span.

To the left of the parking lot, the biggest of Halifax's shipping terminals sprawled along the waterfront, stopping a container length short of the park. Its massive orange-and-yellow building blocks were piled so high you couldn't see the sun, let alone the water. We walked up to Greg and the uniformed officer protecting the scene. Blair gave him our badge numbers, as I pulled my brother aside.

"Why are you here, Greg? Who called you?" I asked, feeling more than a little uneasy. If the average citizen had arrived at two crime scenes, we'd pull him in for some serious Q&A time. Perps often like to take in the show once they've set it in motion.

"Relax, Cam. I have friends on the force, even parishioners."

He nodded toward the young officer in uniform. I didn't know him, but he'd soon know me.

"So why'd he call you?" I asked.

"Thelma attended our prayer service for Pastor Gardner last night. He wanted me to know she'd been found dead. That's all."

I pulled out my notebook and marked the time and place.

"You saw the victim last night? What time?" I asked.

"She left the church at seven. She said she was coming here." Now he was the one who seemed uncomfortable.

"Was he there too? Was Bobby Simms at the service?" I asked.

"Yes, he was. He left shortly after Thelma. Cam, I don't believe he could..." His voice trailed off. He pressed his hand to the crucifix and looked at me with sadness in his eyes I had never seen there before.

"I do, Greg. He's an ex-con with a violent past. Why would that be such a problem for you?"

"What about our brother? Gunner's past is no better, and we still love him."

I couldn't argue the point.

"Gunner doesn't know our two victims. Bobby does."

"I'm sorry, I know. It's not just Bobby. It's all of it. Good people, people of God, are being murdered. If another man of God is behind it, well that kind of news will chase people from the thing they really need: faith in something more."

"Christ, Greg, sorry, but really, where are your priorities? Thelma Waters is right over there." I pointed toward the walking path and the beach. "Maybe worry about her a little and think of the mother Church later."

"That's not fair, this isn't about the Church; it's about the people who need it even if they don't know it. Their souls are suffering, Cam. The level of alcoholism and drug addiction in this city proves it."

I flared a little but swallowed it.

"I have to solve this thing before another body drops, brother. Like I said yesterday, it will be what it will be. I'll need a list of everyone at the prayer service," I said as I walked away, thinking about what he'd said.

Couldn't argue with one thing. Addiction was sweeping the city. Junkies were stabbing each other over crack crumbs like they were the holy grail. College kids were popping ecstasy and making new friends with benefits every night. The prescription-med market rivalled the fast-food chains for volume. Beat it for profit. The Beamer and Cadillac crowd left it all in the rear-view, as they headed home to Bedford and the other burbs every night. Of course, out there the rich and powerful drunks beat their wives behind closed doors like the civilized men they were. I also knew religion couldn't stop any of it. I sure as hell didn't have the answer. My job was cleaning it up.

I looked back as Blair and I reached the end of the parking lot and made our way into the park. Greg looked small behind that white collar. I wonder if Cornwallis knew he was fighting a losing battle.

You see a lot in this job. Most of it ugly, most of it stupid, preventable shit people do to themselves or the people they love. Most of it you forget. Some of it you can't. Blair and I knew Thelma Waters, not well, but we'd spoken with her only yesterday. Seeing her slaughtered—and that was the only way to describe it—meant she'd haunt us. We'd find a way to blame ourselves. I longed for a shot of Wild Turkey, knowing there would never be enough in any bottle to keep her away.

"Fuck," Blair said, turning to look out over the water.

"Overkill," I said.

"No shit."

Thelma's body sprawled at the foot of the cenotaph near a point of land overlooking the entrance to Halifax Harbour. A beautiful old anchor stood sentry near the water's edge. Glance up and you see a wide-open horizon, an endless vista of deep-blue water. Nature's beauty reminding you there is something bigger than you. Something divine, Greg would say. Look down, and you know there is evil. True evil, darker than the deepest ocean current.

Blood saturated her clothes. Her neck was cut wide and deep. I could see bone and tissue in the wound. The irregular oval of her severed windpipe was easy to make out in the mess. Her throat wasn't so much slit as hacked open. There were stab wounds in the area of her heart as well, and I could see what appeared to be defensive wounds on her right forearm. It was overkill, yet it seemed her killer didn't think it was enough. He took the time to make a display of his work. Her arms were spread wide, her feet together one on top of the other. I remembered her crossing her ankles when she was nervous. I fought the bile rising from my stomach as I remembered the living Thelma in that warm, sweet-smelling kitchen.

Her outstretched hands were open, palms up. The left palm was blood-filled, a hole visible in its centre. The right hand held a small blue book. I couldn't see if there was a similar wound under it. Remarkably, her face was untouched. Her head rested on a neatly folded sweater, probably her own. That was perhaps the most disturbing part of the scene. Her face looked so innocent, like she was asleep. The contrast with the gaping wound where her throat should be was difficult to comprehend.

The waves crashed on the rocks a short distance away, the only other sound the clicking of Carla Cage's camera. I still hadn't had the chance to ask her opinion on the Gardner scene, and here we were at another. She walked slowly around the body. Kneeling to frame a shot I knew would include the cenotaph to help position the body in context for a jury. She lowered the camera after the click and looked at the body. I could see pain in her eyes. Her lips moved slightly as though she was talking to Thelma, praying maybe. Apologizing because she knew these pictures would deliver a pain that was unfathomable. Thelma's family would someday see those pictures in a courtroom.

Like Carla, I knew there'd be a trial. We would catch this bastard. I couldn't live if this guy was out there. Thelma's family would never forget Carla's crime-scene pictures. She looked at me. Hardness slid across her face. A silent promise passed between us. I'd catch him. She'd build me a bulletproof forensic case. Or maybe she was asking me to shoot the bastard to spare the family a trial. I was okay with that, too.

Half a dozen cops moved around the scene doing what we do. No one spoke. I'd never been to a silent crime scene. It wasn't that she was cut up so bad; we'd all seen worse. It was the face. Like I said, we see a lot of shit in this job and try to shake it off. A mutilated hooker or street kid is a bad thing, but we sort of expect it. But a sweet-faced, white-haired old lady with her throat hacked up by some animal, well, that's tough for any cop. I didn't know my mother, but figured the others were thinking of theirs.

"Not much blood," I said to Blair as I pulled out my notebook.

"No. He did most of it after her heart stopped pumping. Thank God."

"I've had enough God today. Can't see where He was around here, anyway."

"Hard not to think of Him when you're looking at a crucifixion, Cam. I think maybe the killer is calling God out on this one."

"Got a feeling he's playing for the other team," I said, as I took my first step toward the body. The ground felt a little uneven. My knees felt the way they used to in the ring. After someone kicked me in the head.

✦✦✦

Dr. Ian moved quietly for a big man. Didn't hear him approach, barely heard a sound as he knelt beside the body. Blair and I moved away to give him space to work. Or maybe just to move away.

A uniform was standing about a hundred metres further along the path into the park. Two civilians stood with him. One was looking our way; the other stared out over the water. I'd bet that was who found Thelma. I nodded to Blair, and we walked over.

We told the officer to take a break and took a spot beyond the couple to allow them to look at us and not at the scene. He was a balding forty-something jogger in expensive running shoes with a top-dollar outfit to match. Just in case you didn't know how expensive running suits can be, he wore a bulky gold watch on his left wrist just below the cuff of the jacket. She wore university track pants and a sweatshirt. The shoes were top-drawer, though. Spent the money where it mattered. She was also fifteen years younger than the cash-flasher. She didn't look like the gold-digging type. At least he hadn't rewarded her yet. Blair introduced us, and I took a long look at each. We had one person who saw too much, and one who didn't seem to think he'd seen enough. I started with him.

"What is your name, sir?" Polite usually works.

"My God, how many of you do I have to tell?" He looked at her, putting on a bit of show.

"As many of us as it takes. Now what is your name?" No "sir" this time.

"Luke Weathers, and I expect discretion in this matter. I don't need to be connected to any of this." Giving us aloof with a little disdain now. His eyes still on her.

"I'm sorry, Mr. Weathers, if there is something you are trying to hide, maybe we need to take this downtown. Has anybody read you your rights yet?" That got at least half of his attention.

"What, rights? Are you insane? Do you know who I am? Of course I know my rights. I also know I just arrived to assist my secretary who wandered into this mess. I really don't have time for this, and neither does she. Louise, you must tell them what you saw and be done with it. We've got work back at the office."

"Mr. Weathers, shut the fuck up." Had one hundred per cent of him now.

"What did you say, officer?"

"I said 'Shut the fuck up.' Got it now? You don't tell a witness at a crime scene what to say or what not to say. If you say one more word to her, I will run you in for obstruction. This mess, as you call it, is the brutal murder of an innocent woman. Our witness isn't going anywhere with you. If that is an inconvenience, well, fuck you. Now, did you see anything at all over there or anywhere else in the park while you were running?"

He gave me a hard stare and saw where it got him.

"I ran counter-clockwise, so no. By the time I got to this side of the park, I found Louise standing here with you people."

"Fine, then we don't need you now. But we may be in touch if there are any follow-up questions. You can leave."

He looked at Louise. She looked at the ground. He looked back at me and then tried Blair. Nothing. He turned and headed toward the body. I reached out and put a firm hold on his left shoulder. He stopped but didn't turn. I walked around in front of him.

"Sorry, closed crime scene. You'll have to retrace your steps around the park." I knew he could see his car from here, but I wouldn't let him go to it. I watched as he stalked off in the opposite direction, and doubted if the walk back through the park would cool him off. Blair gave me a shrug. I shrugged back. Usually, we'd feel good after pulling the pompous out of a fool like that. We didn't.

"Sorry about that. I'm Cam Neville; this is my partner Blair Christmas. What's your name?"

She looked up for the first time since my discussion with her boss began. She gave me a half smile.

"Louise Deveau. Don't you know who he is?" she asked.

"I know what he isn't, and that's a witness. You are, and that makes you much more important in my world." The half smile was gone. She was remembering. Tears started to fall.

"I'm sorry," she said. "But, that poor woman. She..." Her hand went to her mouth. This wasn't going to be easy.

"Look, Louise, take your time. We don't need this all at once. Just tell us, did you see anyone in the area when you arrived. Anyone out of place."

"No. I came early to get a run in before work. I got this far and saw a sweater hanging from the anchor." She pointed; we looked. No sweater.

"What sweater, Louise?"

"I put it under her head. I didn't know what else to do." Shit, she got too close. Thelma would play in her mind more than in ours. I was sure she'd alibi out, but we'd need to get some exclusionary DNA.

"Did you move or touch anything else?" Her gaze moved back out over the water, but I knew it wasn't what she was seeing.

"No, nothing. I came over here and called 911 on my cell. I can't..." More tears.

"Look, Louise, I don't think you should stay here. I'm going to send you home with an officer, and we're going to come by and speak with you a little later. Okay? Before we do that, please think hard. Was there anyone, anything unusual when you arrived in the park this morning? Before you came out on the trail, maybe? Were there other cars in the lot?"

"Well, there was that guy who feeds the cats. There's three of them living over by the rocks. He's very nice, he feeds them every day. I don't know his name." I jotted a note. If he was a park regular, we needed to find him.

"No one else, then?"

"Oh, a truck. There was a white truck. It left when I pulled in. I didn't see who was in it though."

"What kind of truck? Do you remember?" Another loose end to tug.

"White. I'm sorry, I don't know much about cars." She looked at me, now desperate to help.

"Can you describe it at all?"

"It wasn't the kind of truck with an open back. It was like the ones you see in the commercials going through puddles and snow."

"An SUV?"

"A what? I'm so sorry. I really want to help you, to help her." She pointed back toward Thelma. "I just don't know cars." She looked back to the water, and I knew the tears were rolling again.

"I'm sure the man who feeds the cats will know. You've been a great help, Louise. Don't worry." I walked over to the uniform and told him to take her home and keep her there. I planned to send a female detective to see her. Sometimes that mattered.

+++

Dr. Ian was through with the body when we returned. He'd need her on a table before working out the sequence of the wounds. Half a dozen officers remained at the scene, huddled in small groups, talking, taking notes, facing away from Thelma Waters. The ME was with Carla. He turned his bulk toward us as we approached.

"Before you start, Detective Neville," his hand was raised as he looked at us, "here is what I can say. Same rule applies today. Nothing in the field is as good as it will be when I get to autopsy. That said, I know you are impatient." He glanced down at his notepad. Carla gave us a blank stare. She looked older, still beautiful but more worn. Dr. Ian resumed.

"Likely cause of death is exsanguination due to a severed aorta. It appears to be completely severed, so it was quick." News we all wanted.

"The bad news for you: she was not killed here. Not enough blood."

Another crime scene to look for. I hadn't even thought about that. I rubbed the back of my neck.

"Let me ask you something else, doc."

He closed his notebook and shoved it into the side pocket of an expensive suit jacket. I realized he was not wearing coveralls today. This case changed everybody's priorities.

"Do you think this is the same killer?"

He pulled his glasses off and began wiping them with his tie.

"You know, of course, forensic medicine is my specialty. But, I confess I do dabble in forensic psychology. This is pure guesswork now, educated yes, but guesswork nonetheless. You'll have to consult with the proper experts." He looked. I nodded. He continued.

"Okay, my guess is no. Not even close. Pastor Gardner's wounds are minimal. The stab wound was post-mortem but could have been almost consecutive to the strangulation, so no overkill. No sign of post-mortem attacks beyond that, aside from what he sustained as the body was moved. No indicators of passion or hatred in that crime at all. Now here..." He gestured toward Thelma Waters. We didn't look. "Here we are dealing with a crime motivated entirely by passion. This killer not only wanted to kill his victim, he wanted to punish her long after death. As though death itself was not punishment enough. If I were to hazard a guess, I'd say a killer who has undergone a psychotic break."

"Psychotic break? We see that a lot in the street, doc, but it never looks like this," Blair said, as he, too, gestured to a body no one looked at.

"True. In most cases, the break leaves a person lost in a world of his own making. Harmless to others, but sometimes a danger to himself. Many of our homeless have suffered breaks." He continued rubbing the glasses with his tie. "There is precedent in forensic psychology for something like this. Some psychotic breaks have led to the most extreme forms of violence. Especially if our killer entered this state with a pre-existing psychopathic personality disorder. I believe this killer has lost touch with himself, and with the world as we know it. He, or in fairness she"—he looked at Carla as though his suggestion that the killer could be female was somehow in deference to her—"we really don't know, but I suspect it is a man based on the physical strength required to inflict some of those stab wounds. At any rate, our killer is now functioning outside of all norms. Sort of a mental virtual reality. Whatever his pathology, it is his entire reality now. It is likely that some form of physical or mental trauma caused the break. Again, this is simply educated guesswork."

"Thanks, doc. Would a victim of sexual abuse be prone to a psychotic break? Or a violent person trying to deny that side of his personality?" It was a long shot, but maybe he'd favour one of our suspects.

He placed his glasses back on his face.

"Either could. But now you are asking me to go beyond where I am comfortable offering an opinion. There are far too many variables. But let me tell you something else about this." He gestured toward Thelma's body. "Don't hold me to this either, but I think maybe this killer has done it before. There is an old case I use when teaching at Dal. An unsolved one from almost twenty years ago. I will dig it out for you. The wound patterns around the throat and abdomen. They are strikingly similar. Not identical but close. The apparent attempt to stage the body in the image of the crucified Christ was not a part of that old case, so maybe it is just coincidence."

Perfect. A cold case to complicate things. Coincidence is an investigator's greatest enemy. Can't be ignored, but sometimes a coincidence is just that. We'd be burning up manpower with that old file.

"How close, doc? And how many people have you shared details of that file with in a classroom?"

"Excuse me." A young uniform interrupted before he could answer. "Sergeant Cage, they need you over there," she said, pointing to an opening in the treeline not far from where we were standing. "The dog found something. Lot of blood, looks like maybe she was killed in there."

That was the first good news of the day. We weren't going to have to go hunting for another crime scene. Gotta take it where you can get it.

+‑+‑+

I struggled with the idea of a cold case coincidence muddying up the investigation, as Blair nosed the car into a loading zone near the old library. I looked up at the street signs. Blowers and Grafton. I smiled. Pizza Corner. There was a time when I thought this place was the toughest strip of asphalt in the city. Every rookie thinks that at first. You do your time on the beat here, and you think you see it all. Pizza Corner sits at the outer edge of the downtown bar district. Halifax is a city with a serious drinking problem, unless you think binge drinking is okay. The city's cluster of universities draws thousands of young people. They find themselves freed from the restrictions of home and set loose on bars competing for their attention with cheap drinks and loud music.

It was two in the afternoon now, and the corner was quiet. In just over twelve hours it would be a steaming mess of drunken drama queens and staggering frat boys, looking for one more chance to hook up. The pizza shops clustered around this intersection draw the drunks from last call. They stand three deep on the sidewalks and wait for the action. Raging hormones, cheap shooters, and college girls are all it takes to bring out the assholes with something to prove.

Most of the fights are sloppy wrestling matches that end before they start. The real trouble comes when some moron gets it into his head to leap into action to rescue his buddy who is at the losing end of a fight. The brawls get out of hand fast. A few split skulls, a couple of dead frat boys, and a bad PR problem for the city convinced the chief to make Pizza Corner part of a permanent night foot patrol where rookies learn to deal with crowd control in a hurry.

I looked down the street to the sandstone arch above the front door at the provincial courthouse. So much of what started in the bars and turned bad here ended up inside that building. My first shining moment on the force, and one of the best fights I ever had behind the badge, happened about half a block from the corner, close to the courthouse.

Not long after I started walking the beat here, I noticed a different kind of victim. Maybe it takes a pro fighter to recognize talent, but I was seeing kids who had felt real pain—good hits delivered hard. Not the sloppy looping punches of drunks. It unravelled slowly because most of the victims were drunk and uncooperative. I put it together, though. Some hard-core street thugs from North Dartmouth were using the Pizza Corner crowd as a gang initiation, or just a kind of blood sport. They patrolled the streets in low-slung cars, hunting for rich white college boys, preferably drunk and alone. Whenever they spotted a guy staggering along on a sidewalk, they jumped from their cars and delivered fast vicious beatings before racing away.

I got lucky and caught up to five of them while they were kicking some kid in the head. They were even more game to have a go at a lone white cop. They got a couple of early shots in, but, like I said, I used to fight pro. I could take a hit. The first kick I landed to the side of a head felt fantastic. I've been paid to do it in a ring, and I've done it on behalf of the club, but to place a solid police-issue boot into a bad guy's skull on behalf of the city, well, that was sweet. I had three of them down and bleeding before I was blindsided from behind and went down myself. I figure three out of five meant I won the fight. The other two got away clean, but they left their buddies on the sidewalk bleeding next to me.

The watch commander was waiting when the paramedics cleared me. He bought me a beer at the end of the shift. Thanked me for keeping calm and not bringing the gun into the fight. I didn't tell him, but I hadn't even thought of the gun or the steel baton on my belt. I just fought on instinct and never felt threatened. I was having fun.

Two weeks later we got the intel from the guns-and-gangs unit. They confirmed what I suspected. It was an initiation. We started targeting gang members seen driving around the corner. They stopped. Sometimes you get lucky and win one. Today, I didn't feel lucky.

"You thinking about Thelma Waters?" Blair asked as he shut off the car,

"Trying not to. Just remembering the good times on foot patrol here. Man, we thought we had it tough then. You Mounties missed out on it."

"Merger only goes so far. We ride horses. You HRP guys can walk the beat. I'm going to grab a donair. Want one?" He opened the door, and the hot humid air filled the car with the spicy smell of donair meat.

"No way, man. You're the only person I know who eats that shit sober. Grab me a veggie slice."

"Your loss," he said as he headed into the nearest pizza shop.

Donairs are made of over-spiced mystery meat the culinary purists at city hall named Halifax's official food. Puzzling call in a capital supported by people who risk their lives on the waves. We send the best fresh seafood all over the world and celebrate meat that spins on a stick, sweating grease over grills, in almost every pizza shop in the city. The hunks of meat draw young drunks and flies; Blair could eat it for breakfast. But then he eats McLobster sandwiches, too, so what are you going to do? I'm not sure which is worse, because I've never been drunk or brave enough to taste what McDonald's could do to lobster.

The food break was a good idea. We needed to clear our heads before the next briefing. I watched a couple of tourists wander past and tried not to think of Point Pleasant Park while I chewed my slice.

I poured a coffee and watched the darkness work its way across the room. Blair stood by the door, reading a newspaper and sweating donair spice. We were back in the office above the mall in Bedford for the late-afternoon briefing. The shock of the Waters scene was being replaced by anger. The entire team was feeling it. You could almost see it. It felt familiar, good. Like a pre-action brief back in Trashcanistan. Close to thirty cops jammed the office. We were lost in our own thoughts. Filling the inner tank with enough hate to pull the trigger if the time came.

Carla's crime-scene pictures helped. They covered a whiteboard at the front of the room. The Sandy Gardner scene filled an identical whiteboard beside it. No one looked at those pictures. Hard to stoke a red-hot hatred when the victim needed killing. Thelma Waters was another story. No one deserved that. We'd feed off her for the rest of this case. I hoped to hell the killer wouldn't give us any more fuel.

Carla joined me at the coffee urn. She wore a tight-fitting pair of black jeans and a matching black turtleneck that clung to every curve. She looked tired, but she looked good. A pleasant distraction. She nodded toward the back of the room.

Inspector MacIntosh, head down, hands jammed in his pockets, paced like he was suffering a psychotic break of his own. You could feel the stress seep out of his uniform. The Mounties in the room kept a close eye on his movements. I figured his career would be made or broken in this room. Promotion or retirement, no other option. He wasn't the type to go down alone. Made me happy I wasn't a Mountie. I'd do everything in my power to solve the case, and that would probably get him his promotion. No good deed goes unpunished.

At least his decision to move the team to Bedford looked good on him. I thought the move was about his inflated ego, but had to admit it made sense now. There was no way the major-crime office downtown would hold this crowd. Blair and I weren't the only new bodies. The full-time major-crime detectives were outnumbered three to one by cops on loan from the other plainclothes units. There were even a couple of uniforms in the mix. Everyone with more than thirty seconds of investigative experience was in the room. Vice cops, the drug team, anti-gang guys, organized crime, and even the clowns from the Outlaw Motorcycle Gang squad. They avoided me. Whole lot of files were going to gather dust for a while. Some bad people were getting a pass. Fine by me. We needed all the help we could get.

I walked toward the whiteboards. Carla stayed at the urn. She'd seen what there was to see. The board on the left was covered with shots of the Gardner scene. I started there. I wasn't ready to face Thelma Waters again just yet.

On the top row, Carla had placed a picture of Gardner in life. Beneath that, shots of his body at the dump. Tights of the bruising around his neck, wrists, and ankles. I found what I was looking for in the third row of pictures. It showed the office above the garage. I looked at the close-up of the drugs I'd seen in the small dish. Satan's head branded the ecstasy pills. Little doubt where they came from. I felt as if everyone was looking at me. I was used to the feeling. Sometimes it was all in my mind.

The board to the right was harder to look at. The shots from the Thelma Waters crime scene were carefully chosen. They were shocking enough to anger and motivate the new team members who hadn't been in the park. I knew they could have been much worse. I looked at Carla and wondered again what promise she'd made to Thelma at the scene.

A large corkboard on an aluminum frame stood beside the crime-scene boards. Pictures of Bobby Simms and Samuel Gardner, the two closest things we had to suspects, sat at the top. The rest of the board was empty. We had nothing to tie either to the crimes yet. That meant Samuel was still off limits, but it was time to bring Bobby in for a serious chat. No way MacIntosh could stop that now.

Blair and Carla came over. The three of us moved behind the whiteboards. Blair held his newspaper rolled tightly in one hand, a coffee in the other.

"Going high-test, partner?" I nodded at the cup.

"Might be a long night." He sipped the coffee.

"Sergeant." I nodded to Carla.

"Looks like you guys picked the wrong time to come out of retirement." Her attempt at humour made me smile.

"Couldn't stay in the country club forever," I said. "Be nice to go track terrorists again, though. At least until this is over. Careful what you wish for, right?"

"If you wished for this, then yes."

"Not this exactly. Just off the task force and out of the port."

"Well, here you are."

"Yep."

Blair had his head back in the paper. I could see it was *The Coast*, a hip weekly that catered to the university students, artists, and the bohemian crowd that gave Halifax a little soul. The three of us sipped in silence and waited for the inspector to stop pacing and start briefing. I broke the silence.

"Let me ask you something, Sergeant. These scenes. You feel anything even close to the same vibe? I mean, you think it could be the same guy?"

She looked up at me over her coffee cup as she took another drink. Seemed to be working it through.

"Why do you do that, Cam? Use my rank instead of my name?" she asked.

"I, well. Because you earned it, I guess."

"Well then, Detective Constable Neville, I've earned the right to tell you not to. It just feels stupid in the middle of this," she said. "This case isn't about rank or the job. This is personal, you know. It's us against something that scares the hell out of me."

"I know, Sergeant. Sorry, I mean Carla. It scares me, too. But we'll win. We'll bag this animal and lock him away. I'm just trying to figure out if it's the same animal. You heard Dr. Ian."

"I think he's wrong. Too much of a coincidence, despite the obvious violence in the second murder. These victims are linked in a way that suggests one killer or group of killers," she said.

"Blair, what about you?"

"Hard to say, partner. I went into the park believing they were connected. Haven't felt anything strong enough to shake that. I'm not sure what Dr. Ian said rules it out. I mean, couldn't the first killer have suffered a psychotic break off the first kill and become more vicious?" Blair tossed an empty paper cup into a nearby trash can.

"Makes sense, I guess, but I think maybe we've got two killers. What happened in the park felt like there was something bigger. Like the killer was releasing something he couldn't contain. Gardner was more like a clean kill and a calculated body dump. Not the same."

"Hmm, I wish he'd released something at the scene. At least we'd have a sample. I do get the feeling he got off on it, though," Carla said.

She walked away to take a seat near the front of the room where she'd be carrying the weight on the forensic side of the team briefing. We watched her go. I wasn't sure if she was disappointed, but the second body meant she'd been taken off the management team. Her talent at a crime scene was more important than what she might have done working directly under MacIntosh, coordinating the investigation.

"Hey, you remember that notation you didn't actually see in Gardner's appointment book?" Blair asked.

"You mean the lyric? 'My sweet lord.'" I hadn't given it any thought in the past twenty-four hours.

"Yeah. Remember it wasn't finished; you said it was 'my sweet lo,' right?"

"Yeah, so?"

"Was the 'lo' capitalized?"

"I think so, not sure. What are you getting at?"

"What if it wasn't a lyric? Take a look at this." He had folded his newspaper into a square, and the only thing showing was a quarter-page ad for The Fog Bank. The picture showed a dancer in a sexed-up schoolgirl outfit. She stood pouting at the camera in patent-leather platforms. Her white stockings came to an end about six inches south of a plaid skirt that would give the nuns at Sacred Heart fits. Her white blouse was tied at the navel. If it had buttons, they were probably never used. A teddy bear hung from her left hand. *Sweet Lo is back*, was the headline topping the ad.

"Thin," I said.

"Maybe. No thinner than a preacher writing George Harrison lyrics. Besides, if he was into kiddy porn, why not a dancer who looks like a little girl? We have to check her out." The grin was back on his face; it felt good to see it.

"She's not a little girl, Blair. I don't think Gardner was dumb enough to get tied up with a stripper. Too much risk." Still, no cop worth the badge would ignore a coincidence. I knew the dancer would be Stallion property and didn't want to rock that boat any more than I already had. I still needed Snake to help me with the video. Trying to draw one of his girls into this mess would not help.

"Let's kick it around after the briefing," I said as I watched Inspector MacIntosh make a move to the front of the room.

╋╋╋

Traffic crawled past on the Bedford Highway below the window. The briefing was over, and Inspector MacIntosh ordered me to stay behind. He was playing head games now, making me wait until he had time to talk.

A white 1957 Chevy pulled into the lot of the old diner beside the mall. The Chickenburger is a magnet for the classic car crowd. Seeing the '57 roll to a stop at the edge of the lot was a harbinger of summer. When the custom cars return to the street, you know winter is gone. I watched the driver pop the hood to show off a chrome-accented eight cylinder. They'd been serving chickenburgers down there for seventeen years before that car rolled off the line in Detroit.

"Neville, let's go."

I followed MacIntosh into a small corner office. He pointed at a chair across from his desk as he took a seat. I leaned against the door frame. I didn't want to close the door. Blair, Carla, and a few other detectives were working the phones and going over the early evidence reports, and I didn't want them thinking I was on the mat already. MacIntosh pulled a small yellow square of paper from his desk blotter. There wasn't much else on the desk. He held it up to me without saying a word. I didn't think he was taking phone messages for me now, but I stepped over and took it. It had a name and a number. I dropped it onto the desktop and returned to the door jamb to wait for the lecture.

MacIntosh placed his elbows on the desk and formed a hand tee-pee that covered his nose. He rested his chin on his thumbs, giving me a studious look. I'd bet he practised the move. His hands were thick, meaty claws, but even they couldn't hide that massive head. The horse tattoo on his left forearm danced a little as he flexed. I tried to picture him in the saddle guiding a horse through the choreographed poetry of the musical ride. Couldn't see it. Probably bullied his way onto the team. I waited.

"I want to hear your side of this before I decide what to do, but let me ask you first, do you have any idea who Luke Weathers is?"

People kept asking me that.

"No."

"No idea whatsoever then?" He peered over the top of his fingertips. I couldn't see through his hands, but I got the impression he was hiding a smile. I felt like I was stepping into a minefield.

"I know he's an asshole who tried to interfere with our investigation. I warned him off, didn't think we needed to charge him, but I'll do the paperwork if you think I should." I didn't bother covering my smile. He leaned back.

"Maybe you should try that. We could all use some comic relief right about now. Tell me, did you swear at Mr. Weathers and force him to walk around Point Pleasant Park unnecessarily?" He leaned forward, back into his teepee.

"That sounds about right, but I'm not sure why we're talking about this shit with two murders to solve." Fuck Mr. Weathers and Inspector MacIntosh.

"Watch your tone, Detective. I am your commanding officer here, and don't you forget it." The teepee was gone, and he was standing now, trying to intimidate with his size. Had probably worked for him in the past. It wasn't working now. He sat on the edge of his desk.

"For your benefit, Luke Weathers is a senior partner in Weathers Mann Oakley. I'm sure you've heard of the firm."

Hard not to, they had their hands in everything in this city. Sometimes Halifax is more like a small town than a small city. I still didn't care.

"He is also a close friend of both the premier and the prime minister," he continued. "The mayor has been trying to get into that club. Having you suspended might get him inside the door. I'm sure he is having that chat with the chief right now." He didn't hide the smile now.

"Won't happen. Now, can we talk about assignments? I thought that was what this was about. Don't really have the time for politics, Inspector." My smile was back. It was hard to keep it there. I knew I'd hear from the chief, but I wouldn't let MacIntosh think I was worried. He moved back around the desk. I figured he'd tell me to find the guy who fed the feral cats in the park. It was what he told Blair to do during the briefing, and I was pretty sure he'd keep us together.

"Your lack of professionalism is exactly why you never made the grade with us. It will cost you your career at some point. You will self-destruct. But let me tell you, it won't happen on this detail. One more report like this, and you are off the case. I don't care what the chief says. I am the lead, and the decision will be mine."

I had nothing for him. He'd either can me or not. I waited.

"In the meantime, I think you can be of some limited use." Time for the cat man.

"I understand your club has a special ride set for tomorrow. I want you on it."

I hadn't seen that coming. Didn't like it. Liked his calling it "my club" even less.

"You may want to run that past the chief." I stood away from the door frame. I hoped my body kept the guys in the room from hearing the conversation. "He wants me to keep my distance. Besides, I don't see how it can help the case."

"I decide what is germane to the case, and I assign assets as I see fit." He was on his feet again, and not leaning on the desk. He was in my face now. "You will go on that ride and you will get a copy of the security tape. You will also find out what that gang of criminals knows about the murder of Sandy Gardner. Buddy up to your buddies. Is that too difficult an assignment, Detective?"

His face was red, his breath coming in short bursts, his temper barely in check. I tried to slow my own breathing. I smiled. He was trying to push me into a move the way I'd tried with Bobby Simms. He reddened more, his fists closing as he took in my smile. Well, fuck you, Inspector.

"You want me to ride, I'll ride. Might give me a chance to check on Bobby Simms. He rides with a Christian club now." I turned to leave. He put a hand on my shoulder.

"You stay away from Simms. You heard the briefing. Special O and the QRT have him in a box now. Don't you spook him."

The Special O unit was the RCMP surveillance team, QRT was ours. They were pros. Bobby would have eyes on him at all times as long as they were told to keep him in the box. The idea was to wait and watch until he screwed up the way killers always do. It made sense, finally. Bobby wasn't getting a free ride after all.

"Whatever you say, Inspector, but I know Bobby, and if I don't try to question him he'll know something is wrong."

He ran a meaty paw through that close-cropped hair and turned away.

"Fine, push him a little. But just for show, are we clear?" He turned back to me.

"Absolutely. If he starts to confess I'll walk away." That's exactly what I did before he had the chance to respond.

I headed out past the other detectives. I skipped the elevators for the stairs. I needed to burn off a little adrenaline. Greg stepped into the hall from a door just beyond the stairs. I only have one younger brother, but I was beginning to wonder if maybe he was triplets. Maybe his direct link to the big guy allowed him to be everywhere at once.

"Hey, Cam, I just called your house. Now I see why I didn't get an answer." His smile lightened my load. Always did.

"Hey, Greg, it's nice to see you without a dead body in the way. What brings you here?" I saw pain spread across his face. Both bodies were people he knew well. "Sorry, Greg."

"It's okay. I'm here because of those deaths. I've set up a temporary chaplaincy office here, so I can be available to the task force."

"Why were you calling me?"

"Are you heading home?" Catholic priests, always a question where an answer belongs.

"Yes."

"Do you have time for a coffee downstairs? I hear it's good."

"Sure, and it is. Let's walk down." I realized I had time, and couldn't for the life of me understand how that could be. The first forty-eight hours in any murder case are critical. I was working two, and MacIntosh had me benched for the night.

"Sure. Your treat." The smile was back.

"My treat? You sound like Blair."

The Second Cup coffee shop sits in the corner of the food court in the mall beneath the office. In truth, the place had nothing in common with a food court. Instead of cardboard pizza slices and grease dripping combo platters, it offered fresh pasta made on-site, sushi that you could actually eat, gourmet pizza that lived up to the billing, and a menu of hearty sandwiches made fresh at a deli counter. A traditional British greengrocer and butcher shop topped it off. Nothing but the best for Bedford. I realized I was hungry as we walked through. I was getting past the image of Thelma Waters.

Greg walked up to order first. I told the tattooed blonde flirting with him from behind the cash register I'd have the same. Blair stopped here every time we were in Bedford. He usually made sure I paid, so I didn't fall over when she asked for twelve dollars for the two drinks. I like coffee, but I can never understand how tossing in a little steamed milk and calling it a latte more than tripled the price. I tossed a toonie into the glass tip jar in front of the cash register.

Fourteen dollars lighter, I headed to the end of the counter where Greg was now smiling at the barista working the handles on the steaming coffee machine. She was an attractive twenty-something with long brown hair and a clear complexion that she did not hide with makeup. She had that natural beauty that made you think of horseback riding and hayfields—maybe haylofts. I waited for her to flirt with Greg. Blair insisted she was in love with him. The fourteen dollars would be money well spent if I could tell him he'd lost her to a priest. She looked from Greg to me, and a small laugh slipped past her white teeth.

"I had no idea there were two of you." Her deep brown eyes locked with mine for a heartbeat, and then she turned her attention back to Greg. "I'm not sure who is cuter." She handed him two large cups.

"I'm spoken for." He raised one of the cups to his collar. "He's not." He handed me the other cup.

"Good to know." She laughed again before turning to fill the next order coming from the blonde bandit at the cash.

We took a table near a glass door that led outside to a patio. The tables out there were full. Another sign that winter was behind us. I sipped my coffee and almost spit it out. I drink my coffee the right way, black. This tasted like a piece of cake run through a blender.

"What is this?" I asked as I placed it on the table.

"Soy, gingerbread latte," he said as he sipped his own. "Great, isn't it?"

I took another sip. It wasn't great, but I knew there was probably caffeine in there, so I stayed with it.

"You should give her your card." He nodded to the steam cloud rising above the coffee machines.

"A little young." I took another small sip.

"You mean younger than all the other women you've been spending time with?" He looked over the top of his cup.

"I mean she's young. I didn't know matchmaking was part of the vocation, Greg."

"It's not. I just worry about you. It's part of what I wanted to talk about yesterday. The things I learned on the Camino." He put the cup down, and my little brother suddenly looked years older.

"Tell me about it." I knew he wanted to, and I needed the distraction.

"The further into the walk I got, the more I thought of you and Lee." Using Gunner's real name. This was going to be a serious chat.

"I thought it was about reconnecting with God or your faith."

"So did I. But I spent two days walking with a man from Northern Spain. Javier is seventy-eight, and he walks all or a portion of the Camino every year. He told me to empty my mind of any preconceptions. To let the Camino speak to me." He took another sip. I did the same. It was beginning to grow on me.

"At first, I didn't understand; but a few days later you joined me on the walk."

"Don't tell me you had visions out there, Greg." I wasn't sure I was ready for this.

"No, no. I mean thoughts of you, and later Lee too, filled my mind."

"If you plan to have this chat with him, you might want to stick with Gunner, and spike the coffee." I didn't want to arrest my older brother for slugging my younger brother.

"His name is Lee, and that's part of it. I didn't know him when he was Lee. You did."

"Same guy, just younger and without a nickname."

"I'm sure that's true to a degree, but I'm just as sure he wasn't exactly the same, nor were you. We were separated for all of my childhood, and I want some of that back. The three of us need it. If you hadn't lost yourself after the war, we wouldn't even have a relationship now." He waited for me to say something.

I wasn't sure what he wanted. You can't go back in time. It wasn't my fault he was taken in by our grandparents. Hell, Gunner and I resented him for it. Maybe he resented us for having each other.

"I'm not sure where you're going with this, Greg."

"I'm trying to do something for all of us. Something else Javier told me about the Camino: it lets you time travel. When you relax into the walk, surrender to it, you can send your mind ahead in time and meet yourself on the same road. When you meet your older self, you weigh your own future regrets. You then promise to do what you can to lift that burden for yourself."

"You're getting a little metaphysical on me here, Greg. Remember, I went to cop school, not a seminary."

"It's simple, Cam, I let my mind wander. When I met my older self, his only regret was not having a close relationship with his brothers. I believe you and Lee will both feel the same way some day. I want to remove that regret for all of us. That's why I want the three of us to ride out to the graveyard tomorrow. We need to forgive our parents for the childhood we didn't have."

I could see he was serious. This mattered to him, and I owed him. If he hadn't come into my life when he did, I was pretty sure I'd be in that same graveyard. It was what I wanted then.

"Well, as it turns out I'm going on the run, so let's see if we can drag Lee away."

Saturday was going to be a breeze. All I had to do was get Snake to co-operate with the police, and convince Gunner to do a little chemical-free time travel with his older self. What could possibly go wrong?

CHAPTER 7

BLAIR AND CARLA STEPPED INTO THE ELEVATOR OUTSIDE THE BRIEFING room and headed down to the parking garage beneath the mall. Blair pushed the button and wondered if he should grab a mint from his jacket pocket. Donair always tastes better the first time. It seems to get stronger as it comes back on you. He should have listened to Cam.

Blair was a happily married man, but even he couldn't help notice how attractive Carla looked in the middle of all this hell. He wondered why Cam never acted on his obvious interest in her. Blair was pretty sure she was interested, too. Maybe he should have Sue invite them both to a barbecue, or even better, one of the Friday night sweats they tried to attend as often as possible. He smiled at the thought of Cam slipping into a sweat lodge, only to find Sue and Carla already inside. He knew Cam would be furious, but would never offend Sue. If they sat through the sweat, Blair was confident Kisu'lk, the Great Creator, would show them the truth about their feelings for each other. That, or Cam would leave the lodge and silently wait Blair out. Delivering payback in the next sparring match. It was a risk, but Blair had faith. He smiled at that notion, too. Blair was a devout Catholic, but now he was beginning to have a deeper faith in the spirituality of his ancestors.

Blair had grown up on the Membertou reserve in Sydney, a cluster of shabby homes behind a white wooden church on a hilltop inside the city limits. Sweats were not a part of his life then. His own heritage was not discussed at home, and certainly not in school. It wasn't just ignored. It was forbidden. There were no schools on his reserve, so he attended the white schools in the city. He was afraid to tell the other kids where he lived, although his classmates told him he was obviously a BFI. He didn't know they meant Big Fuckin'

Indian. When his uncle told him what it meant, he'd had to fight back tears. His uncle soothed him and told him it was really a compliment. Uncle Terry was the only one who spoke of Mi'kmaw heritage then, and Blair thought most of it was nonsense.

Later, he took it more seriously, when he learned Uncle Terry was a survivor of the cultural genocide of Canada's Indian Residential Schools. Blair hated the term now. They were not schools. They were concentration camps, where Native children were locked up and forced to speak English, deny their heritage, and live on vitamin supplements and liquids, just so doctors could see how it would affect their health. Terry told him how they used to eat scraps from the garbage after the teachers' plates were cleaned in the kitchen. Terry was among the first survivors to speak publicly about the abuse. His bravery led to a renewed interest in culture, and a defiant rage among Mi'kmaw youth.

Blair's Membertou was openly called a reserve, another word for slum. It was the militancy among the older kids in his neighbourhood that changed that. With Uncle Terry's guidance, they channelled the anger into a desire to do something positive. They signed up for the free university education offered to Mi'kmaw kids, and slowly the changes began.

Only three weeks ago, on a trip home, he drove through Sydney, the city he had feared so much as a child. He saw closed businesses and signs of collapse. Then, he drove into Membertou to see newly paved streets, new businesses, and signs of fast growth. All because long-ignored treaties with the federal government made First Nations communities a great place to do business. Some of Membertou's earliest university students became the first Mi'kmaw to graduate from law school where they read, and understood, those treaties. They opened the floodgates. Today, his old slum is the pride of the Unama'ki tribe. No one calls it a reserve. It was his first job, as a member of the Unama'ki First Nations police force, that had led Blair to become a Mountie.

"What are you thinking about?" Carla asked.

"Sweat lodges, racism, retribution, and my stubborn partner. You?" Honesty was also a part of the heritage. He smiled, and again wished he'd grabbed the mint.

"Um, well now that you bring Cam up, can I ask you something about him?"

"Sure, Sergeant. What do you need?" He stepped back in the elevator and leaned against the rear wall.

"It's personal, so if you feel a loyalty to him I'll understand."

Blair gathered the thick black hair that hung past his neck, pulling it tight. He released it as he realized it was what Sue called his evasive move.

"I guess it depends. What do you want to know?"

"I noticed how he rubbed the scars around his wrists at the Gardner crime scene. I've heard the stories about what happened to him. I just wonder how much of it is true, and how much is just the usual blue exaggeration."

"Shouldn't you ask him?" Blair knew Cam wouldn't talk about it, and didn't think he should, either.

"Well, I don't want to get off on the wrong foot. A little over a year ago I thought maybe he was interested, but then he shut me down and walked away."

Blair smiled. So this wasn't just morbid curiosity. Perhaps Kisu'lk worked in elevators too.

"So, you are interested in Cam?"

The elevator door opened, and they stepped out into a tiny vestibule with doors on either end leading into the parking garage. Carla blushed as she stepped into the vestibule.

"I guess so. Yes, I am. Please, don't mention it to him."

"Look, Cam doesn't like to talk about his scars. If you think maybe you care about him, you'll have to accept that. Maybe you'll even get him past it. I think that would be good. I can tell you, this is not just the badge rumour mill. What's being said is not even close to what really happened."

She looked up into Blair's eyes with a genuine concern that made him feel good about sharing with her. She might be exactly what Cam needed.

"If he doesn't talk about it, how do you know?"

"We spar together. I've seen the other scars. His ankles, his back, chest, legs, everywhere, really. You have to remember, he was a prize catch. Not quite an American soldier, but still a white infidel in uniform. A sniper, at that. He's joked about it a little with me. If I manage to beat him in the ring, he'll compare it to the beatings over there. They used to put him in the middle of a village square where all the young men would whip him with water-soaked ropes. He was chained and couldn't fight back. The people cheered it on."

"He told you that?" Her tone was challenging, as if she wanted to believe he was making it up.

"In bits and pieces. I shouldn't tell you, but you need to know he is a complicated guy, and maybe that's why he pushed you away. Do me a favour."

"What's that?"

"Don't get involved with him if you think you can't handle all of it. He hasn't had a lot of breaks in life."

"You really care about him."

"If you get to know him, you will too. Just tread carefully."

"Can I ask one more thing?"

"Go ahead." Blair moved toward the door to the parking garage, wanting this conversation to be over. He wanted to go see a stripper about a dead preacher, not spill Cam's secrets.

"His wife. What happened?"

Blair stopped at the door and thought for a moment. He sighed.

"She had a heart defect. Died while he was in captivity. Took a couple of days before anyone found her. I think he blames himself for that. Doesn't make sense, but there you have it. Seriously, Sergeant, I like you and I think you might be good for Cam, but I am starting to get uncomfortable here, so can we leave it alone?"

"Yes, and thank you."

She touched his shoulder as they moved through the door into the garage. Blair headed to his car, saying a silent prayer to both Jesus and Kisu'lk that he had not betrayed his best friend, with a quick postscript that if he had, Cam would never find out. He thought about the fourth level of creation in Mi'kmaw culture, Kluscap, the first one who spoke. Legend had him created by a bolt of lightning striking the earth. Blair finally popped that mint as he started the car.

He laughed out loud. His decision to be the first to speak might well set off a lightning storm of another kind.

╼╼╼

Friday, sunset

The fast-fading rays of the setting sun painted the cross on top of the two-hundred-foot spire a deep ochre, like dried blood in sand. A veil of darkness draped the rest of Saint Mary's Basilica. Irish Catholics built the sandstone cathedral as a testament to their faith in the dying decades of the 1700s. Now, Halifax's first Catholic church sits like an afterthought at the foot of Spring Garden Road.

In the bright sunshine of the day, the sidewalks on both sides of the road are crammed with beautiful people buying beautiful things. Trendy young office workers lug six-dollar lattes past panhandlers who stand invisible at the curb, empty cups in hand. The homeless sit huddled against fire hydrants and utility poles. Halifax doesn't have a trendy Main Street or a Skid Row. Spring Garden is a little of both.

At night, the tide shifts, and Spring Garden is taken over by angry, young rich kids in torn jeans and baggy black hoodies. They scowl and bluster at anyone who walks past and then tweet about it on seven-hundred-dollar phones. The real thugs roll past in Escalades, looking for someone to shoot. Even they wouldn't waste real lead on wannabe hoods.

Two winos huddled against the side of the sandstone-and-stained-glass basilica. They shared the last dregs of a bottle and watched the cars roll past. If they looked up, they'd see the glow reflected on top of the highest free-standing spire in North America. They never looked up.

Inside, Father Greg Neville sat in the front pew. The church was empty, the last of the parishioners from the evening Mass long gone. He looked into the stained-glass tableau suspended overhead. The five panes sat at the top of the wall high above the massive crucifix at the back of the altar. They reached skyward and inward to join at the peak in a classic Gothic arch. They seemed to lean into the basilica above the altar. A miracle of art and engineering that showed God's hand. Local shipbuilders had designed the roof and built it with simple hand tools. It was a classic ship's hull design turned upside down to protect the flock.

Greg worked the rosary beads through the fingers of his left hand, praying silently to the image of the Blessed Virgin Mary at the centre of the stained-glass masterpiece. Mary was his true mother. He'd known that since he was a child. His grandfather said he was born to atone for the sins of the woman who gave him birth. A woman he never knew and never thought of as his mother. The Camino taught him the true price of that ignorance, and he would now change it. He would lead his brothers closer to her as well. Embracing the memory of his earthly mother would be good for his soul. It would help him to better understand the burdens his parishioners faced. He knew that. It would not change what his grandparents had told him.

He was a miracle child, born to do God's work. How else could you explain the son of a killer and a junkie having become the guardian of so many souls? A miracle child just like Jesus, whom he believed to be his brother. He pressed his right hand to his chest. The crucifix, given to him by an earthly brother, a link to the heavenly one. The rosary beads moved swiftly through his fingers as he prayed for Sandy Gardner, for Thelma Waters, and, above all, for the Church. He prayed that the terrible things that were happening would not push people further away. He asked for guidance, asked Mary to lead him, to hold his hand and show him the path. God's will was behind all of this. Greg closed his eyes in prayer. His will would not, could not, lead to yet another blemish on His name.

A tear slipped past a closed eyelid and down the side of his deeply tanned face. He did not reach to wipe it away. It was a mark of his failure. How could he have befriended a man Cam claimed was involved in such horrible, unspeakable things? How could he have failed to see that that man wanted help, wanted his help?

Greg thought of his last meeting with Sandy Gardner. They'd sat in the same chairs in which he and Cam sat only a day ago. A small fire was burning in the pit at the centre of Sandy's impressive patio. Greg had marvelled at the beauty of the place, and he felt the sin of envy as they spoke. He could still see Sandy, one moment sitting beside him, drink in hand, staring into the fire, the next, up tending the flames to no apparent end. Greg recognized the actions of a tormented soul, but at the time he wondered how a man with so much could still feel such torment. He reflected now on how selfish that thought had been. He should have reached out to Sandy and asked what burden he was carrying in his silence that night. Sandy confided that he had demons and wondered if his earthly failures could destroy the good God was doing through his church. Greg had dismissed Sandy's question, assuming the demons he spoke of were in the glass in his hand. Greg knew Sandy liked to drink. At worst, he believed, his friend sometimes used drugs. Greg saw that as more self-indulgence than demons of torment, and he offered no words of support, no opportunity for Sandy to unburden himself. It was the failure of a young priest. One he must learn from now. He moved the tiny beads through his fingers and asked Mary to help him grow through this pain.

He opened his eyes and breathed in the familiar warmth of the basilica. The sharp smell of the industrial cleaning wax mixed nicely with the heavy sweetness of melting wax from the candles that flickered beside the altar. A hint of incense lingered. He loved this church more than any. It had been a sign when he was placed here straight out of the seminary. The place that once offered a spiritual home to so many now stood empty most of the time. If not for the wonderful ladies of the CWL, the pews would be dust covered. Some of them were only filled at Christmas and Easter. The stone walls and spire erected to be seen from afar, to lead the faithful home, were now seen by many as a fortress built to protect hypocrites and liars. Greg and the others who were ordained with him, the new generation of priests, would change that. They would save the Church first and then save its people. For without the Church, the people could not be saved.

A sudden change in the light, reflected in the stained-glass portrait of Mary, drew him from prayer. His gaze was drawn to the rack of candles. The flames moved as one, leaning first toward the back of the church and then the front. Someone had opened, and then closed, the side door. The only one he hadn't locked. Probably one of the homeless men who liked to drink in the shelter of the church walls when they could. They also liked to make a dash for the collection box when they thought the church was empty. He always made sure the box held a few dollars. The collections from each Mass continued to dwindle as the congregation died off. What was collected was never placed in the old wooden box anymore. The bishop liked to joke the money was better spent on wine for the altar than wine for the parking lot. Greg believed money should flow out of the church not into it, but dared not say it to the bishop.

He was surprised to see Bobby Simms walking down the aisle. Simms's shoulders pushed the fabric of a black shirt as he dropped his right knee in front of the altar and lifted his hand to his forehead. He made a quick sign of the cross with a practised ease. He stood and smiled.

"Hello, Father. Thought I might find you here."

"Hey, Bobby, do I detect a lapsed Catholic?" Greg shook Bobby's hand. Felt the strength in a grip that stopped just short of inflicting pain.

"Long lapsed, Father, and almost forgotten. But yes, I went to a Catholic boy's school, was an altar boy, drank the Kool-Aid for a while, but I left the path. I was confirmed right there." He gestured to the space in front of the altar. The same place where Greg and two other priests had lain face down on the day they were ordained.

"Ah, so your conversion in prison was a return to Christ. That explains the strength of your faith. We could always use a man like you here, Bobby. Once a Catholic always a Catholic." Greg flashed a quick smile and then let it fade. "Seriously though, how are you? This is a difficult time."

"I am coping, Father. I have His word and His love." He looked toward the crucifix above the altar as though he expected Jesus to come down and join the conversation.

"Indeed, it is all we ever need. Have you spoken with Cam? I know he was looking for you."

"No, Father, I've been avoiding him. He believes I had something to do with these deaths, and I am sad to say he brings out feelings in me I thought were gone forever." Bobby walked to the rack of candles, and pulled a thin dowel from a box of sand suspended on the side of the metal stand. He held it over a burning candle until the tip began to burn. He moved it over an unlit candle and watched the flame grow. "That's why I am here, actually." He pushed the burning dowel into the sand and turned back to Greg.

"I'm not sure I can convince Cam of your innocence. I did try."

"No, no. God will do that. I know it's been a long time, but I was hoping you would hear my confession. Help me to release the anger and hatred, so I can see him with a pure soul."

"I'd be happy to, Bobby."

The smell of stale beer and sweat slapped Blair in the face as he walked into The Fog Bank. Not the kind of sweat he was thinking about on the drive over Magazine Hill. On the upside, no one here would notice the donair leaking out of his pores. Three dancers wearing stilettos, thongs, and nothing else walked around the crowded barroom. A fourth wearing less worked the pole on stage. Late afternoon had barely faded into early evening outside, but another Fog Bank Friday night was in full swing. Blair grabbed a table near the door and tried to spot the girl from the newspaper ad. With no schoolgirl outfit, there was no way to be sure. The first one to head for his table was definitely not Sweet Lo. The heavyset brunette wore too much makeup, a tight blue miniskirt, and a sequinned silver tank top. The skirt was made of a kind of body-hugging fabric that stretched around every curve. Runners, yoga queens, and the heavyweight divas in the Walmart checkout line wore the same material. The waitress wasn't exactly a heavyweight, but there wasn't much stretch left in the skirt. She moved through the sea of tables easily. Might have been a dancer once, but that would have been before any of the girls working The Fog Bank now were born.

"Hey, honey, what can I get you?" She mauled a wad of gum at the side of her mouth.

"Coffee, black, and a chat with Lo," Blair said.

"Lolita's up next, hon, so you'll have to wait. We got a twenty-buck minimum bar charge, and the coffee really sucks. You sure you don't want something a little stronger?" The gum rolled to the front of her mouth, and a bubble the size of a grapefruit blocked her face. It popped and disappeared inside her mouth to be ground back into shape.

"Make it a Coke then." He smiled "How much do I have to pay to have a chat with you?"

"You're sweet, sugar, but I ain't for hire." Another bubble, there and gone in a heartbeat. "You just stay here, and I'll make that Coke a double." She headed for the bar.

Blair watched her ask for the Coke and caught the eye of the bartender. Bald guy with a head full of ink and enough street smarts to make him for a cop. Blair grinned back, but Baldy just scowled and reached for a phone under the bar. Probably wasn't ordering the Coke.

The naked girl who was on the pole when he came in was now chatting up two men at a table beside the bar, meter running. A deep voice boomed from the speaker overhead as the lights on the stage flashed red, yellow, and white. There was so much reverb it was impossible to make out half of what the guy was saying. Blair heard something about New York, Vancouver, and Montreal before the words blurred into a growl ending in a long exaggerated scream of the name "Lolita." The over-the-top voice of the announcer was swallowed in a sea of whistles and shouts as a dancer strutted to the centre of the stage.

Even in three-inch platforms the girl barely reached five feet. She wore the same private-school outfit Blair had seen in the ad. The skirt had the familiar Sacred Heart plaid he'd seen downtown outside the exclusive school. The gap between the top of the white stockings and the bottom of the plaid skirt was wide. The stockings couldn't reach high enough to meet the hemline. The skirt could pass for a plaid belt. The white shirttails were tied just above her navel, the buttons above undone. The Yardbirds screamed from the sound system; "Good morning, little schoolgirl," indeed. She pranced around the stage, swinging a tattered teddy bear from her left hand, the thumb of her right planted between unnaturally swollen lips. White ribbons held two black pigtails tightly to the sides of her head. They bounced with each step. Her eyes scanned the crowd and locked briefly with each man in the place. She dropped the bear several times during the opening number, and each time she turned her back to the appreciative crowd as she bent from the waist to pick it up, revealing pink lace that left little to the imagination.

As the first song drew to a close, she leaned back on the chrome pole in the centre of the stage. It rested between her shoulder blades as she pushed her pelvis forward and pulled her thumb free. She toyed with the knotted shirttails, tugging gently on the loose ends, as a new song filled the room. Blair's first instinct was to badge his way through the crowd, pull her from the stage, and call child services. Then her eyes locked with his. There was no little girl behind that stare.

He ignored the rest of the show. Instead, he watched as the bartender kept the drinks flowing while trying to keep a close eye on him. He finished his Coke and signalled the waitress for another as he played I-watch-you-watch-me with Baldy. The bartender stopped eyeing Blair. Chalk one up for the good guys. The final song in the set ended, and a naked Lolita picked up her clothes and her teddy bear and made her way to a door near the bar. A few minutes later, she was back in costume and making her way to Blair's table.

Jimmy Williams rubbed his left hand along his jawline, still pissed about Gunner's sucker punch. He kicked his legs out, the heels resting on the edge of the desk in front of him. He'd find a way to hurt Gunner. Priority fucking one, once he had full-patch status.

He held his cellphone up and looked at the number of the last caller. Nicholas Mapp. Williams figured Mapp had serious pull in the club if he could reach out to a burner cell. The way-too-slick car-and-coke dealer said he was impressed with Williams's move on Gunner. Fucking right. If Jimmy hadn't made the move, Mapp would be looking for a dentist. Now Mapp wanted a meet without Gunner at the dealership. Like he didn't have enough to do. There was a party at the clubhouse, and he had to be there to tend bar and clean up with the other prospects. He also had this place to run and the Litter Box Boys to keep in line. Fuck. Still, Mapp might be a guy worth knowing. He had to think it through. Gunner would pull his prospect rocker if he found out, but if Mapp really was a shot caller maybe he could protect Williams and get him that full patch faster. Williams hadn't gotten this far without taking chances.

He glanced at the TV screen above the row of video monitors. The all-news channel was showing that prick Neville and his asshole Indian partner ducking under a piece of yellow plastic ribbon. A headline banner filled the bottom third of the screen, *Murder in Point Pleasant*. The words faded, and another headline appeared: *Woman found dead near jogging path*. Well shit, there's a break. Some bitch gets offed before the cops come sniffing around Lolita. That should buy enough time to find out what she knows. Gunner had left without telling Williams shit, but that didn't mean he couldn't find out for himself. Sure as hell, Neville and his partner looked plenty distracted, and that had to be a good thing.

The knock on the office door startled him. He dropped his boots to the floor with a clunk and leaned over the desktop.

"Open it," he yelled.

Bartender Glen Carroll opened the door, took one step into the room and stopped. Williams glanced quickly at the monitor showing the space behind the bar. Phil was there in Carroll's place. Fine.

"Um, there's a bit of a problem." Carroll's voice was part rasp, part growl. His vocal chords were shot. Williams remembered something about his being forced to gargle bleach or some damn thing in prison. One enforcer who didn't talk, and one who couldn't. Maybe time to hire new help.

"Come in where I can fucking hear you."

Carroll moved into the centre of the room to Williams's desk. He wore a loose sleeveless sweatshirt. It was Stallion blue with 19 on the chest and back. Support gear was forbidden in the club, but the double 19 shirt was an exception. S is the nineteenth letter in the alphabet. Two 19s, *S S* for *Satan's Stallion*. The squares never made the connection, and those who did saw it as a warning.

The shirt hung loose, but it rode high on Carroll's chest before dropping to his waist. The tattoos that covered his hairless head dropped down around his neck and disappeared beneath the collar. They popped back out on top of rounded shoulders and flowed over his biceps. Some seriously dark Gothic shit ran the length of each arm. Daggers, skulls, flames, dragons. Real fucking art. The three teardrop tattoos beneath his left eye marked the death of the fools who force-fed him the bleach. It should have killed him, but it killed them.

The bleach didn't really matter; this guy didn't need a voice. Without saying a word, he scared the shit out of every square who walked into the bar. Williams knew Carroll wanted to get out of the bar and into the real money, but the guy was perfect where he was. Sometimes, you gotta take one for the team.

"Now, what'd you say?"

"Problem, Jimmy." Carroll's face betrayed no emotion. His mouth a flat line. His eyes focused on the floor. Another fucking Phil.

Williams looked at the monitors. Everything out front seemed normal. Phil was behind the bar. If there was a problem out there, he'd be handling it.

"Looks good to me. What's up?"

"Cop talking to Lolita," he whispered.

"The fuck you say?" Williams was on his feet examining the monitors. Sure as shit, the fucking Indian was at a table by the door, and Lolita was with him. Williams looked back at the TV monitor. How could the fucker be on TV and in the club at the same time? Fucking TV news bullshit.

Glen Carroll moved fast for a big man. He headed for the door as soon as he delivered the news.

"Wait. Get back here."

Carroll stopped short. His shoulders met on each side of the doorway, his back to Williams. He turned slowly and walked back into the office. He stood in front of the desk, his hands clasped in front, forearms pulsing in and out as he flexed. Not showing Jimmy disrespect, just a nervous thing.

"Shut the door," Williams said as he stared at the monitor. The bartender did as he was told and returned to the same spot. Williams grabbed the phone, ready to call Phil. He looked at the screen again; Lolita wouldn't say shit to a cop. Maybe this was a good thing. He put the phone down and looked at Glen Carroll.

"You want in the Litter Box pretty bad, right?"

"Yes." He looked up now.

"Ready to prove you're worth it?"

"Yes." Locking eyes with Williams now. Ready to hurt the cop, good.

"You gotta understand something. I need you here, not in the street."

Carroll was silent; his eyes dropped again.

"Here's the thing. I'm busy. Spending a lot of time at the house until I finish this prospect thing. I need eyes and a brain here. I can't have the fucking dancers out there talking to the cops. Can't have them leave the club in the middle of the night either."

Carroll's head dropped further. It was all Williams needed. He knew his bartender had let Lolita leave last night. Fuck, none of this shit would be falling on Jimmy if only that bitch had been kept where she belonged. Let them out of your sight for five minutes, and the trouble follows. Well, no point in punishing the help. Last night it wasn't Carroll's job to control the dancers. Now, it was.

"I know your heart is in the street, but believe me, corralling these bitches can be harder than running a corner. You'd be in the Box but not in the street. We'll find some fucking room on you somewhere and get you the ink first thing. Think you can handle them?"

"I can do that." The corner of his mouth moved slightly; the tiny teardrop tattoos beneath his left eye lifted with it.

"I'll go get her," he whispered.

"Do that and throw that fucking Indian out." Williams sat down to watch the show.

Blair smiled as Lolita explained the cost of a strip-club conversation. Twenty dollars a song for her time, plus bar tab. She touched his arm conspiratorially, like it was a necessary nuisance instead of bar stool robbery. She nodded to the waitress as soon as she cleared that up, and a Shirley Temple arrived at the table before Blair had a chance to respond. Smooth operation—he was now on the hook for twenty plus the drink whether he liked the terms or not. He couldn't wait to see the reaction when the expense claim went through.

"Haven't seen you around before, hon, what's your name?" She sipped her drink through a pink straw. She turned sideways in her chair, keeping her legs out where Blair could see them. She crossed them, and the little plaid skirt rode higher, widening the gap with the white stocking.

"I'm Blair. A friend told me I should check you out while I'm in town. I think he was right." Blair smiled, looking at her legs. He decided to keep the badge out of it, try to play her. The badge tended to put a damper on conversations.

"Oh, and who was that?" Her eyes sparkled as the lids flicked quickly. Turning on the little-girl charm.

"I probably shouldn't say."

"Oh, hon, I can keep a secret. We all can." She smiled over her drink as she recrossed her legs.

"I suppose it doesn't matter. He's gone now anyway. His name was Sandy Gardner. I flew in for a meeting with him today, only to find out he passed away yesterday. Such a loss." Blair kept it vague—like maybe he had a heart attack—to see how she would react. She uncrossed her legs and tucked them in under the table as she lowered her drink and stared at him. No more sparkle, no more little-girl charm. No more little girl at all.

"I'm sorry, maybe you didn't know he passed," Blair said, hoping to keep the ruse going.

"I know he's dead. And I know he would never send you to see me. Who are you?" Anger in the tone now. Not fear.

Blair pulled out his badge and placed it on the table between them. No point in hiding it now. He caught movement out of the corner of his eye, and looked up to see two men walking toward the table. Baldy, the bartender, and Phil Murphy, an enforcer with the Litter Box Boys. This could get interesting real fast. Blair knew the club was a Stallion front and wasn't surprised to see Murphy. He knew the giant would never approach a cop without direct orders. Hell, the guy probably didn't go to the can without direct orders. Baldy pulled Lolita from her chair, knocking it over as her legs tangled under the table.

He whispered something in her ear before slapping the back of her head with an open hand. Blair stood and stepped forward, grabbing the front of Baldy's T-shirt.

"That's assault, asshole. I suggest you apologize before I drag you downtown."

"Fuck you, cop. She ain't gonna file a complaint. Now get out. We don't allow cops or Indians in here."

The guy was leaning into Blair now, whispering the threat like some cheap gangster, hatred in his eyes. Blair ignored the eyes and glanced down at his balled fists. The man wanted to impress. Blair could smell it off him. Worst kind of idiot. Stupid, made dumber by the need to prove how hard he was. He shoved him backward and turned his head to the bigger man.

"You'd better rein him in, Phil, or you're both coming with me."

"Leave now." Murphy wasn't asking.

The tattoo-topped bartender caught his footing and moved quickly back toward Blair. Fast enough to be a threat to the safety of an officer. That was the test, and Baldy just passed it. Sweet. Blair pivoted away, and drove a left sidekick into his stomach. The kick was fast enough to do serious damage all on its own. It was multiplied by the forward momentum of the target. All the air, all the fight, and all thoughts of impressing anyone vanished as the bartender puked, doubled over, and fell face first into his own mess. One down.

Blair barely had his foot back under him when he felt the freight train slam into the side of his head. His vision went black, and then filled with stars as it returned. The light show cost time he didn't have. As his head cleared, he locked eyes with the dancer on the stage, followed her gaze back to the massive hulk to his right. Murphy was hauling a tree trunk with a fist at the end of it back for another shot. Blair knew he had to duck the punch; a second blow would put him down and out. Never live it down, if he was dropped in a bar fight by a guy he hadn't tagged even once. He was about to lose a fight, no question. He just wanted to get something on the judges' scorecard before he went to sleep.

He was off balance; the first punch had him leaning too far to the left to get a kick or a strong right off. He twisted and snapped a fast left jab into the giant's balls as he rolled further left and out of range. He felt the jolt travel from his fist through his arm and knew it had landed strong. Murphy didn't seem to notice at all. He moved forward and drove his right fist with bone-shattering speed. Blair leaned away from it, and the punch missed its intended target, good for his head, bad for his shoulder. All feeling left his right arm as his head was finally clearing from the first shot. He watched Murphy continue to move toward him. No reverse in the guy. Hours in the ring sparring with Cam, a mixed-martial-arts champ, and here he was losing to a gorilla with no technique.

He remembered the lessons learned in the ring, could hear Cam telling him he could be outmatched physically and still win. Fight smart, but fight fast. Trouble is, he'd never been outmatched physically, and he was not feeling very smart. He didn't see the kick coming, but felt it as it caught him in the ribs. He swore he heard the cracking as he sprawled across a table. Maybe it was just the table. He rolled over the top and landed on his feet, buying some distance with his pain.

Thoughts of a fair fight with Murphy danced away with the stars as his head finally cleared. Fight smart. He forced his tingling right arm into action and grabbed the gun from the holster slung under his left. He thumbed the safety and raised his arm, sliding his left palm under the gun for support. Murphy kept coming as Blair felt the weight of the trigger against his finger. His eyes locked on the gun sights as he centred them on Murphy's chest. Everything else in the room blurred as he released his breath slowly and prepared for the familiar kick of the gun. The trigger was about to break when a small hand slid in front of the sight, and Murphy's forward movement stopped. Blair eased the tension on the trigger as he allowed his eyes to move from the sight. Jimmy Williams. The little freak had stepped in front of the gun. His arm was straight back, his hand on Phil Murphy's chest. The big man kept his eyes locked on Blair, but he was out of the fight.

"Got a room full of witnesses gonna say you started this, pig."

Blair placed the gun back in its holster, keeping his gaze on Murphy.

"Fuck you, midget. Your boys here attacked a police officer."

"Loud music. Don't think they heard you say you were a pig. You grabbed our bartender and shoved him, then kicked him. Phil was just doing his job. Protecting the staff and the property. You look like any other drunk Indian."

Williams was baiting him. Blair forced down the rage, post-fight juice. He bent slowly and picked up his badge. Slipped it back into his jacket, trying to use the movement to chill the adrenaline rush. His hand shook. He figured the paperwork wasn't worth it and decided to give Murphy a pass. Another second, and he would have killed the guy. If he had put that in a report, he'd have had to go through the usual psych interviews. He didn't have time for that shit again.

"Okay, little man, we'll call this a mistake. No harm done. Now, I'm here to ask one of your dancers a few questions."

"Sorry. Get a warrant if you'd like to come back. Let us know ahead of time, so we can have a lawyer here. Now get the fuck out."

There was no point in pushing it. Lolita had been scared off anyway. Blair smiled at Murphy as he grabbed his right shoulder and tried to squeeze some feeling back into it. Wouldn't give the guy the benefit of holding his flaming ribs. Had to admit, the guy could deliver the weight. He nodded and headed for the door. Next time.

CHAPTER 8

March 2006, southwest of Peshawar, Pakistan

I WOKE WITH RAGS WRAPPED AROUND MY HEAD AND EYES. THEY WERE stuck in a gash on the back of my head where an AK shell found flesh. It was dry and hard. I must have been out for days. Hurt like hell pulling the rags off. My eyes adjusted to the light as I looked around a small village. Five buildings surrounded a fire pit. A brook ran through from somewhere above. Couldn't see anything beyond that.

I was chained to a rock. The shackles on my wrists and ankles were old and rusty. Dried blood showed around the metal. I pulled. They held. A couple of bearded Osama-looking assholes watched me from across the courtyard. One started yelling. That's when the first beating came.

A pack of kids—the oldest maybe sixteen—came at me with knotted ropes. Thick ropes, thicker than the forearms on most of the kids. A rope doesn't sound like much of a weapon. Soaked in liquid and swung with the enthusiasm of youth, a knotted rope can rip you to bits. A dozen can make you lose your mind. I struggled to my feet, pulling on the chains, but those ropes kept coming. I lunged at the little bastards and fell again.

I fought pro as a cage fighter and won more than I lost. I wanted in this fight so bad tears of rage blinded me. Not being able to hit back hurt more than the ropes. My face pressed into the dirt; mud formed from the spit and tears as I struggled to get back up. I watched a small sandalled foot slide as its owner fought for leverage on the rope. Must have found it, because after that I was out again.

The beatings were a daily thing. Some days they were really bad, like pray-for-death bad. Other days the kids just weren't into the work. I still went down and sucked dirt, so they'd feel the win and leave me alone.

Couple of months into it, a new boss arrived. He spoke a little English. Told me they were trading me to another tribe. That didn't sound good to me. By then I knew the kids weren't going to kill me. I still figured our side would find me and kill everyone in the village. I was looking forward to that. It was all I had. Then, he told me something I liked even less. I was in Pakistan, not Afghanistan. No way the troops were crossing that border to save some Canadian sniper. I was on the wrong side of a line. The old guy pulled Ronald's crucifix from a satchel he carried and placed it around my neck.

"Is important to believe. You are wrong, an infidel. But still, you must believe something, yes?" He pushed the cross down inside what was left of my ghillie and ordered the next beating.

That night I found something to believe in: rage. I was anchored to a rock by two rusted eyebolts. One for my wrist chains. The other for the ankles. The jerking and tugging as I rolled around under the rain of ropes every day had left a little play in the two eyes. I watched two young guards sleeping near the fire. I ignored the pain as I twisted my chains around my wrists and pulled. Slowly, I felt the first eyebolt give. The guards didn't stir. I freed the top bolt after maybe two hours of work. I could smell the rust, or maybe it was the blood pouring from beneath the shackles. The ankle bolt took longer because the blood made the links slip in my hands. A hint of pale blue showed on the distant horizon when it finally let go.

I was free. I had to disappear, fast. First, I needed water and a gun. I moved toward the fire. The chains rattled, and my steps were awkward. Blood pounded my eardrums. The guards were kids, but they were also the enemy, my torturers. They were sleeping together for warmth, guns to the side. I knelt slowly beside them. I grabbed the eyebolt still attached to my chains. I drove it into the skull of the bigger kid. The second kid tried to get up. I wrapped the chains around his neck and pulled tight. His struggle pulled the rusty spike free from his partner's head. He was stronger, but hate fed my weakened muscles. After his final kick, I sat beside the bodies, gulping air. I thought I heard Ronald tell me to keep moving. I touched the crucifix through the rags.

I filled two water skins from the brook, picked up the guards' AKs, and headed out of the village, dragging my chains.

━┼━

Friday, sunset

Sweat dripped from my hair and plastered the T-shirt to my body as I tried to push away the memories. It was a long-sleeved T. I don't like to look at the scars any more than I want anyone else looking at them. I was standing in my garage, trying to suck in as much air as my lungs would hold. I drained a water bottle as I watched the second hand on the Harley-Davidson wall clock. Fast recovery had won me more pro fights than fast fists or feet. Wind is critical in the cage. You gas out, you get knocked out. I train to bring my breathing and heart rate back into the normal range in one minute. I don't get to fight enough anymore, but I try to stay in competition shape. The last time I traded fists with someone, I was still in uniform, and he was dead drunk. It didn't take a minute to recover.

The garage is my escape. I work my body and clear my mind. After Glenda's death, I converted her side into a gym with a small sparring ring, heavy bag, universal weight machine, and an open space to run through martial arts patterns. I spend a lot of my time in the garage. There is still too much of her in the house. Glenda died while I was chained up in a shithole. She spent two days dead in our bed before her friends called police to say she was missing; a couple of uniforms came by and busted the door on a well-being check. I'd been on a few of those and knew what it was like to find a person after two days. I couldn't shake that image of my wife. It was natural causes. Fast, the doctors said. Bad heart finally quit. None of that helped. I'd known her heart was bad. She was born with it. Still, the big hero shipped off to Trashcanistan to play hired gun. I should have stayed with her.

The workout helped me to shake off the memories of Pakistan and Glenda. Unfortunately, they were replaced by the brand new tableau of Thelma Waters. She would not release her grip no matter how hard I pushed my body. The pictures clashed: Thelma in that spotless kitchen, and then on the ground with her throat hacked open. I felt angry and powerless. The anger was fuel, and I wanted to keep it. But anger without action is just stress, and Inspector MacIntosh was keeping me out of the action. Sending me on the Stallion run was just his way of benching me. Snake would let me see the surveillance tape, or he wouldn't. He'd decide what was best for the club, and my riding around with him for the day wouldn't change that. I wandered over to the heavy bag and fired a low left that lifted it on its chain. I stepped back and threw my left leg out, catching the bag high. Liver shot, head shot. Enough to end most fights. I pulled the gloves from my hands and placed them on top of the bag. The workout was over.

I replayed the afternoon briefing in my mind as I towelled off. Inspector MacIntosh gave all the key assignments to RCMP members of the task force. The HRP members knew he wanted a Mountie bust. That kind of bullshit still happens. We just work around it. What he'd done with me was different. He'd singled me out, told the room he'd deal with me following the briefing. His tone said everything. I knew it had nothing to do with some lawyer I'd pissed off in the park. A lot of cops resent my badge, but I'd never worked directly under one who was so open about it. Ordering me to ride with the club was his way of making it clear where he felt I belonged, and not just on this assignment.

I pushed a button on the wall beside the light switch. The overhead electric motor groaned as it pulled the door on my side of the garage up. It's still my side and her side, always will be, I guess. The western sky was a soft blue, the sun beyond the horizon now. Cool air poured in as my breathing returned to normal. I could taste the ocean. There would be fog tonight.

I grabbed my cellphone off the workbench and dialled Blair. The call went to his voice mail. My partner doing the smart thing, unwinding at home with his wife. Probably firing up the barbecue about now. I looked at the door leading from the garage to my kitchen, and decided to change the oil on my bike.

┼┼┼

I own two-and-a-half Harleys. Enough to keep me distracted and in the garage most nights. The half bike is a basket-case 1964 Panhead I keep threatening to rebuild. Grease gave it to me as a project bike before I went to war. We were going to do it together. That plan died when I hung up my patch. Now I just tinker with it. The engine is in a cradle on top of my workbench, waiting for a set of cylinders. I found them at a swap meet and got them for a good price, but so far haven't found the time to put them on. Maybe the desire.

The money bike in the garage is the 1971 Super Glide that belonged to my father. It rests on its side stand beside the bench. It looks nothing like the original '71. The old man had ripped off the ugly stock rear fender, cut and raised the backbone, and raked the front end before he ever rode it. The gas tank sits high; you can barely see over it. The front reaches out so far it takes an acre to turn the thing around. You fight with it more than ride it, the outlaw way.

I take the Glide out once or twice a year, just to keep the parts lubed and to prove I can handle his ride. My father was a violent drunk who liked to give Gunner and me boot-leather lessons in what it took to be a real biker. The childhood Greg missed. He was a small man. All muscle, grit, and hate. He never took his boots off and he stomped around shirtless, making sure everyone could see his Satan's Stallion tattoo and the blood red Demon tat below it. Only those who had killed for the club wear the Demon patch on their cuts or the ink on their chests. He called Greg a useless faggot and wouldn't let him come around. The old man stopped the fist-and-boot routine when he shifted from Jim Beam to heroin, and Gunner dropped him on his ass with a single punch. Gunner at sixteen, proving he was more biker than the old man.

Our father was a bastard, but he was capable of love. He loved that bike, spent hours pampering it when he was sober. Grease made sure a little of that rubbed off on me. I keep my main ride spotless.

With the kinks now worked out of my body, I was ready to give my Softail the attention it needed.

My bike is all about power. When I left the club, I removed the Satan's Stallion markings and painted it a high-gloss black. No flames, no shiny chrome accessories. Just a black bike with a fat tire in the rear and a slim-spoked wheel out in front. Not much to look at if you didn't know what to look for. I stepped over the saddle and leaned forward over the gas tank. My left hand reached under the tank. I pulled the chromed Satan's head choke knob, and felt my way along the space beside each spark plug. I found the small button on top of each head. I pushed and felt the click as each one opened a small airway into the combustion chamber beneath it. The bike might be plain. The engine was a high-compression monster. Without the compression release valves, starting it would be impossible.

I kicked the shifter down into first, grabbed the shoulder-high handlebars, pulled the bike up off the kickstand, and rolled it back slowly until I heard the hissing from the two passages. I kicked the shifter back into neutral, pulled in the clutch lever to be safe, and thumbed the start button. Even with the releases, the starter groaned in protest before slowly turning over the engine. The familiar smell of exhaust rose from the pipes as a heavy rumble bounced off the walls. Both cylinders hissed briefly until the compression releases were forced shut by air ahead of the fast-rising pistons.

I eased the bike back into the driveway. I wasn't going for a ride, I just wanted to bring the oil up to temperature. Drain cold oil and you leave all the contaminants sitting in sludge beneath the cam support plate. Grease still hadn't killed me for becoming a cop. If I changed the oil cold, he probably would. I sat in the saddle and felt the vibration move through my body, blipped the throttle a few times, and listened to the big twin howl. I closed my eyes and let the bike slowly relax into a smooth idle. I reached under the tank and pushed Satan back into place, shutting the choke circuit. The idle stayed smooth. She was ready for a little fun.

I pulled in the clutch lever again and dropped the shifter into first gear. I stood above the seat, planting my feet on each side of the bike, pulled hard on the front brake, and began to ease the clutch lever open as I twisted the throttle. The bike jumped up against its hidden shocks in protest. The front end bottomed on the fork sliders as the rear rose higher. The big cat wanted to pounce. I fought to hold it as the rear wheel shoved against the locked front brake. I twisted the throttle more and released the clutch lever the rest of the way. The tightness in the suspension dropped as the rear began to float between my legs. I twisted the throttle further and quickly shifted into second as the rear tire spun faster. A thick white cloud rose into the darkness and drifted out over the street. The roar drowned out whatever reality show was helping the neighbours avoid reality tonight.

I shifted my hips from side to side, wagging the tail, as the rear tire melted into the pavement. The smoke rolled forward with a shift in the wind, enveloping me and drifting into the garage. I tasted the rubber and smiled, twisted the throttle more, and focused on keeping the bike in place. Zen and the art of the burnout.

One slip and the Softail would launch into the garage, tossing me aside like a rag doll. I eased up on the brake lever a little, daring the machine to break free. A small gloved hand appeared out of the smoke and pushed the kill switch above the throttle. The engine coughed and shut down. The force of the spinning rear wheel against the suddenly dead drive train wrenched the handlebars, and I almost dumped it right there in the driveway.

A wave of anger flared as I turned to see who the hell was that stupid. Carla Cage stood next to me in a heavily padded riding jacket and those tight black jeans. She was pulling gloves from her hands and smiling. The blue-and-white jacket hung loosely from her shoulders like a Kevlar vest. She had it unzipped to the waistline, and I could see the straps of a shoulder harness inside. A tangled mass of brown hair framed her face. Helmet head worked for her.

"My little brother used to do that, until my father stopped paying for his tires." She looked at the screen on her cellphone as she spoke. If she had taken a picture, I hadn't noticed the flash.

"Just heating it up so I can change the oil." I rolled the bike back inside the smoke-filled garage.

"Riding it around the block works. Save you a fortune on rubber." She followed me and began to look around as the smoke cleared. I have a dozen David Mann prints hanging on the shop side of the garage and a couple of UFC posters near the heavy bag. There is also a copy of that magazine cover showing me after the knockout win. Blair put it up, said it made him feel good to look at it after he kicked my ass in a round of sparring. I wasn't sure which was worse, getting caught doing burnouts in my backyard or having her see a vanity shot of me in Stallion colours. I also wasn't sure why I cared what she thought.

Carla didn't notice the picture. Instead, she stared at a self-portrait of Mann. He was riding a black ribbon that fell from the sky to float above a grassy valley. Behind him a topless angel blowing a cloud-filled kiss across an open palm had his back. As a breeze cleared my cloud from the driveway, I saw a blue-and-white GSX-R1000 leaning on its kickstand. The gixxer is a real organ donor's ride. It's capable of a landscape-blurring 300-plus kph. She had a faster bike than I did. Maybe it was her brother's.

"Didn't know you rode, Sergeant." I walked to the small fridge I keep tucked under the shop bench.

"Back with the rank, Cam?" she said without looking away from David Mann's artwork.

"Sorry, I mean Carla. Didn't peg you for a crotch-rocket pilot." I pulled a Coke for myself and offered her a beer. She opted for the Coke. Good choice when you plan to light the fuse under a missile like that before the evening is out.

"Speed helps clear the head. Probably the same way that does." She nodded toward the scorched rubber outside as she grabbed the can from my hand. "Looks like you've been trying pretty hard to clear yours any way you can." She tipped the can toward the sweat-drenched T-shirt clinging to my chest. "Having any luck?"

"No, not really. It's the waiting. Bad for the mind."

She turned away from the Mann painting and stopped short as she caught the mural on the back wall. I hadn't covered the painting of the Satan's Stallion patch. Her eyes moved to my father's glide and the Stallion artwork covering the tank. I knew it was more than a third-generation cop like her could accept.

"Professional standards know about this stuff?" She sipped the Coke and looked at me.

"Probably," I said, feeling a little defensive.

"And you still have a badge? That war-hero thing must carry a lot of weight."

"Why are you here?" I was feeling a whole lot defensive.

I leaned against the kitchen counter, trying to contain the rage. I don't know why Carla's reaction to the Stallion mural bothered me so much, but it did. I left her in the garage to come in for a fresh dry shirt, at least that's what I told her. I picked up a china teacup that sits on the counter beside a matching teapot. The white china was turning a soft cream shade with age. I rubbed my thumb along the lip and looked at the tiny pink flowers decorating the fragile surface. Holding it calmed me. It was Glenda's favourite. Her grandmother left her the china when she left us this house. Glenda used the china every day. She'd say drinking from the cup brought her grandmother back to her, that she would rather drop it and break it and still have those memories than stuff it on a shelf and ignore it. She was holding it the last time I saw her.

August 2005

Glenda sat at the table in her blue scrubs, drinking a final cup of tea before work. I felt awkward walking into the kitchen. We both knew this was our last moment together for a year. We agreed we weren't going to talk about it. She'd leave for work and come home to an empty house. I was going to war. I poured a coffee and leaned against the counter, watching her.

"Stop it," she said.

"What?"

Her close-cropped brown hair framed the most beautiful face I'd ever seen. Brown inquisitive eyes sat above a thin straight nose.

Her lips formed a half smile as she stood and walked to me. She tucked her head under my chin and wrapped her arms around my waist, holding me tight. I breathed in the clean flowery scent of her hair and wrapped my arms around her shoulders. I felt an ache inside. God, if I missed her this much while I held her how would I feel when I couldn't even see her? She felt so small and helpless in my arms. I wanted to protect her, to keep her safe. I kissed the top of her head as she pulled back.

"We aren't going to do this. Right?" She walked back to the table. "I'm worried."

"Don't start." Her smile faded.

"They'd release me. No problem at all."

"It was minor, Cam, forget it." She sat down and sipped her tea.

Glenda didn't like talking about her heart condition. She'd had it since birth and refused to let it control her. She lived with it; it wasn't her life. It reared its ugly head while I was finishing my sniper training. She was lucky enough to be on the job at the hospital when she had a cardiac arrest, as in stopped heart. I wondered what would have happened if she was here in the kitchen, alone when it happened. She looked across the rim of her cup at me, reading me. She put the cup down.

"Look, Cam, if you use my heart as an excuse to stay home, you'll break it," she said.

"What, you want me to go to war? They told us our wives would want us to stay behind." I tried a smile. It felt weak.

"Most wives don't have to worry about a war right here. The kind my husband gets pulled into by the club."

"This has nothing to do with the club, Glenda, you know that."

"Let me finish. I never asked you to give up the club, I never will. But that doesn't mean I like it. Halifax is growing too fast and that means another turf war sooner or later. In Afghanistan you'll be a sniper, far from the front line. Here your patch will make you a target." She sipped her tea again, watching me. "Besides, the army and a real war might change your priorities. You might just grow out of the club."

I didn't know what to say to that. I was going to rejoin the club after the war. She stood and came back to me.

"Look, Cam, my heart is just fine. When I see you in uniform like this, it's better than fine, it sings. It proves you are more than your father's son. I want you to be safe over there, but I also want you to see that you are much more than some street thug. I love you."

Glenda kissed me and walked out of the kitchen. I never saw her again.

I put Glenda's cup back on the countertop. So much for its calming effect. I did come back from the war. I was out of the club. She got what she wanted. I often wonder if the doctor told her something different after that small heart attack, if she lied to me to protect me. If she knew what was coming but still wanted to give me a chance to break free from the club. It keeps coming up that way when I replay it in my mind. She wanted to protect me from myself. Why didn't I know how she felt about the club? Why didn't she ever tell me? I would have quit and become a mechanic, a bus driver, anything else. Would it have mattered? I tossed the sweat soaked T on the mudroom floor, grabbed a clean one from inside the dryer, and pulled it over my head as I walked through to the garage.

I was on my back on the cement floor. I left the garage to shake off the feelings Carla ignited in me. Now I was back and trying to shake Glenda's ghost. A small jack held the bike level above a plastic oil pan. I took an Allen key to the drain plug and turned it. Hot oil poured over my hand. The plug stayed on the key as I pulled it away. I looked at the magnetic tip. No metal shavings. The engine wasn't eating itself.

I could see Carla's boots crossed at the ankles on the opposite side of the bike. She was leaning against the wall beside the old man's Glide. She seemed okay with being here and not talking. I liked that. I didn't like her reaction to the Stallion painting. It bothered me that she had some of that my-badge-is-worth-more-than-yours attitude that my Stallion past brings out in some cops. It doesn't bother me in other cops; maybe her opinion mattered more than most.

I moved to the front of my bike and twisted off the oil filter from the base of the engine. Oil poured out from the opening and began to spread across the floor. Carla laughed and tossed me a roll of shop towels from the bench. I quickly spun the new filter into place and wiped up the mess.

"Maybe you're not such a badass biker after all," she said.

She moved away from the old man's bike and looked at me. I smiled back and leaned against the bench, wiping my hands in the oily shop towel. I still wondered why she was here, but figured maybe it wasn't to bust my balls over my past. I toyed with the idea she was here for reasons that had nothing to do with the case. She seemed to read my mind.

"I want to ride with you tomorrow," she said.

"Don't think so. Not on that." I nodded to the crotch rocket in the driveway.

"Hmm, that's right. You Harley snobs are afraid of modern engineering."

"It's not my party. The club won't allow any Jap crap inside its formation. You could probably run in the back with the other squares on that thing if you really want to go. But I'll be up front in the Stallion ranks."

I let that sit. The fallen rider run may be an open event, but the Stallion members ride at the front. Retired or not, I still had outlaw pride. I wouldn't be caught dead riding outside the club formation.

She moved over to my bike. I ride with a solo saddle slung low in the frame. She stepped over and sat down into it, her knees bent, boots flat on the floor. The low seat fit her perfectly. She grabbed the raised bars and pulled the bike off the kickstand. She looked good, and she knew it.

"I could take this. You ride that." She nodded toward the Glide.

"Sorry, that's for Gunner. It's our father's bike, and he's one of the fallen riders being honoured tomorrow. Only a full patch can ride that bike to a Stallion event."

"I thought you were," she said, stepping off the bike and looking back at the club crest painted on the rear wall.

"Was. I retired my patch long ago."

"Why are they letting you take part in the ride then?"

"It's like the law-enforcement hockey league. Even retired cops can play. Especially if they can put one between the pipes."

"Well, we have a problem then. Inspector MacIntosh ordered me to stick with you tomorrow."

So there it was. I walked over to a set of shelves that ran along the side of the garage and pulled a long, black leather seat from the top. It was a two-up version of the solo on my bike. Not much of a pad in the back, but enough for a passenger with a tough butt. I passed it to her.

"It won't be comfortable, but if you don't mind riding bitch, I guess I can swap the seats."

"I believe you would be the one riding bitch no matter where I sit, Constable."

Guess rank mattered, after all. Well, not if she wanted to ride with the club. When two worlds collide, sometimes things get turned upside down, and she'd have to learn a little about the outlaw code.

"You want to come, that's fine, Sergeant, but you have to leave that rank shit behind. You will be my ol' lady, as in 'property of,' and that means you do what I say, no matter what. Sorry, but that's how it works."

"You can't be serious, Cam. I'm sure there will be women there who ride their own bikes and carry their own weight."

"There will be two kinds of women hanging around the club. Some will ride their own bikes, but most won't. There will be ol' ladies and patch pussy. Old ladies are tied to a club member exclusively and are off limits. Patch pussy belongs to every club member." I watched her stiffen. She had to be a tough independent woman to get to where she was in the world of the badge. She'd either swallow her pride or miss the ride.

"My God, you're serious. You mean you treated women like that when you rode with the club?"

"Maybe, I guess, but it wasn't what it sounds like. I didn't abuse anyone. Didn't have to. The club attracts a certain kind of woman.

The kind that wants the *Property of Satan's Stallion* tattoo above her ass more than anything in the world. Will drop in front of any patch holder to get it." I didn't like explaining the club to her.

"Jesus, have you been tested?"

"Long time ago, Sergeant. I'm fine."

"Good to hear." She handed the seat back to me. "You won't need this. The gixxer is my brother's ride. I have a little custom that should be slow enough to cruise beside you in your little formation," she said.

"Behind me," I said. "The way it has to be."

She looked at me for a moment. Put her Coke can on the bench and started to zip up the padded riding jacket.

"I guess I can be your property for a day, in the line of duty."

"It's a memorial ride, not an orgy, so relax, but we may end up back at the house, and everyone needs to know who you belong to. I know a good tattoo artist, and we can get you done up tonight."

"In your dreams, Neville, in your dreams. I'll just make sure no one sees my ass."

Too bad. I watched her walk back to the gixxer as she pulled on a full face helmet. She straddled the tall sport bike, only her toes touching the pavement. Not smart. She pushed the start button and leaned in over the tank as she pushed it off the kickstand. She popped the clutch and kept just enough pressure on the brake lever to force the bike into a controlled burnout as it slowly rolled forward, and then shot to the end of the driveway. The smoke clouded my view, and I listened to the engine scream as she disappeared into the night. It was going to be fun watching her around the other old ladies. They weren't going to like her. Guess the badge attracted a different kind of woman.

+‑+‑+

The garage door slid slowly down into place as the opening bars of "Simple Man" rang from the speakers above the workbench. I poured fresh oil into the tank and capped it as I listened to Ronnie Van Zant.

I love the pure white-trash wisdom of the song. Stay simple, avoid the rich man's gold, find peace in what you have. Fuck everything else. A Southern rock sermon.

I keep a set of folding canvas lawn chairs wedged behind the workbench. I pulled one out and slid it beside the bike. I cracked open a Coke and tipped it to the speakers as I dropped into the chair. I tossed my feet up on the still-warm exhaust to listen to the tune and relax. As Ronnie sang, I wondered if my badge was the fool's gold I was chasing. Carla's words stung. Her shock that the white shirts in professional standards let me carry a badge. Truth is, they said no. When I came back from the war, I was lost. I quit the club and everything else. My wife died thinking I was dead. The doctors said the congenital heart problem she'd entered life with took her out of it. I wondered if it wasn't a broken heart.

I jumped into the bottle like a world-class coward. It's mostly a jumbled blur of blackouts and drunken runs on the Harley. Greg somehow yanked me out of the self-pity spiral. It didn't happen fast, but he got me sober. I knew if I was going to stay that way, I needed something outside of myself, and it wasn't the higher power Greg was preaching. I needed brotherhood. The kind I'd found in the war and in the club. Trouble was, I didn't want the club, and I wasn't going back to the war.

I tried to become a Mountie. Having fought for the country, I figured I could join its national police force. It was rage more than the need for brotherhood that drove me to the badge. I'd seen the poppy fields and fought the drug lords over there. Knew the heroin trade paid for the shells that had killed Master Corporal Ronald Gosse and put the AKs in the hands of the kids I'd killed. I wanted payback for what happened on the mountain. I wanted to hurt someone for keeping me in chains while Glenda died alone.

The RCMP recruiting officer kicked me to the curb in a heartbeat. No former one-percenter was getting into that gang. The Halifax Regional Police turned me down too. A newspaper reporter on the cop beat caught wind of it and ran a front-page story under the headline *War Hero Not Good Enough.* I'm no hero, and I hate being called one. The newspaper rehashed the same old story. They said I'd battled alone behind enemy lines. The newspaper said I'd killed armed Taliban warriors and fought my way back into Afghanistan. Two sleepy kids with rusty AKs. Some hero.

The day after the story ran I got a call from HRP. The chief had overruled his professional standards officers. Greg watched as they pinned the badge on me. After the ceremony, I gave him the gold crucifix I'd pulled from Ronald's body. I still wonder if Ronald talks to him now that he wears it.

I looked at the Stallion mural on the wall as the music filled the garage. Skynyrd wisdom in simple verse, telling me why I wouldn't feel peace. Not as long as I wanted something I could never have. I needed that bond that comes in a sniper team or with the patch. In the blue-and-gold brotherhood, I was the chief's bastard child. In the blue-and-silver world, the badge put a target on my back.

Gunner blocked a Stallion vote to kill me when I badged up. There are a few in the club who still want to see a bullet sent my way. Despite that, I get more support among the outlaw crew than from the crowd I roll with now. Pull the patch off a one-percenter and you'll find a real patriot. Outlaw clubs treat vets with the kind of respect I have never seen in the square world. That, and the old man's rep earned me a Nomad patch that is still mine if I walk away from the badge. Stallion Nomads are an elite crew, with no ties to any charter. My former bros don't think I'm elite; no charter wants a former cop at the table. The Stallion Nomads don't either, but they say the patch is still mine. I'm sure they've already had a vote on what to do about it if I am ever crazy enough to put it on. Someone will get a red demon with my name on it.

I drained the Coke as Blair walked into the garage. His right eye was a blood-red ball centred in a swollen mass of yellow and green. He looked like he had a baseball tucked in the side of his mouth. He favoured his right leg as he pulled another chair from behind the bench. I could see the pain in every movement as he opened the chair and took a seat beside me.

"Beer might be nice," he said through a crooked smile. At least all the teeth were still there.

I went to the fridge, grabbed him a beer and an ice pack. Wrapped the pack in a shop towel and handed him both. I sat back down to let him drink. He'd tell me when he was ready. He took a long slow drink.

"This place smells like burned rubber." He took another drink. Just another night.

"You look like someone burned rubber on your face. What the hell happened to you?" I let him win the cool contest. Looked like he needed a win.

"Disagreement with the bouncer at The Bank."

"You went there? Shit, what happened? I thought you wanted to check out a stripper, not start a war." I tossed my Coke can into a trash barrel near the door.

"Apparently they don't want us talking to her." He held the ice pack against the side of his head as he sipped the beer.

"So it seems. You arrest him?"

"Nope."

"He look worse?"

"Nope. Never even got a clean shot. Pulled my gun to get him off."

"You use it?"

"No."

"Good. Paperwork's a bitch."

"What I was thinking."

"Glad the head shot didn't cloud your priorities."

"Clouded 'em a bit. I called it in to MacIntosh on the way here."

"What?"

"Seemed like the thing to do at the time."

"Guess he was going to find out. You get the name of the guy who did it?"

"Was Phil Murphy and some bald guy with a head full of ink. Him, I dropped."

"Sounds like Glen Carroll. Dirtbag trying to make his bones with the Litter Box Boys. If he's with Murphy, it sounds like he made it. You saying they jumped you to keep you away from the dancer?"

"Indeed. Fair fight, though. I was on my feet and ready. That Murphy, man can he hit." He lowered the ice pack to his hip.

"Fuck fair fight. We're cops; it's only fair if we win. Let's send a couple of squad cars out and scoop those assholes up."

"Let it go. Jimmy Williams broke it up. Said they had a room full of witnesses would say I started it and didn't identify myself."

"That true?"

"Close enough." He brought the ice back to his face.

"You wanna go to the hospital? That looks pretty bad."

"No, Sue will look after it. I just wanted to bring you up to speed before I went home to show her my pretty face."

"Good thing she married you for your money."

"Good thing." He polished off the beer and tossed the can after mine. He pulled himself out of the chair with the freezer pack still pressed to his side. He was being cool about it, but I knew there'd be payback. I wanted to be part of it, wanted to go out there now and pistol-whip Murphy. The badge carries a lot of weight, but it can be a pain, too. Revenge beatings happened, but you had to be careful. Let the other guy start trouble and then finish it hard.

I knew Murphy didn't throw a punch unless Jimmy Williams gave the order. If that little idiot was unleashing his bull on a cop, the Stallion had something to hide. I'd see the useless prospect in the morning and beat some answers out of him. I wouldn't be taking my badge on the memorial ride. I could start my own trouble. Carla might just see a slice of club life.

CHAPTER 9

Friday night, late

"MY FRIEND, YOU'VE DROPPED THE BALL AT A CRITICAL MOMENT. You assured me you had it under control. Now you tell me a detective is connecting the dancer to the case, to the club. This is bad, very bad." His ear to the phone, Nicholas Mapp waved Jimmy Williams into the seat in front of his desk and spun in his chair, turning away to face the rear wall. "You have just as much to lose as we do, remember that. You tell me he is a lone wolf. That helps. This has to be dealt with on our level now, not yours. Just isolate him for us. I'll take care of the rest. Perhaps there is a lesson in this for you." He spoke just above a whisper, but Williams could hear it all. "This nosy cop, didn't he disrupt a shipment at the waterfront recently, some low-grade shit the Russians intended to flood our streets with?"

Mapp was behind that desk, on the phone being the big man. Ignoring Jimmy.

"Good, that's very good. You see, the difference between a true career criminal and an amateur is always in the planning. The best part of that planning is in the art of misdirecting the police. The most credible false leads make themselves known long before the crime is committed. I've seen it work many times, and I will show you how it can help us now." Mapp turned back, gestured again for Williams to sit.

Williams swatted the side of the chair and walked around the room, making his own point. Little man doing his damndest to show how bored he was with being in the inner sanctum. The office was a cathedral of chrome, glass, and polished marble. It dripped cash and screamed success. Light bounced from every surface and collected like an array of tiny spotlights on the flawless clear-coat surface of the Ferrari in the centre of the room. The '62 250 GTO was a priceless piece of Italian art. The chopper in the corner was more to Jimmy's liking. He recognized the bike as an Indian Larry original. Not one of the copies built after his death. One made by the man himself. Had to be a hundred thousand dollars worth of ego boost, easy. He was sure Mapp couldn't handle the torque that monster put out. The bike never left the office. The Ferrari was an antique and belonged in a trophy case. The chopper belonged on the road. Jimmy belonged anywhere but in Mapp's office.

Mapp was making a show of being on the phone, his back to Jimmy. Too busy. He walked around the car, wondered what Mapp had paid for it, wondered if the value would fall if he pissed on it. He didn't know cars, but even Williams knew this one made a statement. Mapp was money, and in this game, money ruled. Maybe he could deliver Jimmy's patch.

Williams knew being on Mapp's turf without a full patch could cost his life. He'd left the prospect leather in the van with Phil. He was here on Litter Box business, not as a club prospect. That's what he'd tell Snake. Probably wouldn't fly, but it was all he had.

"Beautiful, isn't it?"

Williams turned to see Mapp standing beside him. The phone gone now. Creepy fuck moved without making a sound. Mapp wore a black track suit with silver-and-blue trim on the sleeves and legs. Stallion support wear, for the after-hours crowd.

"Ever take the chopper out?" Williams asked as he walked over for a closer look.

"Jimmy, you don't take a bike like that out anymore than you do that Ferrari." Mapp laughed. "A fender bender in that car would bankrupt a small town. Dropping the bike would be a crime. They are investments, nothing more."

Williams figured it would make more sense to hang a picture of the car on the wall, the bike too. He knew Mapp's wife was a hot piece with an ass that caused car wrecks. Probably didn't ride her, either.

"I want to thank you for your intervention this morning, Jimmy. It's why you are here now."

"What, you offering a reward or something?"

Mapp smiled. He leaned on the edge of the desk, folded his arms, and looked down at Williams.

"There could be a reward. If you think a patch on your back is a reward."

So there it was. Mapp was a shot caller. Jackpot. Williams was in the right place. Had to play it cool, though.

"It's comin'. Just doin' my time, same as everyone else."

"Good to hear. I just wouldn't want your efforts on my behalf to become an issue." Mapp walked over to the chopper. Kept his back to Williams. "There are things about the club you don't know just yet, but I think you must at least suspect the truth." He turned back. "Why else would you choose my side over your vice-president today?"

Williams hadn't chosen Mapp. He just figured Gunner needed to slow down before he ended up in a jail cell. There were witnesses everywhere. He let Mapp think what he wanted.

"A bold and smart move like that is a sign. I read signs, read people. It's how I ended up here."

"So how do I end up here?" Williams wanted Mapp to get to the point. He had to get to the clubhouse to work the party.

"Well, obviously you don't end up here." Mapp laughed and took his seat again. "No, you belong where you are, but I see having someone like you on my team as a worthy investment, like the Ferrari. Having people in the right position means everything, Jimmy. Like the man I was just speaking with. He is in a position to help me, help the club, and maybe help you. He can help because he is loyal to me. Can you be?"

Williams had learned a lot in prison, but the most important lesson was that loyalty, like respect, had to be earned. So far, Mapp was coming up short.

"So who is this guy?"

"I can't say, Jimmy. You should take comfort in that. I never discuss those who prove helpful. Suffice to say he is in a position of some influence."

"Whatever. Just tell me what you want from me."

"Oh, that's easy. There are winners and losers in this world of ours. Most of the losers are gone, in jail or dead. The winners reap the rewards. You can be a winner, Jimmy. All you have to do is keep the police from coming near the club. I don't care if you have to confess to killing that preacher to do it."

"Like fuck." Williams walked to the edge of Mapp's desk.

"Relax, relax, Jimmy. It was a hypothetical example, nothing more. I just need you to know the importance of keeping the club, and by extension those of us who sit above the club, out of this. You do that, and I guarantee you a patch no matter what Gunner thinks. Hell, I'll have Gunner give it to you if that makes you happy."

Fuckin' A, yes. That's what Williams needed. He remembered the Indian. Well, he couldn't be blamed for things that had already happened.

"There's a problem."

"There always is." Mapp leaned his elbows on the desk, and rested his chin on his finger tips. "Tell me."

"That Indian cop was at the club looking to talk to Lolita. We kicked his ass and sent him packing. But he's been around her, so that's around the club."

"Funny. That's exactly who I was speaking with my colleague about when you arrived. Constable Christmas's curiosity about the dancer is our number-one concern at the moment. I'm glad you were upfront about it. I see my judgment is sound. It seems, for now at least, he is on his own. Tugging at a loose string only he can see. That's where you may come in, Jimmy."

Williams looked at him. Waited.

"Montreal has good things to say about you. Says you handle wet work better than most. We think it's time the club put that talent to work on a more delicate matter."

"Don't know what you're talking about. Maybe you should explain it for me." Bringing Montreal into it meant one thing. Mapp was connected well beyond the Stallion Halifax charter. Still, Williams needed to hear him say it.

"Of course. Look, this is not going to be like gunning down a rival dealer or someone stealing crack from the Litter Box. If this happens, and I feel it will, the police will be looking under every rock. Like nothing you've ever seen. There can be no trail."

Williams looked at Mapp. Could the guy really be asking him to kill a cop?

"I see you are puzzled. Let me make this clear. A decision will be made tonight. I will contact you after that happens. If, as I suspect, action is required, we will make certain Constable Christmas is at a certain place at a certain time. I will know the when and where. You just have to be ready. Can you eliminate our problem if that time comes?"

"Fuck, man, I can do that. Had the chance an hour ago. Can you deliver on your end?" Finally, a chance to step up, use his skills, and make his name.

"A patch for a badge. Yes, I think I can handle that."

Gunner tipped his chair against the wall and scanned the crowd. Cheyenne slithered down the chrome pole onstage. Two girls pranced the edge of the stage in heels and nothing else. Cheyenne arched back from the pole and dropped below the crowd. He fought the urge to stand. The clubhouse was jammed. A tight band was playing, the booze was flowing, and the heavy smell of high-grade pot filled the air. Gunner was working.

He watched a street pusher from the Litter Box stagger across the room. The guy's jeans hanging low from the waist. A cluster of ugly gold chains danced in front of the wife beater stretched across his chest. He crowned his gangsta get-up with a silver-and-blue Stallion support cap. The bill in the side-locked position. Another white-trash fool trying too hard to be black.

This ghetto goon was a problem. He kept bumping into people, hard. He was building up to something, about to let everyone know he was the man. Wrong place, wrong time for pissing on trees. Gunner stood. The club's newest prospect, Chucky Hill, was beside the door.

He was tall, but thin. Maybe too thin for a fight. Time to see what he was made of. Gunner nodded to Hill and waded into the crowd.

The moron was stopped in the middle of the dance floor, working his cellphone, making a show of texting or tweeting or some damn thing. Gunner pulled the phone from his hand, and slapped the sideways ball cap off his head. The guy was big, six one and maybe 220, not used to people fucking with him. He spun quickly, looking wild eyed as he shoved his right hand into his waistband, digging for a piece that wasn't there. His hand moved left and right, but then stopped as the realization hit him. Gunner watched as a slight panic crept across his face. He didn't have a gun. He was sobering up enough to realize he wouldn't be carrying in the clubhouse. He looked around the room for support. If his crew was with him, they were staying out of the fight. The guy squared up with Gunner, set to unleash the first punch. He didn't even get his arm back. The new prospect circled behind and swung an arm around the fool's neck, locked it expertly in a rear naked chokehold. He pulled the guy off his feet and eased him to the floor as he choked him out. Quiet, efficient, and no drama. Prospect Hill showed promise.

Baggy jeans, white T-shirts, and locked ball caps flooded the dance floor as a dozen Litter Box Boys moved to the fight. Who the hell would take these clowns seriously? Maybe Gunner was losing touch with the street. He set his eyes on the guy in the lead. He was younger than his friend on the floor, smaller, but big enough. His stride was even and smooth. If he was drinking, he held it well. Everyone in the room was watching. The band stopped playing, Cheyenne stood beside the pole, her eyes on the three leading Litter Box Boys. The prospect moved in from behind him, squared off with the three men, standing between them and Gunner. Kid had balls.

The guy in the lead spread his arms out from his sides, palms open and facing forward, his head tilted slightly sideways as a smile crossed his face. He made a quick sweeping motion with his hand, and the two guys behind him moved to pass him, their hands out palms forward, as well. The prospect turned back, and Gunner nodded. He let them pass, and they bent to help the drunk on the floor.

"Bro, we are truly sorry about this. He's havin' an off day. We'll take him home if that's okay." The guy was definitely sober.

"Do that. When he wakes up and starts worrying about this, tell him he should. If he starts to think about coming here to apologize, tell him he shouldn't. Tell him never to show his face near this house again."

One of the guys picked up the ball cap and the cellphone.

"Leave the cap. He doesn't wear blue and silver again. Take him out now." Gunner's gaze never left the guy in front of him.

"Not a problem. He's all gone, m'man." He nodded to the door, as the two men lifted the drunk from the floor and dragged him to the exit.

"Good luck with the ride tomorrow." The guy trying to keep it casual and friendly now.

"I want you here when it ends. You can explain to me why this asshole was trying to prove himself in my house," Gunner said.

"Sure, but he's..." He started to say something, but thought better of it. "Yeah, sure m'man, what time?"

"Just be here, and he's got nothing to say about it." Gunner figured the hesitation meant the drunk ran the crew, and this guy didn't want to step out of line. Smart guy. He'd be running the crew tomorrow. His first job would be messy. Shit happens. Shit stays the same.

Gunner went back to his chair as the band ripped into a GN'R tune. He wanted to go jam, but the idiot being carried through the parking lot was proof he couldn't kick back tonight. It was one of those rare nights, when the clubhouse welcomed squares along with the regular hang-arounds to a party. Outsiders in the house meant rats in the room, and Gunner stayed ready. No one gets hurt; nothing for the rats to talk about.

He was thinking maybe Jimmy Williams would get hurt, but that would wait. The little shit should have been here working the door with the Hill kid and the other prospects. More than that, he should have been controlling his idiot crew. He'd get here soon enough. Cheyenne had told Gunner about the fight at The Bank. Williams was going to have to explain how beating a cop would keep the police away from the club.

Gunner faced the wall, his guitar slung low. He stomped a foot switch near his amplifier and turned back to the front of the stage. The clubhouse was locked down, the squares gone now, and he was trying to relax. His fingers raced across the fret board chasing the solo that blared from the speakers overhead. Beads of sweat dropped from his close-cropped hair as he leaned over the guitar, eyes closed. He tried to get into the solo, but his mind wandered. The house had the dead smell of cheap perfume and stale beer. Hard to groove when the party's over. He opened his eyes, spun the volume knob down, pulled the guitar over his shoulder, and leaned it against his amp. He was thinking about Cheyenne.

Snake Howard marched into the centre of the room with a wooden gavel in his hand and a murderous scowl on his face. Jimmy Williams was behind the bar cleaning glasses. Gunner smiled at the mean-looking green-and-yellow bruise covering half his face. Snake shot the prospect a look, and Williams swaggered to the side door and disappeared into the office.

Eight full-patch Stallion members were draped over the couches and chairs. They weren't sober, but they were still functioning. It was late for a club meeting. The group looked pissed off. Mostly because the women had been chased out by Snake. They'd be more pissed if they knew the meeting was just a show. Gunner had already reached out to Cam.

"Gunner, shut the fucking stereo off. That shit's been too loud all fucking night." Snake dropped into his chair and slammed the gavel onto a small wooden table to his left. Church was underway.

Outlaw clubs were calling their meetings church before Gunner was born. No one questioned it. Dues are paid at church; business is discussed, and, when necessary, punishment is handed out. Only full-patch members can attend, and missing it was a serious offence. Snake had called this meeting, and he was chairing it down in the main room to allow members to be more comfortable. He didn't like chopping a party short for a vote, but club business always comes first.

A half-finished bottle of Jack Daniels sat on a wooden crate in the middle of the cluster of chairs and sofas. Gunner walked over and raised the bottle, taking a long pull before putting it back on the table and taking the chair beside Snake. He worked through last night's party; today's was just beginning.

"We've got a problem," Snake began. "That dead preacher is going to cause us some grief."

"Fuck 'em. We didn't kill him," Grease said, reaching for the bottle.

"No, we didn't, but one of our girls is involved. And the dumb bitch dropped him beside our house." He stared at Grease; the older biker didn't flinch. "Our former brother knows we have cameras. That means a search warrant and cops inside the house." Everyone looked at Gunner.

"Fuck that. They can't get in here on that weak shit." Dirty Lyle pushed himself up from a leather armchair and began to pace.

Gunner was surprised to hear him speak up. He was the newest full-patch member. His Stallion patch was so clean on his back it almost looked fake. Lyle's loose crop of blonde hair stopped short of his shoulders and framed an angelic face with full red lips, a razor-sharp nose and deep-set blue eyes. His features bordered on feminine, and the older bikers had balked when Snake himself sponsored him for membership. Lyle wore a deep blue, open-collar cotton dress shirt over tight-fitting designer jeans. The clean leather cut and Stallion patch looked like an afterthought. The kid ran a profitable drug pipeline into the university campuses in Halifax. New kid or not, the patch meant he could speak, and the others listened.

"Boys, they'll try to bluff their way in the way Cam did yesterday." He glanced at Gunner as he circled the small group. "That body wasn't on our property, and last time I checked, strippers weren't members. No way they get a warrant on that."

"We can't take the chance with the lawyers. We need to clean the house. Guns, drugs, knives, explosives. All of it," Snake said. Gunner knew the president hated being contradicted, especially by a kid he'd sponsored.

"Naw, shit's safer here," Leroy Moon Eyeking interrupted. Moon patched in while Gunner was serving in Iraq, and the massive biker was voting with his fat ass. "They gotta be watchin' the place. We can't get it out, so I say we leave it sit." Always looking for an excuse to do nothing.

Moon held a beer in each hand. Took a shot from each. Only the tops of the cans showed above the thick index finger and thicker thumb that held them. He always grabbed two from the cooler. Cut in half the number of times he had to get up. His stomach pushed a faded 4XL Stallion T-shirt out into his lap. His shaved head showed more bumps than a back road in springtime.

"They're always watching the fucking place, Moon. We can get around that." Grease returned to the JD. "I say we move it all." He took a long drink and looked at the bottle. Not much left.

Gunner raised a hand and stood. He headed for the bar as Grease sat back down. He pulled a new bottle out, peeled the black plastic wrapper away from the cap, spun it open, and took a drink. He placed the bottle on the bar and watched his bros debate the pros and cons of hiding shit he knew should never be in the house. A couple of guns on hand, no more. That was always the rule. He voted to have the big guns stored off-site in case of a police raid. Big guns brought long sentences. The club voted him down. A street-hardened gang of black thugs living the gangsta life was muscling in on Stallion territory. They ran street hookers and sold poor-grade shit in Dartmouth. The Litter Box Boys were busy keeping the peace in Spryfield, and the Dartmouth gang was taking advantage of that. The bastards were fearless and shot at anything that pissed them off. Shot at each other every second night, just to prove they were tough. Every one of them carried, and as long as they did, Snake insisted on keeping the house fortified.

"Let's give 'em the tape," Gunner said as he moved back to take his place beside Snake. He placed the new bottle on the crate.

"What? How much of that shit you drink?" Moon asked, raising a hidden beer can to his face.

"Fuck off, Gunner, we're serious here," Snake said.

"So am I."

"Fuck me. He's going rat like his brother." Dirty Lyle was back on his feet.

Gunner covered the distance between the wooden crate and Lyle in two quick steps. He grabbed a fist full of perfectly pressed shirt and slammed the smaller biker into the wall beside the picture of Cam. "You're new, Lyle, so maybe you need a lesson in club history."

The others watched, but no one made a move. Gunner was sergeant-at-arms, as well as VP, and discipline was his to hand out.

"Cam is no rat," said Gunner. "Made a stupid life choice for sure, but that doesn't make him a fucking rat. You understand?" He held Lyle just off his feet with his right hand. With his left, he grabbed his face, and shoved it so it was pinned to the wall pointing toward the picture of the victorious Cam in the ring. Lyle remained silent. "He is a member of this club out in good standing. Means he gets respect like any other bro. You call a bro a rat, Lyle, then I got to investigate. If it's true, he gets killed. If not, you get fucked up for saying it."

Gunner released both hands, and Lyle dropped back to the floor. He stood slumped against the wall, his eyes fixed on Gunner.

"He's a fucking cop," said Lyle. "Cop, rat, what the fuck is the difference?" Kid was standing his ground. Good trait for a Stallion. Bad idea at the moment. Gunner's right arm was moving back.

"Fuck, Gunner, hang on." Grease put a hand on Gunner's shoulder. Gunner spun away from the wall and pushed past Grease, trying to walk it off. He turned back from the opposite side of the crate.

"You stunned cunt," Gunner said. "He's been a fucking cop for seven years. If he was fucking ratting the club, they'd have busted down that door long ago. We'd a been in jail before you were even a prospect," he said.

Grease sat back down. Gunner moved quickly back to the wall and brought a right cross with him. The fist smashed hard into jawbone, and Lyle dropped to the floor, unconscious. Grease was back on his feet. Gunner turned back to him.

"He called me a rat, too. You got a problem?" The two stood face to face.

"He had that shot coming. Now sit the fuck down, both of you." Snake leaned forward and reached for the bottle. "Gunner, why should we bend over for Cam and his useless fucking pals? And this needs to be good."

Snake handed the bottle to Gunner, and he sat back down. Gunner took a longer shot. Fucking hand was throbbing again. He took a couple of deep breaths to work the adrenaline out of his system as he passed the bottle to Grease.

"We give him the tape that shows the headlights drive past the clubhouse, go up the hill, and leave. Not the part where the dumb bitch comes here. Nothing but a blurry fucking car. I say we give it to Cam as a favour to a former bro. Not to the cops but to him personally. No need to worry about a warrant or cops in the house if they have the thing." He walked behind the bar and filled a draft beer pitcher with water from the tap.

"Maybe. Maybe. Can we cut it that way?" Snake asked.

"I can." Moon rolled out of his chair, wheezing as he moved to the cooler beside Snake. Grabbed two more beers.

Gunner walked to the still-unconscious Lyle and dumped the pitcher of water on his head. The smaller biker rolled over, coughing. His right hand moved to his belt, searching for a gun. He shook his head and seemed to realize he was safe. His hand relaxed. Gunner looked down.

"Get the fuck up. You're missing the meeting, dickhead." Gunner walked back and took his seat. Lyle pulled himself up and did the same.

"Word gets out we helped the cops, we lose serious cred out there," Grease said.

"Well, then, word doesn't get out," Gunner said. "We make the prospect do it to be safe. People start talking; he never gets a patch. Shit happens." He looked at Lyle. "Cam won't say shit about how he got it. Hell, he's coming to the ride; we can do it then."

"They can't come kicking the door in looking for something they already have," Snake said. "Gunner, I hate like fuck to give anything to the cops, but I think you just solved the problem. Let's vote on it."

Snake cracked the gavel again.

CHAPTER 10

Saturday morning

AN EMPTY STRIP CLUB IS ALMOST AS GLOOMY AS A FULL ONE. WHEN the beer is flowing and the cat calls mix with the pounding bass lines, you can almost taste the desperation. It rolls off the stage where dead-eyed women fake passion on a pole and dream about the big break that will never come. It falls face first on tables where fantasies about attaining the unattainable are drowned in cheap draft. It drops hard-earned cash on lap dances that feel cheap. That's when the club is really rocking.

It wasn't rocking now. Lolita Shines sat alone at a table in the centre of the room. She wore loose-fitting jeans under her blue-and-silver Satan's Stallion support hoodie. The morning sunlight peered through slats in the shuttered windows. The shafts of light bounced off the angled mirrors behind the stage and searched out the darkest spaces. The club was closed. Glen, the bartender, was out back waiting for a beer truck to make its daily delivery, and Lolita was the only dancer out front. She worked the onscreen keyboard on a pink-and-white iPhone. The colour suited her stage image, not her mood.

At nineteen, Lolita was a barely legal headliner. The best kind. Clubs billed her as *Little Lo, The Private School Ho* in newspaper ads in every city on the Stallion circuit from Vancouver to Halifax. The Montreal clubs were better. *Lolita, La Petite Étudiante Cochonne,* they called her in posters there. She didn't know what it meant, but it seemed classier. Either way, she knew what it was about. Fresh meat. If only they knew.

She leaned over the table as she reread the text on the screen. Her long black hair fell from her head like a curtain around the phone. She stared at the tiny screen: "Tatjana, my love, it is our time."

She wanted to answer the text. She knew better. The Stallion members read all of her texts, and she'd have to explain this one.

At least they didn't know her real name. She'd tell them it was a mistake, she had no idea who Tatjana was. In Montreal, they'd taught her that the police watched dancers and read their phone messages, too. Cops were dumb, so she didn't worry about them reading it. They couldn't even figure out how old she was. For three years, she'd danced from Vancouver to Halifax as a nineteen-year-old headliner, and not one cop did the math. They didn't care, probably came to watch her like that Indian cop last night. She hated Jimmy Williams, but was glad he got that cop away from her.

She wanted to answer Samuel's message, but knew she couldn't. The girls had their own code, but he wouldn't know how to read it.

She slipped her phone into the pocket of her hoodie and headed to the backroom. She knew exactly what it would take to convince Glen to let her borrow his phone.

+++

The late-morning sunlight reached over the top of the hill and spilled inside the concrete and barbed wire box surrounding the Stallion compound. Wisps of vapour rose from the parking lot where the first rays began to cook the blacktop. The sunlight bounced from the chrome and glass on fifteen bikes lined up side by side in front of the clubhouse. The lot was big enough to hold twenty half-ton trucks and often did during weekly church in the dead of winter. An old gas pump sat on a raised platform in the darkest corner of the lot. It would be well past noon before the sun found it. A row of wooden tables lined the long wall leading from the front gate to the house. The tabletops were spotless, the bottles and glasses from last night's party gone. Two oversized barbecue pits sat on the opposite side of the gate, a short distance from the tables, a safe distance from the gas pump.

Jimmy Williams directed a stream of water at Gunner's bike. He dropped the hose and grabbed a soap-soaked sponge from a large plastic bucket and began wiping the tank. He was getting the bikes ready for the ride, and he resented washing Gunner's. He knew the prick wouldn't even be riding it. He'd have his old man's Glide, and when that got here, Jimmy would have another bike to clean. When the bikes were clean, Williams had to struggle as he rolled them over to the gas pump to top off each tank. The bikes with Apes were beyond his reach. They would have to wait for one of the other prospects. Gunner had him doing the yardwork alone this morning. Like it was his fault that fucking Indian cop arrived at the bar. He spit on the sponge, and rubbed it into the pistol grip at the top of the shifter.

As he leaned over to pick up the hose, he felt the phone vibrate inside his jeans' pocket. He pulled it out to see a text: "Time to be a winner. Get what you need to deal with it."

Fucking Mapp. As if Gunner wasn't a big enough asshole. Well, he couldn't do shit right now. He had bikes to wash, a run to go on, and then he'd be behind the barbecue flipping burgers all afternoon. He was about to stuff the phone back in his pocket when it began to vibrate again.

Another message: "I've got your back covered. It's been confirmed."

Williams stared at it for a moment. His back covered. A patch for a dead cop? Cops were off limits, mostly. Killing the wrong person was always fine if you didn't get caught. Killing cops, prosecutors, or even reporters brought too much heat, but sometimes it had to be done. You show the balls for that kind of wet work, and you climb fast. If he pulled it off, and kept the heat away from the club, he'd be a hero.

Williams moved to the next bike, thinking it through. Pull it off, and he was in. Fuck it up, and he was dead. Shit, seemed like a reasonable gamble. Still, he'd need the tools, and he was too fucking busy. He grabbed the phone and punched in Phil's number.

━┿━

The smell of coffee filled the open market as Blair limped slowly to the corner cafe. He needed a quality caffeine jolt. The brew at the morning briefing was almost as hard to swallow as the beating. He loved the Second Cup below the Bedford office. He knew it was a chain but still thought of it as a cafe. It had all the flavour but none of the bullshit of the trendy downtown shops that grew quiet when a cop walked in. In Bedford, the money crowd sipped the expensive brew, but they had nothing in common with the artists, pissed-off anarchists, and high-school Goths filling the downtown cafes. Money didn't mind a badge around as long as it didn't get too close. A caffeine boost and a little comfort food were in order. He could smell the freshly baked scones along with the coffee, and he decided what Sue didn't know couldn't hurt her. She'd been pretty upset about the beating, or maybe that it happened in a strip club. He'd had busted, cracked, and bruised ribs before. That kind of pain got his attention. Sleep was impossible, and this time sympathy was in short supply at home.

Two cops walked out of the coffee shop as Blair approached. Both were HRP officers, and Blair couldn't remember their names. One was an older, white-haired guy. His eyes peered out over heavy bags, his broad nose showing a map of red veins. He was carrying too much weight around the middle, had the look of a lifer who was about ready to hang up the badge. The guy carrying the coffee was maybe thirty, had the close-cut hair and squared-away look of a uniform new to the job. One guy on his last plain-clothes assignment, the other on his first. They stopped in front of Blair.

"Shouldn't you be going over there?" The old guy nodded to the far corner of the market.

Without turning, Blair knew the guy was pointing to the liquor boutique. The young cop smiled.

"Problem?" Blair locked eyes with the older cop.

"Yeah, big problem, asshole. Next time your DNA cries for firewater do us all a favour. Grab a bottle and a brown bag here. Don't make up some shit excuse to go to a bar and start a fight. Make a mess the rest of us have to live with."

As Blair moved toward him, the young cop blocked his path.

"It's all right, Ricky, this guy ain't gonna do shit."

"You're right. Can't beat stupid out of a moron, no point in trying."

Blair pushed past and headed into the coffee shop.

He smiled to the brunette barista as he walked in. She touched her temple with a look of concern. He shrugged, ordered, and then eased into a seat by the window. The shop didn't have table service, but he knew she'd look after him. He tried to adjust his position in the seat. The Kevlar vest under his shirt was too tight. He wasn't planning a gun fight. It helped protect his ribs.

He was trying not to let the confrontation with the two morons upset him. But he knew they weren't alone. Most of the team was still upstairs in the office, and more than a few would be second-guessing his decision to go to the strip club. Inspector MacIntosh beat him down for it during the morning briefing. Said he should have been working real leads, not hanging out in bars. Ordered him to forget the stripper and focus on the case. Blair was more concerned about the real cops. He knew the two morons had a right to be pissed off. He had left the fight with his tail between his legs. Left those assholes believing they could beat on a cop. No one with a badge could live with that, and Blair would wear it until he set it right. On the upside, no one from The Fog Bank filed a complaint, and no one knew he pulled his gun.

His coffee arrived. The barista looked at his bruise and grimaced. Maybe it wasn't cool. Three attractive young women sitting at a nearby table broke off their conversation as Father Greg walked past. Blair had walked past the Bedford blondes' club a hundred times and never gotten a notice. Cam's brother, indeed. Greg chatted them up before ordering a coffee, then carried it over and sat across from Blair.

"My, that doesn't look good," he said by way of a greeting.

"Slipped in the shower."

"Well, you must have bounced a few times."

The barista still had the look of concern as she watched Father Greg join him. The attention would have been easier to take if he'd actually landed a good punch. At least the ego bruise didn't show. Hurt though.

"So, Father, things are a little hectic. How can I help you?" Blair sipped his coffee, grateful Murphy hadn't connected with his jaw. He wasn't sure why Father Greg had wanted to meet, and really didn't have the time to chat. He was going to interview members of the Church of Salvation youth group while Cam played biker.

"Yes, I'm sure you are quite busy, and I have to be getting out to Peggys Cove for today's bike blessing as well," the young priest said. "I just wanted to have a word about the investigation." He wrapped his hands around the warm coffee mug and glanced at the people sitting along the counter behind Blair.

"Can you tell me first what Bobby had to say?"

"I guess I shouldn't be surprised that you know we talked."

"It's what we do."

"Yes, I guess it is. I can't talk about what Bobby said." He glanced around again.

"You saying Bobby confessed something, Father?" Blair took another drink. Father Greg kept his cup between his hands.

"Blair, you know I could never answer a question like that."

"No, I guess not. Is he Catholic?"

"I suppose that's fair. Yes, lapsed, I'm afraid, but I think maybe he's ready to come home."

"Well, Father, his home may have more bars than pews."

"I'll tell you what I told Cam Thursday. I don't believe Bobby capable of these things." He held Blair's eyes.

"I appreciate that." Father Greg had made the remark to Cam before Bobby Simms's confession. If he was still calling him innocent, that carried weight.

"Is that what you needed to tell me?"

"No, well, yes, I suppose, but I'm worried about something else."

"What would that be, Father?"

"Blair, you are a strong Catholic, and I feel confident that you believe, as I do, the Church has suffered more than perhaps it should have."

"Lot of bad things have happened, Father. Going to take time for that to go away."

"Indeed, the healing will take time, but I feel it is beginning and I'm afraid of what all this could do to slow that."

"I'm not sure what you mean. This case has nothing to do with the Church."

"Blair, it is naive to think any scandal involving any Christian church will not force more of the faithful from ours."

"Scandal? This is a double murder, Father."

"Yes, yes, and the killer must be caught. I know that. It's just that a person capable of such evil may say anything to justify his actions." He looked down into his cup.

Blair began to get an uneasy feeling. He needed to focus. He watched a brunette in form-fitting jeans and a tight sweater make her way to the counter as he thought of what he should say. She was well into her forties, but her body didn't show it. Maybe that's what he liked about this place. He looked back to Father Greg.

"Father, they all make crazy claims about why they kill. Truth is, we don't care. We look for the who; the courts deal with the why of it."

"Yes, I suppose. It's just that if those claims in some way dredge up old wounds... Well, we can't have that happen, can we?"

"Hang on a minute, Father. If you know something, anything that is going on here, you need to tell me about it now. My head is ringing, so subtle hints may fall short this morning." He sipped his own coffee and looked at Father Greg. The priest's shoulders sagged. Cam's body language behind the collar. Something was bothering him.

"Burying the truth is exactly what chased people from the Church in the first place, Father. Please don't hide behind the confessional." Blair's head began to ache, and he didn't think it was from the punch.

"Blair, please, you know even if I did learn something, I could never share it. The sacrament is the cornerstone of our faith. Jesus granted it first upon his resurrection. We do it now in communion with his risen spirit."

"I know, Father, I know. But you are here. That tells me there is something you want to share. Help us catch this killer, tell me what you know."

"This is not about what I do or don't know. It's about what you can do." The priest's eyes stayed glued to the coffee cup. "When you catch this killer, and I pray that you and Cam do that soon, please find a way to protect what you believe in. That's all I can or will say."

"You mean cover something up."

"I mean think of the Church."

So there it was. The lies of the past on the lips of the future.

CHAPTER 11

I BALANCED ON MY LEFT FOOT, FORCING MY SHOULDERS BACK. My fists were in front of my face, my right leg extended. I snapped three final kicks into the heavy bag before dropping the foot to the floor. Ring rust was showing. Maybe it was age. The kicks should have been at head height. They weren't close. Maybe I was thinking about kicking Jimmy Williams. My morning workout over, I grabbed a towel and headed for the shower.

My cellphone belted out a familiar guitar riff before I got halfway across the garage. Nothing like Bon Jovi in the morning. Blair had loaded the musical ring tone because he knew I had no idea how to get rid of it. At least I knew who was calling. I walked over and grabbed the phone from the workbench.

"How's the head?" I asked.

"Feels like I went three rounds with Phil Murphy. Funny, I'm pretty sure it was only one."

"How's the eye?"

"You know that picture of you hanging above the ring?"

"Yep." I looked over at it.

"Think of the guy lying on the mat behind you."

"That bad."

"Maybe worse."

"How's Sue?"

"Oh, she's fine."

"You tell her where it happened?"

"Yep."

"That was smart." I picked up my towel and draped it over my head.

"Hey, I got hit in the head. Wasn't thinking clearly. You check in with the office yet?" he asked.

"No, I was going to call before I head out on the ride. How was the briefing?"

"What you'd expect. You'd better get ready for MacIntosh. One minute he's ripping me a new one for wasting my time at a strip bar, the next he's making noise about you being a lousy partner for not being with me."

"He's an asshole, but he's right. I should have been."

I didn't say anything about his going and not telling me. He was hurting enough. I drank from a water bottle as he filled me in on the briefing. The Special O team reported on Bobby Simms having spent an hour with my brother at the basilica. I figured they were planning a funeral, but I'd ask Greg when I saw him.

"What's the plan with the dancer?" I asked when he finished filling in the blanks.

"No plan. MacIntosh says there's no connecting the dots between her and the murders. Says we can't afford the resources on a long shot."

"What about the beating?"

"Told him I didn't see who attacked me."

My partner was planning something private. Couldn't blame him.

"When you're ready, I want in."

"Wouldn't have it any other way."

The dancer was a long shot, but I didn't like agreeing with MacIntosh. Maybe I needed to rethink it. The beating could have been Williams off the leash. Could be a thousand reasons for him to want Blair out of the club, and none had to do with a dead preacher and his housekeeper.

"I'll see Murphy and Williams at the house today. I'll let them know payback is coming. Feel Gunner out, too. See what he thinks about his goons beating a cop."

"You think it's connected?"

"No, I thought about it all night. Hate to agree with MacIntosh, but I can't connect it, either. It sure as hell feels wrong, though. I'll see what Carla thinks. She'll be here in an hour." I knew what was coming.

"Carla? You and Sergeant Cage having morning briefings of your own now? Well, can't say I saw that coming. You dog."

"Nothing there. MacIntosh doesn't trust me with the old gang, that's all. Told her to ride along."

"Damn. Can't wait to tell Sue."

"Let it go, Blair. Listen, I'll call Greg to see what he and Bobby talked about." Sometimes I have to refocus my partner.

"Done. I just finished a coffee with your baby brother. Simms was looking for absolution."

"Simms a Catholic?"

"Guess so. Greg can't say what his confession was about, but he does say he still thinks Bobby is innocent. Guess that tells us enough."

Tells us something, but not close to enough.

"We'll talk later. I gotta grab a shower."

"Okay, but I'll want to hear all about your play date."

I hung up.

I twisted the throttle and held the bars steady as the front tire lifted. I kept it up there for half a block before easing it back to the pavement. I slowed, pulled the clutch lever hard against the bar, twisted the throttle all the way and let the clutch lever fly. The bike slid hard right before snapping into a rolling burnout. There's nothing like the smell of scorched rubber and raw exhaust in the cool morning air. Heading out on a run gets my blood pumping. I love to feel the power, hear the bark of a finely tuned, high-compression race engine. I also wanted to see if Carla could keep up. I glanced in the tiny mirror above my right hand as I came to the end of the block. There she was, glued to me. Her front tire beside my rear. Perfect. Last night's gixxer was a pleasant surprise, but it was her brother's ride. She arrived this morning on a jaw-dropping custom, her own bike. Almost slow enough to be a Harley, she said. She had the attitude and the ride.

I laughed into the wind, feeling the pure joy that only comes in the saddle. I dropped my right hand from the throttle and gestured for her to pull up beside me. I wanted another look. Carla was boots in the wind on a Sean's Non-Stock Customs bobber. She didn't have to worry about being accepted into the Harley cult. Her ride was a step above most Stallion bikes.

Green flames swept over the black coffin-shaped tank that rose in front of her. A set of curved risers reached back from the glistening springer front end to put a short set of drag bars in her hands. The V-shaped engine below the tank drove its power into an open primary below her left heel. Its thick black belt spun at better than two-thousand rpm as it brushed the dangling cuff of her black jeans. If it caught, it would pull her off the machine and slam her into the pavement. I listened to the backfiring as she neared. The sidewalk sweepers sticking out of her EVO engine blew a mixture of carbon and unburned fuel into the curb, as she geared down to keep from overtaking me. The only thing legal on that machine was the cop straddling it. The bike was one-hundred-percent badass. The good sergeant was going to fit in just fine.

She matched my every move, every throttle twist, as we rode boot to boot, outlaw style. The sound of our bikes merged into a window-rattling roar. It's only a short blast from my place to the Stallion compound. I glanced over at her and wished it was a longer run.

The morning glow faded as we approached the house. The memorial run is a mandatory mountain of PR bullshit. It started as a way to honour fallen club members and was a patch-only run. It meant something then. While I was off trading lead with the holy warriors, Snake decided to invite every RUB club in Halifax to join the Stallion for the day. The rich urban bikers with their bullshit patches raced to the outlaw clubhouse like groupies.

Hundreds of bikes lined the street leading to the house. Even more packed the parking lot beneath the dump where Sandy Gardner played to his final crowd. The ugly hacking of big-inch engines exploding against rev limiters drowned out the smooth rhythm of our bikes. I cringed at the damage being done inside those machines, as the look-at-me-now clowns twisted throttles on parked thirty-thousand-dollar rides. Just noise, no smoke. Not one of them with the balls or brains to let a burnout give all that pent-up power somewhere useful to go. A black-leather mob filled the pavement, making it almost impossible to get through even on a bike. Carla started to ease back behind me. I grabbed the brake, put my feet down, and let her come back beside me.

"Stay tight. We don't change how we ride into the house for these guys," I yelled to her over the roar. She nodded and stayed beside me as we inched ahead, dragging our boots on the pavement.

Snake was in the middle of the crowd, posing for pictures and back-slapping the presidents of the RUB clubs. Proof that the Stallion was just another riding club. The reporters who came to the event didn't buy it. Our badged brethren knew it was an act. Still, everybody in blue and silver played along. Patches and prospects smiled and mingled with the wannabe outlaws.

"Hey, there's a spot." Carla nodded to an opening between two parked bikes on her side of the street.

I shook my head and looked toward the gate. "Inside," I yelled over the deep barking of her bike.

"It must be full. Look around," she yelled back, leaning closer to me to be heard.

"We have a reservation." I smiled at the thought of parking with the RUB clubs. Never happen.

A uniformed officer stepped in front of us, blocking the gate. Same shit, different day. A member of the Outlaw Motorcycle Gang team stepped up behind him, a camera dangling from a leather strap around her neck. She patted the uniform on the shoulder, said something to him, and then smiled at Carla as she stepped away. The uniform waved us in. Wouldn't be a Stallion party without the OMG crew manning the gate.

A thicker crowd jammed the parking lot outside the house. Almost as many bikers, fewer bikes. The RUB clubs had to park outside, but mingling in the compound was allowed. I backed into a spot along the outer fence; Carla slipped in beside me. I felt my teeth grind as I looked through the crowd to the line of Stallion bikes in front of the house. Getting through the gate put me above the crowd outside. Having to park this far from the Stallion line reminded me of what I'd given up. I was now one small step above a RUB.

"What was that all about?" Carla nodded back to the officer in the street as she removed her helmet.

"Assholes in the biker unit stop anyone the club lets inside the gate. They jot down licence plate numbers, snap photos, make a show of it. Welcome to the one percent." It was out before I realized how angry it sounded.

"Jesus, Cam, you playing the role, or do you mean that?"

"Sorry. It's just such bullshit it still pisses me off. Five-hundred bikes out there get ignored. Two dozen in here get a close look. You and I both know there are better things for that uniform to be doing right now."

"Why bother? They know you guys." She flushed red as she adjusted a do-rag and shook her hair free. "I mean the club members."

"Only members or special guests can ride across that line. They like to see who shows. Members expect it, so it's a drug-and-weapons-free ride. I suppose that's good police work." I tossed my helmet over the mirror on the high side of the bike. She dropped hers over the foot peg below mine. Maybe she had a little ol' lady in her after all.

The joy I'd felt riding here was gone. In its place, a dangerous anger. No way the cop at the gate had me that pissed off. I looked at my father's bike near the end of the Stallion line. Maybe it was more about feeling like an outsider in the compound, being forced into it by MacIntosh. Whatever it was, I had to shake it.

I looked for Gunner among the scuffed leathers and backward ball caps milling around the yard. Instead, I saw a sea of cartoon cut-outs stitched to leather backs. I bumped shoulders with a few as I walked to the row of bikes, Carla in my wake. When I rode with the club, these ridiculous one-piece crests would never get near the house. The easiest way to tell a RUB club from the real thing is to look at the patch its members wear. A single bit of fabric covered in any design is the mark of a bullshit club. The one-percent clubs wear three-piece patches and make sure no one else in their territory does. Prospects wear one piece of the club patch, but only full members wear all three. The diamond-shaped one-percent crest is also reserved for full-patch members.

My anger found a target as I spotted a black-and-white three-piece patch near the gas pump. Black and white doesn't mix with blue and silver in the outlaw world. A rider from a rival one-percent club was pissing on Stallion turf behind the safety of the open ride.

I caught a glimpse of his bottom rocker before the crowd blocked my view. It said *Nova Scotia*. Asshole was calling out the Stallion. There'd be blood, memorial run or not. A real biker will kill or be killed for colours and territorial rockers. Wearing black and white over a Nova Scotia rocker was saying the province was no longer blue-and-silver territory. I wished I had my badge on my belt as I headed over to walk the guy out of the compound. A brawl now would bring in the outlaw-biker detail and end this thing before I saw any security video.

I finally saw his back clearly as I got closer. I shook my head. The fool was wearing a Sons of Anarchy knock-off patch. He was a full rung beneath the RUBs, walking around real outlaws in his made-for-TV patch like he belonged. SOA was a hit inside the clubhouse, but that didn't mean this moron would get away with posing in a three-piece patch outside. I saw two prospects working their way through the crowd. He'd be leaving without his TV colours.

"What's that about?" Carla asked, as she watched the man remove his fake cut and hand it over.

"Nothing. Guy is too much of a poser." I took another look around, couldn't find Gunner.

"Hard to imagine that around here." She looked at the leather-covered RUBs filling the compound.

She had me there.

"I'm going inside. Mingle, but don't mention the badge," I said.

"Yes, sir." She locked eyes with me.

"Sorry. You'll have to show the women out here you know your place or you'll never get inside the house."

"Fine." She turned and walked toward a group of women wearing blue-and-silver T-shirts over tight jeans and black riding boots. I hoped she had followed the no gun rule. It wouldn't help our cause if she shot an ol' lady while I was inside.

+++

The prospects were standing on either side of the steel door at the side of the clubhouse. They were laughing and fist bumping. They draped the Sons patch over the faded wooden fence that hid the door from the police cameras that sprout on the hilltop behind the Stallion property. Good for them; at least there was no blood on it. The fence jutted out from the side of the building, cut ninety degrees, and ran to the parking lot, stopping just short of the line of Stallion bikes. Two nose-to-nose Harley baggers with Stallion logos blocked the path leading to the door. The big touring bikes kept the squares from accidentally wandering from the parking lot to the side of the house. It was a subtle sign by Stallion standards. The open invitation to the memorial run had its limits.

They stopped the celebration as I stepped around the baggers and headed down the fenced alley. The prospect on the left was a long hipless leather strap with sunken cheeks and sullen eyes. His partner was a head shorter and twice as wide. Guy looked like an NFL running back, the Emmitt Smith, tackle-breaking kind. I didn't recognize them. The running back moved in front of me. He'd be the muscle.

"Turn around, man. Private party inside." He pointed to the crowded lot beyond the parked bikes. He looked at his partner when I didn't turn away.

"I'm on the list, except we know there isn't a list," I told them as I stepped up close to meet the muscle. "You try to stop me, you'll get hurt. Patches won't think much of you getting dropped on door duty. You could avoid that problem and just let me in. But then, we also know you'll get seriously hurt if I don't belong. Sucks to be you, prospect. Make a choice."

I was being an asshole, but they were prospects, and I was still pissed off. The running back squared off, making the wrong choice. His skeletal pal put a hand on his shoulder and stepped forward.

"We're outta Sydney." His voice was quiet, no threat in it. No fear, either. "Don't know shit about Halifax. Do know you're not a patch, though. You don't get in without someone clearing it. You're gonna stand back there and wait till that happens. That's the end of it." He grinned through crumbling tweaker teeth. Club was going to hell. I felt a twitch below my left eye. Always happens.

The key to fighting two guys is to avoid it, walk away. Only sensible approach. If you're not feeling sensible, strike first. I was too close to sweep the running back's legs, so I put him down with a driving right elbow. I forgot how much fun it was to beat on a prospect. I didn't mean to break his nose, not really. He curled up on the ground moaning through his hands. No Emmitt Smith in him at all. I stepped over him toward the tweaker. He raised his talons in surrender and backed away fast.

"Hey, man, wait, okay?" He squealed as he backed into a fast-moving forearm smash. His eyes rolled, and he dropped beside his partner. Gunner stepped past him rubbing his arm.

"Why you being an asshole out here, bro?" he asked as we hugged.

"Old habits," I said, rubbing my elbow and looking at the two downed prospects.

"You fucking believe that pussy? Didn't even try you. Pier charter is going to shit in Sydney, man." Gunner looked past me. I could see worry. He didn't want a scene. He stepped past the prospects and squared his shoulders to block the view from the front of the house.

"Hey, Babe, go stand by the bikes and look hot," he said.

A slender brunette with dark skin and deep-set green eyes stepped past the prospects. She was wearing a Stallion support tee shredded just above a diamond-pierced navel. Yoga tights disappeared into thigh-high black suede boots. She flashed a smile as she touched Gunner's shoulder and moved toward the parked bikes. We both watched her walk away. My throat went dry.

Gunner slapped me in the back of the head. I smiled, realized how comfortable I felt here with him. I wondered what it meant, why it was so easy to slip into the old habits and bitch-slap a prospect for fun.

"Who the hell is that?" I asked as I rubbed my head.

"Cheyenne," he said.

"Nice."

"Uh huh."

If he knew her name, she meant something to him. I stopped staring. We turned to the two prospects as the running back struggled back to his feet. Gunner shoved him back down with a boot.

"That one any use to us?" he asked.

"He was ready. Just slow," I said.

Gunner moved to the scrawny tweaker and grabbed the right side of his prospect cut. He yanked, and spun him chin down into the ground as he pulled the leather off. He noticed the Sons of Anarchy colours on the fence as he gripped the prospect's leather. He grabbed the TV patch and tossed it onto the skinny prospect.

"Put that on him and get him the fuck out of here. He just backed his way out of this club."

The heavyset prospect was on his knees now. Blood leaked below his hand as he gripped the bridge of a shattered nose. His eyes were all over me. I smiled.

"Hey, fuckhead," Gunner said. "This guy's my brother; you show him respect."

"Sorry, man," he mumbled through his hand.

"He's also a fucking cop, so don't say shit around him."

His eyes widened. Guess the Sydney charter hadn't told the prospects about the bad seed in Halifax. Gunner and I headed into the house. It was easy being with him. It chilled my anger, made it feel normal. I was surprised at how easy it was to justify the violence with him present. Breaking a man's nose did feel normal. So did missing my brother. We live in the same city but in different worlds. If there was an upside to MacIntosh's order, this was it.

Snake was holding court with the patches as we cleared the hallway. He looked past them when we came in. He walked over and grabbed my right hand in a tight grip, pulling me into his chest. We slapped backs and he pulled away.

"Glad to see you in riding gear. Your patch is still out back if you got the balls to put it back on." His smile was genuine, no malice. Making it clear. I was a retired Stallion today, nothing more.

"I'm here because of the old man's patch, not mine," I said.

My arrival marked the end of the meeting as one by one the bros greeted me. My back was sore and my hand was tingling from the impact on so many patches, but it felt good. I looked across the room to Grease. He was tinkering with a twin-cam engine in a cradle. He didn't look back.

"You coming back to the house after the ride?" Gunner asked.

"Yeah, I got an ol' lady with me if that's cool."

"She a cop?" Sharp, my brother.

"More scientist, but, yeah, she has a badge. She's okay." I wouldn't lie to Gunner or anyone in the club about something that serious. My standing only carried so much weight.

"We'll talk it over," he said, nodding to Snake. "Go see the prospect out back while we do that. And brother." He grabbed my arm. Hard. "You have a problem with the shit went down at The Bank last night, you deal with it on your own time, not here, not now. Fair?"

So Gunner knew about the beating. I held his gaze, couldn't read it. At least I knew where Jimmy Williams was. I couldn't figure why Gunner wanted me to go see the little fuck.

I stepped through the door and stopped in front of a wall-mounted glass case. It looked like a high-school trophy case. No football, basketball, or swim team medals, though. Instead, it held the cuts of the dead or jailed. They were opened and pinned to the back of the case so the full Stallion back patch and the members' personal colours showed. Personal colours run down the front of a Stallion cut. They show rank and accomplishments. My father's topped the small pyramid of leather, still leading the ride. His President and red demon's head patches showing. Mine at the bottom, alone. The prodigal patch. I wasn't sure if it meant I was still good to come back or I was dead to the club. Guess it didn't really matter. I saw Williams at the bank of security monitors past the lockers. My locker sits next to Gunner's. It had been taken over by someone else. Guess they weren't holding their breath.

Williams turned as he heard me approach. Phil Murphy stood to one side. I walked up to Murphy, pushed into his space. "Hear you like to throw those fists."

He looked down at his shoes and backed into the wall. He wouldn't take the bait here in the clubhouse.

"That fucking Indian started it," Williams said.

I slapped him in the side of the head with a backhand. He stumbled out of the chair onto the floor. "Open your mouth again, prospect," I warned, "and the fist will be closed."

Murphy inched from the wall. I looked hard into those dead eyes. He backed away again. He was big enough to hurt me. I was fast enough to kill him. Hard to say if power or speed would win. The time would come.

Williams rubbed his head as he returned to the chair. His tiny fists clenched harder than Murphy's, the knuckles yellow.

"Look, man, you can't call me prospect and slap me around. You're not in this club anymore."

I kicked Williams's leg as he turned in the seat. It would leave a mark, but it wasn't even close to the kick I wanted to deliver.

"That better, prospect?"

"Okay, okay. Look I just want to show you something. That okay?" Swallowing his pride now, like a good prospect. Too bad.

Williams turned back in the chair, and grabbed a wireless mouse, clicked it, and the bottom screen changed. I watched a blurred image of a small SUV roll into the frame from the left and turn into the parking lot across the street. The security tape. MacIntosh was getting what he wanted.

"Is that a Jeep, one of those Suzukis maybe?" I asked.

"Man, I don't know cars," he said.

Brake lights flared as the SUV slowed and began to climb the gravel road where Sandy Gardner was found. Williams clicked the mouse again. The screen went blank.

"That it? Doesn't it come out?" I leaned closer to the monitor.

"Yeah, hang on." He worked the keys. The image distorted as the timer on the screen raced forward. It slowed as a set of headlights came back down the hill and into the parking lot across the street. It turned away from the clubhouse and disappeared out of frame.

"It's all we got. You want a copy?" I could see it hurt him to ask; he was now a rat. Snake was no fool.

"Yes, I do. You sure that's all of it?"

"You want to sit here and watch, go ahead. Couple of hours of nothing till your crew arrives," he said.

"Fine, shut it off and burn me a disc," I said. "Make sure it includes the time stamp."

There was no point in watching the rest. If there was anything Snake hadn't wanted me to see, it was already gone. At least we had something the techs could work with. Maybe even enhance it enough to see what make the vehicle was. Williams handed me a plastic case with a DVD inside. All wrapped and ready to go.

"Listen," I said. "Now that you're a rat and all, do you want some money? I could maybe get you registered as an informant."

He stood and moved on me, fists clenched, showing attitude. I looked at Murphy as I shot the left fist out from my side, catching Williams square with a short jab. He dropped back to the floor.

"Clean that up," I said as I walked away.

I had what I'd come for. The smart thing now would be to skip the ride and head back to the major-crime office. See if I could get back into the case. That would be the smart thing, but I had to ride along and corner Gunner when the time was right. I had to know if the club had sanctioned the beating on Blair, and if it did, why. He'd have to know there'd be payback for the two fools behind me.

I looked to my right, where Carla was inches away on that green bobber. Her left hand feathered the clutch lever as her right wrapped around the brake. A tiny smile showed on her lips, but her eyes were all concentration. Group riding Stallion style is somewhere between a thrill ride and a death wish. We run side by side and tight, with less than a bike length between the front tire of one bike and the rear of the bike ahead. You can reach out and touch the rider beside you. The road captain rolled up beside us and nodded to me as he continued along outside the formation, policing the gaps. If you couldn't keep it tight, he'd order you out of the formation and then hit you with a fine at the end of the run. We were okay. Carla could have ridden back with the RUB clubs who run a looser and safer staggered line, but she insisted on riding beside me in the Stallion formation. She was doing it perfectly. Locking her eyes on the bikes five rows ahead, where trouble starts. If they hit the brake, you hit the brake. If you watch the bike in front of you, there just isn't enough time to react. I could hear the rhythm of her engine matching mine perfectly, could almost feel it. The roar around us was deafening. We rolled through the tight turns along Highway 333.

The memorial run takes only an hour, but by the end everyone is ready for a breather. I could see the turnoff to Peggys Cove ahead and began to relax in the saddle. Carla glanced over at me, and I could see her posture relax as well. Suddenly, the line slowed and we both grabbed the brake levers. I felt the front forks on my bike bottom out as the nose plunged down. I heard the deep whine as the rear tire on Carla's bobber locked up and slid. She recovered quickly, and we both paid attention to the bikes ahead as we approached the turnoff. We rolled into Peggys Cove and parked in a lot behind the restaurant and gift shop near the famed lighthouse. We stepped off our bikes as the line of RUB clubs slowly filed into the lot behind us.

My eyes squinted against the salt sting in the sea air as I watched Bobby Simms pull Greg into the open back of a pickup truck. Bobby, the ubiquitous Christian soldier. The small truck was parked at the lower end of the lot.

Beyond it, I could see explosions of white where waves crashed into the rocky shoreline. One of the RUB clubs had brought the truck and a small sound system for Greg. There had to be three-hundred people huddled in groups around the lot, most not looking at him. Members of the three Christian clubs attending the run formed a semicircle behind the truck, ready for the blessing. Bobby had never made the cut as a Stallion; now he rode with a Christ image on his back. One of the saved. At least I knew where he was.

Carla and I stood to the side, near a winding stone walkway that led to the lighthouse standing over the rolling sea. The light spun slowly inside the red-topped white tower that once guided the fleet through stormy seas to the safety of the harbour below. Satellite guidance had killed coastal lighthouses years ago. This one served now as a beacon to guide tourists to the cove. It worked.

You don't need the weather channel to know when plywood sheets are being pried off the windows in Florida, Georgia, or the Carolinas. Just stand here in Peggys Cove and feel five-storey waves slam the massive granite point beyond the lighthouse. There is no more powerful force on earth than a storm-riled sea. Its mountains of water race forward for days, looking for a place to unleash the fury of the wind and rain that woke them. Peggys Cove is a favourite target. When they hit, the rumble rolls under the soles of your feet. It feels like distant mortar fire. Just more powerful. Most hurricanes hook a hard right and head back to sea when they find the cooler waters this far north. They brush the coast with gales and rolling seas that keep the fishing boats behind the breakwaters and fill the rocks of Peggys Cove with stupid tourists and dumber locals.

More than a million people walk the rolling rock outcropping to take pictures and marvel at the sea here every year. Most leave with little more than a cool wet status update on a Facebook page. But when a storm slips past offshore, Peggys Cove shifts from postcard pretty to killer coastline. This was one of those days. I watched dozens of tourists clamour past the warning signs and point cellphone cameras as waves pounded the rocks. The whitewater clouds jumped hundreds of metres into the air. The bigger the waves, the bigger the crowd of fools. I always wonder if those same people arrived at Busch Gardens when the big cats were being fed whether they'd want to climb the fence to get a good close-up.

Every year, on days like this, the sea claims one or two tourists for its own. The lucky ones get smashed into the rocks. Most get pulled out to sea where they die of acute stupidity, cold and alone, with land in sight and terror in their hearts.

Salt and drizzle slapped my face in a blast of wind, the warmth of the sun on my skin replaced by a sudden chill.

"You realize someone will have to wash this off my bike." Carla rubbed a tube across her lips to fight the salt as we watched Greg lead a prayer from his Chevy pulpit. The lot was crammed with bikes. The salt was coating all of them.

"Sorry. Bike-washing is women's work, and there is salt on my ride, too," I told her. "There will be a bikini bike wash back at the compound. Money goes to charity."

I hoped none of the women caught the daggers she threw my way. Definitely not ol' lady like.

"I was thinking of someone soaping a gas tank not a tank top." She reached over, took my hand in hers. Back in character.

"They don't wear any. You could probably join. Did I mention it's for charity?"

She turned away from Greg and nodded toward a small group of women watching him from a short distance away. She placed her hand gently on my chest and smiled.

"Maybe you can find a volunteer over there," she said. "This ol' lady doesn't wash bikes. This ol' lady carries a gun."

"Point taken. Bring your bike to my place in the morning and I'll wash both. Just promise not to tell them."

The women were no longer watching Greg; they were watching us. Carla must have noticed. She traced her fingers along my cheek.

"Promise not to tell the other detectives, and it might be at your place in the morning anyway." She stood on her toes and kissed my cheek where her hand had just been. She was selling it well. I just wasn't sure who she was selling it to.

"Speaking of the other detectives, you have the video. How much longer do we have to play biker and property of?" Carla turned back to face Greg, gripping my hand.

"We still have work to do," I said. "I need to corner Gunner. Find out if the club sanctioned the beating on Blair, and why. That dancer could be performing at the clubhouse when we get back. If she is, you're going to buy me a lap dance and we're going to have a chat with her."

"You enjoying this?" She let go of my hand and looked at me, same look she showed when she saw the patch on the wall in my garage.

"Look. MacIntosh forced this on me. I just know how to work it, okay?"

I looked past her. Greg was blessing four urns, the newest members of the honour roll. He handed them one by one to a pastor from one of the Christian clubs, who handed them to the riders closest to the truck, the ones who had brought them on their last ride. Bobby was no longer in the truck with Greg. I tried to spot him in the crowd.

With the prayers over, it was time to pour the ashes into the ocean. With the waves pounding, the clubs would do it in the lee of the massive rocks, at the wharf down in the village. Bikers are big on pointless gestures, and no one would leave without a moment or two at the water's edge. Some would toss flowers into the sea to remember those who died in years past. Snake would pour a bottle of Jack for the old man and the other dead Stallion brothers. I knew Gunner would stay up here with the bikes. Neither one of us cared much for pointless gestures or for the old man. I needed to keep our little brother with us. Gunner wasn't going on some graveside run with Greg, and I didn't have time, either. I'd feel guilty if we didn't give him some of the brotherly bonding time he seemed to want. Priests are big on pointless gestures too, and I had to find him before he headed down to the wharf.

+++

Gunner shouldered the side of the sprawling Cape Cod, a cigarette hanging from the corner of a scowl. If the lighthouse draws the tourists to Peggys Cove, the Sou'Wester restaurant gives them a place to leave some money behind. The view in Nova Scotia is free, but so-phisticated tourists like to get their money's worth. The Sou'Wester and the cluster of gift shops below the rocky point make sure they get the full tourist experience. Gunner wasn't paying a dime for the shelter the restaurant offered.

Carla stood at the edge of the parking lot near the road. She was with Gunner's new ol' lady, Cheyenne, and a small group of Stallion women. Greg was in the middle of it, speaking to Cheyenne. Carla smiled my way, a lot of menace in a pretty face. I waved.

"The fuck does he want, anyway?" Gunner asked behind the smoke as we both watched our little brother charm the ladies.

"He came back from that pilgrimage thinking we need some family bonding," I said.

"What fucking family? You a cop, him a priest? That ain't family, bro. That's just embarrassing."

"We look up to you, too. Now fuck off and give him a few minutes."

"You say that behind a badge; guess I didn't teach you your place under the patch."

"Like I said, big bro, 'fuck off.'" I flipped him the finger, a ges-ture that could have gotten a guy seriously messed up in the bad old days.

Gunner smiled as he pulled the cigarette and flicked it off the side of a tour bus rolling past. He raised a middle finger to the faces and cameras pressed against the windows. Bonus photo for them. A legendary lighthouse and a real live outlaw all in one day.

"I see you still embrace your fellow man, Lee," Greg said as he joined us beside the restaurant. A cheek-stretching smile took any sting out of the rebuke. Good thing. Two of us pushing his buttons might be more than Gunner could take.

"They came for the show." Gunner pulled the cigarette pack from his jacket and lit another. I wondered if he'd let it slide if I used his real name.

Greg turned to me. "Cam, Officer Cage tells me you won't be coming to the graveyard after all. That's a shame."

"Sorry, Greg. We wanted to complete the ride, but then duty calls. You know how it is."

"I do, indeed. But, like charity, sometimes duty should begin at home." Greg nodded toward the final group of bikers walking down to the wharf. "Especially at times like this."

I looked at my brothers. A full-patch giant squinting and scarred behind his own angry smoke and a soft-featured mop top peeking out from above a white spec of collar. The badge planted me somewhere in the middle, not pure enough for the priesthood and not dirty enough for gang life. Was I the lost brother or the found one?

"Look at the three of us," Greg said. He was reading my mind. "I wear a collar to atone for our father's sins. Lee, you wear his patch and repeat them. Cam, you curse him by wearing the shield he stood against. Three sons living in a very big shadow."

"Look, Greg, should I call you Father or what? I don't know what the fuck to call you. Doesn't matter. The old man was an ass- hole. Okay? Treated you like shit and kicked the shit out of us, but that don't mean you know anything about him." For Gunner, it was a speech. He took a long pull on the cigarette.

"That's just it. I don't. Not enough, anyway. Just as you don't really know enough about me. You're my big brother, and you are uncomfort- able calling me by my given name. That says enough, and it's why I want us to spend time together. The three of us. We are in many ways one. Children of a broken home, a broken man." He touched each of us on the forearm. Gunner tried to back away, but the building stopped him.

I tried to remember the last time the three of us had stood this close together. I couldn't. Greg was right. Only a fool wouldn't see the shadow of the old man in our choices. He was a gang leader, and his sons joined gangs. Gunner the right one, me the wrong, Greg the biggest gang of all.

"You know what, Greg?" I said. "You're right. For better or worse, we are brothers. Maybe it wouldn't hurt to spend some time together." I wasn't sure I meant it.

Gunner looked at me over his cigarette. He didn't say no, but his eyes did.

"Thank you, Cam," Greg said as Bobby Simms approached from the front of the building.

Today, he wore a loose-fitting sweatshirt under his leather vest. He still looked big, but at least he wasn't busting any seams. So much for the family reunion.

"Well, if it isn't Halifax's most famous brothers. If only I had a camera to capture the moment." Simms smiled. His tone was soft. It dripped bullshit the way it did when he knew Greg was behind me back at Sandy Gardner's house.

Gunner pushed away from the building, standing tall above Simms. Saying nothing, saying everything.

"I hate to break up the party," said Simms, "but Father, I wonder if you'd come down to the wharf with me for the final prayers." He turned away from Gunner, ignored me.

"Well, Cam, as you say, duty calls." Greg backed away from us. "Guess mine comes first. Let's pick this up later. Gunner, ride safe." He dropped the Lee with Simms standing there. Smart.

"Aren't you two coming down?" Simms's tone grew harder as he looked at me. "This is about your father. You can't just stand here and let the rest of us honour him." The smile gone now, his eyes locked with mine.

He was looking at the wrong Neville. Gunner had a handful of Christian vest before Bobby could turn back to Greg. Christ saves, but does he protect fools? Bobby was about to find out.

"The fuck you say, asshole?" Gunner had Bobby against the building now. I saw Carla make a move toward us. I waved her off and stepped in, putting a hand on Gunner's shoulder as Greg pleaded with him to release Simms. As much fun as it would be to watch, I'd never be able to explain to Inspector MacIntosh how I let my brother beat someone he told me to stay away from. I pulled Gunner off.

"Later, prick." Gunner pushed him toward the road. Simms straightened his vest, the smile back.

"My apologies. Love and respect, brother," Simms said to Gunner as he and Greg headed down the hill.

"Asshole," Gunner said, as he stepped away from the building and headed to the bikes. I followed.

"He still connected in any way?" I asked as we walked.

Gunner stopped. Looked at me. A line was crossed. I raised my hands in surrender, and we walked on. I regretted the question about Bobby. It had pissed him off before I had the chance to ask what mattered. We stopped at the glide. Gunner pulled his do-rag and wiped the moisture off the seat and the tiny bitch pad, attached to the rear fender of our father's ride. A suction cup held the square of leather in place behind the saddle. Nothing comfortable, but Cheyenne had a seat behind the VP on a club run. Gunner must be serious about her. He caught me looking at it.

"Problem?" he asked.

"Nah, man. It's what you need. Happy to see it."

He looked past me.

"Cop with you looks pretty hot. Fuckin' bike she rides, shit, nicer than yours, bro." He reached for the cigarettes again. All the tension gone.

"Bike's nicer than most. She carries a big gun, too."

"Like I said, hot."

"Listen, I gotta ask you a question about last night."

He sat on the edge of the saddle, put his right boot on the rear passenger peg, and looked at me.

"That beating at The Bank. The club good with that?"

"You look like your old self, you know bro," he said as he rubbed the do-rag over the bitch pad beside him. "You ride in, nice ol' lady tight behind you. Makes me think of old times. Feel it right here, you know." He pulled the cigarette hand into his chest. "But twice now, you ask cop questions. Maybe it's time you leave."

"Not a cop question, bro. Blair's a friend. Real tight friend. Gonna be payback."

He took a slow drag on the cigarette and shrugged as he stuffed the do-rag in his hip pocket.

"I see Williams is still wearing the lower rocker, see his goon in the back office today. Makes me think they were taking care of business last night. Maybe payback is going to be a bigger problem," I said.

"Shit's complicated, bro. Can't just pull his rocker. You better let it be."

"Fuck that, Gunner. You pulled that scarecrow's rocker in a heartbeat when he turned yellow on me this morning. He wasn't even prospecting your charter."

"Shit's complicated, bro. Not the same."

"So the club's cool with cop beating now?"

He didn't answer. He stood and looked back toward the restaurant. The riders were filtering back from the wharf. Cheyenne and Carla were in the lead, heading toward us. I turned away from them and stepped up to him, put him in a bad place with witnesses watching. This wasn't two brothers now. It was someone challenging the Stallion VP. He raised an open palm to the left as we locked eyes. I knew a prospect or two had been waved off. He put a hand on each of my shoulders. I leaned into him.

"Like I said, complicated right now. That changes, I'll tell you. Let it slide."

I pulled free of his grip and took a half step back.

"Nothing slides. Not a fucking thing." It's the Stallion code, and the club needed to know I still lived by it.

Cheyenne arrived first, wrapping her arm around Gunner's waist and smiling at me. The black boots glistened with a salty mist where they met her thighs. Nature's own stripper glitter. She had a short-waisted, impossibly tight, blue leather jacket covering the shredded T-shirt. Carla placed an arm around me and smiled, not at Gunner, but at Cheyenne. Her jacket was not as tight, but those black riding jeans were. She leaned into me, playing her part. It felt good when she touched me, brought me back down. All eyes in the parking lot were still on us. Gunner raised his right fist in front of his chest. I paused as we looked at each other, then met his with mine. We bumped fists and parted.

"Care to share?" Carla said as we walked to our bikes.

"It's complicated," I said. "Let's just ride."

"What, no party at the clubhouse? No lap dancing?"

CHAPTER 12

Saturday, dusk

LOLITA CLUTCHED HER SKIRT AND BLOUSE IN ONE HAND. THE OTHER held a fur blanket closed over her breasts. The wrap was about warmth, not modesty. She worked hard on stage, and the sweat chilled as she walked through the air-conditioned bar to the dressing room.

Several men waved twenties as she passed, looking for some private time. A drunk in a nice suit waved a couple of fifties as he tugged at the blanket. She paused at the easy mark. She was in a hurry but couldn't leave that money on the table. She looked across the room where Sheilagh was just coming out of one of the private dance booths. Perfect. Lolita caught Sheilagh's eye, nodded to the mark, and then moved in and sat on his lap. She let the blanket fall open as she pulled the fifties from his hand and placed her lips against his ear.

"Got a surprise for you, honey," she whispered, biting gently at the lobe.

She stood as Sheilagh slid into the waiting lap, her red hair brushing his face. Lolita leaned in. Her lips met Sheilagh's in a slow kiss. They parted, tongues lingering in front of him. That's all a hundred buys you, she thought as she left Sheilagh to empty the rest of his wallet.

Lolita wanted to get out of the club to see Samuel before her next set. Everybody worked the pole on Saturday night at The Fog Bank. She'd have almost two hours before the other girls filled out the rotation and it was her time to dance again. She hoped that would be enough.

In the dressing room, she pulled a sweatshirt over her head and slipped into a pair of jeans. She kept her back to the sick midget's camera. She grabbed her purse and headed for the back. She'd almost made it when Glen Carroll grabbed her shoulder as she reached the door.

"Where the hell you think you're going, girl? We got customers out there want some lap time."

"The clubhouse. I'm supposed to dance there before my next set." She knew Glen worshipped the Stallion; she hoped the lie would work.

"Nobody told me nothing about you leaving the club." His raspy whisper was firm, but he released his grip.

"Okay, I'll stay. You call and tell Gunner. I don't want no shit for it." She moved past him and headed back to the dressing room.

"Wait. Hang on a minute. How you supposed to get there?"

"They'll send me a ride. Same as always." She stood still, not moving to the door.

"Yeah, well, that's cool, I guess, but tell Jimmy to call me. I need to know this shit."

"Whatever," she said, heading for the door.

She lit a cigarette as soon as she hit the parking lot, taking a long deep drag as she looked for Samuel's Ford. It slid out of a parking spot and rolled up to her. She jumped in. He looked frail behind the wheel. He was only two years younger than Lolita but seemed somehow like a child. He was handsome, or would be if he wasn't slouching his shoulders and aiming those lidded eyes at nothing. God, she thought she had it bad. She watched him adjust his position, casually throwing his left arm over the wheel as he turned to greet her. Trying to look like he was bigger, older. At least Sam was still trying to be something more when he was alone with her. She couldn't help the smile.

"We can't go far. I got to be back here in an hour."

"Soon you won't have to be inside that place at all, Tatjana." He looked down as he said it. Baby steps.

✦✦✦

Gunner spun the black cap off the bottle of Jack Daniels and leaned against the window frame. He took a quick belt and placed the open bottle on the dresser beside him. He looked down into the compound. The bikes were lined up neatly in front of the house. The old man's glide was in the back of a silver-and-blue half-ton, ready for the drive back to Cam's. He'd let the prospects do it. He didn't want another showdown. He grabbed the bottle again, walked to the edge of the bed, and handed it to Cheyenne. She leaned up on an elbow and let the covers fall free as she took a drink. Looked good and knew it.

The sound of the band thumped through the floor. The party was starting to kick downstairs. Cheyenne stood and pulled him close. The heat of her body felt good. Her feel, her smell, were already familiar, comfortable. Gunner placed his hand on the small of her back and lifted her into him. She wrapped her legs around him and leaned back, her hair falling off her shoulders, her smile full of promise. She didn't say a word, didn't ask him what was bothering him or any shit like that. She just lifted the bottle and took another drink. Fucking perfect.

Cheyenne's body was lean and tan, a natural dark shade, not that bullshit fluorescent copper from a tanning bed. He figured she had some Arab or Indian in her. He didn't give a shit if she wasn't a white chick; she was fucking hot. She had a small tattoo, a vine with tiny blue flowers leading down from her navel. Not Stallion blue but close enough. He knew her back was ink free and wondered if he would change that. He'd never marked a woman as his own; maybe it was time. He took the bottle from her with his left hand. He pushed her back onto the bed, rolled her over, and traced an outline just above her ass with a corner of the bottle. He spilled a shot into the tiny dimple at the base of her spine, leaned in, and licked it. He sat on the edge of the bed, leaned against the headboard, and took a longer drink.

She rolled on her hip and looked up at him.

"We gonna keep the party here or go down?" she asked.

"Little of both."

"How 'bout a lot of both."

He smiled. Where the fuck did this chick come from?

"Can I ask you something?" She reached for the bottle.

So much for perfect. Here comes the feelings shit. He stood and walked back to the window.

"Cam's ol' lady. She's a cop like him, right?"

"Yeah, why?" At least she wasn't asking about him.

"I dunno, she just seems cool, you know. I like her. They gonna party with us?"

"No, baby. Cop is a cop. We can't have 'em here in the house when we kick back." He looked out into the compound again.

"They don't seem like cops."

"Makes 'em better at it, I guess."

"You and Cam okay?"

Now comes the prying.

"Fine."

"Cool. I'm gonna grab a shower. Wanna come?"

He watched her walk across the room. She reached back and slowly stroked the area above her ass. Ready for the brand. He felt a smile burn his cheeks as he turned back to look out the window at the compound. A scowl pulled the smile from his face as he watched Jimmy Williams walk from the gate to the side of the house. He should go down and kick the shit out of the little fuck. Cam was right, that prospect patch should be pulled. Beating a cop, fuck. Snake wouldn't have it, though. Williams was an earner and ran the Box like a pro. He also had support in Montreal, and that complicated everything. Halifax was the mother charter, but Montreal carried more weight in the Stallion world now. Bigger city, bigger profits, more members. Williams had done time with some Montreal guys and had their blessing. Hard to believe. Gunner watched the little fuck swagger out of sight. Killing him would work. No club politics there. A dead prospect ain't much trouble.

He took one more drink before grabbing the cap and twisting it back into place. The real trouble would be Cam, not Williams. Little brother would sure as shit take on the club if he didn't make this right. If the Indian was as close to Cam as he said, there would be payback. Had to be. He wouldn't respect Cam if he didn't go after the prospect. Fuck, one brother wants to get all close and cozy. The other one wants to go to war. He headed for the shower. Fuck 'em both.

The RUB clubs were gone. The real bikers were kicking back in the clubhouse. Jimmy Williams worked the bar, cleaning glasses and serving drinks. The patches were feeling no pain while the band was on stage ripping through "Night Train." The bottles and glassware were dancing behind the bar. Gunner wasn't up on stage. That could be a problem. Most parties he stayed onstage all night, couldn't cause any shit for Jimmy from up there. He was the only patch missing. The best way to avoid trouble with Gunner was to avoid Gunner, so Jimmy decided to make his move. Two prospects were working the door. The compound was locked outside, so it wasn't like anyone was about to crash. Williams signalled to a prospect out of Sydney. The guy's nose was bandaged, and Williams knew his buddy had gotten his cut pulled earlier in the day. He'd be nervous now, wanting to please the patches.

"Hey, man, I got Litter Box business needs to be handled. Take the bar," he said as the stocky young prospect came over.

No out-of-town cherry was going to question him when he raised the Box. They might both be prospects in the clubhouse, but in the street, Jimmy carried weight. Other prospects feared him. They knew about the Litter Box and the way he ran it. The Pier boy gave him a quick "yes, sir." It made Jimmy's swagger a little deeper as he folded his cut, placed it beneath the bar, and headed for the door.

He headed out, sure that none of the drunken patches would notice. And Gunner, well fuck him. Prospecting was a pain in the ass, and he was glad he could finally see the end of it. This would be his night for sure. Fuck 'em all.

Phil Murphy was waiting in a black Cadillac Escalade in the gravel lot across from the compound. Williams didn't ask where it came from, didn't care. It was stolen, that's all that mattered. Good choice, too. Nobody drove the greased-up Caddies except crack dealers. Let the cops chase after them.

"Where is it?" he asked as he jumped into the passenger seat.

"Back seat."

"Drive."

Williams turned in the seat, reached back, and pulled the blanket off his treasure. He grabbed the flat-black MAC-10 and pulled it into the front. Even with the suppressor threaded into place the gun was still a short-barrelled thing of beauty. Be a shame to toss it after the job, but there are always more guns to be had.

Williams's feet rested on a nylon kit bag stuffed into the space under the dash. He reached down and grabbed the handle, pulling it up and sitting it on the gun in his lap. He unzipped the bag and pulled out two clips for the 10 and two balaclavas. Two sets of clothes filled out the bag. They'd change after the job. No residue. He put the balaclavas on the armrest between the front seats and shoved the bag back into place. He slammed a magazine into the gun and held it up to catch the final rays of the sunset as they cut through the windshield.

"Let's take this magazine over the Magazine," he laughed, feeling good about it.

Phil Murphy looked at him and said nothing. The big Caddy idling, not moving.

"Fuck, Phil. Drive over Magazine Hill, will you? We're going to Bedford."

The night slipped past the window as Lolita kicked her feet up onto the dash in front of her. They were more than an hour from The Fog Bank now, too late to make it back on time. She took a drag from her cigarette and smiled, wondering what Glen Carroll was doing. Running around looking for his headliner, afraid to call the clubhouse. He'd spin all night like that till she got back. She would have to take a beating, there was no avoiding that now. Still, she would stay with Samuel. He wasn't saying much, and that was okay. When they were kids, Samuel's silences could last hours, days sometimes. It was nice just to be alone with him. This must be what it felt like to be free. She recognized the bright light off to the left of the highway. A brown and red Tim Hortons sign stood high above the town of Windsor. How many times had they seen that same sign, faces pressed to the window, wishing the driver would stop? The drivers never did. She must have seen it a hundred times and had never once stepped inside the coffee shop.

"Can we get a coffee?" she asked.

Samuel turned to look at her and then glanced ahead at the sign. He flicked the turn-signal lever up. She watched him as the Ford slowed. He was still small but seemed a little older as he relaxed behind the wheel. Like a man, maybe. Hell, she'd been with younger men at stag parties and strip clubs. Hard to think of Sam that way. She wondered if he'd killed Thelma and then dismissed the thought. Sam was no killer, though he was full of surprises. This run to the camp was a big one. She'd ask him when they got there, and he'd tell her everything. They pulled off the highway and into the crowded parking lot. Sam eased the Ford into the drive-thru lane.

"Can I go in?" she asked.

He turned the wheel and found a parking spot near the door.

Lolita wanted to stretch a little. "Come on, let's go act like real people. We can sit at a table and have a coffee together. It'll be fun."

He looked at her, a smile lighting up those beautiful brown eyes. "Sure, we can do that."

Lolita sat at a table by the window while Samuel stood in line to get their coffee. Most of the tables were filled with kids. She looked out at the parking lot. Same thing. Kids clustered around cars in groups, a couple of motorbikes on one side. Plastic-looking bikes. Not the kind the Stallion rode, so she wasn't worried. A few of the kids were wandering between the Tim Hortons parking lot and the McDonald's next door. Most of the boys wore team jackets, *WRHS* on the back in big letters. Lolita had no idea what it might stand for. Just kids hanging out on a Saturday night. She wondered what that was like, wondered why she thought of them as kids. They were probably her age, give or take a year. Still, they looked like babies.

The noise at a table near her drew her eye from the window. Five girls looked back at her. They laughed, all of them. A fat redhead stood, pulled her hair out from the sides of her head, and spun around. The girls laughed louder. Lolita lifted her hand to her own head, touched a pigtail wrapped in white ribbon. She let the hand move to her cheek and down her face, felt the tiny bits of gold glitter. Two boys from another table joined the redhead as she swayed back and forth, flicking her mock pigtails from side to side. All three walked over to Lolita.

"Hey, you retarded or something?" the fat girl asked behind a twisted grin. The bigger of the boys leaned in and gave Lolita's hair a sharp tug. The redhead squealed.

Lolita's purse was on the table, her switchblade tucked inside. She resisted the urge, and instead stood and punched the bigger boy hard. He rocked back. His friend laughed.

"Get her, Lenny." The redhead's squeal turned ugly with anticipation.

The big guy, Lenny, rolled forward off his heels, finding his footing. He glanced at his friend and then at the other girls. Embarrassed now. He pulled back, squared his hips ready to return the punch. Lolita braced; she'd been hit by bigger, she could take it.

The redhead's squeals were lost in a howl as Lenny dropped to his knees in front of Lolita. Samuel stood above him, a bloody knife in one hand, two coffee cups balanced on a cardboard tray in the other. He swiped the blade across the other boy's cheek. A stream of his blood mixed with Lenny's. The five girls fell silent, and for a moment the only sound was the moaning of the boy on the floor.

"Maybe we should take our coffee out," Lolita said as she looked at Samuel.

"Guess so." Sam pushed his way through the door. Didn't look back.

"Why are we going there?" she asked as they headed for the Ford.

"We're going to burn it down," he said.

"That'll be fun."

She looked back through the window as a crowd gathered around Lenny. Maybe Sam could kill. She leaned across the seat, careful not to spill the coffee from its spot in the cup holder. She kissed his cheek as he backed the Ford out and pointed it toward the highway. His eyes opened fully as he smiled.

⊢━━┿

Magazine Hill towers above the Bedford Basin, a bomb blast away from the sparkling waterfront properties of downtown Halifax. The Canadian Navy keeps its powder kegs and missile heads in the underground bunker cut into the rocky hillside. In 1917, a cargo ship stuffed with wartime munitions went off like a floating nuke in Halifax Harbour. The blast ripped a swath through the North End of the city, leaving two thousand dead. It also left a certain sensitivity to explosives on the waterfront. Thus, the magazine inside a hill, although that idea almost backfired, in a big way. The magazine nearly set off a second city-flattening blast when a barge loaded with bombs caught fire at its jetty in 1945. In the end, the bunker held, and now it sits like a dormant volcano while thousands of commuters crawl along the twinned highway cut across its summit. So far, the coughing Jake Brakes are the only things that go boom in the night.

Jimmy Williams craved a different kind of blast. He pushed the button to lower the window as the Escalade rolled over the top of the Magazine. He eased the MAC-10 out and unleashed a burst into the trees and boulders bordering the highway. The suppressor kept the sound and the muzzle flash to a minimum, but the bright tongue of flame still blinded him as the gun spit nine-millimetre slugs into the night. The short barrel jerked up and to the right. Williams grabbed the small strap that hung from the barrel and pulled down, adjusted his grip and poured another stream into the trees, fighting the gun, holding it steady.

He swapped out the spent clip for a fresh one from the kit bag. This was going to be a night to remember. He'd be a legend, Stallion elite. Shit, they might patch him straight to Nomad. A killer's killer. Most would never know why, but that was okay. The chosen few would know. Jimmy was the man.

He ran his gloved hand over the hot barrel, thought about Mapp. Guy had to be wired tight. How else could he know where Christmas and Neville were right now? Mapp was a real-deal motherfucker, no doubt. Williams would have to show him respect, maybe even give him that loyalty he wanted.

"Okay, Phil, this is our ticket. Here's what I want. The fuckers park in the underground lot. We go down and pick a spot near the elevators. That's where we wait. The Indian comes out, he gets it. If we get lucky, maybe Neville is with him, and we get two, but the Indian is our boy."

Phil Murphy didn't take his eyes off the road as he eased the stolen Caddy off Magazine Hill and into Bedford.

Williams slapped him with the hot barrel of the MAC-10. Not hard. He was in a good mood. Murphy glanced over.

"You got us a great car here, man. Tinted windows are perfect, but we still gotta wear the masks cause they got cameras down there."

Murphy reached down, grabbed one of the balaclavas, and struggled to pull it over his head as he drove. Williams grabbed the other and did the same as they nosed down into the ramp beneath the Sunnyside Mall.

Rows of underpowered lights suspended from the cement ceiling dumped a yellow glow into the deep darkness of the underground lot. Cement pillars lined the outer edge of each row of parking spaces. Most of the slots were empty—the stores closed early Saturday night—so there shouldn't be any witnesses. Williams pointed to a parking spot opposite the elevators. A sign pinned to the wall marked it as reserved. Caddy shouldn't look out of place there.

"Back it in, so I've got the angle on the doors and we can get out quick."

He bounced forward in his seat and drummed his fingers on the leather dashboard, the MAC-10 beside him on the seat. He reached up, moved the balaclava back and forth until the eye holes were just right, tested the power window a few times. He noticed the bikes tucked into a corner opposite the elevators.

"That's Neville's ride. Fucking Mapp, man. Yeah."

"Can't shoot him." Murphy expressing an opinion.

"The fuck you say?" Williams pressed the hot barrel into the back of Murphy's hand, pinning it to the wheel, smelling burning flesh.

"Can't shoot him." The big man didn't pull his hand free.

"Fuck, Phil, I heard it the first time. Just shut up. We get the shot, we bag that cocksucker. He's not a Stallion. Let's just hope he comes out with the Indian." Williams grabbed the balaclava and slid it left and then right again, pushed it up a little higher as black wool and sweat clouded his eyes.

+++

Halls Harbour huddles behind a breakwater on the muddy shores of the Bay of Fundy. Fog shrouded the wharf and the weather-beaten homes in the tiny village. A lobster restaurant and craft shop sat empty on the wharf. The Fundy tides are the world's most extreme and dictate the rhythm of the village. High tide, busy wharf; low tide, empty wharf. It was almost midnight when Samuel pulled to a stop in the gravel lot near the breakwater. Cones of light cut through the fog to the fleet below. The boats sat at awkward angles, their hulls planted in the mud. In a few hours, the tide would push around the breakwater and the fleet would rise to meet the edge of the wharf. By then, the parking lot would be filled with half-ton trucks as crews headed out to run the trap lines, but for now, the boats sat alone. Lolita jumped out and walked to the edge of the wharf, leaning over carefully to look down at the deck of the nearest boat.

It was cold, but she liked the fog; it was easy to disappear into it, especially at night. The restaurant and the homes stuck into the side of the hill were all dark. The lights glowing above the wharf were the only ones in the village. She watched Samuel grab two large red plastic jugs from the back of the SUV. She turned back to the boats while he went in search of fuel. She remembered coming here when they were little. She loved the trips, felt free when she was here, even if she couldn't talk to anyone. When the tide was high, and the boats were headed out past the huge boulders that made up the breakwater, she used to dream of being on one, heading out into the water where no one could reach her.

Lolita turned at the sound of a car pulling into the lot. A tan Mercedes eased up next to the Ford. Bobby Simms stepped out. Even through the fog, she could see that grin. Hated it. Simms walked over and stood beside her, lit a cigar, and looked down at the boats.

"Hey, sexy, where's your boy?" he asked.

Lolita looked around, but she couldn't see Samuel.

"What do you want, Bobby?" She looked up at him.

He leaned close, and she could smell alcohol mixed with the tobacco. He reached around and grabbed her, pulling her to him.

"If I want something, I'll take it."

Lolita went limp. Let him hold her tight to his body. She said nothing.

"That's my good girl," he said as he kissed her head and released her. "Maybe we'll play a little later. Now where's Sam?" He looked around the parking lot.

Samuel walked out of the dense fog near the restaurant. The red plastic jugs were gone. Moisture glistened where the wharf lights caught his curls. He had his hands stuffed inside his jacket pockets, probably holding the knife. Lolita thought of her own switchblade. The same one she used on that asshole in Boston and on the bastard's dead body.

"Don't touch her like that," he said as he approached.

"What's that? Come on, Sam, she's everybody's girl. You know that. Lots of Lolita to share. You know girls like her have always serviced men of God like us. Prostitution was born in the temples, Sam." He reached over with his left arm and pulled her close again, puffing the cigar. "So, little man, you called me here. Oh, before you get any ideas…" He reached into his pocket, pulled out a short-barrel .38, and pointed it at Samuel.

"I don't know for sure that you killed your father; maybe someone in the congregation caught wind of his evil ways and put him down. Maybe, but you look pretty good for it to me, so keep some distance." He squeezed Lolita tighter to his side.

"It doesn't matter who killed him, Bobby. His own evil was behind it. He deserved to die."

"Maybe. Whoever did it, he's gone, and that leaves us. You called me, Sam, so what do you want?"

"I'm going to the ranch. We need your alarm fob and keys. They're mine now." Samuel moved closer. "Now please, let Tatjana go."

"Tatjana. Fancy name for a whore, Sam. But I can see you have a thing for her." He pushed Lolita toward Samuel. "You'll learn soon enough. As for the ranch keys, forget it, son. They will never be yours." Bobby kept the gun pointed at Sam.

"There are some things we do need to clear up, and this is as good a spot as any. I'm afraid one of them involves your little tart here." He pointed the gun at Lolita. "I'm afraid she may have to be sacrificed to the bigger cause."

Lolita knelt down where she'd dropped her purse and pulled out her cigarette package. She lit a cigarette and then pushed the small box back inside the open bag. She hoped the purse muffled the click of the switchblade as she pulled her knife hand free. Bobby must have heard it. She saw him start to move the gun, aiming at her face now. She was low on his left side and came up fast, driving the knife high into the head of the big cat tattoo above his collar. He dropped the gun and screamed as he reached for the knife. He stumbled back and dropped. A wet smack rose from the mud bed. Lolita walked to the edge of the wharf and looked down. Bobby was face down in the mud, his arms spread at awkward angles, his legs twisted. He was trying to push himself up. His face fell back into the mud. The bow of a fishing boat cast a shadow over his body.

"I hope he left the keys in the car. Don't want to climb down there after them." Sam stood beside her, Bobby's gun in his hand. He pulled back to throw it. Lolita reached up, placing a hand gently on his arm.

"Let's keep it." He handed her the gun and headed to the Mercedes.

Lolita watched Bobby carefully. There was no more movement down there. She laughed. She'd wanted to kill people before, lots of times. She always thought it would feel bad when she finally did it; it felt great. Bobby deserved it. Maybe she'd feel sorry in the morning. By then the tide would have taken him far from here.

"Look, Tatjana." Samuel drew her attention away from Simms. He held a large ring of keys and a black plastic fob she recognized in the air above the car.

"Let's go to camp," she said as she walked back toward the Escape.

They drove up and out of the fog, leaving Halls Harbour, the mud, and Bobby Simms below. The crest of the mountain led them further east to the ranch. A full moon hung low in the sky above the Bay of Fundy to the left. It cast long shadows through the scrub spruce and pine lining the roadside. Lolita couldn't see the cabins yet, but she knew they were getting close. She wished she could light a cigarette, but the smell of gasoline was so heavy they had to keep the windows open just to breathe. She held her hands out through the window and looked at them in the glow of the moonlight. The blood was dry and looked black against her skin. She smiled as she turned each hand to see the patterns. Killing Bobby Simms was the most fun she could remember having, ever. Stabbing the guy in Boston was scary, but this was fun.

She laughed as she pulled her hands in and looked at Samuel. He hadn't said anything since they'd left Halls Harbour, and she loved him for that. They didn't need to talk. They'd been through it together and now they were getting even. Samuel reached over for the shifter as he slowed the Ford at the bottom of the hill. They rounded a steep curve shrouded by spruce trees and drove into a clearing. The moonlight bounced from the water far out in the bay. It cast a silver glow in the thin fog, a nimbus around the cluster of tiny cabins ahead. Her heart raced as she reached out and placed her hand on Samuel's.

"It looks smaller."

"Not as small as it will be." He pulled to a stop in front of the gate.

A large stone pillar stood at each side of the driveway. Ornate wrought-iron gates hung on each. The black iron rose up from the pillars to form a curled wave on top of each gate, the waves on the verge of crashing into each other where the gates met. A three-metre-high log fence led away from each side of the driveway, enclosing the compound. Near the top of the fence, each log was carved to a point like an old fort. A tiny red light blinked near the top of the fence on the far right. Samuel aimed the small plastic fob and pressed the button. The light went from red to green.

He grabbed Bobby's ring of keys as he stepped out. The headlights pushed his shadow through the gates and across the open field between the cabins and the main house. Lolita could hear the jingle of keys. She watched as he pushed the two gates in, and the iron squealed in the hinges as they moved slowly out of the way.

There was no sign of life beyond. The ranch was empty for much of the year. It operated through the heat of summer and into the early fall, and then on special occasions through the rest of the year. Samuel guided the Ford through the gates and headed for the main house.

She remembered the first time she had passed through those stone pillars. She was eight and excited to be starting her life in this new world. She remembered the thrill when she saw the expanse of water leading away from the bank and the thick growth of evergreens leading in every direction away from the fences. It was a paradise, a haven for a child of war.

She recalled how quickly the safe haven turned into a place of pain, more terrifying than the shells and bullets that took her parents. She was twelve when she left the ranch for the last time. The changes starting in her body meant she was no longer welcome. Her heart raced faster as the Ford stopped in front of the long single-storey house tucked into a treeline that hid the log fencing at the far side of the compound. The moonlight cast deep shadows along the foundation, but Lolita could see the row of windows there. Moonlight never entered, nor did the sun.

"Ready?" Sam asked as he parked the Ford a short distance from the house.

"Do we have enough gas for the cabins, too?"

"Sure. The wood is old; it won't take much."

Samuel lifted the first of the two plastic gas containers. It held twenty litres, and the weight pulled his shoulders forward as it cleared the rear bumper. Lolita reached in and pulled a tire iron from the back as he lugged the gas up the steps. She raced ahead and climbed onto the deck. Ignoring the big wooden doors, she made her way along the front of the house, swinging the tire iron and smashing the windows that overlooked the compound and the water beyond. There were three large windows on each side of the doors. She broke them all as Samuel unlocked the doors with Bobby's keys and headed in with the gas. She listened as he moved around. She wanted to join him inside, but she couldn't.

Instead, Lolita jumped off the end of the deck and walked to the far corner of the house. She knelt in front of the last of the narrow basement windows. She touched the glass with her fingers and tried to peer inside. It was too dark to see anything, but that didn't matter. She knew every inch of the room.

"Do it." Samuel bent low beside her, the gas in the can sloshing beside him. The red plastic glowed wet in the moonlight.

She punched a hole in the window with the curved end of the tire iron, and moved aside so he could pour gas through the opening.

"Yours, too." She moved quickly back to the deck and smashed another of the tiny windows. Her lips and eyelashes tingled as the fumes rose around them. They separated without speaking. Lolita stood near the first of the basement windows she'd broken, Samuel at the second. They each held a small rag. She smiled brightly at him as they ignited the rags and tossed them into the rooms that once held them captive.

CHAPTER 13

CARLA CAGE WORKED THE COMPUTER KEYS WHILE I WORKED the coffee machine in the corner. I still felt the buzz of our ride. The anger at Gunner had melted away somewhere between Peggys Cove and Bedford. We stayed on the secondary roads where she showed me what that ass-kicking custom of hers could do in the tight turns. I let her take the lead when we left. I never had a chance after that. She shot out of every corner like a bullet. When I caught up, we'd be back on the brakes diving into the next turn. She could ride.

I figured the QR teams were out tailing Samuel Gardner and Bobby Simms. I fought the urge to call them to see where our suspects were hanging tonight. Blair was at his desk, and one of the borrowed vice guys was on a phone in the corner. I wondered if Greg was sitting in an empty room down the hall. His car was in the garage. He'd be in the chaplaincy office waiting to comfort any cop smart enough to ask for it. Cops aren't that smart, even cops who've seen a woman crucified in a park. I thought our office would be a little busier. MacIntosh had called us in for a briefing. Looked like he hadn't called the whole team, must be looking for a peek at the Stallion video. I'd call that micromanagement.

I gave Carla a coffee. She was still wearing the tight jeans and T-shirt. Her bandana was sticking out of her back pocket and hanging down behind the chair. Her hair looked like it had never seen a brush. She kept running her fingers through it, trying to chase the helmet out of the head. She looked fantastic.

She was working on the Stallion security DVD, and I could see she didn't want me looking over her shoulder. I headed over to bother Blair instead.

"Hey, partner, how's the head?"

"Fine. You see the cement fist that hit it at the ride?" he asked.

"He was there. Tried to bait him, but he wanted none of it. Gave Williams a slap, and that didn't even get a rise out of him."

"Just as well. I want to try him again on my own." He turned in his chair, slowly.

"We can only hope. Anything new?"

"No new bodies."

"That's refreshing. Any new suspects?" I asked.

"No, but I'm pretty sure we're wasting our time on Bobby. I've been doing some reading about our stripper."

"I don't know. I've been thinking. Maybe they just tossed you because they hate cops. She might be a dead end."

"Now you sound like MacIntosh. He told me to leave it alone and start working real leads." He looked at me with that smile. "You and MacIntosh. That's a super-simpatico kind of team right there."

"Okay, smartass. I must be wrong. Lead me back to the light."

"I think she knows something. She knew who Gardner was, at the very least. Besides, QRT guys reported that Samuel went to see her. That's too much of a coincidence."

"You could be right, but I read the report too. Maybe QR got it right, and Samuel really was just looking for some distraction at a strip club. Doesn't feel like him, but he is a teenage boy. Maybe the QR team will get a better idea of his habits tonight," I said as I glanced at Carla.

"'Fraid not. MacIntosh sent them home. Our Special O guys too."

"Are you kidding me? Why?"

"Said he was sure they weren't runners, and he doesn't think it's worth the overtime if we don't have any solid reason."

"Jesus, what does he think is solid?"

"Don't know. Hate to say it, but he might be right on our boy Bobby."

"What did you find out that clears him?" I asked as I grabbed a chair and sat where I could talk to him and keep an eye on Carla's bandana. I needed the distraction.

"Like I told you this morning, Father Greg thinks he's no good for it."

"He said that Thursday, too, but I'm not sure I buy it."

"That was before Bobby confessed to him."

I stopped watching Carla and looked at my partner.

"You mentioned that, too. What kind of confession we talking about exactly?"

"The kind a priest can't repeat. If Father Greg still says he doesn't think Bobby did it—well, then, that means he didn't confess to the crime." Blair shifted uncomfortably in his chair.

I could almost feel the pain searing through his ribs. The bulk of his Kevlar showed under his shirt. I hoped that helped a little. I tried to make eye contact with him, but I was on his shiner side and pretty sure he couldn't see me. I went back to watching the bandana across the room.

"So what? Shit, Bobby isn't dumb enough to tell the truth to anyone. Not smart enough to know if a priest can keep a secret, either."

"I don't know. I think Bobby might know a lot about religion."

"Did you ask Greg what he said?"

"Tried, but all I got was a lecture on how to protect the reputation of the Church. I have a hunch, though. I think maybe he knows what's behind this and it has him in a knot. Like maybe he wants to tell me but can't find the right way. It's nothing he said, more what he didn't say. A gut feeling," Blair said.

"I told him there was some bad shit in Gardner's house. Maybe that's all he's worried about. Tell you what, maybe I'm giving him a pass when I shouldn't. His car's downstairs; why don't you go see if you can help him find a way to talk?"

"You sure?"

"Yes. We still don't know what the hell we're dealing with. If you got a hunch, we can't afford to ignore it."

"Oh, sure, all of a sudden my hunches matter. Where was your faith last night?" he said as he eased out of the chair.

"I should have been there, Blair, and I know it," I said.

"Good, I plan to dine out on that, so please continue to feel guilty while I go solve this. Maybe go tell the good sergeant how you let me down." He smiled, and slapped the back of my head as he headed for the door.

┿┿┿

My guilt nagged. I should have been with Blair at the bar, and now I was using him to pump my brother for information. Blair was a strong Catholic, and it wasn't right to ask him to push a priest. Still, Greg was my brother, and my pushing him would lead to old resentments. Things could go off the rails pretty fast. I really had no choice. Funny how easy it is to come to that conclusion when you don't want to do something. I was happy with the relationship Greg and I had built over the past couple of years, and I didn't want this case to burn it down.

To distract myself, I watched Carla working her magic on twin computer monitors. She had given up on her hair and had the black-and-silver *Live to Ride* bandana pulled back over her head and tied at the back again. Yellow flames ran down the sleeves of her orange-and-white T-shirt. The T hugged the curves of her body the way her bike stuck to the curves on the highway. The shirt slipped into a pair of black jeans that rode the muscles on her legs. They were tucked into a pair of heavy, black leather riding boots. Her fingers danced across the keys. Biker chick turned computer nerd.

The grainy image from the Stallion security tape filled one monitor. On the other was a box containing what I figured had to be image-enhancement tools. Her mouse was running up and down the list, clicking and sweeping. Tweaking and adjusting.

"How's it going?" I asked.

"Shitty image to begin with, but I think I can get us something."

I watched the right monitor as she worked the box on the left. I could see the image change, sometimes seeming to get clearer, and then hazy again. She'd readjust, and it would go back.

I fired up the computer on my desk to check for the latest updates. A canvas of local tattoo shops had failed to find the artist responsible for the horse on Sandy Gardner's hip. The shops were either reluctant to help, or it had been done out of town. The preliminary autopsy reports were in. His cause of death was ligature asphyxiation. The puncture had been post-mortem. One on the board for Dr. Ian. I clicked open the report on Thelma Waters and read the highlights. The summary was much bigger. Images of her body flashed in my mind as I scanned the list of injuries outlined by the ME. She was dead before most of them were inflicted.

Rage like that meant a serious psychosis or an intimate connection to the victim, maybe both. I believed the killer knew her and hated her. How could a silver-haired church secretary bring that kind of anger out in anyone? I closed the file and rolled my mouse over to the day shift report from the QR team. Shit, what difference did it make now? If the tail had been dropped, who cares where Simms and Sam were this afternoon? I closed the file before I read anything.

I moved to a table near the windows and checked the radio. The yellow LEDS showed it was rolling back and forth across the frequencies assigned to major crime. I turned the volume knob to confirm it was up. Radios are rarely placed in major-crime offices because they can be a noisy distraction. I wanted to be sure someone hadn't turned it down in protest. I was hoping the hotshots in QRT might be moonlighting against orders. They were known for that, and if they were out there, I wanted to hear it.

CHAPTER 14

GREG WAS STANDING NEAR THE ELEVATORS IN THE HALLWAY WHEN Blair stepped out of the office.

"Heading home, Father?'

"Oh, hey, Blair. Yes, unless you'd like a moment in the office."

The chaplaincy office was at the end of the hall beyond the elevators. It would be quiet and private, but Blair didn't want to sit on the leather couch for the chat. The office would give Father Greg a sense of control that wouldn't help with the questioning.

"No, I can ride down with you. I need to grab something from my car. Actually, I'm glad I ran into you. I have a couple more questions."

The elevator door opened, and the two stepped inside. Greg was in his black clerical clothing now. Blair figured he wore it for the cops who came to see him. He still looked young but more priestly.

"What can I help you with?" he asked.

"Father, you told me to do what I could to protect the reputation of the Church, of all churches, right?"

"Yes, and I believe you will."

"If I can, I will, yes. But you are going to have to help me."

"How can I do that?" He pressed the button for the parking garage.

"I think you know something that can help us stop this killer. I believe Bobby told you something. If that information includes the killer's motive, it is crucial that we know. It could be the difference between catching him now or seeing him kill again." Blair leaned against the back wall of the elevator and quickly regretted the move as the pain pierced his ribs. He cringed, and Greg reached over to touch his side. Blair's size often intimidated people. The busted ribs could prove an advantage. He wanted Father Greg to see him as more helpless than powerful.

"Blair, we talked about this. I am bound by the sacrament. You know that."

"Yes, Father, I do, but you are a man of God. Everything the psychologists tell us says this killer isn't finished. You can't stand by and let him kill another innocent person. There must be some leeway."

"You'd be surprised to know how little. I cannot violate a sacred trust. If I knew someone was in danger I could tell you that, but nothing more, and I can assure you, I do not know that."

"I don't want to rehash any of that. I believe you when you say Bobby is not the killer."

"Thank God."

"Still, he may have said something about the killer or at least the motive for the killings. How can sharing that violate anything that is supposed to be sacred?"

Blair could feel the elevator slow as it reached the bottom of the shaft. He didn't want the door to open yet. The intimacy of the small space would be lost.

"You say this killer may make some claims, claims that could hurt the Church. Well, it might be too late. The media mob is already going nuts because Pastor Gardner was found naked and dead in a garbage dump. If you think there is something worse than that, we need to know what that might be."

"As I said, if I knew anything about a person whose life was in danger, the Church would allow me to tell you in order to protect that person. In this case, I believe Sandy's church is in danger. That's the best I can do."

"You have to understand, Father. If we know the killer's motive we may be able to identify a potential victim you know nothing about, or better yet, identify and stop the killer. The thing with these investigations is that we never really know what it is that we are missing. The one small thing that can make all the big things slide together."

The elevator opened into a vestibule with glass doors to the left and right. It was the place where Blair had violated Cam's trust by telling Carla Cage what had happened to him in captivity. He hoped Father Greg would now be convinced to violate a different kind of confidence. Father Greg stepped out first and stopped, his right hand rising to his chest. He rubbed something under his shirt with his thumb as he thought. Blair had seen the move before. He seemed to be weighing his options, so Blair stayed silent. He felt his Blackberry vibrate in his jacket pocket. He stuck his hand in his pocket and pushed as many buttons as he could feel until it stopped. He felt something coming and didn't want to break the spell.

"Okay, I can tell you this. You should take care to protect those closely connected to the Little Maria Foundation."

"What? I'm sorry, Father. I mean great, thanks. Can you help me understand why?" It made some sense if you considered Pastor Gardner and Thelma Waters and their roles with the foundation. It made no sense when you tried to fit a stripper into the mix. Maybe she was just a waste of time.

"Blair, I've said all I can. Please understand that." The thumb worked the fabric of his black shirt as he headed for the door to the right. "I'm parked on this side." Blair followed him out.

━╋━

Jimmy Williams rocked in the seat, cursing the Caddy. At least he could pace in the van. He looked at Murphy locked behind the wheel. Not a move since he parked, not even to adjust his balaclava. Jimmy fought with his again. He couldn't seem to get it right. He moved it up, down, sideways, searching for light. Every time he found the holes, he'd stare at the bikes. The lean black Softail resting on its side stand, the hot cop's green bobber nestled beside it. Be a shame to kill her. Bitch had the look, the bike, all of it.

Even if she got caught in the shit, this was still his lucky night. He'd get the date tattooed somewhere. His thigh would be good. Next to those monster balls, the kind you gotta have to pull off a hit like this. He was gunning for the Indian, but it really didn't matter which cop he killed. He knew that. Any dead cop would keep the rest of them running scared for weeks. They'd be so busy looking under their beds for the boogie man they'd forget about the fucking preacher and stay miles away from Lolita.

He knew Mapp wanted the Indian first, but Jimmy wanted some trigger time with Cam fucking Neville, could taste dead cop in the air. He had to hold back. Get the Indian and Neville, too. Keep Mapp happy, then it would be easy street. He could see himself sitting in the clubhouse, wearing the patch. Smile at Gunner and not say a fucking word. He was going to do all his talking here and now. Fuck Gunner and his brother. All cops need killing, but some maybe more than others. Neville would be at the top of the list, put the Indian at number two. Neville was a traitor. Should have been killed the day he put that badge on. Everybody knew that. Fuckin' Snake should have taken care of this business a long time ago. Soft old man.

He rocked forward in the seat, grabbed the stupid mask again, pulled at the hole where his chin stuck out, tugged the whole thing a little to the right. He caught movement in front of the elevators. Blair Christmas and another man were talking. Man, Mapp had his shit wired fuckin' tight, putting a cop in the crosshairs like that. Christmas faced the Caddy. The swollen mess on the side of his face made Jimmy smile. Phil's handiwork for sure. The other man had his back to Jimmy and Phil. Oh yeah, baby. Fuck yes! It was Neville's curly head. Fucker, all dressed in black like some badass cop. Jimmy stroked the MAC-10, felt a bulge in his pants. Yes, baby.

"Get ready," he said, easing the window down.

Murphy pulled the shifter into drive, and they inched forward.

"Wait, wait, I need them on my side, so stay put until they come out, then just ease ahead a bit." Williams placed the tip of the suppressor on the armrest just below the open window.

Christmas and Neville walked away from him.

"Shit, they're going out the wrong door. Roll around past the bikes. Get to the other fucking side. Hurry up."

He grabbed at the mask again.

The navy blue Ford sedan sat alone in a row of empty slots at the back of the underground garage. Inspector MacIntosh pulled the leather case from the passenger seat and fished for the phone. His hand shook as he pressed the power button and watched the tiny screen come to life. A soft green glow bounced from the plastic trim at the centre of the steering wheel. He pressed the speed-dial button and waited, kept his eyes on the rear-view mirror. He knew this had been coming since he got the call from that stubborn Indian. God, how affirmative action was hurting his beloved force. Imagine, the Royal Canadian Mounted Police force made up of blacks, Indians, women, even people from countries he'd never heard of. Mounties wearing turbans, burkas even. God. Back in his day, every Mountie was a real man—a white man—and every Mountie knew how to follow orders. None of this goddamn freelancing these kids were into today. He'd ordered the Indian to find the man feeding cats in the park, that's it, nothing more. An easy assignment to keep him out of the way. But no, Blair fucking Christmas—like that's a real name–has to go off to The Fog Bank and get into a brawl. Well, Christmas was about to get a lesson in following orders.

"It's me," he said as a familiar voice answered his call. "No, no problem. I'm here. He's probably up there now. I called them both in, and Sergeant Cage too, to make it less suspicious," MacIntosh said. "Look, it's just that he's here because I called him in, and I'm getting worried that could spill back on me. I'm thinking maybe there's another way."

He held the phone from his ear and looked in the mirror, turning his head to be sure there was no one around.

"No, I know what's at stake. I don't think you do. He's one of us, a cop. A quota cop is still a dead cop if he gets shot, maybe more of a real cop if he takes one in the line of duty. I think I can keep this thing bottled up on my end for a little while. We need to take a breath and think it through. Let's not do something we can't undo."

He waited. He knew there'd be a speech. There was always a speech. He looked at the cement wall in front of the car. The reserved parking sign made him smile. God, he loved the little perks. Funny, when you chase power, you think you want the big things: the influence, the ability to control lives, change policy, destroy careers. He knew those things were fun, but they were complicated, sometimes slippery and hard to control.

It was the little things, though—the reserved parking, the better tables at the smart restaurants, the meetings that can't start until you walk in the room—that was real power. The perks that made all the bullshit worthwhile. Of course, his power also helped protect the most important perk of all. With great power comes great pressure. Men who are born to lead feel it more than those who simply fall into power through some quirk of fate. True leaders know they must grasp power, keep it, use it to protect and control those who are unworthy. The burden of true leadership is a price that must be paid. But there are ways to relieve that pressure, to escape for a short time. Great men also recognize that. Others never could, never would, accept that. He must now stand worthy of his power, show his true potential. He knew what was at stake. He interrupted the rambling speech.

"Never mind. Forget I said anything. Just jitters...I know that. Let's just get it done. But before we do, let me ask you. The Russian threat. Was that you?"

He smiled as he listened. The Russians, a brilliant touch. This morning's intelligence briefing included a warning about the Russian mob ordering a hit on an unnamed Mountie. The tip came from a Vancouver addict and snitch. No one knew whether to take it seriously or ignore it. The snitch had told his handler about the Russian mob's plan to kill a Mountie, but said he didn't know where, didn't know when, just knew it was coming in the next twenty-four hours.

MacIntosh had to admit, he couldn't have made that happen. He shut the phone off. Tossed it back into the leather briefcase and stepped out of the car. Smiled at the parking sign.

+++

Blair followed Father Greg through the glass doors into the parking garage. He needed to know what Bobby Simms had said about the Little Maria Foundation. He just had to ask the right question so that Greg could tell him without violating the sanctity of the confessional. Until now, the foundation had been little more than background. Now maybe it was a lead, at least that was something. He'd kick it around with Cam when he went back upstairs. Hell, with Gardner and Waters dead, were there any real big players left in the foundation? Mrs. Gardner probably. They'd need a list from her.

"Father, I'm going back upstairs to get a list of everybody associated with the foundation. I appreciate what you've done for us. Is there anything else, anything at all, that you can tell me that will help focus our search? Help us save lives?" He stopped walking behind Greg's parked car.

Greg turned to him, his hand still kneading the black fabric in the centre of his chest. He looked like maybe he regretted what he'd shared already. No way to help him with that. He would get over it if they caught the killer and saved some lives. He was about to say something when Inspector MacIntosh walked around from behind the cement box housing the elevator shaft. He wore a red musical ride sweatshirt over blue jeans. The tan leather briefcase he carried looked out of place with the casual outfit. A nod to the white shirt, even in street clothes.

"Good evening, Father Neville, Constable." He stopped halfway between the door and the space where Blair and Father Greg stood.

"Inspector. Working on a Saturday evening?" Greg asked.

"Case like this, no one gets a break until we catch the killer. Isn't that right, Constable Christmas?"

"Yes, sir."

"You headed home before our briefing?" The question sounded like a scolding.

"No, sir, just walking Father Neville out. I'll be right up. Cam and Sergeant Cage are upstairs now."

"Good, good. We're going to have to chat about last night, as well. You should never have been at that bar, but you were, and that means he should have been with you. See you up there. Good evening, Father." He moved to the glass door.

Blair pulled his Blackberry from his pocket and pushed the C on the tiny keypad. He lifted the phone to his ear to wait for Cam to pick up. Might as well warn him. He noticed a blacked-out Caddy with low-profile tires and trick rims rolling through the parking spaces behind Greg. It seemed odd. The driver was cutting across the parking grid, not heading for the exit. He lifted the phone to his ear as he noticed the passenger, a kid wearing a balaclava. That was strange. He looked past the kid to the driver and dropped the phone. Big man, big balaclava.

"Father, get down." He grabbed for the priest with his left hand as he drove his right under his jacket for his gun. A lone finger of flame reached out from the passenger side of the Caddy, and Father Greg seemed to leap into Blair's arms. He tried to push the priest down to safety as he struggled to pull the gun out from between them, fighting back the pain from his ribs as he moved. He stumbled backward and down with Father Greg tangled in his arms. He felt a strange vibration. The priest was shaking violently in some kind of seizure. His gun finally cleared, and Blair aimed at the SUV looming above them. He squeezed the trigger four times, fast. He couldn't tell if his aim was true. The gun was slippery, hard to hold. It was taking on a life of its own. He watched it rise higher as he squeezed one more time. The light suspended above erupted in sparks and flying glass. Then blackness. Blair wondered why all of the lights had gone out. He'd only shot one. In the darkness he saw Sue, her beautiful smile. Why was she here? He noticed his ribs were okay, no more pain. Father Greg started vibrating again.

Williams spotted the two cops as the Escalade cleared the entry to the elevators. Too bad Neville had his back to him again. He'd like to see the expression on his face when the lights went out. He locked eyes with Blair Christmas and saw the Indian drop his cellphone. *That's*

right, fucker, it's your time. At least one of them saw it coming. He shoved the 10 through the opening and let loose. He could see the back of Neville's black shirt billowing as the bullets found the target. He let the pistol ride up as the magazine fed the cylinder more lead, needed to clear Neville to nail Christmas. Head shot was all he had.

Shit. The two men fell in a heap on the cement. He pulled on the front strap to bring the barrel of the 10 down into them, but it was fighting him, still pulling up and away with a life force of its own. It went dry before he made the kill shots. He pulled it in and grabbed the final clip, made the switch, and went back to the window. His balaclava shifted as he tried to find the targets again.

"Stop the fucking truck, Phil. Give me a second here."

He jerked the balaclava back into place, and reached out to steady the gun on the lower frame of the window opening. He glanced over the sight to see the two men on the cement floor. They were still, blood spreading around them. Good sign. The sudden flash he saw was not such a good sign. It came from the left side of the blood-soaked black shirt. Christmas wasn't dead yet, and the bastard had his gun in play.

"All right, motherfucker, let's dance." A full-on gunfight now. Yeah, baby. "The cowboys are here. Time for you to die, Indian."

Williams wasn't sure if the high-pitched screams were coming from him, or if Phil was into it now. Couldn't be Phil. He poured more lead into Neville's back, trying to chew his way through to Christmas underneath. The mirror outside his window exploded and fragments of glass and metal sprayed his face. He tried to cover his eyes with his left hand as he kept the trigger pulled with his right. He couldn't keep the gun down with just one hand. It rode high and right again, shattering the doors at the entrance to the elevators, taking out a row of fluorescent tubes too. His balaclava shifted again. He pulled it back in place just as the magazine emptied. The thing went through thirty-two shells pretty goddamned fast. He watched Christmas squeeze off a harmless round into the ceiling before his gun dropped from his hand and his arm fell to the floor above his head. *Bingo.*

"Go, Phil! Go. Go. Go."

He tossed the empty MAC-10 on top of the kit bag. The barrel melted the vinyl. The sour smell of burning plastic mixed with the sweet smell of burned gunpowder filling the Escalade. He pushed the window button to raise the tinted glass back into place. He wanted to pull the oversized balaclava from his head, but not until he was hidden. The window rose up and disintegrated into tiny fragments as it cleared the door. Christmas must have put a hole through the door. Jimmy looked down, felt his legs and his side. *Nothing. Shit, too close.* His head banged into the shifter as he toppled left in the seat. The sound of screeching tires replaced the hissing of the machine gun's suppressor as Phil pulled a hard right turn and shot up and out of the garage. Williams fought with the fucking balaclava and struggled to regain his balance and sit up.

CHAPTER 15

I SAT AT MY DESK, TRYING TO LOOK BUSY, WHILE CARLA WORKED THE security disc. She rolled her eyes as Bon Jovi erupted from my cell. I punched answer.

"Hey, partner." Blair wasn't there. The line was dead. Pocket dial, great.

I smiled at Carla and shrugged as I put the phone back in my pocket. A panicked voice came from the police radio near the window. It was Inspector MacIntosh, and he was in trouble. I heard gunfire.

"Officer down, repeat, officer down. It's Constable Christmas. We are taking fire in the parking garage beneath the Sunnyside Mall. A civilian's been hit. Send backup. Now."

I couldn't believe what I was hearing. Blair was down, taking fire? How could that be? The civilian had to be Greg. *Please, God, no.* I had no gun. I pushed my way into the hall anyway. Carla was beside me.

"Was that real? It sounded like MacIntosh."

"It was. We have to get to the garage. Blair's in a gunfight down there." I looked at the LED display above the elevators. Both were on the ground floor. I ran for the stairs. I didn't know if Carla was behind me. I didn't care.

I slammed into the wall on every landing as the stairway reversed direction. I fought to keep the adrenaline down. I cursed myself for not going home to grab my gun after the memorial ride. I shouldered the wall one last time as I hit the bottom. I was jumping into a gunfight with no gun. I knew it was the wrong move, maybe a suicide move. I knew I couldn't stop as I kicked the push bar on the door and rolled low into the vestibule at the bottom of the elevator tower. There was glass everywhere as I crawled toward the shattered doorway. I could see Blair and Greg and blood just beyond the opening. So much blood. Too much blood. I could taste copper and smell gunpowder. The bloody buffet of battle so familiar yet so out of place here. I saw two heads, two sets of shoulders, no movement. Greg on top of Blair, blood pooling around them. I saw another body, another place. Explosions, jets over head, black smoke. I shook my head, willing the ghosts away.

"Neville, back away from the door and take cover by the wall." I rolled away from the entry to the wall, saw Inspector MacIntosh hiding in an open elevator, his gun drawn, a police radio in his other hand. "Wait," he said. "I've called it in. Cars are on the way."

I looked at him. His briefcase was open on the floor, papers spilled from the elevator into the small lobby. He must have opened it to get the gun. His Blackberry was there. I saw a second cell. A small black phone, a cheap burner. I didn't see another weapon, and I needed one. He was frozen. I'd seen it in battle before.

"Give me the gun," I said. "I'll clear the garage; you help them."

"No, not yet. Sit tight. That's an order."

He clutched the gun and stared wild-eyed at me. No way he'd let it go. The door behind me pushed open. I saw a gun ease out, and then Carla. Why did everybody else have a gun?

"Sergeant, you cover that entry until backup arrives." The inspector wanted both entrances to the vestibule covered. He was defensive now, no sign of fight in him. I crawled to the shattered doorway. I could see a gun near Blair's head, blood spreading toward it.

"Neville, get back."

I rose into a crouch and dove through the opening to the gun, grabbed it, and rolled away from the bodies, coming up in a shooter's stance. The gun felt sticky as I held it forward, gripped tightly in my right hand, the butt cradled in my left. I wished for the familiar feel of the C7 that had saved me in firefights in Afghanistan. The handgun would have to do. I moved my outstretched arms, my eyes glued to the sight at the end of the barrel. Nothing. I raced to the back of the elevator tower and around to the other side, peering over the barrel to the empty parking spaces. I circled around to the front, and back to the scene.

"Clear," I shouted as I ran to help my brother and my partner. I dropped the gun as I knelt beside them.

Greg looked so small sprawled on top of Blair. Neither moved as I lifted my brother away, rolling him gently over into my lap. Carla was beside me now, her gun still in her hand as she reached down and felt Blair's neck.

"He's alive," she said as she moved to Greg.

I should have felt some hope, some relief in those words, but all I felt was death. I'd handled dead bodies before and knew I was holding one now.

Carla looked up at me. "Put him down. We can save him."

I knew we couldn't, but I eased him to the floor anyway. She ripped open his shirt to check the wounds. His chest was gone, bone fragments sticking out of a red pulp of shredded skin. She knelt beside him, looking up at me.

"CPR. I can't, I don't think." She froze.

I leaned over Greg and placed my hands into the bloody mess where his chest should be. I pressed and released as bubbles and blood oozed through my fingers. Carla regained control, leaning over and blowing air into his mouth. We continued our dance with death as I heard sirens in the distance. I felt something sharp under my palm as tears blurred my vision. I thought it was a bullet fragment, but then I recognized it. The crucifix. Sobs came hard now, and I couldn't force my will into his dead heart any longer. I stopped the compressions and looked at Carla.

"Help Blair" was all I could manage.

She moved away. I reached into my dead brother's chest and took hold of the crucifix. I ran my fingers along the chain and felt for the clasp, again. I undid it, my fingers slipping in blood, again. I could see traces of gold but mostly blood as I held it in front of me. For the second time, I slipped it into my pocket and made a promise over a dead body.

I stood as the paramedics moved in. They paused at Greg and then scrambled over to Blair.

"He's got a vest on. Lot of hits on it, God, so many, but I don't think they went through. Holy shit." I heard the words and remembered his slow movements in my garage. Those busted ribs might have saved his life. Maybe Phil Murphy did him a favour. A beating, a blessing. Life can be like that. I wiped my eyes with my sleeve and looked down at Greg. So small, so helpless. Kid never had a chance. Our father hated him; his mother dumped him and ran for the nearest needle. His grandparents forced so much guilt into him it was a miracle he survived his childhood at all. I watched the paramedics ease Blair onto a stretcher. Why had I asked him to question Greg? Didn't I have the balls to question my own brother? Had I killed Greg and another partner?

Inspector MacIntosh was talking to two uniformed officers. Both had the yellow stripe down the side of their pants. Mounties. His chest out for his subordinates, his shoulders swaying as he surveyed the scene. A man in command of the situation. Probably saw a promotion in it. Carla was standing near him now, watching the paramedics lift Blair. I heard the inspector describe a black Escalade. He said it rode very low on an altered suspension, had oversized tires on shiny black rims with chrome accents. Heard him say the gunman and driver wore masks.

One of the uniforms, a pole-thin guy with stubble for a haircut, relayed the information using the radio transmitter clipped to the chest pocket on his vest. His Adam's apple popped as he spoke. A BOLO would go out on the Caddy in seconds. The second officer, shorter, with a belly pushing his own Kevlar, listened to the inspector. His eyes never left Greg. Inspector MacIntosh's gun hung at his side, the barrel banging slowly into his leg as he spoke.

I stepped over Greg to MacIntosh and grabbed the gun from his hand before he could react. I racked the slide back and saw the chamber was empty. I popped the clip and saw it was full. Smelled the barrel.

"What do you think you're doing, Constable?" MacIntosh asked, cowering slightly.

"You saw them," I said. "You saw the shooter, the car, you got a good look. You had time, and you didn't take a shot. You ran into that elevator and left them here to die. What the fuck is wrong with you?" I slammed the clip back into the gun and dropped it on the floor.

"I know you're upset, so I will forgive you that tone, but only once. Now suck it up and act professionally. I handled it by the book. Officer safety is paramount, and I took the necessary steps to ensure mine so I could coordinate a response. You disobeyed a direct order and damn near got yourself killed. Sergeant Cage witnessed that. Sergeant?" The inspector's chest puffed out, his sense of command back as he turned the focus on me.

Carla looked at me as she spoke. "I saw an unarmed officer run into a gunfight to protect his fallen partner and his brother. Bravest thing I've ever seen." I saw tears on her cheeks. Her hands shook at her sides.

"That's the kind of cowboy bullshit we don't need or want," said MacIntosh. "Discipline is the key in these situations. We have procedures, and we must adhere to them, damn it. For Christ's sake, Neville, you're not in some criminal gang anymore. You have to act like a professional at all times. You failed to meet that standard here. By a long shot." He looked at the two Mounties to emphasize the point. Neither looked at him.

I did look at him but said nothing. What could I say? The two uniforms looked at Carla and then at me. The heavyset guy nodded when he caught my eye. Every uniform on shift tonight would hear her version, not his. It was bullshit. I didn't do a damn thing that mattered. I ran through an empty garage when the fight was over. Accomplished nothing, saved no one. My brother was dead, and my partner was chasing him.

"Neville, we are the best police force in the world. As such, we have the best training." MacIntosh pointed to the RCMP uniforms. "At times like this, you must revert to that training. I know you're not a member. But still, the regional force has improved its standards, and you did not meet them here." That holier-than-thou Mountie bullshit again. "I can only hope you didn't destroy any trace while you traipsed around out here."

He was in full command now, all his confidence back. He'd turned his cowardice into proper procedure and my feeble attempt into substandard policing. Fine, I felt two grades below substandard.

"Sergeant Cage, let's snap into it here," MacIntosh said. "Seal off the scene for your team. We'll catch these guys, and when we do, what you find here will put the nails in their coffins. If you screwed up that evidence, Neville, it's all on you."

He locked eyes with me. What I saw was hate, pure and simple. I wanted to think it was fear, but it wasn't. It was hate, fuelled by an overpowering sense of superiority. I wasn't good enough to make the grade on his beloved force, and that meant not good enough to be called a cop. At the moment, I didn't care; maybe he was right. Why the hell did I ever become a fucking cop? If I had stayed in the club, Greg never would have become a police chaplain, and I never would have met Blair. I sure as shit would never be taking orders from some asshole in a white shirt. Guy like MacIntosh would have been buried before he got any rank in a club. Fuck, guy like MacIntosh would never make the grade in any real club.

I watched the ambulance doors close. One paramedic stayed inside with Blair, the other ran around and jumped in behind the wheel. The big truck was moving before his door was shut. Another team of paramedics stood beside a second ambulance. They were looking at Greg's body, wanting to take him away but knowing he was evidence now and had to remain where I'd left him. I looked back at the inspector, his glare still directed my way, a smile on his face now. My right hand seemed to enter the scene on its own. I watched it connect with his chin. A clean shot but a cheap one. MacIntosh dropped. It should have felt good. It didn't.

+–+–+

The highway between Bedford and Halifax was filled with lights, sounds, and sensations, familiar and surreal. I rode hard, grateful I had the bike. I needed the solitude. I kept seeing Greg's open chest and my hands inside looking for life, finding none. Images blurred in my mind. Pulling the crucifix from Ronald, pulling it from Greg. Blood. More blood. MacIntosh falling. Ropes in the air, coming down fast. Pain. I remembered how, after the worst beatings in Pakistan, my mind would somehow leave my body, and nothing would feel real anymore. I had that feeling now, like everyone else knew what was happening, but I was lost, drifting.

The scene inside the hospital didn't help. I leaned against a wall and watched the chaos. Cops filled the corridor and the tiny waiting room beside the intensive-care unit. Most wore street clothes. Many were from the major-crime team, others off-duty patrol officers who had come from home after learning one of their own was down. No one approached me. Word of my attack on the inspector had travelled fast, and none of these cops was about to buddy up to me. *Fuck them all*. The only good cop in the building was in surgery. The hospital was in lockdown mode, standard after a shooting. Shooters have followed their victims here to finish the job. Security guards wearing bulletproof vests stood outside the intensive-care unit, others in the parking lot. Vests but no weapons. Targets. The badges clipped to the belts in the hallway meant they weren't needed. Sue Christmas ran down the hall toward me. She grabbed me and looked up with terror in her eyes. Her pain pulled me back.

"How is he? What happened?" She looked at the blood on my hands, my shirt, my face. "My God, are you hurt, too?"

"It's not mine. It's Greg, he's..." I couldn't finish.

"He's what? Is he hurt, too? How can that be? God, Cam, talk to me."

"He's dead, Greg's dead." I heard the words come out, couldn't really believe them. "Blair's going to be okay, Sue. I'm sure of it. He was wearing his vest."

"Oh my God. He didn't want to wear it. I made him. For his ribs. I told him it would help."

"Well, you saved his life. Most of the bullets hit the vest. One went through his neck though, and he was hit in the leg, too. He lost a lot of blood, but he's going to make it. I know it." I needed her to believe it. I needed to believe it.

She raised her hand to her mouth and looked at me. The sparkle that normally danced in those eyes was gone. It was the moment every cop's wife dreads, not a fear or a nightmare now. It was real. Her shoulder-length brown hair framed the soft features of her face. She looked like an angel, and my heart ached for her. I'd kill for her, and now I couldn't help her when she needed it most. I pulled her into my arms and held her. It was all I had.

Chief Simon Davis stepped off the elevator. Superintendent Lynn Surette was with him. The two highest-ranking police officers in metro were a contrast in styles. She had close-cropped black hair, a stern face, and ramrod posture. Her dress uniform was creased and spotless. The gold buttons gleamed on the front of her tunic, the braids on her shoulders just as bright. He was wearing blue jeans and a pullover sweater. It hung on him loosely. He stood a head above her, his shoulders twice as broad. The ball cap on his head showed a police crest, the only hint that he might be a cop. They headed toward us, but stopped as Inspector MacIntosh stepped out of the waiting room to intercept them. The chief locked eyes with me for a moment. His nod was all compassion. I knew that was about to change.

A nurse stepped out of the glass doors from the ICU. She looked at Sue and stopped.

"Are you Mrs. Christmas?" Her voice was soft, caring.

"Yes, how is he?" Sue stepped away from me.

"He is out of surgery. He made it through okay. They stopped all the bleeding. Now, we wait. He will stay in recovery upstairs for now. They will bring him here to ICU in an hour or so." She looked at the crowded hallway. "I can take you inside the unit now. It is quieter, and you can wait with us. The doctor will be down to speak with you in a moment."

She led Sue back through the glass doors. I wanted to follow, to help her, but there was nothing I could do. I had to face the music. Chief Davis walked up as Sue disappeared behind the frosted glass.

"What's the word?" the chief asked.

"He's out of surgery now. Looks like he'll make it."

"What the hell happened?"

"Don't know, Chief. This makes no sense. We thought Bobby Simms or maybe Samuel Gardner might be good for the murders. But this, neither of them could do something like this." I said. "Last night, Blair got into a scrap at The Fog Bank when he went to question a stripper. Her name was in Gardner's day planner, or we think it was her name."

"A stripper. How does that play?"

"I don't think it does. We both saw it as a long shot. Maybe this is in retaliation for the fight and has nothing to do with the murders. I can chase that down."

He put his hand on my shoulder, shaking his head.

"No, no, Cam, you can't." I don't think I'd ever heard him use my name, always rank. "I'm sorry about Father Greg and I know you want to avenge that. You're too close now."

"Look, Chief, we both know I can get information that no one else can get near. The Fog Bank is a Stallion club."

"Doesn't matter. They won't have it. I have to suspend you." He nodded his head toward Inspector MacIntosh and Superintendent Surette. They were watching us. "You slugged him, Cam. I can't let you walk out of here with that badge. Every uniform out there tonight is talking about two things. The shooting and the blue-stripe constable who dropped the yellow-stripe inspector. I can't let that sit, and you know it."

"Uniform stripes don't mean shit out there, Chief. Too bad they mean so much in here."

I looked past him to the two senior Mounties.

"Well, it matters more than you know. You have to sit this thing out and let me smooth it over with them."

No way I was sitting on any sideline.

"Not going to happen, Chief. You know that."

"It has to, Detective Constable Neville." Being official now. "This is bigger than you. Bigger than Father Greg or Blair. We have a unique policing partnership here, but it's fragile, and you just put it in jeopardy. This model is being looked at nationally now. It is a critical time. I'm sorry. I need to take that badge."

I looked at the chief. I respected him. He'd bent the rules to get me on the force. Still, he was a bureaucrat first and a cop second. Had to be that way, I guess. Well, fuck that. Nothing slides, not a fucking thing. I was wearing my badge on a chain around my neck. I pulled it off and tossed it to him. Inspector MacIntosh ducked back inside the waiting room as I walked past.

✛

I couldn't find my bike in the hospital lot. Couldn't remember parking it. A security guard approached me cautiously, saw the blood, and relaxed. Guess it looked like I belonged. He helped me find the bike, and I headed for the clubhouse. I'd find answers there. I still didn't think the stripper was connected to the Sandy Gardner murder, but I didn't care who had killed Gardner or why anymore. I needed to know if tonight's shooting was connected to Blair's fight at The Bank. The clubhouse held the answer. I thought about Greg as I rode from the hospital to the North End. Thought about his limp body. Thought about Blair and Sue. Sometimes when you ride, the wind pulls tears from your eyes. You get used to riding like that.

Ronald's ghost rode with me. It wasn't the first time. His limp body was still confused with Greg's in my mind. Ronald was my brother over there. I remembered his last words, calling me an asshole with a hero complex. Laughing it off, flashing me the finger and then bleeding to death because of me.

I remembered hiking through the mountains, dragging those chains and feeling dead inside after my escape. I wore his cross then, heard his voice. I wished he'd talk to me now. That same blood-covered crucifix was in my pocket, and I felt dead again. My decision to stay on that ridge got Ronald killed, and I live with it every day. Was I responsible for getting Greg killed? Could I live with that? What had I missed? Did I set it all in motion?

I thought about Bobby. Simms could have been gunning for me and hit Greg by mistake. I pissed him off, pushed him hard to see if he would break. Did he? Could he have been the trigger man?

Made more sense than a Stallion connection. I'd find Bobby. He'd talk. I rolled to a stop at the gates. A prospect stepped out of the shadows. He knew me, nodded, and slid the gate open. I rode inside and backed into a spot at the end of the line of Stallion bikes.

I could smell the pot before I even made it to the door. Inside the smoke was like a morning fog. I saw Gunner sitting with Snake and lifted my hand as he started to get up. Stopped him. Everyone in the bar was looking at me. I looked at my hands. They were shaking. They were covered in blood. I was covered in blood. Jimmy Williams stood behind the bar, he was bloody, too. His face was cut below his left eye. Looked like there'd been a little prospect training going on. I fought the urge to go break his neck. Snake would not allow it. I needed Snake now more than ever. If the Stallion was behind the shooting, I could not approach him as a cop. If the Stallion was not behind the killing, I needed him even more.

The street would find Greg's killer first, and the street stopped at Snake's door. It had ears, and what it heard made it back to the clubhouse, fast. The Stallion grapevine would give up the shooter. The club would know who it was long before the police did. The club didn't have to prove shit in a court. Justice started and ended in this room. There was only one way for me to plug into that kind of information, that justice. I felt every eye in the place as I walked across the bar and entered the back office. I drove my fist through the glass on the trophy case. It felt good. I pulled my Stallion cut off the hook, lifted it to my face, and smelled the familiar sweetness of the leather treatment that kept it soft. Felt the warmth of the leather against my skin. I pulled it over my shoulders and headed back into the bar.

Every patch in the place was standing now, looking from Snake to me. The curved Nomad rocker leading up from my waist to my heart meant he had no real say over this set of colours. I wasn't a member of his charter, I was another member of the homeless Stallion elite. I nodded to the stairs to show him proper respect in his house. He headed up to hold church. The patches all fell in line behind him. Gunner stayed in place, staring at me, a wry smile on his face, joy. I hated like hell to kill that feeling, but I had to.

"You finally come to your senses?" he said as he walked toward me. "Jesus, is that blood?"

"It's Greg's."

"What the fuck? He in a car wreck? He okay?"

"No," I said. "He's dead. Someone cut him in two with a machine gun. Took my partner down, too. I think maybe they were gunning for me."

Gunner didn't say a word. He reached out and pulled me to his chest. We stood there for a moment in the middle of the crowded clubhouse. No one made a sound.

—+—

Every Stallion charter has a space set aside for church. Some have small rooms, some use kitchens or bars. The bigger charters have better rooms. In the mother house, it's like the boardroom in any office. A long wooden table sits in the middle, surrounded by high-backed leather chairs. In this boardroom, the walls are covered in the Satan's head corporate logo printed on rows of flags. Each flag signed by the members of a Stallion charter. The Halifax flag hangs above the tallest chair at the head of the table. Snake was in that chair, waiting as we entered. The other patches were in place around the table. Gunner took his seat at the opposite end of the table, furthest from Snake. I closed the door and stood at the back of the room. A long time since I'd been to church.

Snake slammed a wooden gavel onto a Satan's head carved out of oak on the table in front of him. The meeting was underway.

"Brother," Snake said, "you're standing here covered in blood, wearing that cut. It was yours, could have been again. Not so sure this is how that is gonna work. Don't know that you're ever going to walk out of here. Talk."

"Didn't expect to put it on again, Snake, but here I am." I looked at the faces around the table. "Someone attacked our family tonight, brothers. Gunner's, mine, the Stallion family. Greg was shot to death. Say what you want, he was the son of the founder, too. 'An attack on one, an attack on all. Blood for blood, nothing slides.' Not a fucking thing." The Stallion code.

Snake looked at Gunner. I couldn't see my brother's expression, but I knew he wanted payback as much as I did.

"You know you can't just walk into this thing and then walk out again when this ends," Snake said. "You're a cop, brother. Not many in this club trust you anymore."

"That's my doing. I own it, and I'll try to make it right. The badge was a job, Snake. This is who I am, who I need to be." I realized it was true.

I was never at home behind the badge. It was Ronald's dream for me to be a cop, the opposite of an outlaw, he used to say. The ultimate proof I could rise above myself. I did it for him, for Greg, for two dead men, not for me. I still hated the drug lords who killed Ronald Gosse, always would, but I also knew I'd never been accepted as a cop and wondered now if I would ever be accepted here again.

Gunner stood and walked over to me. He embraced me again as he had downstairs. He turned back to the table.

"Brothers?"

Grease moved first. He was seated at Snake's left. He walked the length of the room and put his hands on my shoulders. A warmth spread from those hands and filled my heart. The cranky old bastard hadn't said a word to me since I betrayed the club. He'd taken it harder than most. Probably because he was more of a father to me than the old man ever was. I watched the tears fill his eyes, knew he saw the same thing. I pulled him close, slapped his back.

One by one, the senior patches stood, and the men I rode with walked to me. There were eleven men at the table; three stayed seated. They were all members who patched in after I left. I respected that. The embraces my brothers gave me were real; those men were not yet my brothers. In the end, Snake stood and walked to me. He looked in my eyes.

"Welcome home, brother. Don't make us kill you."

I was back.

Downstairs, the party was rocking, even without the patches. The band took the stage without Gunner. A top-heavy blonde in six-inch platforms stumbled to the bar. Her *Ride-a-Stallion* T was cut up the middle to reveal a deeply tanned stomach with a jewelled Satan's head piercing just above the navel. A cupid tattoo stamped her left hip, his arrow pointed down into her crotch. Her denim miniskirt was split at the side. From a distance, she was a hot ten, but up close, Jimmy could see the beef-jerky complexion of a meth head. Lot of makeup trying to hide it, but there just isn't that much makeup. She smiled at Jimmy, reached over and touched the gash on the side of his face as she placed an empty glass on the bar. He wanted to plunge a knife into her stomach and carve out that Satan's head, use it for himself.

Williams poured her drink and watched her stagger away, maybe still a ten from behind. He could feel her touch on his face. He reached up to touch the spot. A piece of the mirror must have caught him. Gotta give the fucking Indian credit, he went down shooting. Jimmy hoped he left behind a good scar. Better than a tattoo. He looked past the staggering blonde to the stairs.

Neville was alive? He'd seen his shirt covered in blood. The fuck must have been wearing a vest, but there was no damned way a little Kevlar could have stopped that much lead. He emptied a clip into the bastard's back, saw the shirt take the heat as the slugs cut through. Worse than seeing him still breathing, he was wearing a Nomad patch. Jimmy's crowning moment, gone.

One of the Litter Box Boys arrived and headed to the bar. Good kid. A real earner who didn't go for all that rap bullshit most of the boys were into. Still sporting the baggy jeans, white T, and half-cocked ball cap, but Williams knew his heart wasn't in it. If he was here, it was business. Jimmy flagged the prospect by the door to come back and take the bar. He led the street kid to the backroom.

"Hey, man, some fucked-up shit out there tonight. Cops shutting every corner down. We not going to make the mark tonight, not even close."

No surprise. Even if Neville survived the shooting, the Indian cop should be gone. Cops would turn up the street temperature either way. That would eat into profits, but that was collateral damage. If the Litter Box came up short tonight, tomorrow would be a banner day. Addicts are great customers.

"They saying anything?" Williams asked.

"No, man, just asking shit, but word is some priest got killed, and a cop took some hits."

"Priest, what fucking priest?" Williams knew he'd only shot two people, both of them cops. There was some old fuck in the garage when it went down, but he ran before Jimmy could tag him.

"Don't know, man, but one of the hos saying it's Gunner's brother. He got a priest brother?"

"Yeah, man, he was at the blessing. No one would kill a priest. Hos don't know shit," Williams said it even as the panic began to grow inside. He knew the street girls were the first to hear anything. Even when their mouths were full, their ears were working.

"Look, tell the boys to shut it down. Don't worry about the mark. We'll make it back tomorrow."

"You the man."

The kid headed back into the night. Jimmy flipped open his cellphone. He punched in Phil's number.

CHAPTER 16

Sunday morning

A CAR I DIDN'T RECOGNIZE SAT IN MY DRIVEWAY, NEAR THE GARAGE.
I slowed the bike to a stop in the street and watched the driver's door
open. Carla Cage stepped out. Reaching inside my pocket, I pushed
the button on the garage-door opener and rode past her as the door
slid up. She walked in as I took off my helmet. She was wearing a loose
sweater above her jeans and still had the riding boots on.

"Cam, what are you doing wearing that patch?" There was ten-
derness in her eyes. She looked soft and beautiful in that bulky sweater. I felt something in my chest move. My emotions were raw, and I
didn't want to deal with them or with her.

"I'm back in," I said as I pulled the vest off and hung it on a hook
beside the workbench.

"You can't be serious. They'll fire you. It's bad enough you hit
the inspector, you can't let them see you wearing that," she said.

"That gang I'm out of." I moved away, back toward my bike.

"What do you mean? They won't fire you for what you did. Your
brother is dead, for God's sake, your partner shot. Even MacIntosh
isn't dumb enough to push it." She followed, reaching out and touching the stain on the front of my shirt.

I had no time for this. I couldn't let her plant any doubt in my
mind. I needed the club now and didn't want to hear what the con-
sequences would be.

"Carla, the chief pulled my badge, took me off the case. I decided I am still on it. Probably not a good idea for you to be here.
Bad for your career."

She stood in front of me, looking up but not saying anything. I started to, but dryness in my throat choked it off. She reached up and stroked my cheek. I knew there was blood there, too. I wondered if she was wearing her bloody T-shirt under that sweater. I realized it wasn't a good idea to think about what was under that sweater. I leaned down to meet her mouth as she stood on her toes. Her kiss was soft, like her caress. She pulled her lips away and looked in my eyes, her hand still on my face.

I took her hand, kissed it, and then pulled it down.

"Bad timing," I said.

"It doesn't have to be. We could sleep on it, see how we feel in the morning."

I looked outside. It was daylight. She must have spent the night in my driveway.

"When I wake, I'm going to put that back on. I will find my brother's killer, Carla. The club has already put the word out."

"Then you don't have to put it on. They will find him, and we can arrest him. Don't throw your life away. Father Greg wouldn't want that, and you know it. I saw you take his cross, Cam. That must mean something."

I pulled it out of my pocket. The gold shone brightly through the cracks in the dried blood. She took it and opened the clasp. I leaned forward so she could put it around my neck.

"It was never his, you know." I felt the tears return, let them roll down my face.

"What do you mean?"

I told her about Ronald. I don't know why. I think I just wanted to sort out my own feelings, make sure I was making the right choice.

"So why did Greg wear it?" she asked when I finished.

"I tried to give it to Ronald's family when I got back. They said I should keep it. I felt guilty wearing it, so I hung it here in the garage. I went through a bad spell. Greg pulled me out of it. I gave it to him the day I took the oath. He said he'd wear it as a reminder to pray for Ronald and for me every day."

"Sounds like he wanted to take your guilt away," she said.

"I know. A real fixer, Greg."

"He looked up to you, Cam. He loved you. Why do you think he became our chaplain? He didn't follow Gunner into the clubhouse, he followed you."

I knew that was true, and it had gotten him killed. The chain around my neck now had two bodies weighing it down. I was convinced something I'd done or not done had triggered the violence, that someone gunning for me had killed my brother. I couldn't explain that to her any more than I could explain why I was walking away from the career she loved.

"Carla, I need to get some rest. I have a funeral to arrange."

"Okay." She paused as she turned to leave. "Do you think I'll ever get past this garage?"

"I don't think you'll be able to get past that patch."

┿┿┿

Bad news spreads fast. Satellite trucks lined the street in front of the hospital that morning. I was running on three hours' sleep.

A line of cameras pointed at the pretty people standing along the edge of the sidewalk. The hospital loomed behind them. I'd tuned in at home and knew what they were saying. Words like "shocking," "stunning," and "unprecedented" were being sprinkled liberally over the briefest summaries of the facts. The death of a young priest was the big headline. By now, Greg was being cast as the greatest hope of a struggling faith. He was doing in death what he wanted so much to do in life, casting the Catholic Church in a sympathetic light. That would change, I thought, before this mess sorted itself out.

If Greg was the martyr, Blair was the hero. The cop who took his handgun into battle against a machine gun. Reporters talked about a city holding its breath, waiting for word from the doctors. Halifax, it seemed, needed him to live if it was to survive this grim tragedy. A hero cop clinging to life, it didn't get much better than that for the media. I figured Blair was past clinging by now. I looked across the street to the Halifax Common. People walked dogs, tossed Frisbees, rode skateboards. A city holding its breath looks just like a city enjoying another Sunday morning.

It was easy to slip inside the hospital unnoticed. The reporters were so busy staying on top of the latest developments, they weren't looking beyond the glass lenses in front of them.

The hall was empty now, the crisis over. The nurse from last night was still behind the counter. She smiled as I walked up, told me I could have five minutes, and let me through the frosted glass doors into the intensive-care unit. I was grateful she didn't ask to see my badge.

I get this strange sense of vertigo in hospitals. The intensive-care unit made it worse. I felt the floor tilt under me as I walked past cubicles where the near dead lay below machines that did the work damaged hearts and lungs couldn't. The air was thick with disinfectant and decay. Nurses sat in each cubicle, keeping an eye on the machines and the patients. One patient, one nurse. ICU ratio. A nurse who looked to be about eighteen was busy writing on forms in a binder, her eyes darting up to the patient and back to the papers. The man sitting at a desk outside the next cubicle seemed more relaxed. He leaned back in his chair, watching his patient and the clock. There was a nurse in front of Blair's cubicle. She nodded as I approached, a ton of empathy in the glance. Almost cured the vertigo, she was that good. Only the best in ICU.

Sue looked as bad as I'd ever seen her. Blair looked worse. His bed was surrounded by too many machines for it to be anything but bad. They were anchored to him with wires and tubes that disappeared beneath the white sheet that covered a body I knew to be strong and fit. Funny how frail it looked here. That brought the vertigo back. I could see lights flashing and diaphragms rising and falling, and the comforting digital mountain range running across the front of the heart monitor. The reporters were smarter than I thought. "Clinging to life" seemed pretty damn accurate. I hugged Sue and looked past her at my former partner. I'd never seen Blair so still and quiet. I didn't like it. It had to be harder for her.

"What are the doctors saying?"

"He lost a lot of blood, and they don't know if he suffered any brain damage before they started replacing it. They say the next forty-eight hours will be the real test. All we can do is hope and pray."

I moved over to the side of the bed and took his hand. I squeezed and watched for a reaction. There was none.

"I'm so sorry about Greg, Cam. How are you holding up?" Sue joined me at the side of the bed, leaning into me and wrapping her arm around my waist as we both looked at Blair. It felt good. "My God, who did this?" she asked.

"I don't know, but I am going to find out. I promise you that."

She looked up at me. "The superintendent was here last night. She says you can't do that. They won't let you on the case. She says the chief suspended you. What's going on?"

"It's been a long time coming, Sue. I'm going back with the club. They'll find who did this faster than we ever could with a badge."

She stroked my cheek; I remembered Carla doing the same thing and felt a sense of loss that I couldn't really explain.

"I know it's been hard for you. Blair says you're the only one facing more discrimination than him."

"That's only because the racists try to hide their hate from him, but it's okay for cops to hate dirtbag bikers. No one hides it from me."

"I'm glad you're going with the club. I want you to find whoever did this, and I want you to hurt them. Is that wrong?"

"Of course not. It's the rightest thing in the world."

We held onto each other and watched the machines keep the man we both loved alive.

Greystone Drive sits on the high side of Herring Cove Road in Spryfield, right in the middle of the Litter Box. Thousands of commuters roll past it twice a day. Most don't see it, don't want to. I've burned a few nights there, hunting the illusive urban beast known as the witness. Thought I saw Bigfoot there once, but never so much as a smell of a witness. Spryfield has a hard-earned reputation as a high-crime/low-rent part of Halifax. It's been the battlefield for some of the bloodiest drug wars the East Coast has ever seen. There are third-generation dealers working the same streets, shooting at the same enemies their grandfathers tried to kill. Greystone stands out, a tough spot in a dangerous place.

Gunner leaned his bike into the turn ahead and accelerated up into the public-housing complex turned shooting gallery. I rolled on the throttle and chased him in, knowing the patch would make people more talkative than the badge. Greystone is home to a hardscrabble mix of people on the way down or struggling to get back up. In between, you find drug dealers and prostitutes who decided long ago up isn't worth the effort.

Cookie-cutter triplexes line the small lanes that make up Greystone. Some housing-authority bureaucrat tried to bring a little cheer to the 'hood by naming the side streets Lemon, Orange, and Cranberry, and painting the two-storey units in sunny yellows, reds, and sky blues. Bullet holes look even more disturbing in the happy paint on Cranberry Court. The forensic teams have a system they use in places like Greystone. They photograph the holes left after a round of gunplay. Then they use a permanent ink marker to draw a circle around each hole. Next time they catch a call, they just look for the holes without circles. Saves time.

Gunner rolled to a stop in front of a cheery yellow triplex on Lemon, near Goldfinch. A few bullet holes showed near the door on one of the units. They were all circled. Quiet Saturday night here, at least. I started to ease into the curb next to him. I throttled up and pulled away when I saw the broken glass and needles pooled near the storm drain at my feet. When you only have two tires, you tend to get sensitive about stuff like that. I parked at a cleaner spot near the next triplex, walked back, and checked Gunner's tires. They were okay. He was admiring an RX-8 parked across the street. The car was tricked out to the tune of fifty grand, and it sat there unmolested. Easy to see who was running things in the 'hood these days.

A heavyset guy with short, spiked red hair sat on the stoop in front of the unit on the far left. He looked to be about twenty-five.

He was punching the keys on his cellphone. He looked up at us and clicked a picture with the phone. If the patches impressed him, he didn't show it. We walked over, and he leaned a little onto his hip, making sure we saw the flat black grip under his sweatshirt.

"Delete that picture, asshole," Gunner said, standing over him.

"Delete it? Fuck that, man. I'm gonna tweet it. Badass bikers in the 'hood." He looked down at the phone and kept pushing keys with his left thumb. His right hand was resting on the butt of the gun now.

Gunner was about to grab the cellphone when the door above opened, and a guy wearing a clean, white T-shirt, baggy blue jeans, and a sideways ball cap walked out. He stepped past the muscle on the stoop and offered a fist bump to Gunner. Two guys stepped out on the stoop next door wearing hoodies over the same kind of baggy jeans. Both had their hands stuffed inside the pockets in their hoodies. More guns at the dance. The guy standing with Gunner gave me a long hard look. Pretty sure I busted him once, but I couldn't remember his name. Looked like the smell of the badge was still on me. I hoped it didn't complicate things.

"Hey, man, that guy's a cop," he said to Gunner.

A flash of fear lit up the face of the guy sitting on the stoop. Hate quickly replaced it as he shifted his weight back and tried to hide the gun.

"Not anymore, he's not," said Gunner. "He's with us."

"That's fucked up."

"Yeah, maybe, but it's not your problem, T. J. Your problem is explaining why you weren't back at the clubhouse yesterday. I thought I made myself clear," Gunner said.

T. J., Tyler Jones, I remembered him now. I remembered the bust. We bagged him for selling stolen car parts. Nothing big, but nothing he'd forget. I took another look at the guy on the stoop. I remembered Tyler had a younger brother. If that was him, he'd been hitting the weights pretty hard and probably juicing to help things along.

"Man, I came to see you." He looked at me as he spoke to Gunner. "I went over, but there were cops outside and a bunch of squares hanging around. I had a nine in the car with me and didn't want to bring any heat your way, so I kept on rolling."

"What, your phone not working? Never mind. Fuck yesterday. Look, we need some information now." Gunner doesn't waste a lot of time.

"Sure, man, let's talk inside." T. J. moved past the guy on the stoop. I got the impression he was trying to lead Gunner away to avoid dealing with me.

The redhead stood after Gunner moved past him toward the door. He smiled and looked down at me. "He stays out here," the kid said. If there was a signal between T. J. and the guy, I missed it. The two guys next door stepped down off their stoop.

T. J.'s brother weighed in somewhere north of two-hundred pounds, not much of it wasted. He tilted his head to the left, smiled at me, letting me know this was his turf. He had the look of a guy used to having people do what he said. I ignored him and kept moving toward the door. He grabbed the front of my cut with his left hand and held me in place as his right moved to the gun. I couldn't believe the move. Back in the day, these thugs wouldn't even give lip to a Stallion. Touch one? Not a fucking chance. People in Greystone hate the police. I'd been forced to swallow shit here before. You stand behind a badge you hope people respect, but don't take it personally when they don't. Mostly you try to defuse a situation like this. It works out better for everyone that way. I wasn't behind the badge, and disrespecting the patch was an entirely different thing. Especially in a place like Greystone.

I moved into him before he could touch the gun. I grabbed the back of his neck with my left hand, locking his head in place as I drove three fast rights into his face. He let go of the leather and grabbed my left forearm, pulling it down to try to free his head. I tightened the grip and reached my right around behind his head. I pulled hard, adding to the force he was applying to my arm. His head came down as I shot my right knee up with brutal force. The knee connected with his chin, and he was drooling bubbles of spit and blood before he hit the ground. I straddled him, dropping to my knees and pressing them into his hips to give me leverage. I let loose with my best ground and pound, the kind that had ended fights in the ring in seconds. He was unconscious; but there was no ref here to stop me from raining lefts and rights into his unprotected head.

It was overkill, but it was what Greystone would expect from a full-patch Stallion. I needed the clout the club carried in the street, and that meant protecting its vicious rep. I kicked him once in the ribs as I smoothed the front of my vest. Red would live but he'd be a little uglier, and sore for a while. His phone was still on the step where he'd been sitting. I picked it up and snapped a picture of his bloody face, a souvenir from the badass bikers in the 'hood. I looked at the two guys from the second unit. They hadn't made a move. Smarter than the punching bag on the ground.

"Either one of you know how to tweet with this thing?" I asked.

"Yeah, sure." The taller of the two answered first, and I tossed him the phone.

"Okay, you delete the picture of us and send that one out." I looked at his friend. "You. Clean Stupid up. Then the three of you watch the bikes."

T. J. shook his head and led us inside. The door opened into a living room filled with car parts. It looked like most of it had come from Jap sports cars like the RX-8 out front. T. J. was obviously still in the midnight auto-parts game. Meant the fifty-grand estimate on the Supra was too high. Probably outfitted it for nothing. When Gunner and I ran with the Litter Box, freelancing was forbidden. I figured that hadn't changed, so the club must be into stripping down stolen cars now. Probably into a lot of things I didn't know about. A hallway led past the parts collection to the kitchen. I could see through a window into the backyard where a couple of guys were unloading a grey panel van. They were carrying wheels into a small shed. Something in the fog of my mind was trying to get my attention, but I couldn't force it into the clear. My head was still buzzing a little with the juice from the beating outside.

I stood at the kitchen counter and watched the guys outside through the window as Gunner explained what we needed to T. J. I knew he wouldn't want to give me any information, partly because I used to be a cop, and partly because I'd just kicked the shit out of his brother. One of the guys unloading the van was rifle-barrel thin and maybe fourteen years old. He couldn't lift the wheel he was unloading, so he rolled it out of the van and chased it to the shed. The polished black rim caught the morning sunlight. It was one of those water-cut wheels that were the rage. It had five wide daggers sculpted into the metal. The tips of the daggers met at the hub, the hilts reached out to form a supporting web for the outer rim. The dagger blades glistened with chrome polished edges that really stood out against the glossy-black painted surface. I wondered what they would fence for. You could drop four grand on a set of two like that for a motorcycle, and these rims were huge, had to be off an SUV. And there it was, that nagging thought burst through the fog like a beacon. I turned and grabbed T. J. by the arm.

"Where'd those rims come from?" I shoved him to the window.

"Easy, man." He pulled his arm free. "I don't know. That's some stuff the boys picked up last night."

Gunner moved to the window.

"What is it, bro?"

"Those rims, they could be off the shooter's Caddy."

"Was it an Escalade?" I asked.

"Yeah, man, that could be. We torched one last night." T. J. moved to the back door and opened it.

"Yo, li'l man. Those off the Darkside ride? Cool, man, thanks." He closed the door. "Yeah, man, we gassed one of theirs. Probably sell the rims back to those fools, too."

Slammed and tricked black Escalades were a favourite among the dealers and pimps on the Dartmouth side of Halifax Harbour. The Litter Box Boys were still at war with the Darkside dealers. Had a Darkside hit team taken out my brother? The harder I looked at it, the less sense this case made.

CHAPTER 17

Sunday night

NICHOLAS MAPP'S ESTATE HUGS THE NORTH WEST ARM, DUE SOUTH across the waves from Point Pleasant Park. The Arm is home to some of the most expensive real estate on Canada's East Coast. Those exclusive homes sit just a pistol shot below the streets of Spryfield. It would be tough to spend a night sipping single malt on a patio and not hear the nocturnal symphony of gunplay and sirens heralding the urban decay above. Ignoring it is easier from a private dock.

Mapp's 26,000-square-foot, glass-front sanctuary overlooks his private cove. A two-storey boathouse sits where a wooden wharf cuts the beach. Near the end of the wharf a cigarette-hulled speedboat bobbed in the waves, straining against the lines that secured it. A forty-foot cabin cruiser rose and fell against rubber bumpers that protected its polished fibreglass sides from the dock.

White light poured into the blackness from spotlights suspended beneath the eaves of the boathouse. The light floated in the mist above every surface as the heavy rain bounced. Serpentine streams rolled down the curved glass solarium that covered the pool at the back of the house.

Mapp sat in a canvas deck chair beside the pool, a cigar in one hand, a cut-crystal lowball in the other. He dipped the end of the cigar into the amber liquid in the glass and savoured the flavour of the whiskey and tobacco as he took a slow pull. He wore a thick blue robe with silver trim over a set of black swim trunks. Stallion colours in honour of his guest.

Yves Laroche was swimming laps in the pool, his deep tan cutting the pale blue chlorinated water that rolled over his muscled back. He sliced through the water with long easy strokes. Graceful technique for a thug, Mapp thought. Sometimes these guys still surprised him. Laroche was the president of the Nomads, the most ruthless and profitable charter in the Stallion stable. He hadn't gotten that job swimming laps. The trouble at the Church of Salvation brought him from Montreal. The murders were bad. The fire at the ranch was worse; numbered companies and titles can only hide so much. Behind them hid Laroche's own name. Arson investigators were sniffing around in dangerous territory. Anything beyond a half-hearted investigation would uncover the Nomad president hidden in the records. An unexpected visit from Laroche was bad news. If the Nomads were getting ready to clean up in Nova Scotia, Mapp could be in trouble. He'd have to convince Laroche he could handle cleanup on his own.

The biker pulled himself out of the pool and walked to the deck chair beside Mapp. He was naked. His clothes sat in a heap on the leather sofa at the far end of the pool. Striking blue eyes glistened under woolly blonde eyelashes. The deep tan shaded sharply cut muscles. Beads of water dripped from a smooth bald head. A jagged pink scar dropped from his left shoulder and disappeared under his right arm. The word *Nomad* tattooed in deep blue arched left and up from his navel. It was identical in size and shape to the bottom rocker on his Stallion cut. It ended beneath the Satan's Stallion crest inked above his heart. The small *Cavallino Rampante* over his right hip matched the one on Mapp's own. The prancing stallion signified membership in a different club. Mapp's friends all thought it was a bit of vanity ink to let everyone know he had a priceless Ferrari. They were wrong.

"So, Nick, Halifax is gone to shit. Time to cut and run, I think." Laroche stood naked and dripping as he sipped Scotch from a crystal glass.

"Not everything, Yves, and even what may seem bad will be good again. Trust me." Mapp hated being called Nick, and Laroche knew it. Still, he raised his glass in salute.

"We've made money together for a long time, long enough for me to know I can trust you. But only so far. My brothers wonder if maybe it is time to end our relationship with you."

Mapp knew how the relationship would end. These bastards would cut his throat and dump his body in the ocean. Use one of his own boats to do it, too. That was the risk of doing business with clueless muscle heads. No vision.

"I'm hurt, Yves. The club has nothing to be concerned about. We lost our facility, but we have enough fresh material on hand to keep us in money until we find a new place. We still have the supply line. Our partners are as eager to protect what we have as we are, more so, perhaps."

"The supply is the only fucking reason you are still sitting here talking to me, Nick. Getting into business with these kiddy diddlers was a mistake. You should have stayed with coke. We should all have stayed with coke."

Laroche drained his glass and tossed it onto the patio stones surrounding the pool. Tiny bits of crystal dropped like rain on the surface of the water. If they got past the filter, it would be impossible to save the pump. Mapp clenched his hand tightly around his own glass as he raised it to his lips. The warmth of the Scotch calmed him.

"Look, Yves, I can still save this thing, so relax. Gardner's wife is a better fit for us, anyway. He took too many stupid risks. It's probably what got him killed. Brenda Gardner is more cautious. She cares about two things—money and prestige. We can give her both. She, too, is a pastor and has been waiting to step out of the shadow and into his pulpit."

"Those risks Sandy loved to take were our hold over him," Yves said. "How can we control her if— and that's a big if—we can salvage this thing?"

"We already own her. Sandy was simply the face; she's been the brains behind the Little Maria Foundation from the beginning. She knew what happened to those special children who ended up at the ranch. She's been looking the other way for years. Too late for her to claim innocence now."

Laroche stood and placed his hands on his hips, leaned left and then right, stretching out the muscles in his sides. Mapp wanted to offer his robe to the naked Frenchman. It was the first time he was glad his useless wife and her sisters were off in New York wasting his money.

"Okay, even if we agree that she can run things, I believe it is still too far gone for her to get the chance," Laroche said as he continued the stretching routine. "The police will never walk away from a gunned-down cop. And three murders. This thing is as fucked as it can get."

"Not too fucked to fix. We have a stripper who may be connected to the Gardner murder. You can deal with her. She's one of your circuit girls. Maybe a suicide with a note. We're covered on the Waters woman. It can't come back on us. She had to go, she was going to tell the police everything. Her death sent a strong message to the others who know. Their silence suggests the message got through."

"So we do have a problem," Laroche said. "You ordered her killed and did not consult with me?"

Mapp could not believe Laroche was trying to turn this on him. He'd followed the Stallion rule of three. If three people know about a contract kill, one can always be convinced to talk. The person who gives the order and the person who carries it out are both guilty of first-degree murder in the eyes of the court and can't cut a deal. The third person can go from co-conspirator to witness at the stroke of a prosecutor's pen.

"Look, she made her choice. She told our friend Bobby she was going to the police with everything. He contacted me. I made a decision, suggested a certain level of brutality to ensure the message carried weight. I didn't feel it necessary to bother you with something that obviously had to be done."

"I suppose you are right. The killer: are we exposed? Do we need action there?"

Mapp smiled, noticed Laroche did not mention Bobby's name or ask if he did the work. Smart.

"The only exposure is his. Action against him would be a waste. He seems to have an appetite that could benefit us in the future."

"Fine, I leave that to you," Laroche said.

"As for the priest and the cop, well, that cop may be our out," Mapp said.

"*Excusez-moi.* Or for you *anglais,* 'What the fuck, Nick?'"

"That cop was a member of a special unit on the waterfront. They were supposed to fight terrorists, but all they ever did was get in the way of drug imports. We've been careful, but others have lost significant quantities of product. Thanks to our own friend with the badge, the police here have begun to look at the Russians. The machine-gun hit fits their style, and I managed to plant a little misdirection before the hit." Mapp smiled and sipped the Scotch to let the point land.

"Why would the Russians shoot a cop? Even they are not that stupid," Laroche said.

"They lost more than most groups in these waterfront raids. The priest was simply caught in the crossfire." Mapp drained his glass and then stood to get a refill. "Can I replace yours?" He looked at the tiny bits of crystal along the edge of the pool.

"No, I have to head to the house and my newest Nomad. I'll drink with people I like. You think you can fix this shit, do it. Make it fast, Nick, or this free ride of yours is over." Laroche gestured to the pool, and the view beyond, as he walked to the pile of clothes on the sofa.

—†—

Monday morning

Lolita smiled as she raised a sleeve to her face. The smell of smoke lingered in the fabric. She loved that it was a Stallion support hoodie; she'd never wash it. Phil Murphy opened the door and pointed her into the office, ending her moment of joy. She cursed herself for coming to the club instead of staying at the motel, but the showers here were bigger and cleaner. She was also trying to avoid Sheilagh and her questions. She hadn't even gotten to the dressing room when the giant stopped her and sent her in. She wondered what Williams and his goon were doing here so early on a Monday.

The ugly freak sat at his desk, his legs out, the boot heels catching the edge of the desk. She watched as he flicked the Satan's Stallion Zippo open and shut, showing her the logo like it meant something. The clicking of the lighter the only sound in the office. She turned away from him and looked at the monitors on the wall, one of them showing the empty dressing room. She was surprised he hadn't shut it off before calling her in. On another monitor, she could see a small group of men huddled around the tables furthest from the stage, probably at the poker machines. The rest of the club was empty.

"Take that fuckin' hoodie off. You know better, girl." Williams dropped his boots to the floor and stood behind the desk. Stallion support gear was banned at The Bank. She knew it but didn't really care.

"I got nothin' else here," she told him.

"Like I give a fuck."

Lolita pulled the hoodie off and stood topless in front of the desk, let him look. She pushed an arm inside the open sweatshirt and pulled the neck out through the bottom, then pulled it back over her head with the Stallion logo now on the inside.

"You know why you're here, don't you?"

"Left Saturday night," she said, thinking bad timing was the real reason.

"Where'd you go?" Williams demanded.

"Nowhere. Just went for a drive and started feeling sick, so I went back to Sheilagh's."

"Every time you wander off I got a mess to deal with. You got cops coming here, leaving me to clean that shit up. Who were you with?"

"My brother." She could see the answer confused him. Didn't take much.

"Girl, you lie to me again, and I will take you out back and shoot you. I don't give a shit how much money you bring in. Pussy is pussy, and you can be replaced."

"Not lyin'. I got a brother, and he lives here." She dropped into the sofa across from the desk and began pulling at her tangled hair. Raking her fingers through it, smiling at the smoky smell, still there. Maybe she would hold off on that shower another day.

"Bitch, you smell like shit. What the hell you been up to?" Williams stepped down off the riser, grabbed a fistful of her hair, stuck his face in it.

"It's just rock. Sheilagh had a party last night. Too many people hitting the pipe."

"Rock, my ass. I know what rock smells like." He released her hair and unleashed a hard backhand, catching her on the side of the head. She fell back to the couch.

"You know what, girl, I don't give a fuck where you went. Don't give a shit if you got a brother or if you killed that preacher. I'm the one out there fixin' your shit, and you need to show some respect."

She looked at him, said nothing.

"What? You think I'm shittin' you? Well, you take a look at the news, bitch, see what happened to that cop you brought here. He's dead, outta your life forever. You can thank Jimmy for that."

"You killed a cop?" Could he be that stupid?

"It's time you know who you're dealing with, girl."

He grabbed her sweatpants at the ankles and pulled them off with a violent yank. Lolita didn't see him pull the knife; it was just there touching her cheek. She rolled over on her back as he lowered the blade. She felt cold steel as the fabric split at her waist. She was glad she wasn't wearing her stage panties. They were expensive.

Lolita lit a cigarette as she watched the van pull out of the lot. The freak was gone. She was standing near the garbage bin behind the club. She clutched the front of her hoodie tight with her left hand, closing it around her body. It wasn't cold; she just needed it tight across her chest. The smell coming from the bins didn't bother her. It was better than the smell of that little bastard. It wasn't the first time she'd been raped, and it sure as hell wouldn't be the last. Course, she was told long ago a ho can't be raped. Still, she was sure that's what it felt like when real women got raped. Even if it wasn't real rape, there was something about Jimmy Williams that made her skin crawl, and she needed to clean him off her body. She was more worried about what he had told her than what he'd done to her. If Jimmy really had killed a cop, he was dead. So was she if the club found out she knew. She had to get away. The white Ford rolled around into the back lot, and she tossed her cigarette into the trash bin. Maybe she should burn the club down behind her.

She jumped up into the passenger seat.

"Hey, how are you?" Samuel asked as he put the shifter into gear and headed for the street.

"Great now. Where we going?"

"Home." He smiled at her. His eyes glowed. He looked different since the fire. She wondered if she did, too.

"Whose home?"

"Ours, the Church of Salvation. It belongs to us now. We are going to take over. I will be the preacher. You will make a wonderful preacher's wife."

"Wife?" The laugh burst from her lips. Samuel was full of surprises. It was like he was changing right in front of her. "I can't be a preacher's wife. Besides, you're kinda my brother, you know."

"No, I'm not. Who better, Tatjana? We know everything about each other. We accept all of it. We are one. And now we are free."

Lolita thought about it as they drove. Why not? She called him brother, but that was just something they'd started doing long ago at the ranch. She'd had sex with him many times when they were children. Not because they wanted to, but because they were forced to.

"You think I could be a preacher's wife? I mean, would they let me?"

"Of course. You can be Mary Magdalene. I will cure you of the seven demons of the flesh. You will stand as a beacon by my side. Saved by the love of Jesus. Saved by my love."

Lolita had no idea what Samuel was talking about. She didn't really want to change her name to Mary, but she was sure Lolita wouldn't work as a preacher's wife. Sam often talked about the stuff they taught him in that church. It was stuff he seemed to know about. Maybe she could be cured. She sure as shit didn't want to live in Jimmy Williams's world anymore. How much worse could a church be?

"I want to. I do. I never want to go back there. But the club, they will find me. They will kill us both. Let's just leave here and go somewhere far away."

"No, Tatjana, they will fall before the power of God. His hand is in all of this. In church yesterday, as the fools in the congregation wept, I felt a sudden warmth. A true joy in my heart that can only come from God. He is with us, I feel it."

He turned, looking for traffic as he angled left out of the driveway and up the hill away from the strip club. His smile was like nothing she'd seen before. Maybe God was making him happy. She wanted to feel that kind of joy, but knew she never would. His smile broadened as he continued. Maybe God had made him crazy.

"God showed the people of my village his wrath. They were sinners. I see that now. He chose me. His hurricane set me free. He chose you, too, Tatjana. He spared you when the bombs fell on your town. Once he brought us together, he tested us to measure our faith. We passed that test, and now it is over. Do you see?"

She didn't know what to say, so she said nothing, reached into her bag, and pulled out her cigarettes.

"He purified us in the crucible of pain," Samuel said. "Now, He has killed all who stand in our way. My second father and his white-haired whore. You saw how easily Bobby fell before us. This is our time. We are going to shake the Church of Salvation free of Satan's grasp. We know the hypocrites, know their sins. Satan and all his followers will run from the church now."

It was the most she'd ever heard Sam say at one time, but most of it made no sense. She worried that maybe he really was crazy, that maybe the fire had tipped him over the edge. She'd seen girls crack over weird shit that happened to them.

"That's not the Satan I'm afraid of, Sam. The Stallion will come for me, and believe me, they won't fall like Bobby. That freak Williams did something; if they think I know, nothing will stop them."

He patted her leg and laughed.

"Satan's Stallion. Don't you understand the name? He is speaking to you. He put that godless horde in front of you so you can see Him crush it. Then you too will feel this joy."

He patted her leg again.

"Trust in Him, trust in me. Your new life begins today. We need to find you some proper clothes and introduce you to the elders and church staff. When my mother returns, she will help us take our place at the front of the church. It's what she wants for me."

┼┼┼

"Hey, little perv, getting any?" Yves Laroche asked as Jimmy Williams walked into the clubhouse.

"Matter of fact, I just had a taste. How's the porn business treating you?"

"Just fine, little man, just fine." Laroche slapped Williams hard on the back, almost knocking him off his feet. The big biker laughed.

Williams clenched his fists at his side but smiled broadly at the Quebecer. He could swallow the little-man shit one more time. He knew Laroche's being here could mean Mapp had come through, and it was finally time for him to get that patch. Then the little-man crap would stop once and for all.

"What brings you to the coast, man?" he asked.

"Club business, prospect, club business. Now, make me a coffee before I kick your little ass." The kick came even before Laroche finished saying it. This time, Williams did stumble forward.

Fuck him, Jimmy thought, as he walked to the kitchen to put on a fresh pot. Prospecting is supposed to test character, to prove a man worthy of the patch. Truth is, it's just a glorified hazing ritual, and Jimmy knew it.

It was good to see Laroche, despite his full-patch bullshit. Williams owed him for bringing him into the Stallion world in the first place. They'd met in the Renous Federal Pen where Jimmy was running a porn business with help from a couple of guards.

The guards brought in magazines and DVDs, and Williams distributed them to an eager clientele. Laroche muscled in on the profits, saying Jimmy couldn't continue without Stallion protection. Williams was pissed at first, but quickly changed his mind when he saw how other inmates reacted. Walking under Stallion protection inside a prison gave him rock-star status, and he soaked it up.

In the end, Laroche proved to be more than muscle. He studied everything about Jimmy's operation and found ways to improve it. He didn't want the guards doing the buying outside the prison. He funnelled the orders to a Stallion-owned company with access to the kinkiest shit the inmates wanted. All the guards had to do was pick the shit up and bring it inside. He used the club's clout to reduce the cut the guards were taking. By the time Williams finished his three-year tilt in Renous, the business was thriving, and Laroche had the club running identical operations in every prison in the country. Williams always felt it was his franchise, but as the club member who set it up Laroche got all the profit. Laroche looked after him, though, getting him control of the Litter Box and prospect status with the Halifax charter. The next step was the patch Williams was sure Laroche had brought with him from Montreal. Who else to put it on his back? Snake was standing in front of the sink, pouring water into the coffee pot as Jimmy walked in.

"Hey, Pres, I got that," he said as he walked over.

Snake handed him the pot.

"You find out what the fuck that dancer was doing here?" Snake asked.

"She was dumping the body, all right, but she says she didn't kill him. He was dead when she got there."

Williams was playing it cool as he fed the information to Snake. No big deal, just doing the job. He rinsed out the pot, filled it with cold water, and dumped it into the coffee maker. He dug out the filter basket and spooned in some coffee grounds.

"So who killed the fucker?"

"She says he was into some kinky shit and it went bad. Figures the fucker choked himself out or some damn thing."

"Same shit she tried to feed Gunner. I'm not buying it." Snake ran a hand over his head. He grabbed a thick length of hair, pulled it forward over his shoulder, and then tossed it back. "She say why she brought him here, for fuck's sake?"

"Says she figured you'd help get rid of it. You weren't here, so her brother figured the dump was a good spot."

"What brother?" Snake repeated the thing with his hair. Williams grabbed his own, mimicking the move.

"She claims she got some kind of foster brother here lived with the preacher. Says she helped him clean it up."

"Shit. The cops are gonna get to her pretty damn quick if she's got a brother living with the fucking guy."

Fuck. Snake was so far behind the curve on this thing there was no point in Jimmy even explaining. Yves Laroche walked into the kitchen and headed for the coffee pot. He slapped Williams on the back of the head as he walked past.

"Fuck you." It came out before Jimmy could stop it. "Sorry, man, sorry." He swallowed hard on the apology. Laroche looked at Snake.

"Your prospect, man." He shrugged and grabbed the coffee pot.

Snake's kick was half-hearted, at best. It caught Williams in the left hip and spun him into the counter. Williams leaned, favouring the hip, trying to sell it so there wouldn't be a follow-up.

"Get the fuck out and wash the bikes. We got things to discuss in here. And make sure no one without a patch walks into this house. Got that?" Snake took the coffee pot from Laroche and poured a cup.

Pricks. Make the coffee, don't drink the fucking coffee. Wash the fucking bikes. Jimmy headed for the door.

CHAPTER 18

I SIPPED COFFEE AND STARED AT MY CELLPHONE ON THE WORK-bench. Monday morning, nowhere to be. At least the latest from the hospital was good. Blair was still in ICU, but he'd been upgraded to stable. I wanted to call the major-crime office, call Carla, or anyone who might give me something, anything on the investigation. I should have been working out, but I couldn't get into it. I'd feel better if I pounded the bag, but I didn't want to feel better. I needed to let the hate build. I looked at my father's bike in the corner. Another wave of regret. They just kept coming. I could see Greg straddling the bike. What was it, just a month ago when I was tightening the compensating sprocket on my Harley and he stopped by? Hiding from the bishop, he told me.

Gunner and I grew up hanging in garages. We never owned a hockey stick between us, but we both had tool chests. If you ride it, you wrench it. The only worthwhile lesson of our childhood. The old man never even taught us that. Grease made sure I could strip a bike, and Gunner could, at least, maintain his.

Greg was living the Sunday school life, learning the Bible while we were studying shop manuals, elbow deep in grease. He was one-hundred-percent Neville, though. He learned to ride a dirt bike like a wild man. Saddle fever was showing when he stopped by my garage. I could see him on the Glide, holding the grips and rocking the bike back and forth between his legs, feeling its weight. He asked if he could take it out for a run. I said no. I could have slapped the primary back on my bike in three minutes, and we could have gone for a run. Let him ride the old man's bike once. I could have been sitting in my garage, reliving that ride. Instead, I treated Greg the way the old man had. I made him feel like he wasn't really a part of the family. Nice memory.

I pressed the crucifix beneath my shirt as I pushed the guilt down. I was going to hurt someone, but if I was going to find that target, I needed focus. I didn't have the badge, but I was an investigator, I knew how to break a case. The Litter Box Boys had burned a Caddy Saturday night. A Caddy was used to shoot Greg and Blair, also on Saturday night. Escalades are prime targets for any decent car-theft crew, so it could be a coincidence, but I didn't think so. Everything inside told me the shooters had used that car. I wanted to push hard but knew enough to back off. Get aggressive too fast and you kill a lead. Gunner had more credibility with T. J. and his crew, so I had to let him work it. Waiting sucks.

The garage door was up, and I stood in the opening and watched the tiny wisps rise from the puddles in my driveway as I sipped the coffee. I could feel the hot sun baking my forearms as I stepped outside. Carla rolled into the driveway on her brother's sport bike. The front wheel came to a stop about an inch from my boots. I wondered where her bike was.

"Out of the way. We need to talk, and I really don't want anyone seeing this bike in your driveway." She spoke through an open helmet visor. Guess she wanted her bike seen here even less than I did.

I moved, and she eased the gixxer inside. I punched the button on the control box on the wall, and the door slid down. Being seen with me wouldn't help her career. Being seen with her could be a little more complicated for me. The club knew who she was. This wasn't the time for me to be hanging with cops.

"So, what have you got?" I asked as she leaned the sport bike over on its side stand behind my Harley.

"Some good news, maybe. Inspector MacIntosh may not file charges against you."

She took a step toward my cut hanging on its hook beside the workbench.

"So far no one knows about that." She pointed at the Stallion patch. "If you don't put it back on, we may be able to get you back on the job when this is over."

"I'm not sure I want to go back." I didn't want to get into that discussion. "You sure about MacIntosh? He looked like he was set to hang my badge on his trophy wall. I gave him everything he needs and then some."

"He can't look too eager. You lost your brother, and the media have gone ape shit. They are already saying the Pope should make Greg a saint. Hard to fire the hero brother of a saint. The chief is leaning on Superintendent Surette, too." She ran her finger along the outer edge of the Stallion patch as she spoke. "He thinks he can get her on our side and she'll keep the inspector quiet. He even asked me to write out what MacIntosh had done to help Greg and Blair during the attack. I told him what I saw you do while MacIntosh was hiding in that elevator. He is really pissed. He's still in your corner, Cam, so don't screw it up."

"So why are you worried about your brother's bike being seen in my driveway?"

"Because the chief told me, all of us, to stay away from you until we catch the shooter. He doesn't want you doing anything he can't undo. Like this." She slapped the patch. I let it slide.

"Anything on the shooter?" I asked.

"We have a lead. Looks like the Russian mob was gunning for Blair."

"The Russians?" I didn't see that coming.

"Yes. MacIntosh brought it to the briefing yesterday. Blair had the file on that big ecstasy bust at the port. Cost them millions. Apparently, the tip came in the morning before the shooting."

"They knew Blair was a target?" Rage flared inside. I'd kill MacIntosh.

"No, no. The tip came from some snitch in Vancouver. No one thought the target was on this coast."

I wanted to believe it. A Russian hit was something I could live with. I'd still hunt down the shooter, but at least Greg's death wasn't my fault. Blair's bust was big by any standard. More than two tonnes packed into a container, seven-million pills worth a fortune on the street. That had to hurt the Russians.

"I don't know. Losing product in a bust is part of doing business, even to those guys," I said.

"Used to be. Maybe things are changing. Hope not. Anyway, right now MacIntosh has all resources focused on it. It's the only thing we have."

She looked at me. We both knew that was a mistake. No investigation should take a single focus. Not this early. Not ever.

┿╈┿

We burned up a half hour kicking around the Russian angle. Trouble was, it fit perfectly, and it didn't fit at all. We needed more information. Carla leaned against my bike, half sitting in the saddle, her boot on the front peg as she sipped her coffee. I sat on the workbench. Seeing her on my bike felt good.

"Anything on the Escalade?" I asked.

"We got a break. Someone boosted one from long-term parking at the airport a couple of hours before the shooting. Description fits, right down to the black-and-chrome rims. Sounds like the one MacIntosh saw. Might get lucky with video surveillance from the airport." She walked over to the table where I keep the coffee machine and poured herself another cup.

"There was a black Escalade torched out in Herring Cove Saturday night. Might be the one." I watched her turn.

"What? How do you know that? Are you working this thing? The chief will freak."

"I'm going to work it, Carla, just like you would." I pointed to the gixxer. "What if that had been your brother we were trying to save Saturday night? You saying you'd sit it out?"

"I can't imagine what this is like. If it had been my brother, I just don't know. I'm afraid if you find the shooter, you'll take him out."

"Maybe I'll give him the first shot." We both knew it was a lie.

"Tell me about the car."

"It can't come from me."

"I know, I know. The chief won't have any idea."

"I don't give a shit about the chief. I can't have the club find out I'm talking to a cop about it."

She looked at me, and I saw something shift. A subtle change of light in her eyes, and then it was gone.

"That's right. I'm just another rat worried about his own ass." We were standing on opposite sides of my Harley now, a little over a metre apart. The border marked two sides of the law.

"Damn it, Cam, that's not fair. That's not what I was thinking. It just sounded strange hearing you talk like that. You're not that guy anymore."

I wasn't sure if I'd ever stopped being that guy. You can run, but you just can't hide. A familiar sound rattled the garage door, a string of small explosions. I knew the sound of Gunner's bike gearing down. Running or hiding was out of the question. Carla looked at the door and then at me, fear in her eyes.

"It's Gunner," I said.

"Will you be okay? Will we?" She had that why-did-I-leave-my-gun-home look. Probably the same look I'd had in the parking garage. The banging and popping stopped as Gunner's bike slowed to a crawl near my house. The sudden growl of an engine under load told me he was pulling into the driveway now.

"He's my brother, Carla, we'll be fine. Just act pissed off about the patch. He thinks you're my ol' lady. He'll figure you're out of line, and it's my place to set you straight." I pulled my cut over my shoulders.

"I won't have to act. The patch has to go, Cam, you know it. Now tell me about that Escalade. Who burned it, and where?"

"If I help you, are you going to return the favour?" The engine grew louder as the bike approached the garage door, and then the sound died with a muted cough. I figured we had maybe thirty seconds before he would open the side door of the garage and walk in. He never entered my house through the front door. Last few years, he rarely entered it at all.

"Jesus, Cam, you can't blackmail me. Give me what you have, and we'll find the guy. I'll pull the car apart myself. I'll find trace."

"That's the deal, Carla, take it or leave it."

"Fine. I'll let you know what I find. Now where is the damn thing?"

"It may be missing a few parts; I'll help you with that when I can. For now, check out the spot near the cliffs out by Hospital Point."

"The cable station?"

"Yes, about a kilometre north of there where the old service road is."

"Yeah, I know it."

"Well, what's left of it, should be there."

The side door of the garage opened, and Gunner walked in, a broad smile on his face. It was gone as soon as he recognized Carla.

She pulled my face to hers, kissing me quickly on the lips.

"You know how I feel. Now open the door. I'm leaving." She nodded at Gunner and pulled her helmet over her head as she straddled the sport bike. I raised the door and watched her roll the bike into the sunlight. I knew the kiss was for Gunner's benefit, just selling the ol' lady thing. Meant nothing, meant everything. I watched as she pulled away.

"Hey, little bro, what's a cop doing in the house?" Gunner walked up beside me to watch her go.

"She's trying to convince me I'm making a mistake. I don't think I'll be seeing her again."

"No, you won't. Nomad or not, that comes from a club officer."

"What did you find out?" I didn't like him telling me what I could or couldn't do, but there was no point in arguing.

"Not enough. Not yet, anyway. T. J. called this morning. Says he talked to the guys who stripped it. They say no one was at the warehouse when the thing got dumped. We're going to have to get Williams to chase this down."

"The prospect? He's a moron." Jimmy Williams was a psychopath and a narcissist. He'd make a good fit with the other Stallion patches. But he was also an idiot. There was no way I would depend on him when it came to tracking Greg's killer.

"He's a dumb cunt, yeah, but the Litter Box Boys are scared shitless of him. He puts out the word, they'll find out who dumped it faster than we can."

"So what do we do? Sit here and wait?"

"Nope. Fire it up. I gotta make a cash pickup in the South End, and then we hit the house. Yves is there to see you, so let's ride."

We rolled down Gottingen Street into the North End after Gunner's pit stop for club cash at a Stallion-owned pool hall. Heading into the North End through Gottingen is like moving through a gateway from one Halifax to the other. On the south end of Gottingen, we passed the squat brick bunker of police headquarters. It sits in the shadow of Citadel Hill. The fortress built by the cops and the fort built by Cornwallis keep the poverty of the north from flowing into the moneyed neighbourhoods in the deep south. We slipped through a set of lights and into the gay village with its trendy shops and restaurants. The breeze played with the ribbons of a faded rainbow heart woven into a fence. A tribute to a popular social activist who'd been beaten to death in the middle of Gottingen. I remembered that foggy morning, the blood on the street, the fear in the gay community. Remembered how quickly the fear left, replaced by hope and love, even forgiveness. I'd never seen that after a murder, before or since then.

We rode a few blocks further north where bloodstains are just part of the pavement. No heart-shaped tributes dangling here, no candles, no flowers, no hope, and definitely no forgiveness. A hard-core twelve-year-old slinging rock on a corner flashed the handgun symbol as we approached. His baggy pants hung lower than the usual street style; he had no hips to catch them.

That's where the cruiser lit up in my rear-view. I eased the bike over to the side of the road and saw a second cruiser slide to a stop at the curb on the opposite side of the street just ahead of us. The little dealer grabbed his pants as he scrambled into the Uniacke Square housing project. I knew what was happening. My Nomad patch was new on the street and had to be checked. Guy behind me spotted it, radioed it in, and was told to do the traffic stop to see who was wearing it. The second car was cover. Like we were about to start a shootout on Gottingen Street in the middle of the day. I was pissed. I'd forgotten what it felt like on this side of the law. Powerless.

I got off the bike and put my helmet on the seat as the cop behind me stepped out of his cruiser. I looked across the street. Two cops stood outside that cruiser, one staring at Gunner, who still sat on his bike with the engine idling. He looked back at me, gave them the finger, and took off for the clubhouse. The three cops grabbed at their guns as they watched, but no one pulled. They turned their attention to me. They all knew the familiar *Halifax* rocker Gunner was wearing. It was the Nomad patch they were after.

In the outlaw world, the Nomad patch means one thing. In law enforcement, another. My fellow cops get most things only half right when it comes to clubs. Nomads are one part elite Stallion soldier and one part idiot savant. We are homeless because no charter wants to claim us. Mostly just guys who, for one reason or another, can't handle the club politics that are part of charter life. But point us at a target, that's different. The Nomads are the special forces in the Stallion world, called in to clean up the mess if it involves putting down a full patch or bombing a rival clubhouse. That's the only thing the police care about in a Nomad patch. If a cop in any city spots one, it usually signals trouble. The cop behind me walked up and stopped short. His hand touched his gun butt. He opened his mouth, but nothing came out. It was the same uniform who'd worked the yellow tape at the Gardner scene.

"Hey, Barber, thought I told you not to reach for that gun unless you planned to use it."

"Sorry, Detective, I just...umm, are you undercover here?" His voice lowered to a near whisper. "Should we check your papers?" Poor guy didn't know whether to take a piss or wind his watch. Then again, neither did I. I couldn't ride around under the patch in my own city without word reaching the chief. Just hadn't thought it would be so quick.

"Tell you the truth, Barber, I think you did exactly what you were told to do when you radioed this in. You know who the new patch is. Think you can report that without seeing my licence? I got a meeting to get to."

"Okay, sure, but what about the other guy? Who was that with you?"

"You get the plate?"

"No, I was keeping an eye on you."

"Well, I have no idea who that was, so I guess you let one get away. Now, my papers are in order and my bike is legal. Do you want to do that dance, or do I go?"

"Yes, sir. I mean, I'm sorry if I screwed up an undercover op." He signalled the two across the street and walked away, thinking he was a fool. He'd be feeling much better later in the day when word spread that he was the first cop to find out I'd turned. The story would grow with the telling, and he'd get more than one free beer out of it.

I fired up the bike, feeling like maybe I was the fool. I'd put the patch on to avenge Greg. So far, all it was doing was destroying my career and chasing away a woman who seemed to care about me. I wasn't even sure how long I'd be wearing it. Yves Laroche coming to town probably wasn't good news for me. He was the Nomad president. The patch on my back was his to pull, and I was his to kill.

I rolled into the compound, slipped my bike in next to Gunner's. Jimmy Williams was on his toes, reaching up with a soapy sponge, trying to wipe the mirror sitting just above the apes on Grease's Springer. The bars stretched a good twenty-one inches above the headlight, and he was a good four inches short of pulling it off.

"Maybe you should stand on the front tire," I said as I walked over. He stuffed the sponge back into a bucket of water and began wringing the water and soap out of it without looking at me. I kicked the bucket. The water sloshed up into his face. The adrenaline was still climbing as I thought about the chief. I needed to lash out. It only felt good for a half second before I realized I needed Williams.

"Gimme the fucking sponge." He handed it to me, and I cleaned the mirrors and the top of the bars. He stared in disbelief as I did it.

I tossed it back into his chest. It hit with a wet splat as the soap splashed up into his face. "Fucking clown." I needed him, but I couldn't let him think I was lowering myself.

"You talk to Gunner?"

"No. He just went in." He busied himself with the sponge, refusing to make eye contact.

"Well, we need you to get some information."

"Sure, what do you need?"

"Your boys torched an Escalade Saturday night. You got any idea who in your crew dumped it at the warehouse first?"

"No, no," he said as he lifted the sponge and made a move to soak down Grease's tank.

"Find out. Do it fast. One more thing." I waited for him to quit the shit with the sponge. He looked up.

"Yeah."

I grabbed the front of his vest. It was wet and hard to hold onto.

"That thing at The Bank. The fight with my former partner. If it turns out your boys went looking to finish it with guns, there's gonna be a lot more wet work than you can do with that sponge."

"No way. Glen and Phil—that was something I stopped as soon as it started."

I slapped him across the side of the head. Harder than I should have.

"What your boys do is on you. You got that?"

"Yeah, yeah." He locked eyes with me for the first time. Then looked away quickly.

I headed in to meet with Yves. My adrenaline was easing down into a more manageable range. Abusing prospects was the best anger-management therapy.

+++

I felt the phone in my jeans vibrate as I walked into the clubhouse. I pulled it out, looked at the display. Had to be a record for street intel reaching the top.

"Chief," I said.

"Neville, what the hell do you think you're doing?" No rank again, no Cam, either.

"Finding my brother's killer. How about you?" There was no way he was taking control of the conversation.

"Goddamn it. I told you to stay away from this. Are you wearing a patch? Tell me that's not true."

"Needed some clout, Chief. You took away the power of the badge. This'll do." I stopped in the hallway just inside the clubhouse door. I didn't want anyone inside hearing this conversation.

"Jesus Christ. You lost the badge when you lost control. I had to take it. You'll get it back. Just let things cool down. Don't burn that bridge now."

"You told me I couldn't work the case. What good is the badge if it can't bring justice to Greg and Blair?" The adrenaline was off the scale again. I'd have to go back and slap Williams around.

"Do you know how many roadblocks I blew up to get you the badge in the first place? And even after. To get you off the street and into major crime, I had to promise to resign if you fucked up. I threatened to pull out of the regional policing agreement just to get those fucking Mountie bastards to let you inside the task force. Now, you turn on me. You selfish bastard. What are you thinking?"

"Chief, this isn't about you. It's about my brother."

"The hell it isn't. It is about me, and it's about your partner. What do you think Blair will think?"

"He'll think I had his back."

"Look, Cam, I know you're hurting, but come on. We've both lost men in battle. It happens."

"Greg wasn't in the battle, Chief. Can't let that go."

"Goddamn it, Cam, this is the end of my career, not just yours. There has to be a way to change this. Just let me think it through. Call me in an hour." He hung up before I could say no.

I didn't want the chief to lose his job because of me. He had every right to be pissed, but I had to find the person who murdered my brother. If the Russian mob had ordered the hit, it would be beyond the chief anyway. My hands were shaking as I stuffed the phone back in my pocket and headed down the hall. Gunner, Snake, and Yves Laroche were sitting around the beer cooler when I walked into the main room. Laroche stood first.

"Well, look at you, little man. The fighter is back in the house." He hugged me.

"Hey, Yves." I slapped his back but couldn't say anything more. My throat was too dry. I couldn't sound nervous. I reached into the cooler for a beer. No Coke in the clubhouse. I'd have to be careful not to fall all the way off. I took a swallow to calm my nerves. "So, you here to celebrate with me?"

"It's not that simple, Hammer. You are a policeman. Yet, here you stand in a patch. My patch. Not simple at all. *Très compliqué.*"

Long time since anyone had used my club name, Hammer. Had to be a good sign that Yves was using it now. I reached into the cooler, pulled out another beer, and handed it to him.

"Share a drink with a brother?"

"Your father saved my life. We are brothers till the grave, and I celebrate your return." He took the beer. "But some of our bros in Montreal don't feel the same. No history, you know."

The Nomad charter is a strange beast in the Stallion world, and it was up to the Nomads to decide my fate now. Nomads had no ties to individual charters and no allegiance to me or the old man. A bunch of misfits, burnouts, and stone-cold killers would vote on my fate. Perfect. Over in Afghanistan, I recognized the Nomad swagger in the special-forces teams. As a sniper, my attitude fit just fine. Did I fit in now?

"It is what it is, Yves." I took a long drink. "You told me when I left, this patch would always be mine to wear."

"It is yours. Always will be. But there are those who believe it is time we bury you in it."

Gunner started to stand, but I raised a hand, and he sat back down. This was Nomad business, and I had to hold my own.

"Maybe they should try. But tell them this: it won't happen before I bury the people who shot my brother. Anyone who tries to stop me will fall. Remember, Yves, the old man was also Greg's father. You tell our bros I am avenging the death of the founder's son. The Nomad patch means nothing if the people wearing it stand in the way of that."

Yves hugged me again.

"Okay, I'll send the message. We will avenge your brother first. I just hope Gunner has only one to bury this week," he said.

"Me too." We tapped bottles.

"As long as we agree Greg's death will be avenged, I need to ask you about the club's ties to the Russians."

He looked at me over the bottle and shook his head.

"This isn't a cop asking, damn it. I don't give a shit about any connections. My ol' lady says the cops think the Russians put a hit on my old partner, and Greg got hit because he was there. Can you reach out? If it's true, we want the shooters."

"That I can do." He smiled and took another drink.

CHAPTER 19

A SMALL CD PLAYER PLAYED CHRISTIAN RAP, AND SAMUEL SANG along with every song. The beat was solid. Lolita would have to learn the words. Singing along with the Christians had to beat hip-grinding to Pac. She almost laughed at the prospect. Lolita, a real...no, not Lolita, Tatjana, a real preacher's wife. She sat at the kitchen table, watching Samuel make lunch. The first meal in their new home, he said. He looked so natural working in the kitchen. That silly, maybe crazy, smile still there. It was as though Silent Sam, the kid she grew up with, was gone, replaced by someone else. It was fun to see this new Sam. Still, she knew they were from different worlds. Knew she had no place in this one, no matter what he said about God's will.

The clean kitchen, the bright sunlight, the smell of fresh food, were sort of familiar, like a dream she could glimpse, in the morning, of her grandmother's kitchen. She felt something wet beneath her eye and reached quickly to hide it. She licked the salty liquid from her fingers. When had she last cried? Fuck, she couldn't remember that far back. At the ranch, probably. Funny, how thoughts of her grandmother could carry her back to before the ranch. The fresh-bread smell that never left Nanna's kitchen. The gentle touch as she fixed Tatjana's hair. She felt the smooth cotton of the sundress Sam had bought for her, just like the ones Nanna wore. He insisted she put it on as a symbol of their new beginning.

She could learn to make bread. Samuel would love that. A smile began to creep across her face as she played with the idea of staying. Fuck, it was stupid. A flash of anger forced her to her feet. What the hell was Samuel thinking? She didn't belong here. She had to get out of here, had to take Samuel with her. Why did that idiot Jimmy Williams have to brag to her about killing that nosy Indian cop? He would tell the Stallion she knew. They would find her here. They brought her here to service that sick preacher more times than she could remember.

The reflection of light from the windshield of a car flashed from the driveway. She swallowed air. Could they be here already? No, too soon.

"Samuel, someone is here. Is it your mother?"

"No, her flight doesn't get in until late. It's probably someone from the church dropping by to offer condolences. It will be good for you to meet them."

He rinsed his hands in the kitchen sink and dried them on a towel as he walked toward the front of the house.

"Come on, we will greet them as a couple."

She smoothed the edges of the sundress again. It was loose fitting and dropped below her knees. It felt funny to be covered up like that. If only Sheilagh could see her in such a square outfit. She'd shorten it a bit for Samuel if she could just get him to leave with her.

He glanced out the side window as he reached the door and held up a hand to stop her.

"It's Bobby." He moved back from the glass as he said it.

Lolita looked through the window. Sure enough, the Mercedes they'd left in Halls Harbour was parking near the garage.

"It can't be him. He's dead," she said.

They both watched a very-much-alive Bobby Simms step out of the car and head to the house. Red stains showed through a thick gauze taped to the side of his neck.

The midday sun pierced the canopy of leaves hanging over Waverley Road. Clouds of pollen floated and spun in brilliant yellow shafts where the sun broke through. Carla Cage drove toward Sandy Gardner's home. She kept one hand on the bottom edge of the sun visor; it wasn't low enough to block the flashes of sun. She fought the urge to call Cam. She would tell him what she found in the Escalade but didn't want to talk to him just yet. Her feelings for him were confusing. He was good-looking and intriguing, but he was also a cop, and that broke her rule. Dating a fellow officer was a mistake she wouldn't make again. Still, when she was with him she couldn't stop herself from flirting. It was embarrassing.

Of course, if he wasn't a cop anymore.... No, this Satan's Stallion thing was just a bruised male ego. An overreaction to being kept off the case. Cops were terrible for that kind of macho bullshit. He'd be suspended for it at the very least. If it turned out to be more, and he stayed with the club, he wouldn't be a cop anymore. She could hardly get involved with an outlaw. She felt something when she kissed him, and it was more than the thrill of catching him off guard in front of his brother.

She almost rolled past the driveway. Cam was indeed a distraction. The yellow crime-scene tape and the command bus were gone. The Gardner estate was bathed in those same shafts of pollen-filled sunlight as she pulled into the stone driveway. The house sitting in the full light at the end of the drive seemed lost in a yellow haze. A Mercedes sedan she recognized sat in front of the garage. Samuel Gardner's Ford Escape parked near the front door was a break. Two samples with one stop. Carla needed to pull carpet fibre in Sandy Gardner's office to use as an elimination sample against some found in the plasti-cuffs on his body. She also needed a DNA sample from Samuel. There were eleven hair samples found in the office, and eliminating the three people who lived in the house would help. Tests were being run on hair from Thelma Waters's body, no doubt she had been in the office too. There was too much evidence from the office, too many people had access to it. Still, she hoped the killer had left trace. Ruling out those who belonged would help. It was all just busy work. She could have sent any tech back out here. She just needed to stay active.

She parked beside the Mercedes and pulled out her cell as she sat behind the wheel. Texting Cam was the best approach for now. She had to tell him about the scorched MAC-10 and nine-millimetre shells she'd found in the burned-out Caddy. She still didn't know how Cam had known where to find it, but she was glad he did. The MAC-10 had to be the weapon used in the attack on Blair and Father Greg. She wondered if reporting that to Cam was telling him something he already knew. Maybe his Stallion friends knew who the shooter was. She stared at the tiny screen, trying to decide how to start. Gun found in the Escalade would do it, but she wanted to put a tiny bit of personality in the text. A smiley face after the note was too much. "Dear Cam" wouldn't work. "Thanks for the tip" felt about right. She started with that.

━┼━

The kitchen felt smaller with Bobby Simms in it. He tugged at the edges of the bandage on his neck. Lolita looked at the blood, wondering how he would punish her.

"Well, don't you two look like the perfect couple? That dress does you justice, Lolita. You should use it in the act. The whole schoolgirl thing is getting tired, and you aren't exactly sweet and innocent anymore," he said.

Simms sprawled in the chair Lolita had been in only moments before. Lolita leaned against the counter beside Samuel, her arms crossed. She eyed her purse on the floor, fighting the urge to run for it, grab the knife, and try again.

"I should forgive you for Saturday night, girl. If you forgive others their trespasses, your heavenly Father will also forgive you. Isn't that right, Samuel?"

Sam didn't answer.

"I'll tell you, I should, I really should. I know it. The flesh is weak, though, and I can't get myself there. When I woke in that mud, I thought I was finished. Turns out the Fundy mud caked on my wound—miracle tides, miracle mud. A little divine intervention. Guess you didn't cut anything important in there, sweetheart." He smiled at Lolita. "Climbing up out of there, that was a real bitch, let me tell you. Then, I get to the top and you two are gone. Saw right away you took my church key ring, and I knew where you were going. Thank our Lord I kept the ignition keys in my pocket, or I would have been stranded there. I tried to catch up at the ranch, but I didn't want to disturb the firemen."

"What do you want?" Lolita asked.

"I want to sort this mess out with Sam before the police do. By the way, did you kill Sandy? You're quick with the knife." He touched the neck bandage again.

"She didn't kill him. We found him. He fell or something knocked him over in that chair. God's hand." Samuel stepped away from the counter and placed himself between Lolita and Simms. His smile was gone, the sulking Samuel back. He looked so small. Even sitting in the chair, Bobby dwarfed him. Lolita moved up beside him and looked again at her purse.

"Really? God? I don't know how it happened, but from what the cops are saying it wasn't exactly godly." Bobby stood and moved toward the coffee pot in the corner. Sam backed away. Lolita stayed.

"To look with lustful intent is to commit adultery. He who commits it shall be put to death. His spirit was filled with lust; he was struck down," Sam said.

"I believe that passage refers to looking at another man's wife. Not exactly what your father was into. So, tell me the truth, Sam, were you the instrument of God's wrath? Give the chair a little push after he was hooked up, maybe?" He poured a cup and returned to his seat.

"No, I wish He had chosen me."

"So it was you then." He turned to Lolita as he sipped his coffee.

Lolita stepped closer to the table. Bobby had no right to ask these questions. If Sam had killed his father, he had every right, and it was no one's business. Especially not this asshole. Suddenly, she wished the Stallion killers would show up. Gunner maybe.

"It was an accident. His chair fell over," she said. "I found him, not Sam. I stabbed him to make sure, but he was already dead."

"The mighty Sandy Gardner falls. That's funny that he really falls before a simple stripper. How the hell did he end up in that garbage dump?"

"We took him to the clubhouse. I knew they'd help, but they were gone." She wanted him to know she could go to the club for help. Hoping it would scare him.

"So why the dump?" Bobby sipped from his cup.

"We had to get rid of him somewhere. We were afraid the cops might pull us over or something. We couldn't take him back here," she said.

"I know Sandy had it coming, but that's not much of a final chapter, is it? I thought about doing it myself from time to time. I prayed on it, but blessed be he who stands up under temptation."

"Don't mock scripture, Bobby. You were as much a part of his evil as the others. God will deal with you, too," Sam said.

"Careful what you say about me, Sam. I had nothing to do with any of it. Man, I really bought your father's saviour act when I was still in prison. Thought I was saved, and then I find out his church was knee-deep in that shit. Didn't take me long to see who was calling the shots. I saw an opportunity and contacted some old friends. They put me on the payroll. All I had to do was babysit your father. Make sure he didn't do anything to jeopardize what was happening at the ranch. Guess that gig is over."

"For whoever knows the right thing to do and fails to do it," Sam said. "That is your sin, Bobby."

Bobby stood and moved toward Lolita. He brushed Sam aside and placed a hand on Lolita's cheek. She pulled back, placed her own hand where his had been.

"No sin in sampling your wares now, is there?" He moved to the patio doors and looked out over the lake. Lolita eyed her purse. Bobby turned back before she could make a move.

"Here's the thing, Sam. What happens at the ranch is not evil, not really. I couldn't see it at first, but Pastor Sandy showed me. Look at the two of you. You are alive, healthy. You especially, Sam, living in this beautiful home. You would both be dead or worse, begging in the streets of some Third World slum if he hadn't found you. The church saved you both. Just as it has saved hundreds of children just like you."

"Saved us, are you fucking kidding?" Lolita's hands shook at her sides. "Do you have any idea what they did to us?" Sam moved closer, put his arm around her.

"Most of the kids never saw the inside of the ranch. A few were chosen. So what? Most go to great homes. Even you survived it, so no big deal, right? You two are the real heroes if you think about it, not Sandy. Martyrs, if you want to put it that way. What happened to you covered the cost of admission for the others. You paid a price, like Thelma, a true martyr to the cause."

"We had nothing to do with that."

"I know, Sam. That bit of work was beyond you. Thelma had to be sacrificed in a special way. The foolish bitch was going to tell the police everything. She thought Sandy's death was a sign. She spoke to a few of us about it after the prayer vigil that night. No talking her out of it. Like I said, my job was to make sure nothing got in the way of the operation. I made damned sure her death was a sign to the others in this little church of ours. Their silence is proof that it worked. A little bit of overkill can go a long way in keeping squares quiet, don't you think?"

Lolita could feel the tension in Sam's arm as he pulled her tight. Could feel his body tremble. Maybe she was trembling.

"You know what's funny? I won't get caught. I did a hooker like that in my bad old days. Well, that's kind of cold, she was sort of a girlfriend. Anyway, she needed killing. She was planning to rat, just like our Thelma. I wanted to give her a Colombian necktie, but I couldn't quite get it right, so I developed my own silencer for rats. I hacked out her vocal chords. Did that to Thelma just to revisit the old thrill, you know. Back then, no cop ever looked at me. You think God was training me then, Sam? A little divine preparation for the day I had to be strong?"

"Why are you here, Bobby? What do you want?" Lolita demanded.

"I want this. All of this." Simms gestured around the kitchen. "I am going to be the new voice of the Church of Salvation. The congregation already accepts me as a sign of Christ's power. A prisoner saved. I can take that into the pulpit and rake in the money from the saved and the depraved. Forget the ranch for now, the donations from the TV show will keep us going. Later, maybe we start a similar operation at a new location." He sipped his coffee. Placed the cup back on the table. "Speaking of killing, someone will be taking the fall for Sandy and Thelma. Lolita, you'll just have to take one for the team. I'm afraid you are going to have to kill yourself back up in that office—same as Sandy—and the knife that killed Thelma will be in your purse when they find you."

Bobby reached out and grabbed Lolita's wrist before she could react. She tried to break free, but his grip was too strong. He pulled her from Sam.

"It's okay, Tatjana. God is with us. He protects us," Sam said.

"Psalm 46. A beautiful sentiment. But the only protection you have right now is me, Sam. I can help both of us make all of this go away. We have to sacrifice her. Sorry. No real loss. There will be others. Believe me." Simms reached up and stroked Lolita's cheek again. She felt a chill as he put his hands on her shoulders and forced her to kneel in front of him. She knew what was next. He reached down and unzipped his pants and pushed her head down. She tried to resist, but he was strong.

"How about Romans 12:19, Bobby? You know that one." Sam sounded angry, almost shouting as he said it.

The boom startled Lolita. It bounced off the walls and windows as though the sound was coming from everywhere at once. Bobby's hand fell into his lap beside her face. She turned to Sam and saw a gun in his hand, smoke rising from the small barrel. She saw a drawer open beneath the coffee machine and remembered Saturday night when they had taken Bobby's gun from the wharf. Sam pulled her to her feet. Bobby was slumped in the chair again, his eyes blinking rapidly, his lips moving, but no Bible verses coming now. Blood spread slowly across his chest. Sam moved closer, pushed the gun into the bloody lips.

"For the wages of sin is death." He pulled the trigger again.

The back of Bobby's head exploded. Lolita watched smoke rise from the opening. The clean white wall turned red behind him. She placed a hand on Samuel's shoulder.

"You know, I think I hated him more than the men who came to the ranch. Thelma, too, her especially. I'm glad he killed her," he said. "She could have stopped it. I told her when I was a kid. She told me God wanted it that way, that I had to keep doing it for Him. Told me I had to keep God's secret with her. I believed it, for a long time. I believed it."

Lolita kissed him softly. She noticed another glint of sun through the front window. Another car.

✦✦✦

Carla turned off the car radio. The music was a pleasant distraction but definitely against the rules when she was on duty. She didn't turn off the car's police radio. She just turned it down on routine runs like this. If only her by-the-book father knew she bent the rules all the time. She watched the green bar move slowly across the screen, listened to the swooshing sound as the text left her phone. Not too much, just the basic information about the burned up gun and shells. She did add, "thanks for the tip," and used the smiley face, after all. What the hell. She opened the door and stepped out into a pool of sunlight. She had barely cleared the front of the car when her phone chirped. She smiled as she looked at the screen.

"Hello, Cam." She leaned back on the front of the car, happy that he could not see her silly grin at the sound of his voice on the line. He asked her if she could recover prints from the gun, could she match ballistics to the shells from the parking garage.

"I can't be sure. Prints are a long shot unless we find something inside the clip. I'd bet on ballistics. The gun is burned pretty bad, but it didn't melt. It's at the lab now. Any chance you can tell me how you knew where the car was?" she asked as she watched the front door of the house open. She had to hold a hand up in front of her face to block the sunlight to see who it was. She waved, and held up her index finger as she recognized Samuel.

"Listen, Cam, I'd love to chat, but I'm out here doing real police work." She held the finger up for Samuel again as she listened.

"No, not in Herring Cove. I'm at Sandy Gardner's house. I have to pick up some carpet fibers and a DNA swab."

The phone fell as the feeling left her right arm. She turned at the sound of a crack behind her and saw the spider webbing around the hole in her windshield. She knew it was a bullet hole. She'd photographed hundreds just like it. She fell, bouncing her head off the hood of the car as her left leg quit on her just as her right arm had. She lay on her back, grabbed at the gun on her right hip with her left hand. She fumbled with the safety catch on the leather holster and had to force the right hand into place by rocking her shoulder on the pavement to drag the useless arm back to her side. The gun finally came free. The headlight above her burst into a shower of glass and plastic. Thank God it didn't get in her eyes.

She rolled over onto her stomach and looked for the shooter. It was Samuel Gardner. She pointed the gun with her left and cursed herself for never once pulling the trigger with her off hand at the range. The instructor told her to try it a few times, but she thought it was silly. Gun qualifications were a waste of time anyway, she was an Ident officer. She arrived after a crime, not during it.

A spray of rock chips blinded her for a second as a bullet hit the driveway. She fought to centre the gun on Samuel, her arm moving on its own. There was a girl in a flowery sundress behind him. Why the hell didn't she get out of the way? Finally, the gun settled, and she squeezed the trigger. At least she remembered that much. The gun jumped in front of her, and when it settled back, Samuel was gone. She saw him down on the driveway. He wasn't moving, and the girl was down by his side. The pain began to spread from her right forearm up past her shoulder into her neck and down into her chest. Wow, that hurt like hell. A new hotter pain began to crawl up her left leg. She saw the phone beside her and looked out over the gun once more. Samuel wasn't moving. She dropped the gun on the driveway and grabbed the phone.

"Cam, I'm hit. Call it in. Samuel Gardner just shot me." She couldn't believe the words even as they came out. "No, no. He's down; I got him. I don't know if he's alive. God, Cam, there was a girl behind him. I don't know if I hit her, too. I can't get up. Get me some help."

She looked up and saw the girl in the dress. She was covered in blood, but she was standing. Thank God. Then she saw the gun in the girl's hand and looked at hers, on the ground beside her. She couldn't grab it, not fast enough. The girl screamed and pointed the gun.

"Please don't shoot me."

⊢━┿━━┥

Moments earlier

"It's a police officer. She was here before," Samuel said.

"Oh, my God. Bobby's body. Sam, we're going to jail forever." Lolita stared past him through the window.

"You stay here, and I'll take care of it." He stepped outside.

The fresh smell of cedar bark poured in from the open doorway. She looked back at Bobby's body in the kitchen. A cop. Could she move Bobby? She jumped at the crack of the gun. She stepped out. Samuel stood on the stone driveway beneath the steps. He fired twice more, and she watched the cop fall into a pool of sunlight in front of her car. Maybe God really was looking after him. She didn't believe in God, not the way Sam did. Maybe if she believed, none of those terrible things would have happened to her, but her grandmother prayed and terrible things happened to her. Maybe Samuel knew how to do it right, or maybe he really was just crazy. She jumped at the boom as a flash of fire came from the cop. Samuel dropped. His knees just bent and down he went. One second standing, the next not. He didn't fly backwards like he should have. Maybe God was keeping him from getting hurt, even though he was letting the cop shoot him. Strange God that one.

Lolita knelt beside him. There was a hole in his chest, and blood was bubbling out. He was grabbing at it, trying to make it stop. She felt real tears now, not just a trickle. She couldn't see clearly, and her nose was running. She gasped and gulped for air just as Sam did. She pressed herself into his chest. Maybe if she hugged him, it would stop. She reached under his back and held him tight, placing her cheek to his. She felt the tremors and convulsions stop. She held him tight. She could tell he wasn't breathing. She lifted her face and let her hair fall across his. Her tears dropped onto him, rolling down his cheeks to the driveway. She kissed his open eyes. The gun was still in his hand. She took it and stood.

She tried to smooth her new dress. It was ruined. There was so much blood that she couldn't see the flowers. She turned to the bitch cop. She was still on the ground, on her phone. Bragging about it. Fucking cops, all they did was take. Didn't matter what you had, they'd take it. Making it so Lolita could never be happy, never be Tatjana even if she wanted to. There could only be Lolita. Tatjana died with Samuel. She walked over and stood above the killer bitch. She screamed at her. She hated her, she wanted to eat her and spit her out. The bitch had everything. She probably had pretty dresses and a husband and a kitchen and everything.

Lolita pointed the gun. The cop was bleeding and begging, had her own tears now. Lolita spit on her. She shot her and walked back to Sam.

CHAPTER 20

Monday, earlier

I RAN A CLOTH ALONG THE LENGTH OF THE EXHAUST, FELT THE WARM sun on my back. The bike was already clean, I was just rubbing out a few water spots Williams left behind. He was busy finding out which of his thugs left the Escalade to be destroyed. Gunner made it sucker-punch clear how important the job was before he left. I was weighing the threat from Montreal as I wiped down the bike. Yves wouldn't kill me. We had history. But there would always be Stallion members who would, founder's son or not. I committed the ultimate betrayal. I was a cop. There was no undoing that. I had the patch on my back again. Pulling it off was no longer an option. My only out was a body bag. That was fair. I knew it. I didn't care. I wanted Greg's killer. If it was a Russian hit, I'd want more than the hit team. I'd attack the Russians who had called the shot. That would put the Stallion at war in Montreal, Toronto, and Vancouver. I could never walk away if I started that.

My cellphone chirped. It was sitting on a cement curb behind the line of bikes. I grabbed it and sat behind my bike. It was a text from Carla. She'd found the Cadillac and the gun. I felt a rush of adrenaline. The Litter Box boys did burn that SUV. Someone in the Box knew who'd been behind the wheel when those shots were fired. The club could reach out and touch the shooter, Russian or not. I would do the touching. But if a Russian hit team had used

Litter Box help, why didn't the club know? It made no sense. Didn't have to. Like we said in special ops, "Kill 'em all, let God sort out the bodies." Kept most of us alive in the war. Might work now. I dialled Carla.

"Hey. Any prints on the gun? Can you match it to the shells at the scene?" I asked.

No prints, she was waiting on ballistics. She wanted to know how I'd known where the Escalade was.

"When people torch cars around Spryfield, the club knows, Carla. Think about it."

She was cutting me off, claiming to be too busy being a real cop. Cute.

"Good for you. I'm just washing my bike. You still with the truck?"

I didn't like the answer. She was back in Waverley. That scene was picked over. If she was doing follow-up there, she wasn't doing anything to help find the shooter.

"When you get the report back, will you—" I heard a gunshot and her phone clatter. "Carla, what's happening?" I knew the answer. She was under fire.

I stood and paced out past the row of bikes. More gunfire, three more shots and then one so close to the phone it distorted. She was returning fire. Even through the phone, the sound of a firefight stirred up the familiar mix of terror, anger, and disbelief. Her voice was strained and higher, but she was back on the line.

"Carla, slow down. Is he down? Is it over? Are you safe?"

"I'll call it in" I said as I heard a woman's scream. Had to be the girl she said was standing with Sam. The hysterical voice was close to Carla's phone, too close. I heard another shot. I fought the urge to keep listening. I hit the kill switch and dialed 911.

"It's Detective Constable Cam Neville. Officer down at the Gardner scene in Waverley. I don't have the civic. It's the same scene we worked Thursday. Sgt. Carla Cage is under fire there now, and she's alone. I heard gunfire over the phone and then lost contact. She said it was Samuel Gardner, but I think there may be a second shooter, sounded like a woman. I am headed there now."

I knew I was talking too fast, but I also knew the operator had instant digital playback. I turned to my bike and saw Gunner and Snake standing there.

"What the fuck was that 'Constable Neville, officer down' cop shit?" Snake asked. I ignored him and looked at Gunner.

"It's Carla. We were on the phone, and she took fire. I gotta go."

"Like fuck." Snake stepped out to block me. I was about to drop him when Gunner stepped between us.

"It's his ol' lady, Snake. You met her." He placed a hand on my chest as I pushed toward the bike.

"Fuck. We all go," Snake said.

They headed to their bikes as I mounted mine. I thought about what Gunner said. Was Carla really my old lady? Could she be? Was she even alive? I snapped open the compression releases on the side of the engine and punched the start button. The bike fired, and I jammed it into gear. The engine choked on the sudden spray of gas as I opened the throttle too quickly; it backfired and recovered. The power train grabbed with a violence that almost tossed me from the saddle. The bike swerved right, then left, as the rear tire spun, fighting for traction. The front wheel pulled up as the rear found what it needed. It wasn't pretty, but the bike leapt into the street. In seconds, we were on the MacKay Bridge crossing the harbour. Lane splitting is illegal in Nova Scotia. I didn't care. I shot up between the cars headed for Dartmouth, but that wasn't fast enough, so I moved out around the Dartmouth-bound traffic and squeezed between two oncoming cars, then pushed it all the way to the guard rail on the far left, forcing oncomers into their passing lane. I needed the drivers to see me if I was going to get through. I shot toward the tolls at more than double the limit. I glanced at the blurred image in the vibrating mirror above my left hand and saw the two tiny headlights chasing me. Gunner and Snake weren't far behind. I choked down the fear. It had nothing to do with the wild ride.

+++

We hit the Waverley Road and rolled up behind a cruiser, its red-and-blue lights popping, its siren screaming. I swallowed the urge to pass. We'd get there faster with him clearing traffic ahead. The Waverley Road traces a series of lakes to Fall River. A biker's dream roller coaster of hills and sweeping turns. Today it was a nightmare, as the cop kept jamming on his brakes in the turns and then accelerating again. I pulled the front brake and then twisted the throttle, matching his slow-and-go pace. Snake was inches to my right. Gunner's front wheel split the small space between our rear wheels. One bad move, and we all drop. Outlaw riding is tight, but this was insane. I could see the cop yelling into his mic, all nerves, responding to an officer-down call and cursing the three bikes crowding him.

Sandy Gardner's place sits in the middle of a straight run between two of the most severe curves in the road. The cop slid the cruiser to a stop across the driveway. We dropped into single file. I hit the brakes and stood on the pegs to look beyond his car for Carla. I was so busy looking for her that I didn't see sand at the edge of the driveway. The rear tire found it and shot out to the right as the brake locked. I knew the feeling, there was no arguing with it. The bike was gone. I pulled my left leg out from under the frame as it dropped and began sliding along the stone. I stood with my foot on the high side. The bike slammed into the rear of the cruiser, and I rolled over the back of the car, landing on the ground beside it. I scrambled to my feet and headed into the driveway.

"You, stop now, goddamn it."

I looked back. The officer was out of his car now, his gun levelled over the open door toward me. He backed tighter into the small space as he looked at Gunner and Snake. He looked to be maybe twenty-three. His hand shook, the gun barely in his control. A second cruiser was parked inside the driveway. Whoever put it there would be as jumpy and trigger-happy as the first cop. I raised my hands.

"Hang on, hang on, I'm a cop, Detective Constable Cam Neville," I said to the guy behind the car. "I called it in." I turned to Snake and Gunner. "Don't fucking move." I saw Gunner grab Snake's arm. Would the old man really pull on me here? A problem for later. I had no time to pave the way for them.

Constable Lori MacLean inched around the front of the other cruiser in a crouch, her gun pointed at me. I flashed on the smile I'd seen on her face when she'd stood beside Greg the last time we were here. No smile now, but no panic either. One of our unmarked cars sat just beyond her cruiser. I recognized Carla's biker boot twisted at an awkward angle in front of the car. My knees buckled, and I let one drop to the stone driveway.

"It's okay. Let him in," MacLean shouted to the terrified cop behind me. "We have two down here. I can't get close enough to check, but I think they are both dead. We need to secure the house before we can get close enough." She turned away, her gun pointed at the house. She was frozen in place.

I ran to the boot. As I cleared the car, I saw Carla, face up in the driveway. Shards of what looked like broken glass glistened red in the pool of blood reaching out from her. I looked toward the house and saw Samuel Gardner on the ground, surrounded in his own nimbus of red.

"There may be another shooter, a girl. She may be inside. Let's just hold tight until backup arrives." I shouted the order as I moved to Carla. I gently pressed my fingers to her throat. Her eyes opened. I felt my heart roll over in my chest.

"Hang in there, Carla, help is on the way. Can you move?"

She struggled to rise. Her eyes closed again, and she fell back to the driveway. I turned back to Constable MacLean.

"She's alive. We need to clear that house now. We've gotta get paramedics in here fast."

I felt Carla's blood seep through my jeans as I knelt beside her. Her gun was in a lake of blood. It was probably still operating, but I couldn't risk it in a firefight. Blood could jam a weapon. I needed a clean gun, fast. I could hear sirens and the sound of two Harleys racing away, engines howling under load. I could feel the sun's heat on the black leather on my shoulders. I needed to move, to clear that house, but I couldn't abandon Carla.

"Sir, should I go around back?" The young cop was crouching beside me now. He looked at my colours, but said nothing. I looked at his name tag,

"Get me your big gun, Constable Dill. I don't have a weapon." Every cruiser has a pump gun in the trunk at the least, a fully automatic C8 if Dill's cruiser was up to standard. If the shooter was inside, girl or not, I was going to cut her in two. He ran back for the gun. I moved to the front of MacLean's cruiser without looking back at Carla. I couldn't help her by kneeling there. The sirens got louder. One would be an ambulance. It would be held back a safe distance from the house until this scene was secure. I couldn't let them sit there and wait while Carla was bleeding out. The cop shoved a tactical shotgun into my hand, no C8 but more than enough gun.

"Okay, you go around to the patio on the right side. Go fucking slow, you hear me. There's a girl here somewhere, and it's a safe bet she has a gun. Constable MacLean, take the left beside the garage. I just want you two to get eyes on the backyard, make sure she doesn't run, okay?"

"Are you going in?" It was MacLean.

"Yes, I am. Just cover the sides."

I moved to the doorway, did a fast pulse check. Samuel was dead. *Good for you, Carla.* The front door was open about an inch. I moved up the steps and pushed it in with the barrel of the shotgun. I should be waiting. I should have MacLean and Dill stacked up behind me. There is a right way to do it, a safe way. First officer in breaks right, second breaks left. You chase your gun along the wall, looking for targets, knowing the middle of the room is covered by the third member of the team. I wasn't waiting for backup. I didn't want witnesses. I knew the house well enough to play the odds. If she was inside, the girl would likely be all the way in the kitchen or down the hall hiding, not lying in wait inside the small foyer. I rushed in and dashed across the floor, slamming my back against the knee wall that jutted into the kitchen entrance. Nothing. I dropped to my stomach and eased my face around the wall. She'd be looking higher if she was waiting. The kitchen was clear, boiling water spilling out of a pot popping and hissing on the stovetop. I saw the pot before I heard the hiss. That was a problem. My pulse pounding in my ears blocked everything else. I had to take a deep breath and gather my senses. Not hearing is as bad as not seeing; it could be fatal.

The sound of the gunshot was unmistakable, and I probably would have heard it even with my pulse pounding in my eardrums. I rolled back behind the knee wall and pulled my legs under me. The shot came from the hallway beyond the kitchen. I was calm. Being under fire is easier than thinking you might come under fire. When it's real, you can fight back. I dumped a round high into the open doorway to keep the shooter down as I ran past to take a position in the kitchen. I caught a glimpse of Bobby Simms sitting at the table and spun, putting the shotgun on him. The trigger was about an ounce shy of breaking when I eased up. He was not a threat. I leaned out and took a quick glimpse into the hallway.

The girl was sitting on the floor, staring at the gun in her lap. She was small, looked to be maybe thirteen. The front of her dress was covered in blood. I thought maybe I'd hit her, but she raised her head and looked at me. She lifted the gun, and I dove to the right. I slid into the patio door in a shower of broken glass as I heard her second shot.

"Get out. Get out," she yelled. "I won't go back. You can't make me. Fuck the Stallion."

I could hear the sobbing from the hallway. I thought it would be easy to shoot her when I saw Carla in the driveway. I tried to put that image back in my head, but all I saw was a tiny, broken girl with a gun in her lap. I couldn't kill her. I had to disarm her before she shot anyone else. I moved to the wall and inched my way past the kitchen table to crouch next to the opening to the hallway.

"Hey, are you still there?"

She answered with another shot. The pot jumped from the top of the stove, spraying water over the floor. She wasn't aiming, just shooting. I wanted to rush her, but it would be suicide.

"Hey, let's talk. Just you and me. Okay?"

"Fuck you. You think I don't know a Nomad. You're gonna kill me. I know it."

"Hey, come on now. Why would I want to do that? Just calm down, okay?" I looked at the Nomad patch arching up the front of my vest and wondered at her observation skills during a shootout.

"Go away," she cried. "Just leave me alone. Fuck that midget. He killed that cop, I didn't do nothin'."

I waited, didn't know what to say as her sobs grew louder. I looked around the kitchen for a way to distract her so I could disarm her.

"You don't want to do this. Please, there has been enough killing." I looked over at Bobby Simms's body. "What happened to Bobby?" I hoped I could draw her into a conversation.

"Fuck him too, he killed that woman and said I had to take the blame. For killing Sam's father, too. I already told Gunner I didn't kill him. That stupid preacher killed himself. I didn't break any rules. Just leave me alone." She punctuated it with another blind shot into the kitchen. The sobs stopped; she was angry again. Good, angry is easier to deal with.

"Look, I am not going to hurt you. No one is, we can sort this out."

"No, you're going to kill me because of that dead cop. I know it."

She wasn't making sense, but she wasn't in shock. She knew I was wearing Stallion colours. She did not see my back, just the Nomad patch. She had to know the club well to call it from that and the few badges on the front of my cut. She had to be the dancer Blair had gone to see. He said she looked like a kid.

"Hey, come on. Lolita, right? That cop's not dead. She's going to make it. I just want to get you out of here. The cops are coming. You hear that?" The sirens outside seemed constant as more and more officers arrived.

"I'll kill them all. I'll kill you."

Her voice sounded different, calmer. Not good. I heard movement. She was standing. I pressed my back into the wall and pulled the shotgun tight to my chest, tilting it slightly toward the doorway. She walked out and swung the gun my way. She wanted out, and I was her ticket. I hesitated and felt the burn as she took a shot.

The kick of the shotgun hurt more as the butt punched the inside of my left thigh. She fell back into the hallway; her gun dropped beside me. I kicked it away and rolled into the doorway.

She looked like a broken doll on the floor in front of me. Blood poured from a hole just below her throat. She looked so young. I'd seen dead kids who were a lot younger. You could never unsee them. This one was mine, and there was nothing I could do to change it. Her head was tilted to the side, facing the open door to Sandy Gardner's bedroom. I wanted to turn it back away from that place. I picked up her left wrist to check, but I knew I'd find nothing.

+++

The mobile command bus sat in Gardner's driveway again. The weather was the same, too. That's where the similarities ended. This time I was sitting inside, waiting for the chief. I was covered in blood, Carla's, the girl's, and mine. A compression bandage on my left shoulder leaked red. The paramedic who put it there told me Carla was unconscious with strong life signs when the ambulance left. He figured another five minutes out there and she would not have made it. Maybe killing the girl had an upside.

The list of people I've killed is too long. It was too long when the first man started the list. For a sniper, a kill is intimate. You never forget that shape locked in the centre of the reticle, clear and moving with life one second, and then gone. Blown into the air in a final death spiral by a .50-calibre armour-piercing slug. I'd seen too many men explode like that, and could replay every one. I killed two men in close combat, too. Got caught in a firefight on a narrow street. A close-up fight is a crazy scramble of images and sound. The world flips upside down, and things happen in a timeless kaleidoscope. I remember seeing the bodies after the fight. I didn't have that same connection with the moment they died; it was all just confusion and motion. I rubbed my inner thigh where a bruise was forming. As I touched it, I could smell the discharge from the shotgun, feel the recoil again, and see the girl floating backwards into the hallway. That was intimate.

The chief stepped into the bus and stood above me.

"Jesus, Neville, you okay?"

"Great." He'd seen enough combat to know the question and the answer were meaningless.

"Take that damn vest off, will you? We need to talk about this."

I ignored the request.

"What the hell happened?" he asked.

I told him what I knew. What I'd heard on the phone. What happened in the house. It was the third time I'd told the story, but I filled in more detail this time, more for me than for him. Best I could figure, Carla had stumbled into some kind of fight between Samuel Gardner and Bobby Simms. I took a sip from a can of soda someone, maybe the paramedic, had given me.

"Another thing, Chief. That Ford outside matches the one on the security tape from the clubhouse. I think Samuel killed his father. Girl inside said Gardner killed himself, so I'm not sure. She said Simms killed Thelma Waters and was pinning it on her."

I didn't know how Bobby ended up dead. A falling out of some kind? It didn't matter, no great loss. The girl I'd killed was another thing; she did matter, and she still didn't fit anywhere in this puzzle.

"You think she is involved?" he asked, reading my mind.

"Damned if I know. She recognized the Stallion patches on the front of my vest. Said I was here to kill her because of the dead cop." What had she said about a midget? Jimmy Williams? Blair? She wasn't talking about Carla. Adrenaline pushed all the pain from my body and patience from my mind.

"Why would the club care if she shot Sergeant Cage?"

I swallowed, tried to hide what I was feeling.

"I don't know."

"She puts the gang in this until we figure it out." He looked at my vest again.

"Snake gave me that tape, Chief. Can't see him doing that if the club was involved. Could be she was just a runaway stripper afraid the club was looking for its money."

I didn't want him thinking too hard about the club. I thought about Yves Laroche. I thought he'd come from Montreal because I patched back in, but maybe he was here on Nomad business. Would Gunner know? I needed to talk to Yves alone.

"We're going to have to pull Snake in, anyway." The chief moved to the window of the bus and looked out on the driveway. I knew he was looking at the blood where Carla had fallen. He'd been an officer in Afghanistan. He'd lost his own people in battle before. I'd lost Ronald that way, and I still fight my own demons over it. I hoped Carla wouldn't be added to the list for either one of us.

"Chief, this is a clean shoot, and everyone here knows it." It was more of a question than a statement.

"Yeah, MacLean and Dill say they heard her shoot several times, only heard two blasts from the shotgun. That graze on your arm isn't self-inflicted. The shooting is not my concern."

I waited.

"Cam, you took over this scene and killed a girl, wearing those colours. You don't even have a badge. I can maybe finesse that, say you were undercover, but you gotta drop that vest now."

"Chief, I want to know who killed my brother and shot my partner. This doesn't change that. If it turns out the club was somehow involved in that shooting, I have a better chance at justice this way."

"Revenge isn't justice, Cam. You need to think this through." He looked out the window and then back to me. "Regret is a heartless motherfucker. It will eat you alive, son."

"Can I leave?"

He looked at me and said nothing for a moment. Something passed over his eyes.

"Go."

Someone had pulled my bike out from under the cruiser and stood it on its kickstand. The front and rear turn signals were gone on the left side, so was the mirror. A large black stain under the cruiser told me I'd lost at least half the oil and maybe some gas. It started on the first try, that's a tight engine. My shoulder throbbed as I pulled the clutch lever. I headed slowly out onto the Waverley Road and wished my brother was still beside me. I regretted yelling those orders at Snake and Gunner like some asshole cop. All they were doing was trying to stand with a bro, and I turned on them the minute I stood beside that cruiser. I knew how that looked. Snake would not let it slide, and I needed the club, now more than ever.

┿┿┿

Monday evening

Gunner took a drink from the bottle, looked around the table at his bros, wondered about his brother. Snake slammed the gavel into the block at the head of the table. The patches were ready for church. Killing a member was the most serious business ever discussed at the table, and the tension ran high. Yves Laroche sat at the corner nearest Gunner.

"Let's do this," Snake said, looking at Gunner.

"Brothers, the Hammer has to go down." Yves spoke first. "Gunner, I am sorry, bro. You know I love you both, but he turned on this club a second time."

He was right. Gunner hated hearing it, but Cam was showing all blue and no silver, he admitted. He couldn't save him. When it was time, he'd do it himself. Cam deserved that much.

"This has to be on us," Snake said to Yves.

"He's a Nomad. We clean our own mess."

"He's a founder's son first, a Nomad later." Grease rarely spoke at club meetings, and everyone turned to him. "I want to know what he did before I vote. I want it from Gunner."

Gunner leaned back in his chair, not sure what to say. Cam had made a choice, the wrong choice. Could be his ol' lady had him twisted up, but even that couldn't excuse it. Club first, bitches second, always. He'd turned his back on the club again. Worse than that. He was out there giving orders to cops, wearing a Stallion patch. That was not something that could be forgiven. Fuck.

"He made his choice, Grease." Gunner stood. "We went to Waverley with him. Had his back. His ol' lady got shot."

"Shot by who?" Grease asked. The others at the table seemed willing to sit back and let Grease and Gunner talk this through before the vote.

"Don't know. When we got there, the cops were there. He told us to stay put. Went in with them."

"Ol' lady make it?"

"Don't know." Gunner looked at Snake.

"I'd say no. I could see her on the ground. She wasn't moving. Lotta blood." Snake ran his hand through his hair and looked at Yves.

"I say we hear him on it," Grease said.

"No, no, he never steps in this house again." Yves stood.

"Last time I checked this wasn't your house, Yves." Snake stood.

"Wait." Grease raised his hand. "Man loses his brother and his ol' lady. Gonna make some poor choices. Maybe we owe him a minute at the table."

"You know this decision is not going to be made at this table," Yves said. "This has to go to Montreal."

"No. You can pull that Nomad rocker in Montreal, but if we want him back you can't take him out. The constitution is clear on that. I'm not saying we want him. I think maybe we don't. I'm saying we hear him." Grease looked at Snake. They were the only two founding members still wearing Stallion colours, the only two left who had helped write that constitution. No one would argue the point with either.

Snake stood and paced toward the door. He paused, looking at the flag from the mother chapter. He placed a hand on the fabric. Gunner knew it was his father's signature Snake was holding.

"Yves, we hear him out and we take the vote with him in the room. If he dies, he dies in this room with everyone sharing it." He looked at Gunner.

"If he dies, no one shares in it. I do it alone," Gunner said.

"Settled then." Snake reached back to the tabletop, grabbed the gavel, and slammed it again. Church was over.

†††

The sun dropped into a red free fall beyond the container pier as I arrived at the clubhouse. The gate was closed, and I had to wait for a hang-around to let me inside. If the hang-arounds were manning the gate, the prospects had to be guarding the house itself. That meant church was in session. Good. Everyone I needed would be in one room. Well, not everybody.

I parked my bike in the line and dropped my helmet over the remaining mirror. A prospect ran over to look at the damage. Jimmy Williams was standing beside the main door with Phil Murphy. The only way he could provide security was to bring help. I needed answers, and I would start with Williams.

"Get in the fucking house, both of you," I told them. "Hey, prospect, take this door," I yelled at the guy checking out my ride.

Inside, the main room of the clubhouse was empty. Everybody was upstairs in church.

"I just killed a girl. Pretty sure she was one of your dancers."

They both looked at me. Williams recovered faster. "Where? At the club?"

"No, she was at Sandy Gardner's house. Know anything about that?"

"Fuck."

"Fuck what?"

Williams looked at Murphy for help. Murphy looked at me and stayed put. I was pretty sure it was the patch he was avoiding.

"I asked you a question, prospect."

"Look, I'm sorry. It's just you, are you still a cop?"

I punched him with a short fast right jab. His head rolled back, but he stayed on his feet. With my left shoulder taped, I couldn't get enough in it to knock him down. He looked at Murphy again. This time the big guy made a slight move. I stepped up to him, and he eased back.

"Nicholas Mapp says I shouldn't talk about her," Williams said as he rubbed his chin, a defiant look in his eyes.

I knew Mapp. Not well, but I knew who he was. A rich asshole trying to play bad boy when I was still riding with the club.

He thought his money could buy him a patch, but it never got him past hang-around status. He wasn't good enough to wear the patch, but the club used him in other ways back then, mostly to launder money through a used-car lot he owned out in Lower Sackville. He was running a much bigger operation when I returned from the war, and I figured it was built with club money. Still, there was no way Snake would let him give orders, not even to a prospect.

"You a fucking car salesman or a prospect for this club, idiot?"

"What?"

"Mapp doesn't give orders to us; we give them to him. Talk."

The defiance was replaced with something that looked like panic. I hit him with another jab to help him focus. This time I ignored Murphy.

"Okay, okay, her name is Lolita. She's fucking crazy. Thinks that preacher's son is her brother. I had to keep you, keep the cops, from getting to her. Mapp told me to do it. It's about protecting the club, man, that's all."

The pounding in my ears returned. My fists were clenched, my hands shook. I tried to swallow it down but knew I was losing.

"Keep the cops away how?" It came out slow, quiet.

"He gave the order. I didn't mean to shoot no priest."

He was backing away, trying to get behind Murphy. I kicked him in the chest. He flew backwards, breaking glasses, overturning tables. I was going to kill him. We both knew it.

Murphy stepped into my path. Fair enough. I looked at him. There was nothing in his eyes. He knew where we were headed. Didn't seem to want it. I didn't either. I couldn't take him. I knew it. Not because he was bigger, but because a bullet had taken my left arm out of it. I'd need everything to take a monster that big. I saw Greg, covered in blood in my arms and knew I had to try. Lifting my hand to my chest, I felt the crucifix. Saw Blair in that hospital bed. I needed to slow my pulse and ease back on the adrenaline. Eight years in the ring had taught me that.

"You leave the Caddy at the warehouse?" I asked Phil, looking around for a weapon. He nodded.

"You pull a trigger?"

He shook his head.

"You wanna walk away? This isn't about you."

He raised his right hand and looked at a fresh burn and nodded, showing good judgment for the first time.

"Good. Go look after the door. No one gets in here. No one."

Murphy headed to the door as Williams scrambled away from me toward the bar. I followed. He disappeared behind it, and I could hear glass breaking. I stopped short as I reached the bar. The gun came out first; he was close behind it. I didn't hesitate, drove a fierce front kick up into the barrel. I felt the heat, nothing more as the gun exploded and spun up away from his grip. He'd missed. I grabbed his hair and dragged him out from behind the bar, drove a knee into his face, felt his nose break. I tossed him into an overturned table, heard wood crack and more glass break. I walked over and picked up the gun. I knelt beside him and forced the barrel into his mouth. I could feel the slack come out of the trigger. I waited for the explosion as I looked into his eyes.

"Bye, bye, motherfucker."

"What the fuck you doin', Hammer?" Yves asked. The whole crew was in the room. I ignored him.

"He killed Greg," I said, as I pushed the gun harder. Gunner moved in and pulled Williams out of the mess.

"Mapp told me to," he gurgled.

I didn't see the knife come out, I doubt if anyone did, but everyone in that room knew the sound of a blade cutting through leather, skin, muscle, and tendon. If they didn't before, they did now. The sound repeated over and over. The unmistakable wet sucking sound stopped. It was followed by two quick thuds as Williams's prize cowboy boots dropped from his lifeless body. Gunner tossed the dead prospect aside and turned to me. "You okay?"

I was still covered in blood.

"Yeah, fine," I said as I put the gun back on the bar.

"Anyone here still think he's a cop? Any vote needed?" Snake said.

I looked around the room. My brothers locked eyes with me one at a time and nodded. I knew what the vote was about. I'd just survived it.

"Lock down the house. We need to clean up this mess," Snake said.

"I'm leaving. This shit isn't finished yet," I said. I looked at Gunner. He nodded and we both headed for the door.

✠✠✠

Nicholas Mapp opened the door, wearing money. Gold chains dangled from his neck, an ugly gold watch hanging low on his wrist. His ankle-length white silk robe probably cost more than everything I was wearing. We followed him to the pool where he offered us a drink. I declined. Gunner walked to the bar to pour his own. We agreed, coming over, that I would question Mapp. Gunner could play Blair's part and watch, or maybe just drink. We didn't trust Jimmy Williams enough to walk in shooting. I needed the truth. If Mapp ordered the hit, I also needed to know why. I couldn't shake the club free of this thing, no matter how I looked at it. The club got Greg killed, I could feel it. Gunner said no way, but we both knew Mapp could be working some scheme with Yves Laroche and the Nomads. The only way to keep a secret is not to share it, even within the club. Especially within the club.

And then it all turned upside down. Inspector Carl MacIntosh walked into the pool house, wearing a terry-cloth robe over swimming trunks. He was carrying a glass of Scotch. A fat cigar hung between his fingers. He stopped short when he saw us. His face told me enough. Gunner moved fast, pulling his gun and grabbing the inspector by the shoulder. The glass of Scotch dropped, shattering on the stone floor.

"Who the fuck are you?" Gunner demanded.

"Easy, Gunner, easy." Mapp was on his feet. "He's a friend. It's all good, my brother. Relax."

MacIntosh's eyes never left mine.

"Sit the fuck down, asshole." Gunner shoved him toward a deck chair.

"Look, Detective, I can explain this." MacIntosh found his voice as he sat in the chair.

"You shut the fuck up before I let my brother kill you. The only guy doing any explaining is this little prick." I grabbed Mapp and pushed him back into his chair. He laughed as he fell into the seat.

"Look at you—back in the game, giving orders and taking no shit. God, that takes me back." Mapp lit a cigar through the laughter. If he felt any guilt over Greg's death, he didn't show it. "Great to see you in the colours again, Hammer. I guess it's too late to see you back in the octagon. A little old for that, I suppose."

"Got a fight or two left. I see you've moved up in the world." I walked to the edge of the pool, looked out over the dock and the boats outside. I nodded toward MacIntosh. "Making new friends in powerful places?"

"Yes, I suppose I am. But then, I thought you'd moved up in the world, too, although our mutual friend here tells me you are not much of a cop. No surprise, I guess. Stallion Forever and all that," he said.

"Yeah, well things change and things stay the same, Nick." I walked back, stood above him. I couldn't look at MacIntosh. I didn't know how this was going to play out, but his being here meant there was no going back for either one of us.

"Things change, things stay the same," Mapp repeated to no one. He still looked comfortable in the chair. Not a worry in the world. In control. A small black cellphone sat beside a silver iPhone on the table beside him. Something about it was familiar.

"I guess that means you are a two-bit spineless weasel, a richer one for sure, but still the same old dickless Nick." I slapped the cigar from his hand.

"What the fuck?" He struggled to get up. I pushed him back into the lounger.

"Gunner, you better let your brother know things have changed around here," Mapp squealed. "Neville, I don't know who you think you are, but you better think again." He did defiant well.

I grabbed the front of the silk robe and pulled him to his feet. "I'm the last guy you will ever see in this world, unless you answer some questions."

"Hold on, hold on. I have protection. Nomad protection." His eyes caught the Nomad patch on the front of my cut. "Okay. If this is about that idiot Williams, I can explain."

"Start with why you sent that idiot out with a MAC-10."

"He was supposed to take care of that nosy Indian. Our friend here set it up nicely."

"Now wait just a minute." MacIntosh was pushing to his feet again. I looked at Gunner. He slapped him hard across the face with the gun; blood began to pour from his cheekbone. It felt good to see the bastard pistol-whipped.

"Boys, come on now, you don't know what you're getting into here." Mapp tried to pull free of my grip. "We were just protecting a nice bit of business we had going with that dead preacher. We have it in hand now. The Waters woman planned to tell you, so she had to go, too."

He looked up at me as he said it. Like killing Thelma was somehow my fault. I had enough guilt, I wasn't going to own that.

"The Indian was sniffing too close and had to be put down. Strictly business, boys. We all know that can get messy. I've got the Russian mob on the hook for it, so the club is clear. We're good. I am sorry about your brother, though. Really, that was not necessary. That fucking moron Williams thought he was shooting you." Mapp smiled as he said it.

So Greg did take my bullets. And Blair was targeted by his own inspector. Mountie to Mountie. My breath came in shallow gulps; my heart raced.

I pushed Mapp back into the lounger. His robe opened, and I saw the horse tattoo. I turned and looked at the tattoo on MacIntosh's forearm. I always thought it was a tribute to the musical ride; now I saw that it looked more like the one Mapp and Gardner had.

"Tell me about that." I lifted my boot and pressed the heel into Mapp's hip.

"Hammer, back off," Mapp pleaded. "Jesus, man, I'll tell you. Relax, okay? Gunner, call him off."

Gunner stayed with MacIntosh. I pressed a little harder with my heel. Mapp tried to squirm away but there was nowhere to go. Finally, I saw fear in his eyes, then resignation. He was ready to play for a deal. The weasel not far beneath the bluster.

I sat on the edge of the chair next to his, my elbows on my knees, my head in my hands when he finished. The slide show from Sandy Gardner's laptop played in my mind, stopped on the little girl with the empty eyes. I looked up at Gunner.

"You know about this thing?" I asked my older brother.

"Nope."

"Yves?"

"His party, I guess," he said.

"How many kids you run through that place?" I asked Mapp.

"Not a lot. We don't need volume. You have to understand, Hammer, the movies we make with just one kid are worth a fortune. No distribution needed, virtually no overhead. It's all encrypted and moved through a secure server in Korea. Our customers get what they want instantly. We pick the kids carefully, reduce our exposure to risk. That's where Gardner came in. He did the shopping overseas and brought the chosen few in with orphans headed to legit homes." He was drinking his Scotch, had the cigar lit. Schooling us on the finer points of his kiddy-porn empire.

"All the kids Gardner's agency brings in have to go to Montreal once they clear Immigration here. A few get lost in the paperwork and end up at the ranch. Easier than you think. Not everyone can get a new mom in a minivan or a puppy. Cost of doing business. It's the business we're in, gentlemen."

"So how does he end up dead with a set of cuffs on his wrists?" I wanted to know what set all of this off.

Mapp smiled as he described exactly what Gardner liked and how he and Laroche used it to control him. Gardner was into bondage, asphyxiation, and kids. How does that even happen? It sickened me, but not as much as Mapp calling it "business."

I walked to the edge of the pool then circled back, pacing. Sex and drugs are the big money-makers for the club. That wasn't going to change. I knew a lot of members who didn't get involved in either business. I was one. But we all knew about it, so I guess we carry some guilt. We could live with the guilt, as long as we knew those in the game followed the club rules. The sex trade, like any profitable club business, was based in the belief that man-made laws are bullshit. As long as politicians legislate morality, the Stallion will cash in by serving those with a shaky moral compass. In the sex trade, youth is the blue chip. Couple of years south of legal is the golden age. No way would the club touch kiddy porn. Outlaw clubs live by a strict code. They don't exactly agree with the government's arbitrary rule on the age of majority. When it comes to sex, the Stallion code lets Mother Nature pick the date. Puberty is the magic minute. Any kid past that is fair game. If she's ready at thirteen, she's ready. Clubbers are fathers who expect to do time some day. Drawing that line is their way to protect their children from perverts when they are gone. It's a line the club would kill over back when I rode. Gunner's face told me that hadn't changed. What these guys were up to was not Stallion business, no matter what Mapp said.

"Everyone involved get that horse?" I asked. MacIntosh wouldn't look up. Mapp answered.

"No, that's exclusive. Costs a lot more than one of our movies. Guys pay a fortune for one of these. Well, some pay a fortune. For others, it's a reward for special services." He looked at MacIntosh as he said it. "Our own little stallion. It's reserved for those who pop the cherry on one of the new ponies. Boys, this is Stallion approved."

I didn't buy that. No way this was club approved.

But Laroche approved. I knew that was another thing. The Nomad president ran the Stallion porn business in all the federal prisons. He helped build an online porn empire for the club, and no one asked any questions as long as the money rolled in. Stallion lawyers taught the club the importance of secrecy. The club's biggest legal concern was being ruled a criminal organization under Canada's untested anti-gang laws. The Stallion didn't want to be the test case. So, small cells operating within the larger club ran every illegal operation in secrecy. It would be easy for the Nomads to run a kiddy-porn operation without drawing attention from the rest of the club. First, Stallion charters don't question Nomad operations, and second, no patch would question another member about business. Only cops and rats ask questions like that. Secrecy protected the club, but it also opened the door for this kind of operation.

"Come on Gunner, Hammer. This is just business; you have to let it be," Mapp said.

"I can't do that," I said to Gunner. "We're talking about kids. Fucking babies here. No way the patch stands behind that."

Suddenly, I wanted to drop the vest and pick up a badge. I knew what would happen to Mapp if I could get him behind bars—true outlaw justice. Then I looked at MacIntosh, and the badge felt even dirtier. The outlaw justice would have to happen outside of prison.

"Look, man, this sucks," Gunner said. "I know it, but if Yves got some shit going outta Montreal, we got to bring it to the table. He's running it in our backyard; that means we can kill it, but we gotta do it right. Nothing more we can do. That shit bird is right, man. This garbage is Stallion business."

"Fine, we vote on how we deal with the kiddy porn," I said. "What about this asshole? He took Greg out. That's not about the club."

Gunner walked over to the lounger. Mapp was fully recovered now, confident he was untouchable, protecting a valuable bit of club business. Gunner pulled the gun from his belt, it looked small like a .22. It exploded like a cannon as he shot Mapp in the stomach. Definitely not a .22.

"That's family business, different thing." Gunner tossed the gun to me.

I put one in Mapp's chest and another in his head. MacIntosh stared at me. Gunner looked at him. His fate was mine to decide. I walked over and stood beside him.

"Why?"

"I, umm. He forced me to protect the operation. They have pictures."

MacIntosh looked past me to the pool.

"Pictures of what?"

"Me, some kids. Look, it's not what it sounds like. Obviously, I underestimated you."

He looked at Gunner and stood slowly. He opened the robe, showing us he was unarmed.

He walked to the bar and poured a drink. I could see it happening again, exactly the way it did in the minutes after Greg was murdered. I watched his body language change, his chest expanding, his eyes locking on mine as he sipped the drink, assuming his command posture. He tipped the glass toward Mapp's body.

"I believe what you just did was a mistake," MacIntosh said, "but it shows me you are men of action. You are ready, willing, and, more importantly, able to do the unpleasant things that must sometimes be done."

"There was nothing unpleasant in that." I pointed the gun toward Mapp. "The only unpleasant thing around here is that tattoo on your arm and how you earned it. And how many other kids you tortured, how many of their tormentors you protected."

He sipped his drink, looking over the top of the glass, the same way he looked over his hands when he lectured me about Luke Weathers.

"Look, gentlemen..." I could feel another lecture coming on. "We still have a great opportunity here. As for the sex, you have to understand it is a perfectly natural thing. Some men—quite often men of power and great responsibility like us—need certain forms of release. All we are—"

I shot him before he finished. His body fell into the pool. I offered the gun to my brother. This time he took the head shot. For Greg.

Gunner was on his cell as we walked toward the door. A cleanup crew would be here within the hour. They'd burn the place, maybe take the bodies out in one of those fancy boats tied to Mapp's dock. I took back the gun and wiped it clean inside and out. I popped the clip, emptying it of the remaining shells. I pocketed them and slammed home the clip. Then I looked for a serial number; it was gone. That didn't surprise me, the name did. I looked at my big brother.

"A Baby Eagle .45?"

"Bought it for Cheyenne." He shrugged.

"Well, it's got two bodies on it now. Maybe get her the nine," I said as I tossed it into the pool.

We left the door unlocked and headed out into the evening chill.

+–+–+

I could smell disinfectant, fear, and death as I walked down the narrow corridor. The shining hospital floors accounted for the disinfectant. I wondered if the fear and death were coming from me. Kid Rock was singing about holding on through the tiny earbuds I wore. His raspy voice above Slash's guitar licks. I heard him sing about seasons changing and memories. The song carried me to another place, another season. I wasn't sure where that was, but I knew I'd never find my way back, not all the way back. The slow push of the music moved me forward in the wide hallway. I was disconnected, floating just outside the space and time my body filled. The ache in my right finger was my only anchor. I could still feel the pinch of the trigger break as the .45 spit death into Nicholas Mapp and Carl MacIntosh. I was used to the feeling. The phantom ache followed every kill back in Afghanistan. Now, like then, I knew the kills were justified, but, like then, I was lost afterward. I needed to find the anger again; it was the only way back.

Up ahead, a door opened into the hallway. Sue stepped out. Her face lit up as she saw me. Her smile cut through the fog and brought me back to what was important. Maybe I don't need anger anymore.

"Cam, how are you?" She hugged me as I pulled the earbuds free. I flinched as she held me.

"What's wrong?" she stepped back. "Are you hurt?"

"Just a flesh wound. I'm better now, Sue. Much better."

She looked at me and then hugged me again. More gently this time.

"Go see him, he's awake, Cam. It's amazing. I am just going for tea. Can I get you something?" she asked.

"No, I'll just be a minute."

"Take all the time you want," she said as she walked down the hall.

Blair's smile blasted away any doubt that lingered as I stepped into the room.

"Man, you look like shit," I said as I walked to the bedside.

"Fuck you very much, partner," he said through a broad grin.

His skin was chalky and seemed to sag under his chin. His thick black hair was matted against the pillow. A yellowish stain showed at the centre of the bandage wrapped around his neck. I smiled. He'd never looked better.

"Nice to see you out of intensive care."

"Yeah. Listen, Cam, I'm sorry about Greg, man. How are you holding up?" His smile was gone.

"I'm okay. Funeral is Wednesday, that'll be rough. Just glad I'm not going to two."

I put my hand on his. He didn't ask about my suspension or my return to the club. I figured Sue was keeping it from him. He didn't need the stress.

"Tell me about it. You believe this shit? A Russian hit? Man, those guys are out of control. Gunning for cops. Well, this cop is going to do some gunning of his own. I get out of here, we find the triggerman. Get some payback for this, for Greg."

I didn't say anything. Just looked at him. Didn't know what to say.

"What is it? You know something. Tell me, partner."

I thought for a moment. "It's done. Don't think about it. Nobody left to pay back. No shooters. No shot callers. You just heal, brother."

He lifted his hand out from under mine, grabbed my wrist and held tight. His eyes locked on mine. A tear rolled down the side of his face into the gauze.

"Thank you, brother. You okay with it?"

I nodded. I knew he'd never raise it again or ask any questions.

"How are we doing on our case, anything new?" He changed the subject.

"Long story, partner, but you were dead on with the stripper."

"Superior detecting skills. My people are natural trackers. We see the little things you white men miss."

"I see you weren't shot in the ego."

We both smiled. It felt good.

"So, just to restore your ego I will let you tell me exactly how she fit in," he said.

I thought about what Mapp told me.

"Most of this comes from the club, so it's not going to be in the official record. Apparently, they sent young or young-looking girls his way on a regular basis," I looked at him. I could see he wanted to ask. I knew he wouldn't.

"Okay, officially I don't know either. Fill me in," he said.

"It looks like Sandy Gardner was into a dangerous kind of auto-erotic asphyxia. We'll never know for sure, but it looks like his own kink got him killed when his chair tipped over and things went too far. Can't say I feel bad about it."

"Self-strangulation and kiddy porn? Guy was one sick bastard," he said.

"And then some. Seems he got off with his hands and feet cuffed to his favourite chair and a noose around his neck. He'd get Sam to hook him up nice and tight so he could watch that slide show. When he couldn't take it anymore, he'd have his way with the stripper, or Sam, or both."

"And then work on the Sunday sermon?"

"Something like that, yeah," I said.

I left Blair's room when Sue returned. I knew she'd have questions, and I didn't have any answers. A slender, white-haired man in creased pants and a cardigan stood in the hallway outside the room. Superintendent Wilbur Cage was a familiar face, although I'd never seen him out of uniform. Cage was a fast-moving, buttoned-down cop, who ran the patrol division like an army general.

"Detective Neville? I ran into Constable Christmas's wife downstairs. She told me you were here." He reached out to shake my hand.

"Yes, sir."

His eyes locked with mine. They seemed heavier, slower some-how, than the fast-moving, decisive eyes of the man I'd seen in pa-trol briefings. Cage was a second-generation cop who knew the risks of the job. Seeing his daughter fall victim to the biggest risk of all weighed heavier than the usual burden of command. A wave of panic rolled across my chest as I realized I had no idea if Carla was alive or dead. I was so lost in my own hatred I hadn't even bothered to check.

"How is she?" I asked.

"She's going to be fine, thanks to you." The warmth of his smile was a physical thing.

"No, sir, I got there too late to help," I said.

"No, you risked your life to clear that scene. Going in without backup so paramedics could get to her. I was fully briefed on what happened, Detective. You saved her life, son, and I won't forget that." The smile beamed as he touched my arm. The same way Carla did it.

"Is she awake? Can I see her?" I suddenly felt an overwhelming need to see her. It was fuelled by guilt. I had not even followed her to the hospital. I just watched the paramedics take her away and then went chasing vengeance like every asshole I ever locked up.

"You sure can. She's sleeping now, but come on. She's in ICU. I'll tell them you are family." He had me by the elbow now, leading me toward the elevator.

He spoke softly as we walked.

"Detective, I know you are going through something horrible right now. What happened to your brother, your partner. The chief is concerned, as well. You have to know, you are valued in this depart-ment. You are exactly what the HRP needs. Don't throw away every-thing you've gained these past few years."

There was no command in his voice, no anger. I could feel his concern, and suddenly felt sad. It was nice to think I was his idea of a good cop, but then, he didn't know I was also a murderer. I was glad I'd left my leather with Gunner. Superintendent Cage might be offer-ing an olive branch out of gratitude, but I was pretty sure he wouldn't be leading a full-patch Stallion to the ICU to visit his daughter.

Wilbur Cage left me in the hands of that same ICU nurse I'd met before. I don't think she bought me as family. She did still think I was a cop, and that was enough to get me to Carla's bedside. Carla was surrounded by the same array of equipment that had kept Blair alive after the shooting. A soft yellow glow played across her face, reflecting the steady flickering from one of the monitors. Somehow, she looked stronger than Blair had, like she was just sleeping peacefully. There were no bandages on her face or neck, maybe that was it. Maybe I just felt good seeing her.

The ICU was still and dark, a lamp above the main nursing station the lone exception. The clicking and hissing of life-saving machines seemed to come from every angle. I reached for my phone and my earbuds. I didn't want to hear the rhythm of a hospital, didn't want to be in one. I needed to think about what I'd done, where I was heading. I selected the original Skynyrd live album and listened to Ronnie Van Zant call me to a simple life. I wondered how mine had gotten so twisted. I'm not sure why I pulled that album from the list. Maybe it was the guilt over leaving Carla. That guilt was familiar; it was like my feelings about Glenda. We'd spent the better part of a summer hiding in Grease's shed making out to Skynyrd live. It's why I don't listen to the album much anymore. Yet, here I sit in the dark, watching the cotton sheet rise and fall above Carla's chest and listening to Glenda's music. I felt a tickle on my cheek as I watched the sheet and thought of my wife.

┿┿┿

Wednesday morning

I prayed hard during the funeral, the same prayer I used when I was being tortured. *God, if you are real, get me through this.* It worked in Pakistan. I hoped it would work again. The basilica couldn't hold the crowd. Gunner and a team of Stallion patches lined the sidewalk outside. They wouldn't enter a church filled with cops. At least Greg finally managed to fill it. I tried to be happy for him, to feel something other than the hole in my chest. A lot of people said a lot of things I didn't know about my kid brother. He liked cooking, the blues, practical jokes, and old movies. Every new insight into the kid in the box drove the pain deeper. He was in that box because of bullets sent my way. I would never get past that. Blair managed to get paroled from the hospital for a couple of hours. He was in the aisle in a wheelchair at my side. Sue sat with me. Carla didn't make it, she was still in the hospital. At least she wasn't in a box beside Greg.

The true hell that was the Church of Salvation didn't make any headlines. Solid chance it never would. I knew Greg would like that, so I wasn't going to do anything to change it. The truth about Sandy Gardner was buried with him. There were damaged kids out there, and no one was going to avenge them. Nothing could undo the damage. What was the point in trying?

Halifax reporters were locked on some bullshit Romeo-and-Juliet saga. In the age of entitlement, the modern star-crossed lovers skipped the suicide and killed everyone else. The preacher's son and the stripper. His father forbade it. Church leaders Thelma Waters and Bobby Simms tried to enforce the will of Gardner, if not God. Samuel and Lolita killed them all and went out, guns blazing. More Tarantino than Shakespeare. No truth in it, but a great story that just kept on giving. Fuck it, let it be.

As for Greg's murder, everyone with a badge was accepting the Russian-mob theory. Greg was collateral damage in an unsuccessful hit on Blair. They believed the gunmen were either dead and dumped offshore, or hiding in some Russian back alley. Close enough.

Couple of major-crime guys told Blair they were looking into a fire that destroyed Nicholas Mapp's house. No bodies found, and his cigarette-hulled speedboat was missing. Guess the cleaner took a souvenir. Inspector MacIntosh wasn't missed at the funeral. Everyone figured he was avoiding me. Too late for that.

I slid into the back seat of the black Lincoln behind the hearse. I was alone. A booming roar filled the air as we left the basilica. Two motorcycle escorts guided Greg to his grave. Six traffic cops rode in close formation on identical white Harleys up front. Six full-patch Satan's Stallion members followed behind the family car. I looked back and saw Gunner in front, Grease beside him. I listened to the rumble from the front and rear.

Snake missed the funeral. He was in Montreal raising hell about the Nomads torturing kids on his turf. Laroche would have to die. The Stallion members ride under a patch. It stands for something more than brotherhood. It stands for a code where a man's word means more than any written law or contract. The club could be brutal, but the Stallion code forbade what was happening at the ranch. If it allowed the kiddy porn, the patch would lose its lustre in the dark shadows where it shone brightest. Especially there. The places where violence is expected and respected. Where rules are clear, and those who break them know death is coming.

The soothing rumble of the bikes rolled around the interior of the Lincoln as the city slid past the window. I watched it go by, wondered where I fit in it. Shooting Mapp and MacIntosh was right, but it was still murder. I was a cop-killer, not a cop. I didn't regret it, but those bodies stood between the badge and me. They also cemented my status in the club. I was a blood Stallion now. Blood in. My past was washed away in their blood. I wasn't sure I could stand under the patch any more than I could behind a badge, but only my death could remove it now. Blood out.

Greg's funeral procession was a spectacle. The sound stopped people on the sidewalks. They watched the bikes and the hearse but looked away as they caught a glimpse of the family car. Sometimes, turning away is the best we can do.

ACKNOWLEDGEMENTS

I'd like to take a moment to thank those who helped this book make the journey from a vague idea in the back of my mind to the story you have before you. First. Nat Sobel—so much more than an agent—who saw something he liked in the earliest draft and then patiently guided the project through several drafts until he felt it was ready. Nat's partner Judith Weber brought a fresh set of eyes and her considerable skill into the mix in the final stages of our journey. Adia Wright handles rights, and had my back all the way.

At Nimbus and Vagrant. Thank you to the Yoda of editors—that good she is—Elaine McCluskey. She took a veteran journalist's eye to the project and proved to this reporter that not all desk editors are created equal. Senior editor Whitney Moran, thanks for giving Elaine and me all that rope.

On the law and disorder side, hundreds of police officers have generously shared their time, feelings, and thoughts with me at hundreds of major crime scenes over the past three decades. You are all in here. Thank you to RCMP Staff Sgt. Scott Warnica and Const. Sandy Matharu for reading through and pointing out errors in legal and police procedure. Those that remain are left for story-telling purposes and do not reflect on the considerable talent of those two men. Cam was a Mountie in one draft, but then Scott laughed and said, "Not in this lifetime." The story beats up on the RCMP, but that's Cam's payback, not mine. Halifax Police Sgt. Sandy Johnston became an unknowing participant as she and I routinely met at late-night and early-morning crime scenes. Watching her work a scene brought Carla Cage to life and to this story.

Thank you as well, to those one percenters who reluctantly and slowly let me enter their world and their clubhouses over the years. They shared the stories behind their choices and even took me along on a few rides. Thanks for taking the pencil along, guys; yes, I know what you are saying. Remember, this is fiction; your clubs are still clubs. Mine is a gang.

A quick note on PTSD. I believed it marked the end of the line for me. It didn't. Thank you to Vanessa McColl for guiding me, slowly, back to the keyboard. Dr. John Whalen, thank you for playing hardball with me when I was finally ready. Dr. Jonathan Fox, thank you so much for knowing what to say and when. This book, and its author, are here today in no small measure thanks to each of you.

This book has a soundtrack, and I'd like to thank the many talented artists who helped me block out the PTSD noise and focus. Where songs appear in the story they were playing as I worked. If you enjoy listening as you read, this book goes well with Lynyrd Skynyrd, Slash, Kid Rock, and Metallica.

To Mowgli, the world's worst PTSD dog and best office manager, thanks pal.

Finally and most of all, thank you so much to my loving wife and family for holding me up and believing.

PJ

LOOK FOR PHONSE JESSOME'S NEXT CAM NEVILLE MYSTERY, COMING FROM VAGRANT IN FALL 2018.

More crime fiction titles from Vagrant Press

Shortlisted for the 2016 Arthur Ellis Award for Crime Fiction, and Dartmouth Book Award for Fiction

978-177108-350-8

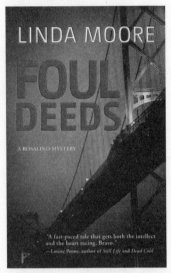

The first book in the Rosalind series is a highly engaging mix of crime, theatre, and environmental justice

978-155109-946-0

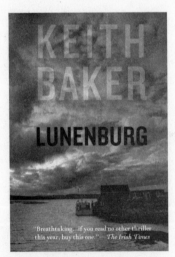

Riveting crime thriller set in Lunenburg, Nova Scotia

978-177108-309-6

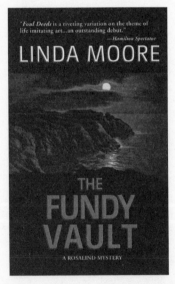

Anticipated follow-up to gripping literary mystery Foul Deeds is "a page-turner with gravitas" (Patricia Reis)

978-177108-421-5